The Appeal of Ebony Jones

The Appeal of Ebony Jones

Nikesha Elise Williams

NEW Reads Publications

Copyright © 2018 by Nikesha Elise Williams

Library of Congress Cataloging-In-Publication Data

Williams, Nikesha Elise.
    The Appeal of Ebony Jones/Nikesha Elise Williams

Romney, this book wouldn't exist without you.
Thank you.

Part 1

"Though he slay me yet will I trust in him. I will surely defend my ways to his face."

— Job 13:15

"If surviving lions don't tell their story hunters get all the credit."

— African Proverb

1.

"On the charge of second degree murder how do you find?"

Ebony listens to the monotone voice of Judge Marisol Shaw trying to glean whatever information she can about her own fate, her own future before the jury announces it to the world. With closed eyes, and shallow breath, Ebony listens to the fidgeting silence in the room. The tap, tap, tap of pens against pads scratching out notes, or sketches for the journalists required to turn her story into copy, or an edited package before she is ushered to wherever she's supposed to go after she's acquitted or convicted of the crime she knows she did not commit. She listens to the held breaths around her. Her mother, Ayana, behind her. James, her boyfriend, and her attorney, beside her. She listens, but she does not see. She refuses to see, to look at the jury make a decision about her that she's not sure they're qualified to make; to render judgement on a situation they weren't apart of and therefore could never understand.

She listens as the jury forewoman stands to her feet, the thin paper of the verdict sheet rustling against the cheap fabric clothing her thighs.

She clears her throat, "Not guilty, Your Honor."

Exhale. The room exhales. Ebony exhales. James exhales. Ayana behind them exhales. Ebony lifts her eyes to see the jury chose the Black woman to be their forewoman. The only black person on the jury of six. She stands in authority, in the first seat of the jury box closest to Judge Shaw. A man and another woman sit in the seats on the row beside her. Two more men and a third woman sit on the second row. Ebony fixes her gaze on the juror disappearing behind the forewoman. The man hiding behind her hips and ass. The man with the thinning comb-over, jowly face, and forest green V-neck sweater worn atop a denim button down shirt. The top button at his throat is closed. Ebony stares at him from her hard seat at the defense table. She looks through the forewoman's thigh gap to the slinking man behind her. The one who's clothes choke the truth out of him, before she wonders why the forewoman is still standing.

"On the lesser charge of manslaughter, how do you find?" Judge Shaw asks.

"Not guilty." She looks at Ebony and grimaces.

The forewoman said four words in the high-pitched squeak of someone who talks over their larynx, "Not guilty. Not guilty." She is still standing. The paper still rustling against her sides and then in her hands as she looks away from Ebony and back to Judge Shaw. The forewoman waits for her cue. Ebony ignores the cacophony of the rising anxiety in the room as those gathered wait in frenzied impatience for the final outcome. They wait for their gossip, their tea, their story, their package to be told to them, not caring that the woman who will live out the consequences of what is written on the forewoman's paper is in front of them.

Ebony ignores their jubilant anticipation and focuses on the pained expression of the forewoman and the slinking man behind her. The man whose ruddy face is exploding with sunburn beneath fluorescent lighting, and the woman whose side-eye in stolen glances says get ready.

"There's only one more charge left," James whispers to her.

She hears the excitement in his voice, as if he's done the impossible.

"On the charge of culpable negligence, how do you find?"

The forewoman looks directly at Ebony. "Guilty, Your Honor."

2.

"You can't win them all," Ebony whispers to James.

Her voice is resigned and relieved. No longer anxious about the fate she now knows, yet still uncertain of what is to come. James drops his left ear to his shoulder to rid it of the wetness of her words; her breath that still lingers in his ear. His defeat in front of the court. His failure before the world. He stacks the files in front of him, slamming folders and papers together, angry at himself for sacrificing his life for her. Angry at her for her casual flippancy; the ungratefulness in her disdain for him and his shortcomings.

She is condescending in her silence, acquiescent to her fate, and defiant in her truth. James looks over at his devil in a white tux and only receives the side of her face. The strength of her jawline, the cut of her cheek bones, dusted with a golden shimmery glimmer, and the outer corners of her eyes where a black line was dragged hours earlier to make her look like a cat. He looks away. To the judge. To the woman he used to prosecute cases before. The Latina who welcomed him with a fruit basket and a note that read "we need to stick together" on his desk when he first went to work for the State Attorney's office. The office he left for the woman beside him. The woman convicted of a crime she refused to admit she committed. The woman whom he told he loved and she withheld her response because of her prescient sense they would end up here, standing side by side in court. She in white, he in black, and the weight of a guilty verdict laying bricks of silence between them as the rest of the courtroom chatters their response behind their wall of conspicuous responsibility. Anger is only the beginning of what is building inside of him.

Judge Shaw bangs her gavel to bring order to the explosive noise in the courtroom. James feels the heat of his rage flowing through his veins with the successive knocks of wood on wood. His wrath for the jury's conviction, his irritation with the people rejoicing in his misery, his resentment for the woman who still can't muster a compliment, encouragement, or even a simple "I love you," in his hour of need.

Judge Shaw bangs the gavel twice more. Silence covers the courtroom.

She says, "The court thanks the jury for their service. You are dismissed."

In shaky stilettos, Ebony watches as Judge Shaw turns to her. She pulls the hem of her white tuxedo jacket down to lay flat against the wide waistband of the matching pants. She folds her arms in front of her. Nails from her right hand find the back of her left hand. She rakes against her scratched skin as she faces Judge Shaw. Finding comfort in the uncomfortableness of reopening scars and scabs she's had since she was twelve, indulging her nervous habit to scratch what doesn't itch, Ebony stares into the Judge's eyes. She tries to see if she can spot anything that resembles more than an insouciant, nonplussed feeling.

"Ms. Jones, you are convicted of culpable negligence in the death of Judge Barker Gordon. Since you are on house arrest, you can remain in home confinement until your sentencing, set for two months from today."

Ebony nods in understanding. Her head bobs slightly back and forth on her neck, even though there is nothing else for her to answer affirmatively to. She does not stop her bobble until she feels the tug on her arm. The loose grip of James's ashen hands pulling her by the elbow force her to drop her arm. Her nails stop their graze through her warn, unhealed skin. He pulls her through a side door at the front of the courtroom — the area where felons are escorted in and out — away from the general public. Away from the people who participate in the justice system only from a comfortable distance.

"What happens now?" Ebony asks as they walk down the marble steps of the Duval County Courthouse.

"We go home," James says.

"We?"

"Yes. We."

11.

The terse cut of his words keeps whatever remark she planned to say behind her lips. They file down the last four flights of steps in the same brick laid wall of silence they built between them after the verdict was read. Once they reach the bottom, James leads her to a side exit door. A guard opens it for them. They step out and down onto the concrete outside.

Ebony is face-to-face with the Sikes & Stowe auto body shop. She is face-to-face with downtown Jacksonville and the scene of the crime she did not commit, where her gun, her Lady Smith, went off without her permission. She sees the parking meter where she waited. The meter she stood next to. The meter she tried to grab ahold of when she was slammed back and forth against her car. The meter he stumbled next to. The meter he tried to grab ahold of as he fell to the ground. The meter she drove away from knowing her Lady did something not of her own intention.

"Ebony. Let's go." James tugs.

She walks reluctantly. Moving two paces behind James, he drags her, at first by the elbow, and then by a loose grip around her second and third fingers across the street where she watched him cross, to the chain-link fence that guarded the lot where he used to always park. The only difference now is James's sedan occupies the space that used to belong to Barker. Her car still belongs to the state, still evidence in a crime they say she committed.

He opens the door for her with one hand, the other still holding on to her fingers. He is slow to release her. Slow to drop his fingers from hers. Slow to look away from the parts of her body to close the door. He has yet to look at her face, to face his failure in her convicted countenance of disapproval. He pushes the door shut gently. The lock barely clicks into place. James reinforces the closure with a push of his hip before he crunches around the grassy, gravelly lot to the driver's side door. Ebony watches him shove himself into the car with as much force as a defeated zebra trying one last time to get away from a lioness that's already pounced and torn into it's hindquarters. She sees his hurt and his pride.

The need in him to receive what she cannot, what she refuses to give. The apology on her tongue that is not enough. The trivial "I love you" scratching the backs of her teeth. She keeps the cage in her mouth from uttering anything to aggravate his wounded ego. He starts the car and roars the accelerator. It's the cry of a dying animal attempting one last time to evoke the sympathy of it's predator before surrendering to a prey's death. James pulls away from the scene of death the jury found Ebony responsible for.

"What does culpable negligence mean?" Ebony asks as they get caught at the light on Broad and Duval.

It's the light that caught Barker. The light where she interrupted his morning routine with his own greeting: "Good morning, Gorgeous." The light he waltzed away from to speak to her that led to the crime she did not commit.

"It means you acted recklessly bringing your gun with you to talk to Judge Gordon and caused his death. It's a third degree felony."

James squints in the late afternoon sun as he makes a right on Broad Street.

"What does that mean?"

"Three-to-five years in prison, but you don't have to worry about that."

"Why not?"

"Because this is just the beginning."

He makes a right on red at Duval Street and passes the fire station that responded to treat Judge Gordon. Ebony gazes from the passenger window as James takes the same route she did six months ago. Her arms are folded across her chest restrained by her seat belt. Her hands are in action. The nails of the left scratch the back of the right. She watches their section of the world go by as she remembers how she escaped then, as he escapes now.

"The beginning of what?" Ebony asks. She stares out the window and watches the dilapidation of two old paneled houses on Jefferson blow by.

"Remember when I requested the mistrial after they allowed the tape of your questioning to be shown in court?"

"Yeah, so?"

James drives through Monroe and makes a right on Adams.

"That'll be the basis of our appeal. The officers and the State Attorney tried to coerce a confession out of you, even though I was standing right outside the door. Judge Shaw shouldn't have allowed the tape, but since she did we'll use it in our favor to claim prosecutorial misconduct."

Ebony scratches and watches her escape route go by on the opposite side of the street that she took six months ago. His pace much slower than hers when she was behind the steering wheel of her damaged car running for her life. Now they run together. Side by side away from court, the jury, the judge, the cameras, and a verdict they did not want. One he almost guaranteed she would not get. Broken promises. The future in front of them is filled with the detritus of their mistakes, her lies, his over-confidence and broken promises of their past, reemerging for a reckoning in their present. A present hanging on an appeal that sounds more far-fetched than the original plan.

"Stop that," he says looking over at her.

Ebony puts her hands beneath her thighs as he eases into the evening rush hour traffic hampered by a sea of cars, orange construction barrels, and shifted lanes no one knows how to navigate. The radio is off, the air thick between them. Neither of their breaths is audible. They ride in contemplative silence. She remembering the face of the forewoman given the task to deliver her bad news. The one juror she thought was her ally made into her enemy.

He mulls the probability of slicing across traffic, slamming into the concrete barrier, and flipping into the river. How long would he live? James drives across the Fuller Warren Bridge toward the complexes of hospitals and insurance company towers. Hospitals and companies that could not save his mentor from the vengeance of his girlfriend. The man he admired, esteemed, and modeled his own career after, was gone at the hands of the woman who sits on her fingers to keep from clawing away at her own chance of survival. Ebony shifts the weight of her ass side to side on top of her hands as she looks out from her side of the car. She focuses on the tops of the whitewashed buildings standing taller than the canopy of tree leaves, the cranes in the sky above both that are supposed to signal momentum in the city's long neglected downtown and downtown adjacent neighborhoods. All she sees is progress on top of poverty. An appeal on top of a conviction. His plans to save her on top of her imminent sentence.

James slows as he turns into the subdivision. The street in front of him is blocked by three news trucks. Insignias emblazoned on all of them. 9 News Now, WNNB, Channel 2, they're all staked out in front of or behind the second house from the entrance. Ebony's house. His temporary home since they started prepping for trial. They're waiting for them.

"Get down," he growls.

He pulls their sun visors down to obscure the view of the camera's shooting in through the front of the car to capture them coming home. Ebony unbuckles her seat belt and crouches down to the floor of the car. She takes off her shoes, and folds her diminutive body beneath the glove compartment. James drives forward through the reporters, hitting the garage door opener as he goes. With his head bowed between his arms, he looks over his shoulders and pulls forward into the garage, ignoring the reporters and photographers with their microphones and cameras pointed toward all the windows of the car. He does not put the car in park until the garage door is completely closed behind them and he knows no one snuck under to try and get an exclusive interview he was not in the mood to give.

"You can get out now," he says in a softer voice.

The automatic locks click open as James steps out of the car. His own contempt keeps him from going to Ebony's side to help pull her from the floor. He opens the door from the garage into the house and disappears into the laundry room. He does not listen for steps behind him. He does not check to see that no one is harassing them with questions peppered through the closed garage door. Tunnel visioned on nothingness, working hard to clear his head of everything he walks into the master bedroom, her bedroom, and takes off the suit jacket that has become too big over the last three weeks of the trial. He tosses the black jacket onto the new lavender comforter spread across the bed. He kicks his scuffed wingtips into a corner by the stack of papers he accumulated during their prep. The papers fall, fly and spread. He does not go to get them. He does not move to reorganize them. He can't save his defense that did not work; he cannot save his woman who won't tell him the truth. He cannot even save himself. Defeated, damn near destitute, and dropping weight from stress, James loosens the skinny off black tie from his neck and leaves it on the dresser in front of the rectangular mirror, where he forced all of her confessions. All but one. His belt and cufflinks with EAJ engraved in them, her initials, are placed next to the mirror. He leaves the room in dress socks, suit pants, and an untucked black shirt with the sleeves rolled to the elbow.

"You left me," Ebony says, coming through the laundry room into her house.

"No I didn't. I told you to get out."

"And then you left me."

"You were taking too long. What am I supposed to do? Wait? This is your house. You know where you're going?"

"Clearly."

"Then what's the problem?"

"Nothing, James. Nothing." She mumbles, "I told you this shit would happen."

"What was that?"

"Nothing. I'm going to change my clothes."

Ebony pads barefoot into her room, grateful she held on to her words, that she did not let her feelings and emotions cloud her judgement to say "I love you" when she knew he would turn on her the moment he didn't get his way. She shakes her head as she passes his piles. His junk squandered on her bed, dresser, and floor and steps into the walk-in closet. She is overcome by the sea of white and black.

James's suits and her ensembles for court. Their costumes worn to evoke emotions and illicit favorable verdicts did not work. Their cosplay was a bust. Ebony drops her shoes where she stands. She shimmies the tailored tuxedo jacket off of her shoulders, unhooks the wide waistband of her pants, and runs through the buttons of her white blouse until all the fabric is pooled at her feet and she stands in nothing but a wife beater, no bra, and black boy shorts. She leans against the wall of the closet, arms folded, hands scratching, eyes closed. She breathes in the stuffy air in the attire that started it all. What she was wearing those years ago when her air conditioner broke, the repair man canceled on her, and Barker showed up angry, unannounced, and uninvited.

"Rest in hell, you son of a bitch."

Ebony leaves her mess in the closet, ignores James's mess in the bedroom, and walks out of her room and down the hall to see James sitting in front of the TV. The local news is on, Dawn Anthony is talking about them.

We have new video just in to the 9 News Now newsroom of convicted felon Ebony Jones, arriving home with her attorney, and former Assistant State Attorney James Parnell. We've slowed down the video and highlighted Jones in the clip. You can see once she notices she's on camera she ducks down out of sight of our cameras. New tonight on "Dawn in the Evening," Owen Major is live outside of Jones's home in Mandarin. Owen, did Jones or Parnell say anything as they arrived home.

Dawn, we've heard nothing from Ebony Jones or Attorney James Parnell since the forewoman in the jury read the verdict convicting Jones of culpable negligence in the death of Judge Barker Gordon.

"So are you just going to watch them talk about us, like we didn't just live through this shit?"

"It's your favorite show and your friend. I thought you'd want to see how she portrayed you?"

"It's not that serious."

"But it is?"

"What the hell is that supposed to mean?"

"Just what I said, Ebony. It is serious."

"No shit."

He looks up at her. "Stop scratching."

She drops her hands. "I'm supposed to be going to prison for up to five years for some shit that I didn't even do."

"Apparently, you did. The jury didn't believe your story."

"My story?" Ebony shrieks. "You concocted the script for half of the bullshit I said up there on the stand. It was our story, James. We lost together."

"No, you lost this case. We had them, Ebony, until your cross."

"You mean the cross where you lost your shit at the table and looked like you were about to cry, like somebody stole your fucking bike? That cross," Ebony seethes.

James turns around on the couch, "I mean the cross where you let your fucking attorney, your boyfriend, be surprised because I didn't know you were stalking Judge Gordon since the day we met. I told you the whole time, no surprises. And what did you do, you lied, and you left me fucking surprised, and out to dry in open court. You gave me the rope and I hung myself like a dumbass. Yeah, I lost my shit, but it doesn't take away the fact that you lied."

"Don't curse at me."

"Is that all you can say? Get mad at me for cursing back at you because you know you're fucking wrong."

"I'm wrong, and now I'm the one going to prison for it. So let's not act like you got the shitty end of the deal here."

"I ruined my career for you."

"No one told you to do that."

"You're fucking ungrateful, that's what you are."

James stands up from the couch and leaves Ebony alone in the living room angry at herself and her portrayal on television. He pads from the carpet of the throw rug to the cherry hardwood of the floors, down the hallway, and back into her bedroom. He reclaims almost everything that was his. He rushes his arms into his suit jacket, shoves his tie into his pocket, throws his belt over his shoulder, and then walks across the room to slip his feet into his shoes. He doesn't tie the shoes, nor does he tuck his shirt. The cufflinks are left on her dresser, in front of the mirror where he heard her lies, thinking they were the truth.

He walks out of the room, to the front door and opens it. Camera lights immediately swing to capture his face, the cacophony of questions from reporters deafens them all. He hears noise instead of words, conjecture instead of consideration, conviction and condemnation instead of sympathy, empathy, or understanding.

"Why did she do it?"

"What does Ebony Jones plan to do now?"

"Is she ready to go to prison?"

"Do you plan to file an appeal?"

"Is this hard for you since you're her lover and her attorney?"

James doesn't answer any of them. He keeps walking to the curb where his car is not parked. Where he remembers he pulled in to her garage for the first time in all the time they've been together. He keeps walking past the live trucks, across the street, and down the road into the bowels of the subdivision, away from the reporters tethered in front of cameras where they announce the news as he makes it. He marches down the pavement passing driveways with two or three cars lined up, manicured lawns, basketball goals, and bikes with pink tassels. Well fed cats dart beneath cars or on to porches as he walks. The deeper into the subdivision he goes the louder the crickets, and frogs, and birds become. It is a moonless night, and on this side of town the stars are always visible. The three stars of Orion's belt, the only constellation he can name, that he can always make out, burn above his head. He walks with the hunter above him replaying everything he knows, everything he's been told. The lies about her family and then, finally, the truth after her first appearance in court. The dubious circumstances of how they met, the reason she was late for the Mayor's luncheon, the content of the conversation she had at the luncheon with Soleil, her three trips to the courthouse, the lie she told when he caught her, and the shooting she admitted only after she was a wanted woman.

James circles the cul-de-sac and marches back the way he came, still thinking of her. The dependence she had on him when she couldn't leave the house, shackled by an anklet that tracked her every step and left a nasty rash on her skin. Her nervousness and anxiety she only expressed through involuntary scratching. The backs of her hands carrying the track marks of her true feelings. Her love, her anger, her frustration, her irritation, her uncertainty, is all buried in the scabs on her skin. She stuffed herself in the nails that scraped through her flesh and allowed him to make her body his home. She enveloped him to make him forget he was angry at her. The way she held his head, rubbed his arms, and stroked his chest when he was unsure of the motions he should file, the arguments he should make, the defense he should run. The only thing he was certain of was the feeling emanating from the both of them. Their love that was unspoken but understood. Now he wonders if he is the only one standing in the middle of misunderstanding.

He walks back to Wexford Chase Road and makes his slow return to the house from which he left, the woman he wants to run from, but can't, the gaggle of reporters relentless in their pursuit for an exclusive, and the mess he's made of his own life by his own choices.

"You're back," Ebony says as the front door slams shut behind him.

"Forgot I parked in the garage. Didn't want to look like a jackass walking outside and turning right back around."

"They didn't follow you for long. Dawn had some expert on the show to talk about us. About what they would do if they were you. How I still have a chance."

"What did this expert say?"

"She said you should file a motion for a new trial based on the request for the mistrial over prosecutorial misconduct."

"I told you that in the car."

"She also said that request will probably be denied and then you should appeal to the first District Court of Appeals."

"Uh huh."

"And file some other motion so I can stay home. Some type of bond."

"I'd already planned to do that."

"You didn't tell me that."

"I didn't have the chance to," James says, coming to sit beside Ebony on the couch. "You've been jumping down my throat since we left court."

"Well, I'm sorry to ruin your disposition. I just got some bad news today."

"It doesn't matter."

"Why the hell not? Three-to-five . . .is a long time."

"Because this is just the first round."

"And what if we exhaust all of our appeals and I still have to go to prison."

"If it gets that far we'll be before the Supreme Court and the whole country will be on your side, as long as you stop fucking lying."

"You seem real sure of yourself, Counselor?"

"I may not know you, but I for damn sure know the law."

3.

*Thank you for joining us tonight on "Dawn in the Evening."
Tomorrow night you will hear my exclusive interview with Ebony Jones.
We sat down before her trial to talk about what happened the day Judge
Gordon was killed, why she's not prepared for prison, and the one thing
she revealed after our cameras stopped rolling.*

Johnnie mutes the television mounted on the wall of
her bedroom. She sets the remote on the nightstand beside
her bed and picks up her sweating white water bottle. The ice
inside rattles around as she tips the black cap to her lips and
tosses her head back.

"You want some?" Johnnie asks, holding her hand out
to Nathan.

He takes the bottle from her and tips it back to his
own mouth.

"It's water." He raises an eyebrow handing it back to
Johnnie.

"I know."

"How long has this been going on?"

"Since the funeral."

"Cold turkey?"

"Yup."

"What made you do that?"

"Death has a way of putting life in perspective."

"I guess I could have come home sooner." Nathan
slides beneath the sheets beside Johnnie's naked legs.

"You never had to leave."

Johnnie keeps the rest of the sentence to herself. She
doesn't tell him that she needed him most when she was
drunk with jealousy, filled with fear over what she had done,
and burning with bitterness over his flagrant philandering.
She doesn't say they had both made enough mistakes to forgo
his abandonment. She opens her legs to Nathan's petting
nose and allows him to make another apology with his
tongue. He doesn't hesitate to oblige. He kisses the inner
sides of each thigh. Thighs he hasn't touched in months. He

squeezes each, appreciative of their new thickness. The weight that's settled in to them since Johnnie's been out of work and off the bottle. He kisses his way up the inside of her legs until he can feel the heat of her sex rising from her body. He is overwhelmed by the smell of them from their first round of the night. The smell of their combined sensations as they each became one with one another. He hovers over the beginning of them until he plunges face-first into what he's being offered.

Johnnie's legs are drawn up to her breasts to give him space to make amends. He kisses the outer corners and works his way in until he can suck on her caramel colored lips. He takes them both in his mouth and soaks them until dribble falls onto her body and forces her to open her legs wider. He adds his fingers, using just one to spread the elixir of his mouth up and down and over her inner workings. He lingers on the bundle of her most sensitive nerves, winding clockwise and counter clockwise, until he feels a pulse under his power. She throbs under his pressure, the apex of her pleasure pushing forward from its secret place beneath the thin layer of wispy, unwaxed hairs to the center of her mound.

Nathan lay prostrate on the bed beneath the covers, his face in his wife, his tongue working over her religion, worshiping at the altar he'd neglected for the six months he'd been gone, and the two years before that, when they'd both neglected each other. He prays with the most nimble part of his body against hers. Using his dexterity to illicit her love, he laps up every drop she squeezes out. Tongue to the tips of his fingers, his mouth to his whole hand he pulls and tugs, licks, laps and loves, cups and covers her sacred place until she releases her legs and uses her arms to pull on the back of his head. She cradles him with her hands pushing his face down and pressing her lower body up. Her ass is suspended in the air, hovering over the sheeted mattress. Johnnie balances on him, holding on until her vision clears, but the fog remains over her eyes. She closes her lids and squeezes her lashes together as she reifies the sensations of her body.

Opening her eyes again, she tries to bring clarity to the concupiscent. Her brain identifies the two fingers working her walls, the thumb roiling her power, the lazy tongue lagging a half beat behind everything else, dipping and darting where it can, tapping a different frequency of her flavor along the spectrum of her femininity. She identifies the feelings and falls back into the fog of her body, the information from the synapses too much to compute, she lingers in the languid susceptibility of her sex.

Toes grip the bed, her thighs press up into his, elbows on his back, hands around his head, she pushes, and he bends to her whims, diving deep into her skin. He blows a steady hot stream of breath against her soaked body, tapping just two fingers against the pit of her peach until her tap turns on and splashes the bottom of his face. Nathan drinks her in, laying flat against her, his beard against her growing bush, his mouth receiving the rush of her well.

With one arm, he pulls her body back down to the bed placing her to where she's poised for his entry. He is swift in his invasion. He mounts her to her meridian, holding himself at his zenith until the vibrations around his length make him slide back and forth, out and in, in a rhythm all their own. She adds to his drumbeat with a twisting freestyle, moving her hips over and around his until the jazz they make is completely improv. They touch and feel their way toward the finale. Nails into shoulders, fingers in hair, knuckles kneading dimpled muscles, teeth tearing into ear lobes, bodies beating against one another, up and down, until the final chords of their conquering clang out of their bodies, and the last notes of their symphony are hammered out of their limb strings.

Connected but at rest, the harmony of their sighs sings through the semi-darkness of the room. The TV glows blue before them. Nathan rests his head against Johnnie's stomach. He sinks against her softness, against the evidence that she's borne him two children, the defiant part of her body that refuses to snap back no matter how many leg lifts or bicycle crunches she punishes herself with. He melts into the bevy of her belly, eyes closed to the rings of stretch marks below her navel that wrap themselves around her waist, ass, and hips.

Johnnie unmutes the television.

More video we want to show you tonight from Ebony Jones's Mandarin neighborhood. Shortly after she and attorney James Parnell arrived back at her home, our cameras captured Parnell leaving out of the front door. He walked toward our cameras, crossed the street, and then down Wexford Chase Road away from Jones's home. He did not say anything to us as he left or when he returned.

"They need to just leave my man alone," Nathan says. His voice is scratchy and groggy as it vibrates against her stomach.

"I just can't believe they convicted her," Johnnie says.

"I don't know why you're surprised. This is Florida. North Florida at that. Might as well be Mississippi the way some people act around here."

"It's not that bad."

"And she's not Samuel L. Jackson in *A Time to Kill* either. She got no sympathy."

"No sympathy would have been a conviction on second degree murder. They liked her a little bit."

"Not enough to let her off. Probably because your girl's a stalker."

"Yeah, I didn't know about that."

"James didn't either from what I can tell. Dawn said he had a meltdown in court when she was being questioned by the state attorney. I bet if he ever regretted leaving his job for her, it was right then."

"She definitely didn't make it easy on him. I just don't think it's her fault."

"You just feel bad because he died on your table. You can't save them all."

"I know." Johnnie turns up the volume, drowning out his offering of absolution. Forgiveness she doesn't deserve because she knows she is more guilty than the woman being vilified on TV. She knows Taylor, her mentor was right, she was slow, and lagging, dragging out the surgery because she couldn't keep up, inevitably inviting death. His words still haunt her.

What I saw was a surgeon whose team was working, but you, the leader, the surgeon in the room, was always one step behind. Your hands were shaking."

"I'm going to take a shower," Nathan says.

He pushes his body away from Johnnie, taking the sheets and the spread with him. They drop to the floor as he slides off the edge of the bed. She watches him as he drags his feet across the carpet past their closets and into the bathroom. He disappears behind a wall. On the TV they are showing video from court. She can see the profile of her own face in the front row on the defense side of the courtroom behind Ebony and James. Soleil, Ayana, and Dawn are there too. Their faces aren't shown but she knows her row. Johnnie doesn't remember which day the video is from. She can't recall when in the three-week trial this footage was actually taken. She zeros in on her own half-shown facial expressions. The nods of her head, the tightness in her jaw from the clenching of her teeth that forced her to swallow her truth.

She looks at the cut together images and remembers sitting beside Ayana, both of them rocking on their bench, their reasons entirely their own.

It was me. It was me. It was me.

The refrain in her head, she rocked her body and ground her teeth to keep from standing up, to keep from saying "Excuse me" as she squeezed by Dawn and Soleil to the aisle, crossed the apron, and told Ebony to switch places with her. She sat in court and held her tongue; and her body to keep from telling the state attorney she got it wrong. To keep from saying it should be The State of Florida versus Jonelle Edwards instead of Ebony Jones.

The video cuts to another clip; this one shows Ebony walking into court. The white pencil skirt hugs her voluptuous frame as she takes confident steps into the courthouse. The sun, on that particular day, glinted off the even cut of her straightened, jet black hair, that bounced on her shoulders as she was jostled between James and the stable of reporters who peppered her with questions every morning as she went in. Johnnie remembers their shouts of, "Did you do it? Why did you kill the Judge? Do you hate police?" The kinds of questions asked just to get a response. The kinds of questions that were spontaneous and impetuous, inartful, and for Ebony, unavoidable.

Johnnie remembers the day she walked in to court just before Ebony did. The silence that greeted her as she made her way up the stone steps, followed by the burst of commotion as Ebony and James rounded the bend from a hidden corner. The rush of reporters, and cameras behind her working to be first to capture the same stoic expression from James and turn of the head from Ebony, as they ignored the clamoring chorus of professionals who acted more like petulant children demanding to get their way with each unbelievable and exacerbated question after another. The histrionics made Johnnie stop at the metal detectors and watch the frenzied hyperbolic revelry unfold in front of her. Each question louder and louder and more tasteless than the last.

In the bed she shivers with the guilt that was not adjudicated for her.

"She didn't do it. I did," Johnnie says.

"What did you say, Babe?"

She jumps in the bed. "Ooh, you scared me. I thought you were in the shower."

"I came back out to get you."

Nathan holds out his hand for Johnnie to take. She reluctantly reaches for him. Fingertips to fingertips she follows him into the steaming en suite. A sage candle burns on one sink and a lavender candle burns on the other. The sweet smelling smoke rises into the air and becomes vapor, thanks to the steam rising from the shower. Nathan opens the door for Johnnie into the glass encased stall. She steps in and immediately sits down on the slick bench directly in front of the streaming water. He closes the door and sits beside her.

The only light comes from the candles. Their figures are obscured in the flickering flames. Shadows dance across their faces as the medium force drops of water from the shower fall on them.

"Is this how it's going to be now?" Johnnie asks.

"Say it again," Nathan says.

"I said, is this how it's going to be now?"

"How what's going to be?"

"Us?"

"What do you mean?"

"Are we just going to go back to being the perfect married couple, and not address the teacher's assistant in the room."

"I don't believe we can," Nathan says.

"Then why are we pretending we don't have shit to sort through."

"Because it's easier to rekindle a relationship, than it is to work through the baggage and bullshit that made us fuck it up in the first place."

"I heard the first step is admitting your baggage and bullshit," Johnnie says, turning her head to look at Nathan's wet face.

"Is that right?"

"That's what they teach in AA."

"You've been going to AA?"

"Online."

"Is that even the same?"

"Don't do that."

"Don't do what?"

"Don't discount what I'm doing to accept my share of the blame. To admit my baggage and bullshit. I shared. Your turn."

"I don't have anything to admit to, Johnnie."

Nathan turns to her with open hands in his lap and pleading chestnut eyes.

She sighs. "You really believe that, don't you?"

"Johnnie, I didn't do anything."

"Then why is Danielle so familiar with her that she's still asking about her, even though she's moved to a different grade, with a different teacher."

"Because she and Lisa had a bond . . . I guess."

"Still on a first name basis I see."

"What?"

"I guess Danielle isn't the only one who bonded with her."

"She was her teacher, Johnnie. What do you expect?"

"Soleil was her teacher. She was just an assistant."

Johnnie can still hear the sound of their laughter and see the looks on their faces, his face, when Danielle announced she was home.

"Dani still saw her everyday," Nathan interrupts her thoughts. "They had a bond."

"They had a bond, huh? I guess I'm supposed to be Boo Boo The Fool."

"I'm not saying that, Johnnie, and you know it."

"I don't know what you're saying, Nathan. So far, you haven't said shit."

Lying bastard. I don't even know why I let him come back home. He abandoned me, took my children and left me holding the bag and the bills, while he fucked around with the teacher's assistant.

Johnnie releases her hair from the sex loosened puff at the top of her head. Her curls fall slowly to her wet shoulders. She sets the ouchless elastic on the bench beside her and fingers her hair until it lays flat around the sides of her face.

He can't even look me in my eye and tell me he didn't sleep with her. Danielle had a bond. She's six. She'll get the fuck over it. Just like a man to use his child as an excuse for his fuck ups.

Burying her face in her hands, the water from the shower beats directly on the crown of her head. The mass of tight corkscrew ringlets droop and drip with the weight of the water. Johnnie folds her body over her legs and lets the water beat across the span of her back. She focuses on her toes, painted plum. Johnnie rakes her hands through her toes, webbing her feet until she pulls her fingers all the way through to her shins. She sits up slightly, resting her elbows on her thighs, her arms covering her breasts, her long, fallen, wet hair shrouding the rest of her body.

Nathan reaches to touch her.

She swerves.

Don't fucking touch me. Lying ass.

"I didn't know your hair started going gray," he says, drawing his hand back.

"Just started. Stress. I guess."

"Over what? You haven't been to work. What could you be stressed about?"

Are you fucking serious?

"I also haven't been getting paid, but still paying all the bills here. My savings can only last but so long."

"I went back to work."

"Good for you, Nathan, but until a second ago I didn't know that, and there's been no contribution here."

"I haven't been living here."

"My point exactly, now tell me why."

"Because you needed to get yourself together."

"I already said that. I've done that. Now tell me why you don't live here."

"Because you needed space?"

"Because *I* needed space?"

This is a fucking joke. Johnnie stands from the marble bench directly beneath the water. Arms folded across her chest, her back to Nathan, she closes her eyes and waits. *Why can't he just tell the truth. I told him I killed a man the day it happened, but he was too stuck on protecting the fucking teacher's assistant. I told him I was an alcoholic. I told him I've been doing AA. Just say you fucked her. It's not that hard.* She licks her lips and opens her mouth. The water pours in. Johnnie holds it, swishes it from side to side, and then spits it down the drain. She sighs, unfolds her arms, and brings two fingers to each temple. *This is ridiculous. I can't believe we're even doing this right now.*

"So everything is my fault?" Johnnie asks, massaging circles into her head. "I'm an alcoholic and I needed space. I'm an alcoholic and I needed time to get myself together. I'm an alcoholic and . . ."

"Why do you keep saying that?" Nathan stands up from the bench.

"Because I want you to hear how easy it is to tell the truth. I'm an alcoholic. Your turn."

"Johnnie, I have told you the truth. I am telling you the truth." He grabs her wrists. "I left because I thought you needed space to get clean, to get sober."

"So you left me for six months and it was for *my* benefit?"

Johnnie sees the affirmative answer fighting to get out of him. She looks at the lie he's trying to tell and won't allow free.

"Don't bullshit a bullshitter," she says, wrestling her arms loose. "I'm a lot better at it than you."

"What's that supposed to mean?" Nathan takes a step back to look at her in the dim light.

He can see the weight she's picked up in the stretching of the skin across her thighs. The muscles that used to show through her scrubs now covered by cellulite. He hides his concern beneath the shower head. The falling water obscures the look on his face. Her body was always her point of pride. Kale and walking, Pilates and yoga, green smoothies and organic produce. She was a walking billboard for healthy living. Alcohol was her only vice, and even that kept her lean, taking her liquor straight, no flavor, no chaser. A life she no longer models. *Too much weight and she's going to lose all her shape.*

He sees the weight in her breasts is multiplied. The bags that used to hang from her body with little lift and no shape are now fuller and plumper. The dark berries of her nipples, always erect from nursing two children until well after their first birthdays, point slightly up instead of down. The gray strands of her hair blend in the with the sandy brown of her natural color. He reaches out to try and finger her curls. She swerves.

"You used to love it when I washed your hair."

"I loved it more when you told the truth."

"I'm not lying about anything, Jonelle."

"Then I'm just supposed to forget that you and the teacher's assistant were downstairs rolling around on the floor, watching *Frozen* with Danielle like this isn't my house, and she's not my child. I'm supposed to have amnesia about that?"

"I'm not saying forget it, or have amnesia . . ."

"You're not saying shit."

"I'm saying nothing fucking happened."

"Just because you say it doesn't make it true."

"You're looking for me to tell the truth about something that never happened."

"You changed your soap and cologne after nearly two decades of wearing Old Spice and I'm supposed to believe nothing happened."

"Am I not allowed to buy new cologne?"

"So it's just a coincidence that it's the same scent she was wearing when she left here in that fucking ugly car."

"Nothing happened, Johnnie."

"I don't believe you, Nathan."

"Don't believe me. I'm not admitting to shit I didn't do." His anger is sudden and abrupt. He grabs the loofah and bar of soap.

I should have just stayed in the hotel. She never did like to listen to anybody but her damn self. I don't know why I thought she would listen to me now. If it's not what she says, her perspective, her opinion, then it ain't real. She's worse than a child.

"Danielle asked me why I don't take her to the zoo like you did with Miss Jessie. I'm supposed to believe nothing happened? You really do take me for Boo Boo The Fool?"

"Don't make your insecurities, my transgressions," Nathan says, stepping out of the shower.

"Fine. Go ahead. Runaway."

"I'm not running away. The water is getting cold."

"This water is not cold."

"Once your blood stops boiling maybe you'll feel a difference."

The glass door to the shower slams behind Nathan. Johnnie hears the aggressive power of his wet feet marching across the tile and onto the carpet of the bedroom and closet. The sound of hangers clanging reach her as the force of the shower-head lessens. She hears him pulling clothes and then the sound of his feet, once more, marching through the room until the door slams behind him.

Johnnie sits back down on the shower bench, arms at her sides, breasts hanging free, head leaning against the lone marble wall in the otherwise see-through shower. Goosebumps rise on her flesh as the cool water pours over her skin. The only warmth she feels is the wetness falling across her cheeks and down the side of her face.

4.

Standing in the middle of the bathroom floor amidst a circle of tissue and trash bags, Soleil looks at the empty racks and shelves surrounding her. Bare hangers line the thin bars in the tiny four by six walk-in closet. The clothes that used to hang there, dresses and suits, outfits for galas and soirees she was forced to attend but never allowed to participate in, are stuffed in the bags at her feet. All the clothes he bought are stuffed in the bags. All the clothes he touched, including her running shorts, tights, tank tops, and sports bras, are in the bags. All the things he violated by just being him are in the bags.

After six months, all she has left to get rid of Barker are the three bags at her feet that will join the three bags of her broken bed, destroyed rocking chair, and shattered ceiling fan, she already heaped in the dumpster. The shattered ceiling fan that fell from where it was hanging by wires. It initiated her purge and forced her to confront what she had been content to ignore since he died. The bags are also filled with the balled up wads of tissue filled with the tears she didn't cry over him, or his death, but the tears that fell after listening to the TV tell her something she didn't want to hear. Something she didn't expect. The verdict she wasn't ready for. The verdict she tried to deter with her own testimony, even though she was a witness for the other side.

The tissues are her tears for Ebony. Her tears for the woman who helped her when no one else could. She mourned over her loss, their loss, as the forewoman read the verdict aloud with a steady voice and smug conviction. She screamed out loud and scared her nosy neighbor, Ms. Jay, who hurried over with her puffy Pomeranian yipping at her heels, to bang on her door and to find out what was the matter.

She, too, had been watching the news, keeping up with the case, and had a vested interest because of her proximity to Soleil. The victim's abused ex-girlfriend, the suspect's unlikely friend, the personified motive as to why the suspect stalked the victim, armed with a gun, and confronted him and killed him. Soleil let Ms. Jay in and allowed her to sit on her sofa as they watched the rest of the coverage together. The neighbor she hadn't spoken to until earlier in the afternoon when she lugged out the first round of trash, and found her standing outside her door with her obedient dog at her feet. The second encounter brought them side by side in front of the television with Ms. Jay trying hard not to ask deeper questions beyond the ones she'd already learned the answers to from the news.

In front of Ms. Jay, Soleil held back her tears. Instead, she and the old woman from across the breezeway sat knee to knee, listening more than talking, two coffee mugs filled with tea between them. She flipped the channels from Cori Shannon and Brock Aldridge, to Cameron Addison and Cohen Bartlett, to Dawn Anthony and Linden Beale. They watched clips of Soleil's own testimony, Ebony's testimony, and listened to the replay of the verdict every half hour after it was read. They watched video of Ebony and James leaving court and arriving at her house. A house Ms. Jay did not know Soleil had visited, had been invited to, and had shared a drink with Ebony, Dawn Anthony, and Johnnie, the mother of her now former student.

Soleil kept the details of what Ms. Jay didn't know to herself. After ninety minutes of watching different people say the same things, she yawned and told her neighbor, who was falling asleep on her couch, she felt better. She was just shocked at the verdict but would be okay. It took her another thirty minutes for her to get the woman to swish across her apartment in her pale pink track suit to the door, followed by a two-minute round of "I'm so sorry," and "I didn't know," and "He seemed like such a nice guy every time I saw him around."

When the door closed behind the pompous dog and gray haired woman, in the sequined hat to match her track suit, Soleil leaned against it. She sank her body weight against the door cooled by her air conditioner. It was cold against her bare back. She was still in the bike shorts and sports bra from her run before the verdict, when she took a hammer to everything in her bedroom except the nightstands, dressers, and mirror. She listened to the steady beat of life running through her. Two fingers to her wrist, she felt the pulse of blood pumping through her body. She leaned against the door, relished the coolness against her skin, closed her eyes and welcomed the silence around her, despite her racing thoughts.

> *On the charge of culpable negligence, how do you find?*
> *Guilty, Your Honor.*
> *She doesn't deserve to go to prison for this.*

This is when her tears began to fall. When she realized her heartbeat was normal and stable and she didn't have to wonder what time he would show up, because Ebony had made sure he would never come back. Just like she told her. *Do something to make him never come back.* The memory ignited more tears. The tears she never cried in front of him. The pain she never let him see. The hurt she never showed he caused. She laid back against the door and listened to her body at ease. With fat tears rolling down her face, one by one, she listened to what her heart sounded like without fear, without anticipation, without the angst of his choleric confrontations. Instead, she felt the fissures that come from grief. *You're free.* The mouthed phrase Ebony told her when they stood face-to-face in the police station.

The tears fall as she wrestles grief with regret in her new normal. All she had known for the six months of their relationship was his abhorrence, his revulsion, and his pointless suspicion. But even his death, his killing, his murder, the crime for which her friend was found culpably negligent, did not bring her peace. The revelation from his mother that he behaved just as his father, did not bring her peace. His funeral, his burial did not bring her peace. The circus of Ebony's arrest, court appearances, and final trial did not bring her peace. His image was always before her eyes, open or closed, lucid, or dreaming, he was there. In the stares of people who watched the news, read the papers, and caught up with the blogs, he was there in their gaze as they looked at her and saw him. Pictures of him, of her, the lone shot of them together. The group photo of her, Barker, Ebony, James, and Dawn. The picture he was not supposed to be a part of. The picture Ebony insisted on. The last picture of him taken during his life. He wore a dark gray suit, with widely-spaced, black pinstripes, a crisp white shirt, and a lavender tie with an intricate knot she later learned was called an Eldredge. In the photo she matched his accent piece. Her iridescent gown complemented his tie. The gown he forced her to dress in after he fisted her up three flights of stairs and violated her in the tiled rectangular entryway just inside her front door.

The dress.

It is the memory of the gown that sent her lurching from her lean against the front door. With wide eyes and a racing heart she hurtled into the bathroom, flung open the accordion closet doors, and found the dress hanging in the black garment bag he brought it in. It was the first piece of clothing she pulled from the racks and dropped to her feet. It was followed by several more garment bags of clothing he'd bought for whatever function they were attending. When Soleil finished pulling the garment bags out, she then pulled down everything he ever saw her in until the hangers that survived her tirade of absolution swung back and forth on the closet rods, squeaking their own freeing whistles of expurgation.

Now she stands in the bathroom before the empty closet, with three bags of clothes, the tissues she used to dry her eyes, and the box of oversized garbage bags ready to be rolled open to help her cleanse even more.

Soleil turns away from the closet to face the bathroom mirror. Her eyes settle on their next target. She pulls a bag from the open cardboard box, thrashes it open and tucks it in one of the drawers of her vanity so it stays agape. The makeup palettes lining the countertop around her sink, fall into the bag one by one. Make Up For Ever, Nars, Urban Decay, all with the shades of blue, purple, and red brushed down to the black plastic of their casing, they all clang as they hit the tile floor beneath the open bag. *This didn't even look good on me. Had me walking around looking like a corpse, trying to hide what he did.* The thick full coverage foundation is next, followed by the copious amounts of black eye liners, liquid, and pencil, she used to cover the prints from his hands or his fists. Pressed powder, color corrector, concealer, lipstick, and lip stains all fall into the bag. Bronzer, highlighter, and finally his toothbrush. She even tosses her own toothbrush and toothbrush stand into the bag because they shared space with his. The only thing that's left on her counter is a clam shell soap dish, and a bar of something scented with essential oils meant to relieve stress.

She is not done. Soleil kneels to the cold tile floor and opens the cabinets beneath the vanity. Right in front she finds what she is looking for. The mother load of her makeup collection. What she bought just days before his death. What her friend Troy insisted she have. The six-hundred dollar airbrush makeup machine complete with compressor, airbrush gun, and a cleaning kit. *What a waste.* She heaves the hulking metal block machine into the bag. It clangs against the plastic palettes, and packs, and bottles, until it makes a decisive thud against the ground. She is not done. Soleil tosses the starter bottles of foundation, blush and highlighter, contour, and bronzer, concealer, primer, and even a facial cleanser all into the bag.

In the back of the cabinet she sees a box she doesn't recognize. A box he bought. White on one side. Black on the other. A sleek, futuristic looking hair dryer with a round fuchsia nozzle pictured on both sides. The hair dryer he bought when he suggested she'd look better with straight hair than "those tangled, matted curls" she insisted on wearing.

He said, "Why don't you blow it out, Gorgeous."

She answered him, "I don't know how."

"You could try," he said with a lecherous grin she gleaned was no longer suggesting.

He sat on the toilet and stared at her as she stood in the mirror and blew out her hair even though she was still learning how to hold the dryer and work it and the roller brush at the same time. He complimented her on a job well done. He glared down at her with an appreciative gleam in his eyes, while the keloid crow's feet at the corners of his face crowded his gratitude with dubious intentions. His fingers raked through her straightened hair. He asked, "Do you like it, Gorgeous?"

Only two months in to their six month saga, she still hadn't learned which questions she was supposed to answer honestly, and which questions she was supposed to answer with only the responses he wanted to hear. She said, "No."

She remembers her answer was decisive and his grip was tight. Her shoulder length curls stretched well below her bra strap. His hand choked everything from the nape of her neck down. He held her until she agreed it was "gorgeous, pretty," and made her look more attractive. She only used the dryer once.

Soleil drops the box in the bag. His money. His investment. Wasted. Trashed. Discarded to die a dumpster death and resist decomposition in whatever landfill the county deposits its detritus. She glances around the darkness of the cabinet to see if there is anything else of him that she's missed, anything else he bought, touched, used, breathed on, defiled with his presence. All that's left are the bars of soap he never used because he never stayed more than a few hours at a time. Even if he spent the night, he left well before morning truly began.

She decides against tossing the bags of Epsom salt since they soothe her after running, a sport she only took up after meeting him. She leaves the bottles of bubble bath she bought in bulk before she knew who he was.

That's enough.

The vanity cabinet slams shut with finality. It is clear of him just like her countertop, just like her closet. These are the spaces he inhabited in her home. The bathroom and the bedroom. He never ventured into the living room like Ms. Jay, or a friend, or a neighbor, or a guest. He didn't bother with the kitchen because they always ate out. The bathroom and the bedroom. He was only after one thing. He only visited for one thing. He only broke one thing.

The half full bag behaves as she ties it into a knot. She heaves it and the three bags of clothes her shoulder. Carrying them out of the bathroom and to the front door. She takes them down the three flights of stairs and across the parking lot to the dumpster. She does not check for raccoons or armadillos as she tosses the bags in. She drops her load and walks back home. At the top of the steps, Ms. Jay is there, standing in the crack of her door, her dog peeping through her open ankles.

"Still taking out the trash?" She asks.

"I just finished."

Soleil turns the handle to her open door and steps inside. The door closing behind her sets off a slight echo. There are no more clothes, no makeup, no bed, no rocking chair, no ceiling fan, or hair dryer, or tooth brush to catch and muffle the sound of the slamming door. It is loud and defiant. As defiant as the woman who cleaned out her closets and cabinets, and had nothing on the way to replace what she'd thrown away. Anything on Amazon was still two days away, and all the malls and Town Center were closed.

She walks through the bathroom and looks at the empty spaces around her. In the closet are jeans and her school polos. Knowing what she's wearing to work in the morning, she leaves the closet and bathroom and walks through her bedroom into the living room. The gray sofa is her new bed. The teal velour blanket her only cover. Still in her sweat dried bike shorts and sports bra, Soleil lays down against the cushions. Her body relaxes into the pillows. She takes deep breaths to slow her heart from her activity and waits for her new normal to return; for the sanctity of silence to become hers once again. The quiet consumes her as heavy lids droop over exhausted eyes, with one last lucid thought, before sleep, she says in a yawning voice, "It's time to go."

5.

Dawn drags her bare feet across the thin peasy carpet of the hallway outside her condo. Heels in her hand, blazer draped across her arm, purse slung across her body, she fingers the key ring in her hand until she feels the door key she is looking for. Looking up, she stops just before her door.

"What are you doing here?"

"I started watching the coverage at five and was surprised to see you instead of Julia. Then I saw you at eight and then at eleven, and I could tell something was wrong, so I came over."

"Why are you here?"

"I just told you," Victor says standing up.

"No. You told me you thought something was wrong with me. It's not. Why are you here? It's after midnight."

"Because you looked upset on air, so I came with the intention of making you feel better."

"Why is that?"

"Are you going to grill me, or are we going to go inside?"

"I'm going inside after I find out why you're here."

"I just told you. Damn, Dawn, must you be so difficult?"

"The last time you showed up, unannounced and without invitation, did not end well for you."

"You were rude."

"And you weren't listening, and then you belittled me and my work."

"I'm sorry."

"Are you?"

"Open the door, Dawn."

"Go home, Victor."

"Do you really want me to leave?"

Dawn frees her feet from her frozen stupor and steps close to her door. She smells him as she turns the lock. His scent is thick and earthy with slight sweet notes. The full mixture of aromatics that can only be detected within kissing distance. He hovers over her short frame as she leans into the unlocked door and allows just enough space for her body to fit in. She steals a glance at his masculinely angular face from her space in the doorframe. *He can't seriously believe I'm going to let him in.*

"Let me in, Dawn," he pleads.

"Why?"

"Because I'm here."

"And. Presence does not automatically mean entrance."

"Does it automatically negate it?"

Dawn smiles. "We've had this conversation before."

"We have." He returns the smile.

"Why are you here?"

Victor sighs, "I wanted to see you."

"You've seen me. Go home."

"Do you really want me to leave?"

"That's the second time you've asked that question."

"It's the second time you haven't answered."

Dawn drops her shoes and blazer at her feet. She pulls her purse from across her side body and it joins the pile of belongings inside her threshold. Stepping back from where her body holds the door open, she watches it close on Victor's leering face. He ducks his head backward to avoid the door knocking him in the forehead. She smiles at the closed door with a satisfactory grin.

"Dawn. Don't be like that," Victor says from the hallway.

"Last time you were here, you said we didn't have shit else to talk about. So why do you want to see me now?"

"I just apologized."

"That rushed "I'm sorry" was not an apology. It's not your golden ticket to get in either."

"Last time I was here, you told me to Google you. I'm not the only one who needs to rush 'I'm sorry's."

"And yet you still texted me first when the trial started."

42.

"I wished you well. What's wrong with that? You're the one who opened up tonight and told me you might be staying in Jacksonville. I didn't ask you anything about that. I didn't need to know that. I didn't want to know that, so clearly you've been thinking about me too."

Dawn opens the door as wide as the hinges and doorstop allow. "You shouldn't be so presumptuous."

"Thank you."

"For what?"

"For opening the door."

"You're welcome."

"I'd rather talk to you face-to-face, than to look like some creeper for your neighbors to call the cops on."

"I wouldn't mind seeing you get arrested."

He sees the playful smirk at the corner of her mouth where her real smiles begin. "I bet you wouldn't," Victor says, taking a step forward into her condo.

"I didn't say you could come in."

Dawn pushes the door closed so, once again, there is only enough space for her body.

"I guess you really do want me to leave."

Dawn doesn't answer. She walks away from the door and let's it close behind her. She sidesteps her furniture and the row of beanbag chairs and walks to her bedroom. Unzipping the back of the teal sheath dress, she pulls it from her shoulders and lets it fall on the carpeted floor as she walks into her en suite. She hears the faint sound of her front door closing and the single turn of the lock. *He decided to stay.*

Dawn opens the shower stall and turns on the water. Letting it heat up she faces her mirror, reaches behind her back, and unhooks the clasp on her dove gray bra. She pulls it off one arm at a time. Her matching thong underwear follow and are left with the bra in the middle of the bathroom floor. She grabs her shower cap from atop the faucet, covers her hair, and then steps into the steaming shower. She does not look around to see if Victor followed her trail of clothes to her nakedness. She does not turn around to find out if he is watching her from the hallway as she lathers in the darkness.

43.

She soaps, she rinses, she stands beneath the rain shower head and listens to the gentle drops of water fall on top of her plastic covered hair.

She stands until the water becomes cool to her warmed body. Stepping out of the shower, she finds no one with her.

I thought he came inside.

She picks up her underwear off the floor and takes them to the dirty clothes hamper inside of her closet. Wet feet leave prints on the cream carpet as she walks into the bedroom where she left her dress. It goes in the closet on top of the pile of her other work clothes that have to be taken to the cleaners during her weekend errands. She walks dripping wet, back into her bedroom where she pulls her silk robe from where it hangs on the post of her headboard. The fabric clings to her damp body despite the loose bow.

Dawn yawns as she walks out of her bedroom and into the living area. Victor is sitting with his back to her on the navy leather sofa. His fingers drum an unrecognizable pattern on the seat. She squints to see him clearly in the darkness. He took the liberty to close the drapes over the floor to ceiling windows. The light over the stove is the only thing that keeps them from being shrouded in black. Dawn moves toward it. In the kitchen she can see his profile as she absent-mindedly opens and closes drawers along her countertop, until she finds the box of matches she's looking for. With one strike, a flame begins to burn the red sulfur at the tip of the wood. She lights the three candles on the marble peninsula and then blows out the match flame.

"Why didn't you come in?"

"Someone once told me I shouldn't be so presumptuous. I thought it best if I just sit here and wait."

"Wait for what, Mr. Russell?"

Victor turns to face her from the sofa. She walks from the confines of the kitchen into the living room and sits on the red beanbag chair angled toward him.

"To see what kind of mood you were in, Ms. Anthony."

"It's late; I just got off work. What kind of mood do you think I'm in? I'm tired."

"You failed to mention your friend was just convicted of murder."

"It wasn't murder," Dawn corrects. "And we barely know each other."

"You're close."

"It's work."

"You're still close."

"Why are you here?"

"I think we're past that question now."

"Do you?"

Victor says, "I think the better question is, why did you let me in?"

"I didn't."

"You did."

"I did not."

"You left the door unlocked."

"And that was your invitation to intrude?"

Victor doesn't answer. He stares at Dawn's face. The intensity of her eyes against the clear serenity of her skin. He ignores the angry flare at her nostril and reaches for her. She allows him the pleasure of moving a wayward lock of hair out of her eyes. He lingers his caress on her cheek, then her chin, until his hand comes to settle on one unsheathed knee.

"You know, this is what you were wearing the very first time I came up here."

"You were early."

"And you weren't dressed. Did you do that on purpose?"

"Why would I be nearly naked, the first time I ever invited you in, on purpose?"

"The same reason you're nearly naked now, even though you've repeatedly asked me to leave."

"Did you come early on purpose? Is that why I caught you sitting outside my door at the first stroke of a new day?"

"It's the same reason you're letting me sit here with my hand on your knee with your legs parted, knowing you have nothing on underneath."

"Go home, Victor," Dawn says, standing up.

"Why?"

"Because attraction or not, good sex or not, this isn't going to work. This isn't what I need?"

Dawn walks in front of Victor to the door. Her robe blows open as she goes. She turns the lock and knob, and opens the door wide. He doesn't move. He doesn't stand. He sits, watching her insist on what she does but does not want. His mind assesses her face, reads the emotions she's trying to hold back.

Always playing hard to get. Women always pretend they don't have the same needs as a man, then have more toys than Toys R Us when they're too proud to pick up a phone.

He watches her face as it moves from decisive to indecisive in the blink of her eyes. Her assured steps gave way to shaky hands. The strong pull of the door followed by her light lean, as if she'd rather leave than force him to. He watches her run from her womanhood, from the part of her the night hours were made for. He watches as she shifts her weight from foot to foot, her thighs rubbing together as she sways, rubbing her own secrets she's trying to deny, the covert skin kisses she's determined to make into lies. He looks from her naked feet and ankles to the contrast of her licorice skin against the stark white of the robe. The plunging neckline reveals the rise of one breast, the air-dried skin, and shows off the attention of one nipple. He finally comes back to her face. The face he learned said a whole lot more when she wasn't speaking, than any word that could ever come out of her mouth.

He learned how to read her smiles. The anchor smile everyone received was her comfort; pulled corners, open mouth, slight space between the top and bottom rows of her teeth. Then there was the genuine smile. The one she smiled when she was thankful, pleased, gracious, flattered, humbled. It was wider than the anchor smile, her teeth bared together almost like a child learning to control their face. It was big and boisterous, and often accompanied by nervous laughter that brought her back to her composure and her anchor smile. Then there was the real smile. More rare than the Cullinan diamond. It began in her eyes and burned with pleasure across her face, making her lips spread slowly and her cheeks rise to the peaks of their apples. It crinkled her nose, left her face awash in the light from her teeth and, at the very end, showed off a singular dimple on her left cheek. Victor looked at her face now and knew her real smile was in there, but he had to find it, and she had to be willing to let him.

He stood up from the sofa, crossed the room to the front door in two swift strides, pressed his palm against the heavy wood and closed it.

"Go home, Victor."

"You don't want me to go, as much as you want me to stay."

"That line only works in songs and movies. Go home, Victor."

"Make me."

Dawn reaches for the door again. He moves out of her way to see what she really wants. Her hand grabs the knob but doesn't turn the lock. She drops her hand, walks away from his aura, and settles into the navy and white arm chair. *I can't believe I'm doing this.* Victor goes back to sit on the sofa. Dawn pulls her robe closed and tightens the outer belt into a double bow at her hip. She crosses her arms across her breasts, and her legs tight at her upper thighs. Her foot bounces in the air. Victor smiles, knowing the vibrations from her toes are running all the way up the length of her legs.

Dawn asks, "Why are you here?"

"I came to see how you're doing," Victor says.

"I told you I was tired."

"That's how you're feeling. Being tired is temporary. I asked you, how are you doing?"

"Right now it's all one and the same."

"I have a question," he says with a rise in his voice.

"Ask, since it's clear you won't let me sleep."

"Why were you on all day?"

"It's my job."

"You know what I mean."

"I don't have the answer to that. I was told to anchor the five, six, and eleven, along with my show. I did."

"Then what did you mean when you text me you might be staying in Jacksonville, after all?"

"Just what I said."

"I thought you already had a network offer."

"I do."

"Then why would you stay here?"

Dawn shrugs. It's followed by a sigh and then silence. *He wants to have a heart to heart now? I need to just send him home.*

"Why do you do that?" Victor releases an exasperated sigh of his own.

"Do what?" She asks defensively.

"Shut down and become another person."

"Because I'm not at ease. I'm tired. I don't know your motives. And this is a conversation we can have during normal business hours."

"So we're strangers now."

"We're certainly not together."

"I see."

"Why are you here, Victor?"

"Why do you keep asking me that?"

"Because the sooner you tell me why you're really here, the sooner I can decide whether or not I want to be bothered in whatever proposition you're going to make."

"Everything is business to you."

"It makes life simpler that way."

"Going through life with your emotions cloistered, and your heart walled off to friends and lovers, is not living."

"Don't lecture me on what living is. You're in my house, wanting something from me. State your purpose or go the hell home."

"There she is," Victor says with disgust. "I wondered how long it would take for the bitch inside you to show up."

"Did you just call me a bitch? Get the fuck out."

"No. You want to know why I'm here. This is why. I can't forget the woman you really are when you're not putting up a front, like you're the baddest bitch to ever walk the face of the planet. The woman I got to know through text, email, dates, conversation, quality time, versus that mean and shrewd person you pretend to be on TV. You're good at your job, I give you that, but you're not your job. When you turn that shit off, you're a great woman. The woman I can't forget."

"You could have said that out there." Dawn points toward the door.

"I'm gone."

Victor jostles his way toward the door, turns the lock, and swings it wide.

"I don't want to go to network as just another correspondent," Dawn yells from the chair.

The door closes.

"Julia's being put under review. While she's tested I'm filling in, but they also offered me her chair. Main anchor, and I can still do *Dawn in the Evening*."

"What do you want?" Victor asks.

"I want both. Network doesn't always come calling, and who knows if I say no, if they'll come calling twice."

"But you want more time on the desk?"

"I do. I also want to see Ebony's case through the appeal. I know James is going to file it. I can feel it in my gut. Her case is the kind of case names, personalities, and bylines are made from. Think Robin Roberts during Katrina."

Victor walks away from the door. He comes to stand behind Dawn. His hands land on her robed shoulders. He massages them through the thin material, kneading the knots that form from sitting too much.

He lowers his face to her ear, "Is that all you want?"

"I want this. But I don't think it's going to work," she answers, relaxing into the power of his hands.

"Why is that?"

"For starters, you just called me a bitch."

"I didn't call you a bitch. I said you have one on standby inside of you. Kind of like an alter ego. Like your very own Sasha Fierce."

"Sasha Fierce is a much nicer name than Bitch."

"I'm sorry, Ms. Anthony, for referring to your mean news lady alter ego as a bitch."

"You're not forgiven."

"Then I hope you plan to punish me."

Victor reaches past her shoulders over her chest to her folded arms. He grabs her hands and pulls them up until her arms extend above her head and she has no choice but to stand up right. She tugs his hand and takes the lead, making him follow her to her bedroom, he did not breach before. She stops just before her bed and turns to face him. Even with him looking down on her they are not eye level. His cocoa face is illuminated by the lights of the scant city skyline from the undrawn curtains. Dawn pulls the purple graphic tee over his head by the hem of his shirt. His body is still as thin, lean, and chiseled as she remembered. He takes the liberty of unbuttoning and unzipping the dark wash denim jeans. With a slight tug of her hand they fall to the floor. Gaze to gaze he grabs the belt of her robe and pulls it apart. He checks to see if he has permission to go further. Her stare through her bangs is bold and daring. He obliges. Reaching his hand inside, he tugs one string and then the other until the knot comes apart, and the wispy robe flows open to reveal her naked body. He slides down his own underwear and steps out of his flip-flops, so they are naked together.

Dawn turns away from him and tosses the pillows from the bed onto the floor. She pulls back the sheets and tan duvet. Victor opens the nightstand drawer and pulls a condom from the box inside, along with the lipstick disguised device beside it. Clumsily they slide in to the bed together. He flicks the switch for the lipstick and the pink tip vibrates to life. He places it on her flat belly with the tip of the stick hovering over the cavern of her navel. He lets the toy entice her womb from the inside out as he lowers his face to hers.

He offers his lips. She accepts and raises his offer giving her tongue. He accepts her wager and they broker a deal between them, sealed with kiss after kiss after kiss after kiss. They explore the mouths they had been missing with frenzied insistence until he pulls away breathless. His hand leads the way as his fingertips brush over her shins, up her knees, and across her body to her breasts. He kneads the lopsidedly perfect mounds until her nipples are more erect than before. Lowering his face once again, he takes one into his mouth. He kisses, he sucks, he tugs, he suckles, leaving it wet and sensitive in the cold conditioned air, and then does the same with the other. Her hands find the back of his head and pull and tug at his ears, as she licks her own lips.

Victor reaches one hand to her mouth appeasing her oral fixation. She grazes her teeth against his index finger, then takes the whole thing into her mouth, sucking it from base to tip until her jaws pop. He moves his lubricated finger down between the span of her breasts near the vibrating lipstick, over her mons, until it hovers at the center of her peach. Using the one finger to part her slick, engorged lips, he teases her, moving it back and forth over the outer protection until she groans her impatience.

The guttural growl is his permission to move forward. Victor picks up the buzzing toy from her belly and pulls her further down on the bed by her hips. He hooks one arm around each thigh and parts her open, submerging his face in her. He inhales her scent, her wetness, and her hunger for him. He tongues her greedily, making figure eights, and spelling his own name across her clit until she squeezes her thighs around his head. Dawn uses what strength she has to rock her body across his face. She rolls her hips in circles as his tongue sweeps across her equator, and his nose nudges her toward a nervous breakdown. He buries himself in her bundle and then backs off. She strains her head on her neck to see, until the sensation of the lipstick forces it back on her pillow. The buzzer is on its highest setting in its most intricate pattern. At the height of her own euphoria she creams around the body candy; her yoni hyperventilates it's liquid exhale.

Victor licks her once more, pushing aside her lips with the power of his tongue and reaching into where he knows she wants the rest of him. He suckles her until his own jaws pop. Unhooking his arms from her legs, he raises his head to see what he'd been waiting for, the burning satisfaction in her eyes, the glow across her face, the wrinkle in her nose, and the single dimple in her left cheek. The real smile he worked for, as rare as the Cullinan diamond, or the dark side of the moon on a moonless night. Poised at her precipice, he glides into his own warm, wet heaven knowing that whatever it is she's feeling, is real.

6.

James watches Ebony wrestle the pillow in the bed beside him. Her bed. Her pillow. Her room. Her house. He watches her battle the demon that only visits her at night. The monster that makes her fight in her sleep. The chimera that commands her attention. The dragon she can't slay and refuses to talk about. He watches her fitful sleep fully awake, despite the hour; three in the morning. He looks at her body as the fear of whatever she can't escape grips her. Her involuntary reaction to whatever makes her afraid is evident in the grip of her fingers on the top sheet, the strain of her throat against the pillow, and the unintelligible murmurs and mumblings coming from her lips. He watches her dream with fright, not knowing that in her sleep she is being chased by a two-headed monster that looks like both of her mothers. The mother who birthed her and gave her, her name and the mother Ebony chose for herself.

In his wakefulness, James can't see the green scaled lizard-like creature with dueling heads of Ayana and Marilyn. He doesn't see their heads circling around her in tsks of judgement. She stands on the edge of a mountain, or a window sill, or the lone piece of molten rock in the center of a volcano while her mothers upbraid her with their silent wrath of looks, stares, and glares, that condemn her, convict her, and sentence her to more time than what culpable negligence calls for. They blame her for the death of the man who deserved to die, they criticize her for her complicity in Soleil's abuse, and they denounce her good deed with the reel of her arrest. The mothers confront her as she struggles to stay balanced on whatever ledge she's standing on, while the backdrop behind them is her own life story: the lonely dinners, the late night rides to meet a pusher named Joe, waking up uncovered and cold in the old Buick, going to school with necessarily stolen lunch money, befriending girls who didn't like her, staying late at her new mom's house, even though she was uninvited, the accident, the flames of the fire that took the mother she desired, and the flippant comment from the woman who was lucid enough to remember she was a mother.

Ebony sees her years behind her two-headed dragon. The silent moments of her middle school and high school years, the college she couldn't wait to get to, the university dorm room she never made trips home from, and the graduation she invited no one to. She sees her first job at a private fitness studio, her colleague's client who ruined her life, the colleague's client who became her so-called boyfriend for three months. Ebony watches her assault and her answer with the purchase of her protection, her rape and her rebellion with her Lady to his forehead, the lie that led her to meet James, their year together, his year of blissful oblivion erased because of his insistence on getting to know her. Ebony watches the highlights and lowlights of her life play behind her mothered dragon as they gird her in silence, tongues slithering in castigation, waiting for her to choose in whose footsteps to follow. The four eyes of their two heads burn with the telepathic questions, *"Will you be a convict, a felon, a delinquent, or will you be a symbol, a crusader, a citizen of the world? The choice is yours."*

"The choice is mine," Ebony says, waking up breathless.

"Tough night?" James's voice is flat, cold, and distant in the darkness.

"Is it cold in here to you?" She sits upright in the bed and leans against the cushioned headboard.

"No. You were probably just sweating in your sleep."

"How long have you been awake?"

"I haven't gone to sleep."

"You've been watching me this entire time?"

"You fell asleep on the couch with the TV on. I turned it off and put you in the bed. I was drafting motions in the kitchen until my eyes got tired, so I came in here to lay down, but the sandman never came."

"Have you been drinking?"

"I had a glass or two of that SoCo in the cabinet."

"Please, don't drink that."

"Why not?"

"You know why."

"He's dead, Ebony."

"I'm aware. I'm guilty, remember."

"Only of not knowing how to use your gun."

"Tell my mothers that."

"Mothers?"

"Ayana and Marilyn. The dream was about them."

"Which one did you punch?"

"Neither. Why didn't you wake me up if you saw me fighting in my sleep?"

Because I just wanted to look at you. I wanted to watch you without you talking back.

James leaves her accusatory question unanswered. He avoids the bait to fight, her default when the conversation turns to what she doesn't want to talk about. He allows the silence to subsume them so she can't pick a fight he doesn't want to participate in, all to cover up what she still doesn't want to talk about. Her family. Their sore subject. The mother, brother, and sisters she told them she had, and then later told him were her neighbors who looked after her and died in a car crash. Then there was her real mother he found on his own by representing her and running a background check. The mother she refused to acknowledge. The mother he called on his own. Ayana. The woman Ebony referred to as a drug-addicted bitch. The woman he spoke to and learned was still struggling with the mistakes of her past. The neglect of her child for prescription pills that made her forget she was a mother. The use of those pills to escape what she lost, her parents and her boyfriend, and to cover-up what she wasn't ready to cope with, the postpartum love she didn't feel toward the child she never wanted. The child she only showed up for when the neighbors no longer could; when the nice nuclear family next door was taken from them both. The couple she knew before she became pregnant. The couple who never called the department of children and families on her, despite her abuse by neglect.

James leaves Ebony's demons alone. He doesn't pick at them. He doesn't ask to know more about them. He doesn't back her into a corner to tell a lie she will later have to apologize for and tell an even more complicated truth. He waits in his own silence. He tests his own tactic to see if he gets more of a response by doing nothing, asking nothing, saying nothing, and implying nothing, than he would if he poked, prodded, and punched with his words, treating her as a hostile defendant, and acting like the prosecutor he was trained to be by the man she killed. He lays beside her in supine position, eyes on the tray ceiling, hands folded across his bare chest, and listens to her wrestle with the words she's choosing to say next, instead of the ones she knows she needs to tell. He listens to her suck her teeth, blow air through her nose, and wrestle with her pillow to find the side that is cooler.

She turns her body toward his, rolling toward him aiming her bosom at his shoulder, and throwing her arm across his stomach. He braces himself against her spoon that is meant to elicit comfort in their closeness, instead of allowing herself to be loosed by the truth. James takes her fingers and puts them back at her side. *Here we go.*

"It's hot," he says.

She rolls away, back to her corner, back to her side, back to her thoughts, the dream of her demons. Ebony lays in the bed, the nightmare invoked sweat cooled on her flesh that rose with goose pimples in her sleep. She shivers beneath the sheet and fingers the lip end of her peach pillowcase. Her hands move from the bedding around her to her own body. She pulls down the boy shorts that rode up her ass as she tossed and turned, along with the wife beater that provides no warmth and irritates her nipples, hardened by the cutting chill of the air conditioning.

Ebony swings her legs out of the bed and stands up. *Why is he even here? I need him, and he can't even be bothered.* She walks to the nine drawer dresser in front of her and avoids looking at the mirror. She avoids seeing the face her mother gave her. The eyes she never knew with insights she was never allowed to ask about, staring back at her. In a drawer in the middle of the bureau, she pulls out a golden sweatshirt. She throws it over her head and pushes her arms through the sleeves. She leaves the hood over her unwrapped, uncovered hair and slides between the sheets, knowing James is still awake.

"They were a two-headed dragon," she says breaking the silence.

"Who?"

"Ayana and Marilyn."

"Oh.

The silence returns. James waits for what he needs to be told. He waits for the information she intends to impart with open ears and heavy eyes. Tired but unable to fall asleep, unable to shutdown his brain, unable to keep from thinking thoughts about his case, her case, their case, the case they almost won. Almost.

"I was standing on the edge, or at the edge, or on the only piece of something," Ebony begins again. "Basically, it was a scenario for suicide all around, with one wrong step. Ayana and Marilyn were staring down at me. Their heads were on long necks that kept me caged in front of their bodies, watching my whole life play out on some screen behind them."

"What do you think it means?" James asks.

"I don't know. They didn't say anything to me."

"You did."

"What did I say?"

"You were mumbling when I walked in, but I couldn't make out what you were saying. Then when you woke up you said, 'The choice is mine.' "

"It was like they were challenging me. Trying to make me choose which path to take in life. Be a delinquent like Ayana or a good woman like Marilyn."

"I don't think your characterizations of either one of them are really who they are or were."

"You weren't there, and you don't know."

This is what I get for opening my mouth. I don't know why I even bother. James drops his chisel, refusing to pick at the argument he knows could be next. Warm, awake, and ready to fight, he lets her stew in her own selective memory. Her vilification of Ayana is only justified by the canonizing of Marilyn.

"It doesn't matter anyway," Ebony continues. "It wasn't like I was standing on some fork in the road in the dream with their heads suggesting a path to take. The way I see it, anywhere I step there is danger or death."

"Seems like you figured it out. Good night."

He rolls his body toward her ready to be the spoon. An arm around her waist, he scoops her up into his body. With his hand and forearm through the front pouch of her hoodie, he holds her tight. His face in her hair, he smells the coconut and hibiscus products she uses to moisturize her scalp. His eyes close over the sweet smelling strands as the bounty of her blessing settles in his unaroused lap.

"What's wrong with you?" She asks.

Through the fog of descending sleep he says, "Nothing. It's just been a long day."

"I know. I was there. I was convicted, remember."

"I never said I forgot."

"Then why are you acting like you're the one facing three-to-five and not me?"

"I'm not."

"You are. You left me in the car in the garage. You walked out and didn't say where you were going. You barely spoke to me when you came back in. You watched me damn near break my neck fighting in my sleep. You act like someone pissed in your Cheerios today and not mine."

"Why do you do this?"

"Do what?" She asks, pulling his arm out of her pocket.

"Pick a fight about bullshit."

"I'm not picking a fight. I'm asking a question."

"I answered you. Nothing is wrong with me."

"You don't act like it."

His eyes flash open. "Ebony, how am I supposed to act? I lost my case. My girlfriend may be going to prison and it's up to me to figure out how to get you out. I know you were convicted, but the pressure is not on you right now. It's on me to try to figure out how to fix what you fucking started."

"So you blame me?"

"Ebony. You're to blame."

"I didn't kill him."

"It's me you're talking to. Not the judge. Not the jury. Not Dawn or your little friends. It's me. You stalked that man for a year and then you shot him at his job."

"He could have killed me."

"You're right, he could have, but you're not the one dead, now, are you?"

"So if you thought I did it from the beginning, why even take my case?"

"I ask myself that question every day. Does it even matter? Who else was going to do it? The public defender?"

"I could have gotten my own attorney, James."

"How? With what money? You'll be lucky if you're able to keep this house."

The truth shuts her down. The reality of her finances quiets her questions. She hasn't worked in six months. Hasn't had a client, a Skype session, or anything to bring in income. The year salary worth of savings will be depleted in months, and the mortgage will still be due.

"I know," she agrees in a sobering voice.

"Then let me sleep so I can figure out what we're going to do next."

"We?"

"Yes. We."

"Whatever," she mutters.

"What's that supposed to mean?" James sits upright in the bed.

"Just what it sounds like."

"Be more specific."

"There won't be a we in prison. There won't be an us in prison. There will just be me. Let's not act like *we're* affected in the same way."

"I didn't say we were. I just said I'm affected too, but you fail to realize that."

She huffs and pulls her body up. "How is that;" she asks as her nails find the backs of her hands in the front pocket of her hoodie.

"Did you ever stop to think how leaving my job — no — my career, for you would affect me? My income? My own damn mortgage payment?"

Slitted eyes and a smirking mouth relay nothing.

"No. You didn't did you," he continues. "I've been dealing with your shit for six months. Immersed in your story, your case, your drama for six months. All I'm asking is for you to shut up, lay down, and let me deal with my own shit for once, because you obviously don't give a damn."

"Go home, James."

"Don't worry. I'm already out the bed."

With her back turned, she listens to him as he grabs his clothes off the floor, and his belt from the dresser. She is satisfied with his reaction, vindicated from her own guilt. *And this is why I didn't say I love you. I couldn't. I knew he was going to act like this. A guilty verdict and he's brand new. I love you don't mean shit until it's tested.*

The alarm beeps twice. It is disarmed. It beeps again and announces the garage door is open. The car alarm clicks. The engine rumbles to life. She listens until she hears the metal of the garage door meet the ground, and the gravel crunching on the street outside. Alone, unarmed, and too cold to get up and reset the alarm, she lays in the bed, balled in the fetal position, hands scratching in her hoodie, facing the way James just left. His imprint is still in the bed. His pillow still smells like him. She looks toward the front of the room, eyes connecting with the bottom of the mirror mounted on the wall above the dresser. Refusing to look at her own reflection, she looks just beneath the border of the glass at the nearly empty dresser. Nearly. He left his cufflinks.

Sterling silver, polished to shine, bearing her initials. EAJ. Ebony Ayana Jones. Her mother's initials reversed. Ayana Edwina Jones. She stares at the letters, the initials, the representation of who she is, until the E and the A blur in her dreary sight and become one. The letters send her back to where she was, standing on the edge of something, pleading and proselytizing before her silent, judgmental mothers, as her life plays out behind them with no path forward.

7.

A faint noise pulls Ebony away from a new edge. This one positioned amidst the clouds of a gray sky. She can't tell if the noise is coming from her two-headed monster made of her mothers or from the unending deep beneath her, beckoning her because there is nowhere to go but down. She stands on the edge girded by the two heads and four eyes that don't speak, or sigh, or huff, or puff or breathe fire to intimidate or get their way. Encircled, she is unburnt but unable to break the chain of their entwined scales. She is unable to move beyond where she stands statue still in their sphere of bobbling heads and beady eyes. She stands in their circle watching her life play over and over, her choices, good and bad, on repeat. The loop ends with a pronounced ding. And then another, and another and another, until she is convinced it is coming from beyond the upbraiding glares and accusatory stares of her silent mothers. She is convinced it is coming from beyond where she stands. It is coaxing her and coming from below where she is. She moves a tentative foot from the edge on the thin ridge of whatever peak they have orbed her on, into the foggy abyss around her. The one move sends her free falling into the subterranean atmosphere, her legs pumping as if she is running through the wind toward the incessant ding until the sudden jactitation of her legs tangles her feet in the sheets and startles her upright and awake in her bed. The ding sounds again. It is her doorbell.

Ebony wipes cold from the corners of her eyes, and blinks until her pupils focus on her own face in the mirror in front of her. The doorbell dings. She looks at the old school alarm clock on the night stand beside her. The small square box with just two buttons and no USB port or iPhone jack reads in red block numbers eleven a.m. The doorbell dings.

Who the hell is at my door now? I swear it better not be another reporter.

"Coming," she yells as loudly as possible.

Her voice is strained, filled with sleep, and comes out as a tenor instead of her normal alto. She takes her time untangling her feet from the top sheet and then places them on the carpet beneath her. The doorbell dings. Walking to the door she pulls her wedged boy shorts from the crack of her behind, and then bends down to pull up one sock. It is her barrier from whatever abrasive material was used to create the ankle monitor leashed to the top of her foot. The only thing that has stopped the itch that started the moment police slapped it around her leg back in March.

Ebony unlocks and turns the handle of her decorative front door as the doorbell sounds inside her home once again. She stands face-to-face with her doppelgänger, her twin, the older version of herself. Ayana.

"What are you doing here?"

"James said it would be okay if I stopped by."

"He's not here. Do you want me to give him a message for you?"

"I came to see you."

"How did you get this address? Did . . ."

"No. James didn't give me your address. I saw the house number on the news last night and the reporters had already said what street you lived on. I looked it up on the property appraiser's website to make sure and I found you."

"And you thought that after fifteen years without seeing each other, or speaking, it would be okay for you to just drop by unannounced? You *and James* thought that was okay?"

"I told James I had the address and he said it couldn't hurt to take my chances to see if you would open the door."

"I thought it was him."

"Doesn't he have a key?"

"He doesn't always use it."

Ebony stands with the majority of her body behind her door. Only her head peaks out from the opening. She stares at what her own face will look like in another twenty-five years. The slight sag in the skin due to the loss of elasticity. A wrinkle here or there. A pimple or two on the fleshy skin just beneath her lashes, parallel to her nose, and clear eyes unclouded by any yellow tints, red flecks, or the bluing circumference around the rim of the iris. She stares at her future with disdain as she notices where her curly grade of hair comes from. The only difference is length. Ayana's is cropped close, currently waved to her scalp because it is wet. Ebony's hair is still tamed by a pressing comb and flat iron as part of her trial costume, but she usually wears it wild and free like in her mugshot. Her mane, her crown and glory is also often mistaken for a wig, like the arresting officer assumed when he tried to check her hair into evidence.

"Are you going to let me in?"

"I'm still trying to figure out what you want."

"To see you."

"You see me. You've seen me for the last three weeks on trial. What more do you need to see?"

"Let me rephrase. I came to check on your well being."

"You wanted to see if I had taken enough pills to forget what they said I was guilty of? Sorry. I'm not you. I don't self-medicate and forget my problems."

"Okay. I thought I'd get in the door before you started blaming me for my bullshit, but I see for all the time you spent around the Washingtons you didn't pick up on Marilyn's manners or southern hospitality."

"She died before I could be refined in the Washington school of charm."

"She wasn't that damn charming."

"And that's the fastest way to get thrown out of my house and you haven't even made it in."

Ebony pushes the door closed but it jams on Ayana's foot.

"We can either do this now or later," Ayana says in a husky voice. "I know where you live and you can't leave. Make a choice."

The choice is mine. Ebony recalls her dreams knowing her conscience has prescience and was trying to prepare her for what she faces now. One head of the two-faced monster. This one alive, well, and just as menacing, dressed in a green cardigan, patchwork jeans with the cuffs rolled to the ankle, and matching forest green and white striped Adidas.

"Let's get this over with," Ebony says, walking away from the door.

"Don't you think you should put on some more clothes?" Ayana locks the door behind her.

"For what? It's my house."

"For one, you have company. For two, what if James were here? And for three, who comes to the door in their underwear? I could have been a Jehovah's witness or the cable people, or lawn service, or security people."

"You're not company. James has seen me in less than what these boy shorts don't hide. And you have no right to come to my home, uninvited, and then criticize my clothing when I have on the same amount of clothing you used to wear to drive to God knows where to get your medicine we both know wasn't medicine."

"You just don't waste any time letting people know what you think about them."

"The only person who has time to waste is God. I ain't him. Life ain't forever."

"I see why he slammed you against your car," Ayana mutters.

"What did you just say to me?"

"I said I see why he slammed you against your car. You may not like me, but you still came from me. All of you, including your smart-ass mouth."

"Don't curse at me."

"James said you would say that."

"Well, what the fuck else did James say, since you two seem to be so fucking chummy these days."

Ayana smirks. "He said you would eventually curse me back."

"I only operate on a similar level to which I'm being treated."

"Is that a fancy way of saying I started it?"

"You said it, I didn't."

Ebony plops down in one of her striped armchairs in the living room. She offers no tour, and gives Ayana no choices of where to make herself comfortable. Ayana chooses one of the bar-stools and perches herself at the peninsula, her small green clutch rests on the bar beside her. She allows the awkward silence to add to the intensity in the room. She looks over at Ebony pulled into the fetal position in the armchair, hands in her front pocket, her eyes closed, lashes fluttering, but wide awake. The way she tried to fake sleep after the Washington's died and she didn't want to be bothered with her own mother. She looks over her daughter's long straight hair held in a loose ponytail, the edges a mess of cowlicks and curls from an evidently rough night of sleep. She looks over the hair she barely remembers brushing. The intricate styles Ebony used to come home with after sitting between the knees of another woman. She would waltz in the house well after dark smelling like Sulfur 8 hair grease and peppermint essential oil. The scent would linger and awaken her from whatever drug or alcohol induced stupor she had decided on for the day, or week if she had enough money.

Ayana looks over the body that used to be her own. The small but shapely breasts, wide hips, thick thighs, and more ass than she or most men knew what to do with. Where her own genetics and predilection for chemical substances over actual food kept her stomach flat, she can see Ebony's body is a sculpted work of art. Her thighs are thick with the weight of her ancestry and the muscle she toned, her ass is big because of her heritage, and the squat hops James told her she does across the ring when she used to have clients. Ayana looks over her daughter. Her lean, cut up arms reminiscent of Angela Bassett's portrayal of Tina Turner. The delicately arched eyebrows free of filler. The pout of her lips, plump even in restful, pretend sleep.

She breaks the silence, "You have a nice house."

"Thanks."

"It makes sense you would live in Mandarin. This is where you began. Your house even looks a little like ours did before we moved."

"We had more walls."

"Open concept just became a thing in the last decade."

"I guess."

"I watch HGTV, too, you know."

"So you have cable now," Ebony goads.

"Yes. I have cable now," Ayana answers proudly.

"I thought it was a luxury you couldn't afford. That's what you used to say."

"I used to say a lot of things."

"You used to say a lot of lies about why we didn't have stuff. Cable was a luxury but your "medicine" was a necessity."

"I guess those lies rubbed off on you?"

"James told you that too, huh?"

"He just wants to understand you."

"Did you tell him lying runs in the Jones's bloodline."

"I don't know what runs in the bloodline except dying young. I've lived longer than both of my parents, despite my best efforts not to be here."

"There's some honesty. Maybe there is some hope for me yet."

"Are you going to be sarcastic and bitchy all day or are we going to have a real conversation?"

"You don't want to talk to me."

"Ebony, if I didn't want to talk to you I wouldn't have crossed the bridge."

"Don't act like you're doing me any favors by crossing the bridge. You used to cross all the bridges for a lot less. Hell, you'd have probably thrown me off a bridge if it would have gotten you your drugs faster."

"I was a shit mom. I know that. I own that. But I'm not the one who was just convicted of a crime and facing prison time. So you can shit on me all you want, but that doesn't change your circumstances, sweetheart."

"I'm not your sweetheart."

"I'm sorry. Was that a name reserved for your precious Marilyn."

"Go home, Ayana."

"Oh. So we call mothers by first names now."

"You never acted like a mother, so why would I treat you like one now? I didn't call you mom when I was a kid, so what makes you think I'm going to do it now?"

"Touché, dear heart. Touché."

"My name is, Ebony."

"I know what your name is."

"Then act like it."

"Ebony. Can I at least have some water?"

Ebony takes her hands from her hoodie, unwinds herself from the chair, and moves across the cherry hardwood to the tiled kitchen floor. She pulls a plastic cup from the cabinet and fills it with water from the refrigerator tap. She places it on the counter in front of Ayana and then hops up on an opposite counter away from her. Arms folded across her chest, nails against her skin, she studies Ayana as she gulps the water until the cup is empty. The sound of liquid barging down her throat is the only noise that cuts through the heavy silence.

They examine each other. Eyes trying to covertly scan the other's body, the changes in their faces and features, habits and minute idiosyncrasies only they would know about the other. They come to the same resolute conclusion, *she looks the same, just older.*

"I see you're still scratching at your problems," Ayana nods toward Ebony's hands.

"Habit. I'm trying to stop."

"I know." Ayana takes another long gulp, draining the glass. "You've been doing that since you were twelve. I don't think you're going to stop no time soon."

Ayana sets the glass on the counter and pushes it beside her purse. She looks across the kitchen to where Ebony sits on the countertop looking down at her. She looks at the grimacing face and cold eyes and remembers when it was etched into the skin of her twelve year old. The face that looked up at her in the dark, the only light aglow from the television screen, where a van lay crumpled in flames, beneath the wreckage of a semi-truck. The face glared into her then with unabashed tears, rolling in succession. She said nothing with her mouth, but her eyes said everything, the way she looked from the television to the woman in front of her, wishing she could have made her trade places with the family that perished in the flames. Ebony looked up at her from the TV screen then with shame, blame, and regret, not knowing Ayana felt relief. Relief she expressed in the groggy language of her hangover, "I'm the only family you got, girl."

Ebony's face looks down at her now with the cold and hateful grief she had then at twelve. Stubborn in her silence, judgmental in her gaze, and prejudiced in her opinion.

Ayana sighs. "Say what you have to say, Ebony."

"When you talked to James, did he say where he was going today?" Ebony asks reluctantly.

"You don't know?" Ayana toys.

Ebony folds her lips and holds her thought, *I wouldn't ask you if I did.* She sighs. "No. I don't."

Her sigh is the first sign she has given anyone else that she is not as well as she may appear. That there is a storm brewing inside of her. A hurricane of emotions fueling her fury and sadness, her angst and regret. Her thoughts of should I or shouldn't I. *Should I tell James to drop the appeal and just do my three to five.*

Her sigh is the only symptom of her inner sickness. She knows it is weighted with anticipation and frustration, incompetence and a lack of confidence. *I don't know where he is, what he's doing, and if it's even really for me. He could be trying to get his old job back and lying to me about the appeal. I couldn't blame him if he did.*

Ebony rolls her eyes at her own tell and waits for an answer. Ayana relishes the moment to turn the conversation. She drinks the last of her water, then sets the cup slowly on the counter. Fidgeting, she twists from side to side on the bar-stool, moves her purse from her right to her left, and finally settles to drumming her fingers on the granite countertop. Ebony and Ayana. They play a game of chicken with the information one is seeking and the other is holding on to for ulterior motives.

Ebony hops down from the countertop where she was seated and walks over to the wall mounted landline phone.

"He said he was going to his mother's house," Ayana blurts as Ebony begins to dial.

"Thank you."

The gratitude is more formality than genuine. More platitude than anything else.

"He probably needs to be there," Ebony says, walking back to where she was perched.

"I don't follow."

"Nothing. He goes to see his mom when he's stuck about something."

"Is it you or work this time?"

"We're one in the same."

"He's still representing you?"

"Apparently."

"Then let him go and get all the motherly advice he needs."

"Hopefully, it's good advice."

"Mother's always give good advice."

"Present company included?"

"I'm sure I said at least one thing to you, that you remember, that's come in handy in your life."

"You're right. It's just one."

"I can take it." Ayana sighs. "What did I say that's been so helpful?"

"I didn't say it's been helpful."

"What did I say, Ebony?"

"You told me to never settle for anything less than what I want, and when someone can't give me what I deserve . . ."

"Take the shit anyway," Ayana joins for the end of the mantra.

"I think that's the only thing you ever taught me that I remember."

"Perhaps."

"But it was the best thing."

Ebony smiles. It is a temporary peace offering. Ayana accepts with one of her own. Their similarities sit in the distance between them. Mother and daughter. Ayana and Ebony. Separated by painful misunderstandings of the past and wounded egos that won't let them humble their pride in the present, they observe and survey what the other has learned about life in their absence, and agree that perhaps motherly advice is sometimes still the best and only medicine.

8.

He had to cross the river on I-95 North to get to where he is now. With intention, he exited the highway at Golfair into the heart of Moncrief. Not the upcoming acreage of North Jacksonville, not the hot zone of Northwest Jax, he is simply on the Northside that is stereotyped by its headline crime. He drives deeper into the neighborhood made up of rugged, red tinged, asphalt roads passing gas stations galore, every kind of chicken shack from the commercial, Popeyes and Church's — those two right across the street from one another at one corner — to the ones owned by local entrepreneurs with handmade signs of red paint lettering that read fried chicken, fried fish, gizzards, fries. He passes liquor stores, food marts with "We Take EBT" signs flashing in the window that sell lottery tickets, malt liquor, cigarettes, hot Cheetos, and maybe a banana. He passes independent Chinese restaurants, beauty supply stores, and the legal loan sharks, the predatory payday loan places that allow people to cash and give away their entire checks with the promise of "free money" now.

James obeys the posted speed limit signs as he drives down Moncrief Road. He hangs a right on Bronson Lane and takes it to Longspur Avenue. He drives until he passes the church he was raised in, that is in desperate need of a new roof and paint job, and wonders what's become of its building fund. He drives down the block where he learned to walk, ride a bike, kiss girls, and lie to his mother. He is deliberate in his slow creep down the sleepy street. He passes small house after small house, some well-kept, others not, and some vacant lots overtaken by trees and shrubs and the critters that live in trees and shrubs. His big-bodied car comes slowly down the avenue lined by tall leaning trees whose roots take over the curb and before long, the street. He arrives at his destination. The small red brick house with the white front door.

James pulls into the driveway, cuts the engine, and closes the door to his gold Impala. Jingling his keys in his hands he strides to the door, takes the one step up onto the concrete porch and pushes his key into the lock. It turns with an easy spin and James is back home.

"Mama, it's me," he says closing the door behind him.

Inside, the smell of years of fried chicken, catfish, and porkchops assault his nose. The smell is baked into the walls just like the grease stains on the wallpaper behind the white, four burner gas stove. James walks inside. The small three bedroom, two bathroom house is antiquated in style, but it is still home. The entryway is small, the kitchen off to his right, also small and square. A stove, a refrigerator and freezer, a sink, a few countertops, and a few cabinets. There is no dishwasher. The appliances aren't stainless steel. The refrigerator and freezer combo is side by side and not the French door design of the new millennium. When he was here he was the dishwasher. Now the job belongs to the nurse he hired to help his mother and father, who has early onset Alzheimer's.

"I'm surprised to see you here," his mother says.

"I told you I would stop by."

James takes a seat on the cracked brown leather sofa in the living room beside his mother. His body sinks into the center pillow of the couch that's about six inches lower than the rest of the cushions from years of wear and tear. The worn leather gives in to his weight without protest.

"You've said a lot of things over the last few months that weren't true, so why would I believe you when you said you was coming over here?"

"Mama, I just got here. Are you really going to start right in on me?"

"Boy, I'm grown and so are you. Ain't nobody got to worry about your feelings. You don't like what I got to say . . . Leave. That's why you ain't been coming around here in the first place."

"That's not true. I've been busy, you know."

"Yeah, I know. I seen you and that girl on the TV. You even got the news lady tangled up in ya'll mess."

"I didn't know what was going to happen when we took the picture. It was just a picture."

"And now it ain't. It's evidence. You better hope the State Attorney don't try to come after you for collusion. You know she's a vindictive SOB. Excuse me, Lord."

"But she won."

"I know. So when you going to ask for your job back?"

"Damn, Mama . . ."

"Boy, you better watch your mouth in this house and when you talking to me. I don't know who you think I am, or where you think you are, but cursing at Mama's is what we don't do."

"Yes, Ma'am."

Chastised and silenced, James sits back against the sofa and turns his attention to the TV his mother has on mute with the closed captioning playing. A book of sudoku puzzles sits in the lap of her white terry cloth housecoat with a floral design. A book of word search puzzles, and another book of crossword puzzles sit on the right arm of the sofa. Puzzles she only began playing once her husband got sick. Puzzles she plays as a precautionary measure, determined to keep her own mind sharp while the man she loves loses his.

"Rachelle," an old raspy voice croaks.

"I'm coming. Hold on."

James's mother stands from the sofa and shuffles quickly through the doorway space along the half wall separating the kitchen and the living room. He hears his father croak her name once more until she reaches him.

"What you in here fussing for, now?" He hears her ask from the bedroom.

He doesn't hear his father's response. Diagnosed three years ago, the Alzheimer's has progressed slowly. His father, James Parnell, Senior still remembers names; his wife Rachelle Parnell, his two sons, James Jr. and Joseph, and the basic layout of the house he bought and paid for from his job at the post office.

"He just wanted some water and for me to fluff his pillows," Rachelle says coming back into the room.

James notices she moves more slowly coming back to sit beside him than she did when she got up to check on his father. Short and stocky, his mother stands no taller than five foot two. Her weight is evenly distributed. No noticeable or excessive gut, but heavy and solid in her arms and legs. Arms that used to hold babies all day long at the daycare she owned, and the legs that supported her body as she ran behind children, cooked their breakfasts and lunches, and cleaned up after them when the day was over. She plops down in her seat beside James, sinking him even lower into the center cushion.

"How's he doing?"

"Go on in there and see. He still your daddy, even if you don't come around."

"Mama, I know."

"You don't act like you know. You ain't been here in forever."

"I told you . . ."

"I know. You've been busy. But you should never get too busy for family. You can even bring that girl with you, if you want, since she still home."

"She can't come, she's still on house arrest."

"She been on house arrest since she killed that man."

"Mama, I told you she didn't do it."

"I know what you told me. But I know what I saw in that courtroom."

James huffs. "I'm going check on Pops," he says, standing from the couch.

"You'll be lucky if he still remembers who you are, you ain't been here in so long."

"We have the same name. I doubt he forgot me."

"Mmhmm."

James walks into the room where his father lays propped in the bed, with his eyes closed. His hands hold a rough piece of wood and a sheet of sandpaper. The only thing he's allowed to have that reminds him of his part-time carpentry work he used to do after his shifts at the post office. James takes the block and sandpaper from his father's loose fingers and sets it on the nightstand with his glass of water. He sits on the quilted spread atop the bed covering his father's legs.

"Hey, Pops," James says striking up a conversation. "I came to see how you're doing. How you holding up. Hopefully, Mama don't be getting on your nerves too bad with all her yanging."

"Who, you?" James Senior asks, opening his eyes.

"Pops, it's me," James insists. "Your first born. Your favorite."

James Senior reaches for his son's hand. James takes it and clasps it between his own and holds on tight.

"I saw you on TV," his father says after studying his face awhile. "You were on TV every day."

"I was?"

"Rachelle watches you. You a judge."

"No, Pops. I'm a lawyer."

"Naw, you a Judge. I saw you in the black robe. Where your glasses?"

"Pops, I don't wear glasses. Remember, I have good eyesight like you."

"I don't need no glasses, but you have on glasses every day on the TV."

"No, I don't."

"I know what I saw," James Senior roars insistently. "You on the TV in a black robe, in court, with glasses on. And you had more hair. Why you cut your hair?"

"Pops. That wasn't me you saw. You're talking about Judge Mathis. That's what Mama watches during the day."

"I know what I saw," he yells again. "Rachelle. Rachelle. Rachelle."

"What is it, Jamie?" James's mother asks rushing into the room.

"This man from the TV, tried to tell me that he ain't no judge just because he took his glasses off and cut his hair."

"Jamie. This is our son. James Junior. Remember?"

"Our son is Joey."

"We have two sons, Honey. Joey and James Junior."

"Two sons?"

James Senior questions Rachelle's assurances. She nods her head emphatically and strokes the unbrushed mat of gray and white hair atop his head. She grabs the glass of water from the nightstand, tilts the pink straw toward his mouth and lets him take a sip. Rachelle replaces the glass and continues stroking James Senior's hair. One hand atop his head, the other caresses the side of his face, she hums an old hymn until she can feel his breathing slow. It takes three verses before he drifts back into the light sleep James found him in.

"Come on outta here if all you gon' do is rile him up," Rachelle whisper yells.

"Mama, I didn't know I was going to upset him like that."

"I told you he wasn't going to remember you."

"But it's me, Mama."

"Everything ain't about you, boy."

"I thought you were just exaggerating."

"Why would I lie to you?"

James leaves the question as it was intended. Rhetorical and unanswered. His mother takes a seat in front of the silent TV and resumes her puzzle. James watches from the carved doorway in the wall. Her hands move swiftly through the nine boxed game of numbers. Her skin makes a swishing sound across the flimsy recycled paper pages. Skin the color of his own. In fact everything about her is in him. His build, his height, his features. He belongs to his father only in name. James Senior wasn't a towering man, but he wasn't short. Average height, and a lean build, his attributes went to his second son, James's brother, Joseph. The brother with three children by three different women and who is

77.

always looking for a quick come up instead of trying to invest his time and talent into a long-term project for an extended period of profits.

James sees the family portrait still hangs on the wall behind the sofa. It used to be the centerpiece of the wall. Taken when he was sixteen and Joseph was thirteen, both his parents sporting hair close to their natural colors, and in control of all of their faculties. He resents the emblem to an easier time. To a time when all he had to do was go to school and make good grades and play with his brother. He resents the present loss of youthful innocence and vigor encapsulated in the family photo. His father dressed in a simple blue suit and red tie, his mother complimentary in a navy Sunday dress, wearing a combed out roller set, her thick hair draping her shoulders, and her bangs curled before her eyes. He sees the unsmiling lips of he and his brother, eyes alight with mischief despite their promise to each other to look hard in the picture. He shakes his head at what used to be so simple, regretting his wishes to be grown and to get out of the house as quickly as he could. He stares at the nuclear family on the wall that's been demoted from the centerpiece of the display to an accompaniment.

In the center of the wall is another black family. Not their own, but theirs. A man and woman, and their two daughters. The First Family. Barack, Michelle, Sasha, and Malia smile back at him from the center of the wall as if they are a beloved aunt, uncle, and first cousins you can't wait to see on summer trips up North. Their official family portrait in a golden oval frame takes up prime real estate on the wall of notable people. Beside them in four eight-by-ten frames affixed in a square pattern are pictures of black Jesus with a golden halo and knotty hair as if the Lord was considering growing locs. Beside black Jesus is Martin Luther King. The iconic black and white image with his finger on his cheek that covers one side of every church fan, with a local funeral home advertisement on the other. On the second row is a color photo of Nelson Mandela and next to him, a black and white photo of Malcolm X. Thought leaders, a revolutionary, and the Lord don't even measure up to the success of the Obama's, smiling proudly from the center of the wall.

"Boy, you gon' stand there all day staring into space, or you gon' tell me what you really came here for?" Rachelle asks, not looking up from her puzzles.

"Do I need a reason to come by and see you and Pops, Mama?"

"If this was three months ago, I'd say no. But since you ain't been here, and you didn't call until you was down the road, I assume there's a reason for this pop up now. Your girlfriend put you out?"

"I have my own house, Mama."

"You don't act like it. I drove by your house last week, tooted the horn, got out and rang the doorbell, and tried to peep inside that complicated side window you got with all them cutouts . . ."

"It's called a mosaic, Mama."

"I don't care what it's called. I know I tried to look through that thing, and I guess your neighbors felt sorry for me. The man next door came outside and told me you ain't been there in weeks."

"I go by and get the mail, and feed and walk Caesar."

"Well, I'm glad to hear that. A foreclosure notice could be sitting in the box and a skeleton in the hallway, and you wouldn't know it because you got your head stuck so far up Ebony's, behind you can't see the forest for the trees."

"Mama, it's not even like that, and I'm not going to lose my house."

"Are you sure? It's not like you got a real job. I know that girl ain't paying you for your services and expertise. Not in money, anyway."

"Mama!"

"Tell me I'm lying."

James sighs. "I liquidated some assets to make sure the mortgage is paid up."

"I liquidated some assets," Rachelle mocks. "Don't you sound smart and fancy. All that means to me is you cashed in some stocks or heaven forbid, tapped into your 401K. I hope you know what you doing."

"I do, Mama."

"No, you don't. If you did you would've left that convict a long time ago, found a good, wholesome, church going woman, and given me some grandbabies by now."

"You already got three from Joey. Why you rushing me?"

"That's not the point. And don't back talk me, boy. The bible said be fruitful and multiply."

"The Bible also say love your neighbor as yourself, and judge not lest ye be judged."

"I know what the Bible say, boy. We not talking about that part right now. You may think you can shoot out some kids forever, but time ain't forever. Shoot out a baby when you forty, fifty-years-old and see if your knees don't give out trying to chase around after they little behinds."

"Okay, Mama."

"Don't okay mama me. I don't need your okie doke. Ebony might fall for your BS, but I'm your mama. I birthed you. And I raised you."

"I know, Mama."

"Then you better act like that girl is guilty and going to prison so you can get your old job back and move on from her convict behind."

"We still have an appeal."

"That you don't have to file."

"Yes. I do.

"No. You don't."

"Yes, I do. Mama, I love her."

"Like Tina say, what's love got to do with it?"

"What's love got to do with what?" A deep voice yells from the front door.

"I guess it's all my children in here today," Rachelle says, standing from the couch.

"Hey, Joey," James mutters.

"What the hell wrong with you?" Joey asks, slapping his brother's hand and pulling him upright for the standard black man's hug.

"He mad, 'cause he know I'm right," Rachelle says, wrapping her arms around Joey. "I keep trying to tell your hard-headed brother to leave Ebony's shifty behind, but he don't wanna listen."

"Mama, I'm with James on this one. I've seen her behind shift, I wouldn't want to leave that either."

"Boy, don't come in my house with that gutter talk. If that's your only conversation, you can go back out on Moncrief with that. We may be in Moncrief, but I am not of Moncrief and you ain't either."

"I'm just saying, I know why he ain't leaving."

"Joey. Tread lightly," James cautions from his lean against the wall.

Joey sits in the recliner that matches the sagging sofa. "I didn't mean no disrespect, Bruh Bruh. I'm just saying, if I was you, I wouldn't leave Ebony, until she left me."

"That's why you got three kids now, because you don't know when to leave."

"Where are my grandbabies, Joey?"

"At school."

"You picking them up?"

"In a little bit. I'm on break."

"On break from what?" James asks.

"From work, what else," Joey defends.

"Boy, you know you ain't got no job. I don't know why you come in here with all these lies."

"Mama, I told you I'm working for the carwash service that runs out of Town Center. I detail the cars."

"So you expect me to believe you on break from a job at Town Center, and you came all the way across the bridge, on your break?"

"That's just how much I love you, Mama."

"Boy, you full of it."

"You right." Joey laughs. "I came to see pops."

"He in there sleep. Leave him alone. Your brother done already upset him once today."

"James!" Joey says accusingly.

"I didn't know he wasn't going to remember me. He thinks I'm Judge Mathis."

"Damn, Bruh."

"Watch your mouth, Joseph. I done already told you."

"Sorry, Mama," he mumbles. "That's tough, James."

"I know."

"Welp, he still remembers me, though."

"That's because you over here every day mooching off of mama and pops."

"And there he is. Mr. I think I'm better than everybody else. I do what I gotta do for mine. Ain't nobody asking mama and pops for shit."

"Joseph."

"I'm sorry, Mama. But James needs to hear this," Joey says, standing from the recliner. "You walk around with a chip on your shoulder, thinking you better than everybody else because you went to law school. Look at you now. Pussy-whipped just like the rest of us out here. You running behind some tail that won't even say 'I love you' back. At least I know I could be back with any of my baby-mama's if I wanted to."

"Is that your argument?" James smirks from against the wall.

He looks over at his brother. Their father's doppelgänger. Average height, lean build, mocha brown face, dark wavy hair, thick eyebrows, and a lecherous grin. Dressed in a plain white T-shirt, khakis, and black work boots, he is a far cry from the mischievous thirteen-year-old smiling from the family portrait at the far end of the living room wall.

"You know I'm right," Joey eggs on. "That's why you not saying nothing."

"I don't have anything to say," James begins. "I don't have anything to defend. We don't run in the same circles, we don't do the same things. We don't have the same goals. We don't have the same aspirations in life. We don't even go after the same women. I went to law school. I got a job. I saved my money. You wasted mama and daddy's money. They took out a second mortgage to try to put you through school and you didn't even finish, more concerned about knocking up these chicks you mess with than doing something with your life. I don't have to defend nothing I do to you or anyone else. Mama, I'm gone."

"James, don't go. Your brother just saying what everybody's thinking." Rachelle stands from the sofa.

"If that's what y'all think of me, that I'm so pussy-whipped that I can't see the forest for the trees, then maybe it's best if I do leave."

"James, that's not what I said."

"Yes, it is, Mama. You don't believe Ebony, that's fine, but now you're saying you don't believe in me or my choices either. I'm a go. I'll come back by and see Pops another time when it's just Laverne here taking care of him."

"Thank you for getting her, James. She's a big help around here."

"You're welcome, Mama."

James walks to the front door, his mother's bare feet shuffling behind him. He opens the door and steps outside.

"Bye, Mama," he says, hugging her over the threshold.

"I love you, Junior," Rachelle says with her head buried into her son's neck.

"I love you, too, Mama."

"You know you don't have to go through with this."

"Yes, I do."

"Why, Junior? Tell me why."

"Because I love her too."

"Then you better get yourself together and win before they come after you."

"I know, Mama. I know."

James walks away from his mother's embrace with the lingering scent of her ivory soap and raw shea butter wafting around him. He gets in the car knowing she is staring out at him. He starts the engine to see his mother and his brother in the doorway of the little house. Joey raises a finger to get his attention before he backs out the driveway. James lowers his window as his brother jogs over to the car.

"Wassup, Joey," he says curtly.

"I just wanna know there's no hard feelings from what happened in the house."

"We're good, Joey. I gotta go."

"Hold on. Hold up for a minute."

"How much you need?"

"Damn, James, why you gotta be like that?"

"Be like what? That's what you want, right? Some money."

"No. Well, yes. But you ain't gotta come at me like that, like I'm not good for it."

"Joey, don't worry about it. I don't even want it back," James says.

He lifts his butt from the driver's seat, and pulls out his wallet from his back pocket. He opens the black leather case and pulls out all his cash.

"That's a hundred and twenty dollars."

"Thank you, Bruh-Bruh. I promise I'll pay you back. I get paid Friday."

"Don't even worry about it." James throws his car in reverse. "Keep it. When you get paid, take a hundred and twenty out, and set it to the side and use it for when you wanna ask me or Mama for some money."

James backs down the driveway, forcing Joey away from his car. He drives away from the small red house of his youth; away from the old church where he was taught to make a joyful noise. He drives away from the neighborhood of aging matriarchs and knucklehead grandsons and great-grandsons. Following the speed limit he takes New Kings Road away from Moncrief, away from his childhood, his mother, his father, his brother, and back toward I-95. He takes the highway across the bridge back to the Southside to the life he's made for himself. Exit after exit passes until he is thirty miles away from the truth, the voices of reason he's left ignored and unconsulted in his choices. He drives until he's forced to make another choice without the contributing comments of his DNA. He exits the highway at Philips instead of staying on for another two miles to go to Old St. Augustine Road. Choosing the exit for where he wants to be instead of where he should be, the exit for the call he answered instead of the career he made, he drives the streets until he reaches the home that is not his, with the woman inside he can't leave. His brothers words a refrain in his mind.

I wouldn't leave Ebony, until she left me.

9.

It's been nine months since Ebony left James alone on the Riverwalk. Nine months since he realized he was in love. Nine months since they strolled arm in arm along the St. Johns wearing light jackets and thin scarves, the extent of their winter wardrobe, even if it was the middle of December. He was in a suit on break from a court case. She was in the area before a session at the gym. They met for lunch at the Landing, despite its slim selection of restaurants. Sitting outside on the bank of the river at Fionn Maccools, he had the Dubliner and she had Guinness Beef Stew. Her hair was pulled into a ponytail at the middle of her head. A cascade of curls fell down to her shoulders and crowded in with her hot pink scarf, and forest green bomber jacket. Her back was to the sun, but it still glinted in all its glory off the water, and the pink of her scarf, bathing her face in its warm light. She ate her stew slowly as she talked. He gazed at her while she spoke, listening but not, admiring the construction of her features. One hand on his corned beef sandwich, he reminded himself to take a few bites every few minutes, so he could actually have lunch during the hour recess. He looked without listening, wanting to know everything he could about her.

He interrupted, "So . . . tell me something,"

"What do you want to know?" She played along.

"What were you like as a child? Were you precocious, rambunctious, petulant. Did you get into a lot of trouble?

James asked his question with a smile, but it was met with a furrowed brow and a flash of darkness across her face.

She shook her head and said, "You'd have to ask my mother."

"I'd love to," he responded, thinking it was an invitation.

She didn't offer anything else. Didn't extend anything more of herself. She stopped talking and took quick gulps of her still steaming stew from her spoon. He continued through his sandwich and fries until his plate was empty, save for the dill pickle spear he didn't plan to eat.

"How's your mom doing?" she asked, eyes focused into her bowl.

"Good," he answered with a self-assured nod. "Just trying to take care of my dad. I'm thinking about hiring someone to help her out, because he's only going to get worse."

"I told you."

"I know, but you saw how she acted when you suggested it. I just don't know if she would be offended if I did it without telling her. My mom's a proud woman."

"I remember."

"I just don't want her to take it the wrong way."

"What way would that be?" Ebony asked, finally dropping her spoon.

"I don't want her to think that by me hiring somebody, I think she's not qualified to take care of my dad."

"But she's technically not."

"It's not that simple with my mom."

"I guess," Ebony said, focusing back on her stew.

"She thinks because she owned and ran a daycare that it's the same."

"But it's not."

"I told her that. And you know what she said to me?"

"What's that?"

"Once a man, twice a child, Junior. That's all we can look forward to in this life. I didn't get him when he was three. But now he's seventy-three and my baby."

"You can hire the nurse for one day," Ebony suggested. "Let them know it could be temporary or permanent, and see how it works out. That way you're not out of any money by paying too far in advance, and you're still considerate of your mother's feelings."

Ebony didn't see the light in his eyes at her suggestion. She finished the last spoonful's of her stew as James gazed at the pulled back curls at the crown of her head. His own mind running with adjectives to describe her;

thoughtful, sensitive, caring, compassionate, with a big booty to boot. His eyes fell in love with her sporty body when they met outside his office nine months ago, when she was trying to pay a ticket, and he was waiting until the news crews vacated the premises of his building. He was intrigued by her wit as she joked with him about their happenstance meeting. He was impressed by her strength as she went round after round with him in the ring of her gym, helping him slim his forming comfort-food gut. But that was all in the beginning. In the first few months of their meeting. Nine months in, this was the first time he'd seen her mind at work for something more than to convince herself, or him, that they could overcome the level of physical activity they were exerting. It was the first time she'd spoken a truth to power to compliment and convince him of his own truth, without aggrandizing herself in the process.

"Let's take a walk," James said standing.

"Good. I can walk off some of this Guinness."

He threw down a one-hundred-dollar-bill and they stalked off from their table, walked inside the restaurant, and back outside to the Riverwalk. He led the way, walking in the direction of the courthouse, even if he was blocks away at the waterfront. They passed the empty bandshell always set up in the open area of The Landing. They walked past Hooters, and Chicago Pizza until they reached the gazebo setup to provide shade for walkers, joggers, and their dogs on a hot, sunny day at Hogan Street.

It was there under the gazebo where they stood looking out over the river. Standing between two bridges, they gazed at the Southbank. The condos, the apartments, the hotel, the few tall buildings rising above the water. He laid against one of the pillars and she laid with her back against his chest. They looked out over the river as if they had one mind, and one thought, and moved with one body. As if their two had become one in the middle of the day with all of their clothes on. He looked out from over her inclined body, her lavender scent inviting clarity, and he asked the question that had been on his mind since the first time he laid in her bed and felt open enough to be honest.

He bent his lips to her ear and said with the gentleness of the afternoon breeze, "I want to meet your family."

He felt her body stiffen against his chest and stomach. She became rigid where she was once pliable.

"I think it's time," he said, ignoring her physical warning sign.

Ebony stepped away from his embrace, backward toward the railing guarding the water. Alarms went off in her mind and every thought was *no, no, no, no, no.* The flash of darkness James forgot he saw earlier at the table, tinted her olive skin in hurt and anger.

"I have to go," she said, looking at her wrist that didn't hold a watch. "I have to pick up some equipment from Academy before my next session."

Ebony walked away from James without waiting for his response. She walked away without hearing his protest. His offer to walk her back to her car. She hurried away from the gazebo back toward The Landing. She moved at a full sprint by the time he stumbled back to the edge of Chicago Pizza. He watched her run past Fionn Maccol's where they'd had lunch, where he'd seen the capability of her compassion in the bat of her lashes, and the slow measured words from her mouth.

He walked away from The Landing and started up Hogan Street, bewilderment in his slow stride. His calls of "Ebony, wait up," unanswered and ignored. He reached for his phone as he crossed Water Street. James ignored the time, cleared the home screen, and laid his finger over the green phone symbol. He dialed her ten numbers by heart walking and waiting for the connection to be made, for the phone to ring, and for her voice to pick up on the other end. It never did. She never answered. He hung up and dialed again as he crossed Bay Street and walked past a bank. She did not answer. She did not ignore his call, but she did not answer. He dialed again and waited to leave a message. His stride a little faster, the wind in his throat, he left a breathless message apologizing for the abrupt end to their date, concerned for her well-being, hoping that they could get together for dinner, and that he looked forward to meeting her family whenever she wanted to make it happen. He crossed Forsyth with his confidence clipped, and turned left down Adams checking his breath, concerned it could be rancid from the sauerkraut on his sandwich. He reached Julia Street and shook his head to clear his conscience. The hasty end to their afternoon replayed in his mind, always in her voice. *I have to go.*

He kept walking to the courthouse knowing his case was about to be back in session, hearing Ebony's voice in his head every step of the way as he questioned — W*hat did I say?* James jogged the last two blocks passing Pearl Street and didn't slow down until he turned up the courthouse walk at Clay Street. His heart pumping, his mind racing, he climbed the few stairs in twos, entered the front oversized glass doors, and flashed his badge to the security guards to skip the line for the metal detectors.

The marble staircase took him to the fifth floor. The courtroom he was presenting in. The courtroom he returned to being an assistant state attorney in. He took a seat beside the state attorney and waited for the judge to gavel the court back in to session. In court for the rest of the day, he argued without vigor, he made his case without punctuation, and persuaded the jury without charm. He talked, and he spoke, but he did not debate. He made words into sentences until the judge gaveled that he had done enough for the day.

His mind left the law in the courtroom. Skipping the walk across the connecting bridge back to his office, he left his work for the paralegals, exited the courthouse, and walked across the bright green lawn to the parking garage that held his car. He checked his phone. There were no missed calls and no text messages. *I have to go.* Her unceremonious dismissal of him gave him the strength he needed to resist the temptation to send a text of his own, but he broke. He kept seeing the sun on her face and the glow from her scarf. He kept hearing her suggestion, *Hire the nurse for one day*. He didn't remember the cold steeliness of her answer when he asked what she was like as a child. With rose-colored glasses obscuring his memory, he broke and called her before and after court for the next two days, apologizing for something he didn't know he did.

The next week he left one angry voice mail, accusing her of being silly and childish. He unleashed his anger at Ebony in court. Invigorated by his own waffling emotions, he objected to be objectionable, debated for the sake of feeling like he was doing something, and performed in the drag of a well-trained prosecutor until the jury had no choice but to rule as he wished.

James won the case, but had still lost his own internal war. He left one last voice message on the first Wednesday of the new year. All he said was "Happy New Year." She called back the next day and wished him the same. She didn't ask about his Christmas, or how he spent the New Year. She asked about his family and said she spent her holidays alone. She didn't color in any detail of her three weeks away from him, nor did he offer to do the same for her. She invited him over for dinner and he readily accepted, angry at himself for his own earnest, anticipatory eagerness.

In the newness of the year, she assuaged his concerns with a kiss at the door. Ebony offered herself as his gift, already unwrapped, wet and ready to give and receive. He fell into her body, and allowed her lavender scent to provide the kind of sex tinged clarity that only half clears the mind. He kept on his rose-colored glasses and took her suggestion for his parents. She helped him find Laverne and was beside him when he broke the news to his mother. He was reminded of her thoughtfulness and compassion, and forgot the flash of darkness he saw in the moments he asked her to reciprocate the familial closeness he readily gave away. He forgot the three weeks where he'd been ghosted, determined to be damaged, and relegated to her rubbish. His selective memory cherry picked the moments that lingered at the front of his mind, and discarded the anger and anguish he didn't want to relive. He remembered the feeling of her against him, as they stood naked, with their clothes on, gazing out over the river. He remembered breathing with one heart, thinking with one mind, and feeling with one body, as the river dazzled beneath the sun and the scant skyline shined in the distance. He forgot the tenor and timbre of her voice when she said, "I have to go." That total recall was erased as if it had never happened.

He remembered what he thought was love with the prescient sense to keep it to himself. He did not know his unspoken confession would determine his decisions months later, as he descended into her truth and uncovered her two families. The one she spoke of with fond girlhood memories, and the other she didn't acknowledge existed. He was unaware that his caged emotions would keep him shackled to her, despite his own subconscious's better judgement.

Pulling up in her driveway, two unfamiliar cars parked in front of her door, his brother's words haunting him in his ears, *I wouldn't leave Ebony, until she left me.* He remained unsure of what to do with his unrequited love. The wanderlust that always led to her. He opened the garage, pulled in, and hit the button to enclose himself in the carbon monoxide filled darkness around him. The poisonous atmosphere that could consume him if he let it. James cut the engine, open and shut the door, and made another decision based on what had been left unfulfilled. He entered another house that was not his. Ebony's house. The house where she would kiss him and straddle him with the reckless abandon of love, that the flashes of darkness across her face never allowed her to say. Instead, she would criticize him, affirm her future with prison, and believe in Dawn and the news more than the man at her side.

"I'm back," he yells after the beep of the alarm.

"Stay decent," Ebony yells back. "We have company."

He stands between her bedroom, and his car in her garage. Just like when they stood between the bridges and he decided to cut open his body and invite her in, he is now between two bridges, between two decisions, with no room for indecision or doubt.

He picks his poison and moves forward into her house, lavender candles burning clarity into his conscience, drowning out the clarion call from deep inside of himself that says he knows better.

10.

"Good afternoon, ladies," James says walking into the living room.

"Why are you being so formal?" Ebony questions from the couch. "You remember Soleil. Have you met Ms. Nona?"

"Mrs. Gordon, how are you?" James asks, walking over to where she sits in one of the multi-colored striped armchairs.

"I'm well, James. Really good, actually."

He kneels down to hug her.

"I don't know if I ever told you," he says nestled into her neck, "but I'm so sorry for your loss. Judge Gordon meant a lot to me."

"I know, James." Ms. Nona releases him.

"The last few months have been hard."

"I know, James."

"I'm sorry."

"Listen to me, James, and listen to me good. This is not your fault. This is not Soleil's fault. And this is *not* Ebony's fault. Barker was my son. He was also my ex-husband's son. I could not love out of him, what was born inside of him. He's gone now. Let's just accept what happened as God's best."

"Yes, ma'am," James says standing to his feet.

He looks down over the regal old woman. His eyes go directly to her uncovered scar. On her chest, just below her collar bone, the thick keloid of scar tissue is shiny, and glints with whatever lotion or moisturizer she uses on her skin. He had only met Mrs. Gordon a handful of times before the trial. Always at events with Barker, and always in an evening gown or cocktail dress with a matching scarf bustled at her neck. Then, he thought the scarf was one of her elderly affectations, something she did, she wore, to harken back to a time gone past, until she sat on the witness stand. He didn't see her as she came into the courtroom, and he didn't pay attention to her when she passed between the prosecution and the defense tables. It is only after she sat down and was sworn in, and began answering questions about her son, his mentor, the victim Ebony is convicted of being responsible for killing, did he notice her bare neck.

It was the first time in all their run-ins, in all of the years he had known Barker, and had been mentored by him, that he'd ever seen her — in a photo or in person — without something around her neck. She sat in open court in a scoop neck purple blouse, he realized during her testimony, was intentional. She was there to show off the damage done to her. To show off the future that could have faced Soleil, Ebony, or another woman, if her son had not been taken from the world when he was. She said as much on the stand. *No woman deserves to have done to them, what was done to me.*

The physical revelation and the verbal acknowledgment in the courtroom caught the state attorney by surprise. She stumbled through questions and quickly handed James the reins to shape the narrative of the case. James was grateful for her openness, for her willingness to show off her naked skin, and lay a stronger foundation for his defense, for Ebony's defense.

He never knew the man who mentored him the way the women around him knew him. He never knew the condescending, malevolent reprobate who got hard from the sight of women cowering beneath him. He didn't know the man whose charm, which contributed to his ascension in the Navy, and then through the legal system, also used his charisma as a means of control and sexual domination. Unable to attend the funeral, for the sake of appearances, he mourned in his own inner turmoil, and outwardly defended the woman who still believes she's not responsible for his death.

Absolved by Barker's mother, James kneels and leans in to Mrs. Gordon once more, and sighs his thanks. She envelops him against her chest again. His head swaddled against the silk of her short sleeved white blouse, he closes his eyes and soaks in her absolution for himself.

"What brings you by?" James asks, standing a second time.

"I came with Soleil."

James turns his attention to the woman Ebony thought she was saving. The light woman, whose skin has been burnished bronze by the sun. The woman who also testified for the prosecution, but laid the foundation for the defense. She sits on the white suede sofa with her feet folded beneath her. Her tan canvas and cargo topsiders are on the floor in front of her. The assortment of yellow, marine, and salmon colored pillows are huddled in a pile across her lap, nearly hiding the light wash of her denim jeans. She, too, wears a white shirt, only hers is cotton, and has a V-neck instead of scoop, which brings the attention up to her face where a jagged half-moon scar rests above her left eyebrow. The scar made by a spiked titanium ring instead of a knife point. As smooth and discolored as the second smile cut across Mrs. Gordon's chest, identical to the scar over Ebony's own left eyebrow. The two halves that made his whole defense, the identical scars imprinted and branded by one man, the common denominator between both women.

"How are you doing?" James asks.

"Doing well," Soleil begins. "I cleaned out my apartment last night, and I went shopping this morning and ran in to Ms. Nona. We had lunch and were talking about the trial. She said she wished she could talk to Ebony. So I gave your girl a call and she said come on by, and here we are."

"I came to tell Ebony that I plan to ask the judge for the minimum at the sentencing when they do the victim impact statements," Ms. Nona says.

"Me too," Soleil adds.

"Thank you, both, but I don't think we're going to get that far," James says.

"Why is that?" Soleil asks.

"Because there's still the appeals process, which I'm working on now."

"In case that doesn't work," Ms. Nona cautions, "I just wanted you guys to know that I don't plan to make it like Barker's loss has somehow stopped the world."

"It for damn sure hasn't stopped mine," Soleil says.

"Thank you." Ebony sighs.

A single tear falls from her right eye. She wipes it away with the back of her hand and then dabs at her left eye. Tears flow, despite her best efforts to stop them before they start. Both hands come up to cover her face. To hide the emotion she doesn't want anyone to see. Knees hugged into her chest in the arm chair, her head in her hands, she lets the warm water slide from her fingertips to the base of her palms. It drip drops into her lap, staining her jeans with her own rain release.

James steps around to her side. He bends to the ground beside her as he knelt next to Ms. Nona. His hand finds hers. Tugging, she complies and falls out of the chair into his arms. Her small body fits in the lap space he creates for her. He buries his head in the loose curls of her freshly-washed mane, and rocks her back and forth from where he crouches beside the chair He rocks and hums a random tune in her curls until she takes her hands down from her face, and wipes her eyes and nose against his turquoise graphic tee. Standing up with her in his arms, he slowly lowers her to her feet. Ebony wraps her arms around his waist and lays against his chest, breathing in all of him.

"You've lost a lot of weight," she says stepping away.

"So have you." He helps her sit back down.

"Five years is a long time."

"You're not going to prison for five years," Ms. Nona says.

"Even still, three years is a long time. That's the minimum."

"You're not going to prison for three years either," James says.

"Just because you guys don't want to see me punished, doesn't mean the judge feels the same way."

"Judge Shaw knew Judge Gordon, and she knows me," James says.

"Barker is dead, and I'm not you, James."

"My point is, she knew him a lot longer than she knew me. And because she knows me, my ethics, she knows I wouldn't leave my job unless it was something serious."

"Barker was careful, and ethics don't matter when the heart is involved."

"He wasn't that careful," Soleil says. "He scarred us both."

"James," Ms. Nona calls. "What made you leave your job?"

"That's a question even I don't know the answer to," Ebony says.

"She's my girlfriend."

"Exactly," Ms. Nona says.

"I'm not sure I follow."

"She means girlfriends are temporary," Ebony explains. "You have no obligation to me. I'm not your wife. So why put yourself at risk?"

"Got it." James nods.

He takes a seat beside Soleil on the couch and kicks off his flip-flops. He delays answering the question he barely has the answer to. *Because she's my girlfriend* is not enough, and he's not sure he can explain the feeling inside of him that compelled him to forego all logic and jump off a legal cliff with a woman, and neither of them is strapped with a parachute.

Because I love her.

That's not good enough either.

James talks himself in and out of answers as he sits on the couch, pressing the cushions, adjusting his weight, all eyes on him. Soleil offers him a pillow from her lap and he takes it. It is the same pillow that was between them when they watched the news together; when she made her confession. *"Short, dressed in black, with long, curly hair. If the woman is black, I fit the description."* James balls up the pillow in his own lap until his fists are buried in the cushion, and the fabric covers his wrists with warmth.

He says, "I was sitting right here when she told me what happened. I made her turn herself in because I didn't want to get in trouble. The longer she was a wanted woman, the more credible it could become that I was somehow an accomplice."

"So you were going to turn me in and leave?" Ebony asks.

"I was," he answers without looking at her. "You railroaded me when you told me what happened, and you know it."

"So what changed your mind?" Soleil asks.

"When they tried to force the confession at the police station."

"It wasn't like I was going to write or sign anything," Ebony says.

"That's not the point. I'd seen the state attorney do that so many times. That's kind of our thing. I've done it. Force a confession, settle the case, keep the conviction rate high, the case load low, and our time in court little to none. That's how we operate. Going to court costs money. Money the city doesn't want to say it has. Even though I was pissed at you. When I think about it, I get mad all over again. I didn't want you to become another statistic in the system. You deserve better from the justice system despite what you did, and how you told me was fucked up."

"That's noble of you," Ms. Nona says.

"It's not always about me, as my mother tells me."

"Is that why you're still here?" Ebony asks.

"I ask myself that question every day. Why am I still here, when leaving you would make my life so much simpler?"

"It's because you believe her, right?"

"Soleil, at this point, what I believe doesn't matter. What Ebony believes happened doesn't matter. She doesn't remember intentionally pulling the trigger, I wasn't there, Judge Gordon can't speak from the grave, and the jury has already spoken. Once a case goes to court, it's not about the truth anymore. It's about who can tell the best story and make the jury believe their version of events. When a case goes to court, it's only about who wins, and who loses."

"So now what, since we've lost?" Ebony asks softly.

"We don't lose until the Supreme Court says we lose. Until then, there is always an appeal."

James's statement leaves the room in silence. Ms. Nona and Ebony are in the two arm chairs across from each other. James and Soleil are side by side on the couch. His words remain suspended among them. He absorbs his own truth he's been reluctant to accept. Accepts the fact he must draft the appeal he doesn't want to file. He must remain counsel for the woman he loves, who refuses to acknowledge if she loves him back. He must stand by the side of the woman who's trapped him in lies, fights against the truth, and needs him to work a miracle so that she can remain free.

He stands up from the couch, exits the women's circle in the living room, and heads into the kitchen.

It doesn't matter why I left my job, or why I'm still here. I have to do this.

"Anybody want a drink?" He asks from behind the peninsula.

"Water, please," Ebony answers.

"Me too," Soleil adds.

"Same," Ms. Nona says.

James comes back into the living room with four checkerboard-glass tumblers. Three of them have ice inside to cool the clear liquid. He hands the glasses to the women.

"What is that?" Ebony nods toward the glass in his hand.

"Hold on," he says taking his phone out of his pocket.

He reads the message on the screen.

Any word on an appeal?

Damn, can I file it first.

James clears the message, and drops his phone back into the pocket of his loose fitting jeans and sits down on the couch beside Soleil.

"What was that?" Ebony asks.

"Nothing important."

"What's in the glass?"

"You already know what this is?" James takes a sip of the brown liquid.

"I asked you not to drink that."

"Then you should have poured it out two years ago, after he left."

The television clicks on in the middle of a commercial.

"What is this?" Ms. Nona asks.

"I have it set on a timer," Ebony answers. "It comes on right before the news begins."

"She means before Dawn comes on," James corrects.

"How is she doing?" Soleil asks.

"Haven't heard from her since the verdict," Ebony answers. "Her minions were out here last night, but she wasn't."

"What's she talking about tonight?" James takes a gulp from his glass.

"Me. What else?"

11.

"Tonight on *Dawn in the Evening*.

You'll hear my exclusive interview with Ebony Jones, who was convicted of culpable negligence in the death of Judge Barker Gordon.

Jones and I met at her Mandarin home, just days before her trial began last month.

We discussed what happened the day of Judge Gordon's death, why she says she's not responsible, and new information into the 9 News Now newsroom tonight . . . what our sources say about her plans to appeal her conviction."

Dawn's mic clicks in the studio as the sound comes up on the intro package she wrote for her exclusive interview with Ebony. The interview she broke up into six parts to satisfy the segments of her hour-long show. She looks at the screen beneath her prompter and watches the video as it transports her back three weeks to a late morning, after her argument with Victor. The first piece showing what it took to get to Ebony's home, transform it into the makeshift set, and then the introduction of the subjects, Dawn, Ebony, and James in the background. She looks at the screen showing herself and the brown-skinned woman in all white, just like she dressed for court every day, and waits for the package to end with the close-up of her subject's eyes before the camera. The close-up she kept in for dramatic effect, to give viewers the feeling they, too, were peering into the windows of Ebony's soul. The shot she wanted her viewers to see and determine if the judgement from the trial was correct, if their own version of the verdict could withstand whatever truth they gleaned from the woman who says she did nothing wrong. Her mic clicks.

"I prepared Ebony by telling her she didn't have to answer every question I asked. It is a warning and a lifeline I give to all of my interview subjects.

My first question was why did she kill Judge Barker Gordon.

Her attorney James Parnell refused to allow her to answer.

My second question was admittedly a roundabout.

I asked why she brought a gun to the courthouse.

Her attorney also refused to allow her to answer that question.

My third question was altogether different.

I asked about her family, about her mother and father, and whether she had any siblings.

Jones's attorney did not object to the question, but she did.

She stood abruptly from the interview set, unmic'd herself, and disappeared into another room.

It was several minutes before she returned to her own living room to resume the interview she and her attorney agreed to.

When she returned, she answered my first question and so many more, maintaining the entire time, that she did not kill Judge Barker Gordon."

The mic clicks.

"How long is this piece?" Dawn asks aloud.

"This segment is six-and-a-half minutes," Kelly, the producer, says through Dawn's earpiece. "There's a taped tease at the end, so it will take us all the way through to the break."

"I'm going to the bathroom then."

Dawn turns off her mic from the battery pack hooked to her calf brace, and hops down off the high desk chair. She walks out of the studio, through the nearly empty newsroom, to a hallway off the front doors of the building. She makes her way down the hall and steps into the bathroom. The ladies restroom is more than just a long room with enclosed stalls. The first door takes her into the dressing room filled with bright bulbs framed around a large mirror. There are open shelves filled with her spare jackets, dresses, and slacks, an iron and ironing board, and a can of starch sitting on a shelf with her makeup case, edge control, paddle brush, feather comb, and coconut oil.

Dawn takes another door into the cold bathroom, and it closes on her butt. She stops in its threshold, ill prepared to continue what she came in for. Standing in front of a sink with brown paper towel wadded and dabbing at her eyes, is Julia Gillé. Dawn did not expect to see her. She thought she was already gone. She thought she had already disappeared into whatever abyss elder anchors go to when they're put under review, and are waiting to learn if they still have a job.

Dawn arms herself with her own hubris and strolls to the stall in front of her. *Just ignore her* she tells herself as she passes the brunette woman with the blonde highlights, running mascara, and smudged lipstick. She walks into the stall, closes the door, and clicks the mic pack at her calf as she sits on the commode.

"How much time do I have?" She asks aloud.

"About three minutes left in the package and then a two thirty break."

"Jennifer, is that you?" Dawn asks.

"Yes, ma'am. Do you need something?"

"Hold on."

Dawn clicks the mic off, and then back on.

"I had to flush," she says. "What's the next segment?"

"The one on how she turned herself in," Jennifer answers in her ear.

"Have we gotten anything new from James about if, or when, he will file the appeal?"

"Not yet," Kelly jumps in. "I just checked both of our email lists. No response yet."

"I would really like to have his confirmation. Not just our expert's opinion."

"I'll keep checking," Kelly says. "Try texting him."

"I did, earlier this afternoon. No response."

"Then expert opinion is all we have."

"Okay. Time?"

"Ninety in the package plus the break."

"Alright, I'm on my way back."

Dawn switches her mic off again. She steps out into the open bathroom to see Julia still there. Dry-eyed and stone-faced, she stands with her back to the sink, laying in wait. Dawn does not pause in the open stall. She strides to the sink beside the woman who waited for her, head shaking, remembering when Boyce threatened to swap anchors, and revive the long dead *Weekday Roundup with Julia Gillé* and cancel *Dawn in the Evening*. Running one hand under the automatic soap dispenser, and then the other, she looks at her own face in the mirror and smirks as she rubs the foam over her hands and between her fingers. *I guess he wasn't completely overreacting about the anchor changes.*

Dawn focuses on her own eyes, lined in black, lids heavy with glued on feather lashes that blend into her own with a thick coating of black mascara. She runs her soapy hands beneath the faucet, still staring at her face, knowing Julia is beside her watching her stare at herself. She smashes her burgundy-stained, matte lips together, as she shakes her hands in the sink.

"You are so fucking full of yourself," Julia sneers.

Dawn places her hand beneath the towel dispenser and waits for the rough brown paper to descend in her hand. She says nothing. She does not turn her head from her own visage. She does not acknowledge the woman waiting to get a rise out of her. Dawn turns her hands over and over across the paper towel, crunching the napkin to create a noise to overtake the accusations, both spoken and unspoken.

"You think you're too good to even speak to me now?"

"I never said that," Dawn says.

She tosses the used napkin into the white circular trash can with the open mouth, placed between each set of sinks.

"You didn't have to say it."

"What do you want from me, Julia?"

"Dawn, we're in the break?" Jennifer says in her ear.

She reaches down to switch on her mic, "Okay. I'm coming."

She turns it back off.

"You thought you were hot shit when you first got here with your own show."

"No, I didn't."

"Yes, you did. Thought that because you started something in whatever podunk town you came from, got picked up here, that I was just supposed to bow down to you and let you take my chair."

"No, I didn't. I was hired to do a job. I did it."

"And now you're doing mine."

"I didn't ask to."

"You didn't say no either."

"What do you want from me, Julia?"

"I don't want shit from you, Dawn. You're the worst kind there is. Smile in your face and stab you in the back."

"I didn't stab you in the back, Julia. Boyce stabbed you in your chest and you didn't see it coming, and now you're blaming it all on me."

Dawn walks away from the mirror she's stared in for the whole confrontation.

"One minute, Dawn," Kelly says in her ear.

She reaches down to turn on her microphone, "I'm walking out now."

"I have a show to do," Dawn says over her shoulder.

"You could have said no," Julia yells at her back.

"I haven't said yes."

Dawn waits to exhale until she steps out of the door from the makeup room and into the hallway. Her high-heeled steps carry her quickly back to the set. The movement forces her heart to beat faster in her chest, and her breath to catch up with the rest of her body. She steps into the bright lights of the set, lit for her licorice skin color, and takes her seat atop the lone anchor chair. She adjusts the lapels of her burgundy blazer over her black sheath dress.

"Thirty seconds," John, the floor director, yells from behind the cameras.

Dawn lifts the mirror sitting beside the laptop on the rolling under table of the anchor desk. She moves a lock of her long bangs out of her eyes, smashes her lips to spread the color, checks her teeth, and then put's the mirror back down.

"Ten," John yells.

He counts down the rest of the numbers with his fingers held high in the air above his head.

The mic clicks.

"You're watching a special edition of *Dawn in the Evening.*

My one-on-one conversation with Ebony Jones.

She is convicted of culpable negligence in the death of Judge Barker Gordon.

Jones tells me, after she turned herself in, she was forced to spend one night in the Duval County Jail.

She describes what it was like being among the inmates, why she says she was victimized despite the crime she was then accused, and now convicted of, and the legal gymnastics her attorney and former prosecutor, James Parnell, had to pull to allow her to spend the time leading up to her trial on house arrest.

She says it had to do with the evidence she turned in, and the fact she had always been a law abiding citizen."

The mic clicks. The extended package rolls for this section of their interview. Dawn picks up her pen off her desk and scribbles on the paper scripts in front of her. Though her iPad with her scripts are beside her in digital form, she always prints a paper copy, just in case something breaks. Her hand moves with a mind of its own across the paper as she thinks back to the confrontation in the bathroom. Julia in a hot pink, calf length, sleeveless dress and white jacket, nude pumps, and full makeup, until she cried it off. She was dressed and ready to work, but unable to take her seat. Unable to take her chair. Unable to read the prompter. Unable to do her job.

"Dawn."

She turns to the voice that called her name. It is Boyce Butler peeping in to the studio from the newsroom.

The news director. The man she told Julia she should redirect her anger toward.

"Did you go over the paperwork?" He asks.

"I just got it yesterday when I came in. We had a long day with the verdict. I glanced at it, but I haven't gone completely through it."

"We need to get that done. I need you to look it over."

"Did you send it to my agent and my lawyer?"

"I didn't forward them a copy yet. I wanted you to see it first and get your thoughts on the draft."

"Send it to them."

"When do you think you'll have an answer?" He presses.

"I know I won't have one right now."

"Alright. We need to get this done."

"I know. I saw Julia," Dawn says turning back to her camera.

Boyce doesn't respond, and she doesn't look to see if he untucked his head from where he peeked into the set. She doesn't look to see if he waddled away ashamed of the conniving secret he tried to hide, the betrayal he did not want to admit. The desk vibrates. It is from her phone. She turns it over and sees a message from Victor. Two more vibrate through as she unlocks the screen.

This is good
You are good
You look damn good

She taps out a hasty "thanks" and then turns the phone back over. Facedown, she puts it off to the side of the desk, out of range of the camera. She waits for her cue. Waits for her producers to come into her ear with instruction, for John to raise his hands, and direct her where to look. Dawn clears her thoughts and stares straight ahead at the words she wrote. The words she will read next. The words to set up the next segment.

"One minute out, Dawn." Jennifer says in her ear.

Her concentration breaks. She stares down at her doodles on her scripts and sees words. Her own cursive handwriting that formed letters. A message to herself — I'm not your enemy. It is scrawled at the top of one script. Hasty. Without the perfection, precision, or deliberate insistence of the framed Post-it note in her office. The anonymous note that haunts and comforts her. The note that is a message and a warning, a lesson and a cautionary tale, all wrapped up in four simple words in fading red ink. "I'm not your enemy." In her own hand, it is her reminder to stay humble, to stay hungry, to stay vigilant, and to remain flexible. She tears the corner of her script with her message and grabs her phone from the side of the desk.

"Thirty seconds," Kelly says.

Dawn removes the phone from its see-through protective case, and places the scrap of paper with the message inside, facing down. She sees John's hands move into the symbol for fifteen seconds. Dawn places the phone back in the case and sets it on the desk, screen side down, her message facing up.

I'm not your enemy.

Dawn looks up into the camera at her words and waits for John's hand to reach the fist for zero. She waits for the mic to click.

"In our next half hour after the break . . .

The question I asked Ebony Jones about what she would do once she learned the verdict . . .

And what we're learning, new tonight, about how she's doing now that she's been convicted of culpable negligence in the death of Judge Barker Gordon, and faces . . .years in prison.

That's next on *Dawn in the Evening*."

The mic clicks.

12.

Wednesday, September 16, 2014

If you're convicted, what do you plan to do before you go to prison? And secondly, if you're acquitted how do you plan to celebrate?

"She didn't do it."

Johnnie mutes the replay of Dawn's interview on the morning news. She fell asleep on the black leather couch watching bits and pieces, every time it came on, and pretended to be asleep when Nathan tried to coax her upstairs to bed. He walked back in the house ninety minutes after he left with two boxes of pizza and a six-pack of beer. She laid on the couch ignoring him, telling Tyler and Danielle, "No," she wasn't hungry. They finished their dinner in awkward silences interrupted by sparse conversation, leaving her alone to her thoughts, influenced by the information flowing from the TV screen. She laid in the darkness of the living room, facing the glowing screen of the muted television, well after normal television had gone off, after syndication of talk shows, judge shows, gossip shows, and blogs-turned-into shows had gone off, and infomercials had taken over. She laid in the glow of the television replaying Ebony's answer.

"I'm going to take lots of long walks outside in the air for several days, weeks, months even."

Johnnie laid in the glow of the television trying to envision what it would be like to not go outside her front door. To not be able to walk to the mailbox at the edge of the driveway. She laid on the couch erecting bars in her mind to imagine the feeling of being imprisoned in her own home. For the police to be notified if she went further than the closed door confines of the garage. If she set foot out the back door to enjoy the open space of the yard, butted up to the retention pond in this section of her subdivision. She laid on the couch in the prison of her own making until the jail bars became real, and the passing of time became unbearable as her subconscious took over and made her dream dreams of elongated days and extended nights, for years and decades to come. She dreamed of sloppy meals and timed showers, rationed, thin toilet paper, and getting tampons from the commissary. She dreamed of scheduled visits and not seeing Danielle until she was a mother in her own right. She dreamed until it was lights out in the prison she created, and blackness greeted her at the end of her regimented day. The deep of darkness hugged her until she could feel hands, arms, shoulders, and a chest around her body. Her eyes flash open into the Old Spice laden polo Nathan is wearing.

"You want some coffee?" He asks.

She nods in the affirmative, and then bends down to find the remote to turn up the volume on the television she muted. Ebony is on the screen. Nathan hands her the mug of caffeine, completely black without sugar and without milk, kisses her cheek and says goodbye to her back. Tyler and Danielle, her children, say good morning and goodbye as she holds the trance of the television.

She hears Nathan say in the distance, "Mommy's not feeling well, right now. Danielle, I'm going to take you to the bus stop this morning, and Tyler, I'm taking you to school since you've missed the bus. How many times do I have to tell you to get off the phone and go to bed at night, so you're not late in the morning."

"I know, Dad." Johnnie hears Tyler say.

"You better act like you know. Let's go."

They leave through the garage. The alarm chirps until all the doors they opened, close. She remains mesmerized by the shots on the screen she had already seen, listening to questions that had already been answered, mumbling to herself, "She didn't do it."

Johnnie quiets the excited utterance of her conscience and places the coffee mug in the stainless steel farm sink. She leaves the TV on, despite her disagreement with the judgement of the supposed convict. She leaves the beacon to cognitive dissonance playing, as she takes the stairs to the second floor. Walking with intent and purpose, she grabs a clean bra, matching panties, and a tank top from her dresser. In the closet she steps out of yesterday's jeans, and T-shirt, and under clothes, and pulls a pair of black shorts from a hanger. Naked, and arms loaded down with clean and dirty clothes alike, Johnnie drops the clean clothes on the edge of her sink, then takes the dirty clothes to the hamper waiting beside the shower. She steps in, turns the water on, and sits on the bench. The cold water sprays over her body until the hot water heater kicks in and showers her with warmth. She sits to soap, wash, and rinse until the hot water runs warm, and the warm water runs cool, until the steam abates and her scalp begins to feel cold. The same chorus replays in her mind and comes out of her mouth, "She didn't do it."

Johnnie reaches to turn the handle stopping the flow of water. She gets up slowly from the bench, steps out of the glass door, and pulls her towel from the shower bar. Wrapping her body in the thick terry cloth, she walks to the vanity where her clothes rest. Her hands clear a space in the mirror for her to see her own reflection. Deep set haggard eyes greet her; eyes that closed but didn't sleep, eyes that were unseeing but not at rest. Her mind, also not at rest, accuses her in earnest. *They say the truth will set you free. Yeah, well we'll see about that.*

Johnnie blots her wet face with a wash cloth laying on the edge of her vanity. She goes through the motions; brushes her teeth, exfoliates her face, unwraps her towel and lotions her skin, and moisturizes her hair. Eyes meet the mirror. Stress greets her gaze. *The truth will set you free.*

Turning her back on herself, Johnnie steps into her clothes one layer at a time. The boy shorts ride up her newly developed, alcohol-deprived behind. A custom bra that cuts across her already ample breasts, give her a muffin top in the too little cup size. The T-shirt clings to the new weight on her waist, and she has to jump into her jeans and hold her breath to zip them up. She turns to face the mirror. Fatigue frowns back at her. *The truth will set you free.*

Johnnie picks up her towel from the floor, hastily hangs it on the shower rod, and quickens her step out of the bathroom, past the closets, through the bedroom, down the hall, and back to the flight of steps. She doesn't stop until her feet are shoved into her sandals at the foot of the steps, and the alarm beeps to secure the house. The sound nearly drowns out the television. The news is off. The talk shows of women gabbing around tables have begun.

We're following the case of Ebony Jones this morning, who was convicted of . . .

"She didn't do it."

Johnnie silences the world and herself, closing the door to the garage.

Her motions are involuntary. Unlock the car, get in, open the garage door, adjust the mirrors. She catches her eyes; exhaustion personified. She shakes her head, and backs her red Camry down the driveway and into the street. She hits close on the garage door and drives by memory, out of her neighborhood and onto Fort Caroline Road. She leaves what was once an affluent African-American enclave. The signs of generational lack of care more apparent than the neat lawns of first in a generation homeownership, when she and Nathan first moved in. She turns on Townsend and then on Merrill, until she gets to 295. The highway will take her to her only destination.

Johnnie drives in the scant traffic of the late morning. She makes it from Arlington to Mandarin in under twenty-five minutes, and finds herself parking in front of the second house from the entrance of the infamous subdivision. Her car is the only one there. She parks in the still rising sun, the newly planted tree not developed enough to provide her vehicle any shade. All her resolve is in her feet, to make them get out of the car, march up the walk, and step up on the porch of the woman she needs to switch places with. She repeats as she goes, "The truth will set you free."

Johnnie rings the doorbell.

There is no answer.

Johnnie rings the doorbell again. A faint, "I'm coming" comes from deep in the house behind the door.

She waits until the lock turns. The door swings open. A short olive-skinned woman with curly hair, pokes her head out.

"I didn't expect to see you here?"

"I know you can't go anywhere," Johnnie begins. "I thought you might like some company."

The door opens wider. Johnnie steps forward, accepting Ebony's invitation inside. She shuts the door behind them and leads the way into the kitchen. Johnnie follows behind the woman with the naturally wagging ass in black bike shorts and a gray sweat shirt, deep into the house. She makes extra effort to lift her leaden feet, so they don't drag across the cherry hardwood floor.

"What brings you by?" Ebony asks, plopping on the sofa.

"Just wanted to come by and see you," Johnnie says, taking a seat on one of the bar stools. "I haven't seen you since you took the stand, and I couldn't be there for the verdict."

"You didn't miss anything."

Johnnie nods. "How have you been holding up?"

"Good, I guess. I'm home. I'm kind of used to the house arrest, now that I finally got the itching to stop. It's when I have to go to sleep that my mind starts racing."

"Same."

"What are you so stressed about?"

"Stuff at home. Plus seeing you on trial and knowing I worked on him. Well . . . I tried to work on him. It . . . It . . . It's just been hard to watch."

"Try living it."

Johnnie nods.

An uncomfortable silence settles around them in the house. Ebony's home is absent the creaking noise of an aging house settling on its foundation. There are no clocks on the wall or standing in corners, to mark the seconds and the minutes of the day, or to chime out the hours. The microwave and stove don't beep, there's no hum of laundry from a washer or dryer, and there's no chatter of children, teen or adolescent, to halfway listen to. Ebony's house is silent and subsuming. Johnnie shifts back and forth in her seat, trying to convince herself to do what she seemed so sure of, staring at her reflection in the bathroom mirror. *The truth will set you free.*

"You want anything to drink?" Ebony asks.

"Water please."

Johnnie is grateful to speak. "How is James?" she asks.

"Hell if I know," Ebony says, bumping around in the kitchen. "He comes in and out, but he hasn't really said much except that he has to work on the appeal."

"That's good."

"I guess."

"You don't want him to represent you on your appeal?"

"I don't know. I don't know what I want. I'm just trying to get through the day."

"I've been there. Hell, I'm still there."

"You're married, right?" Ebony asks, handing Johnnie the glass of water.

"Yeah."

"What's your husband's name again?"

"Nathan. We've been together sixteen going on seventeen years."

"That's a lifetime."

"I know."

"Has it been a good life?"

"Up until the last few years it has. When Dani was born, my daughter, she's five, everything changed."

"How?"

"Nathan stopped working so at least one of us, would be home with the kids. We have a son, Tyler. He's fourteen about to be fifteen. I picked up more and more shifts at the hospital, partly because I was that good, and because we needed it."

Ebony nods her head for Johnnie to continue. She nods to allow someone else to unburden their soul for once, instead of being in the spotlight. She looks over to where Johnnie sits perched on the bar stool, eyes cast down, her curly puff at her eye level, and waits.

"The last few months have been the hardest. I had to step away from work and Nathan moved out."

"Why? If you don't mind my asking."

"No, it's alright," Johnnie answers. "He's moved back in, but he was sleeping with the teacher's assistant, but won't admit it. And I had my own stuff going on. We needed to be apart."

"James and I are together, but it seems like we're apart. I see him every day, but it's not the same."

"Relationships get like that sometimes." Johnnie sighs. "The fact that he's still around, still working for you, still helping you, it means something."

"Doesn't seem like it," Ebony says looking down. Her fingers gently rake across the backs of her hands.

"When you guys make it through this," Johnnie says lifting her head. "You'll see it was all worth it. I remember when Nathan and I first got together. We didn't have anything between us but debt, bills, and an "oops" baby."

"Does your son know he was an accident?"

"No." Johnnie laughs. "We got married because we had a baby. I was in my fourth year of residency, and Nathan was still trying to get a job. You go to school and major in all the fancy things *Forbes* says will make money, like medicine and engineering, and you still struggle to find work, just like everybody else who was sold a dream for five hundred dollars a credit hour."

"If not more."

"Exactly. So we were struggling; to pay bills, buy diapers, clothes, food, get to work. Everything. All we had was each other. Then he got a job, I became certified and a specialist, and all those extra titles doctors pick up to charge more. Tyler got older, was potty trained, the bills were paid, the ends met. We moved out of our shitty one bedroom

116.

apartment on the Westside and got our house in Arlington. We were the American dream. We no longer needed each other. We just wanted to be together, and now, I don't know if that's true anymore."

"James and I never needed each other. It was always a want for us. At least for me anyway. But sometimes he just pushes too hard. He pushes me too hard. He wants everything when he wants it, and the way he wants it. He's impatient."

"And you are?" Johnnie asks.

"Destructive," Ebony says.

"So you destroy the relationship, rather than try to fix it? I'm there."

"Not like this."

Johnnie doesn't correct Ebony's assumption. She doesn't compare her relationship, her marriage, her guilt with the woman who was rendered an actual guilty verdict. She drains the glass in front of her leaving the sweating cubes to rattle around inside.

Coming over to where Ebony sits, Johnnie asks, "Have you seen anyone else?"

"I saw Soleil and Ms. Nona yesterday."

"Who's that?"

"Remember the lady with the scar who testified?"

"Yeah."

"That was Barker's mom."

"Now I remember. I met her at the funeral. Why did she want to see you?

"She and Soleil came by to tell me they were going to ask the judge for the minimum during my sentencing, when they give their victim impact statements."

"That's nice of them," Johnnie says looking down into her hands.

"Yeah, but it doesn't mean anything. Whatever they say is just a suggestion. The judge still has to follow the mandatory minimum and whatever other legal bullshit."

"I thought the judge had the final decision and discretion on sentencing."

"I guess we'll see what Judge Shaw decides in November."

"I wish it wasn't you," Johnnie sighs.

"You've said that before."

"I know. I just wish I could have saved him when he was in the ER."

"You've said that before too."

Johnnie knows Ebony is giving her the space she needs to say whatever she's come to say. Her guts and gumption to set the truth free dissipate. Everything inside her screams "run" in bold font, all caps with triple underlines.

Johnnie sighs. *The truth will set you free.* Her subconscious is less convincing than it was nearly an hour ago. She looks toward the silent television housed in the red wood built-ins, occupying the wall across from them. Her eyes jump to the outdated *New Yorker* magazines on the cracked glass coffee table. The last issue from the first week in April, weeks after Ebony's arrest. On top of the *New Yorkers* are a few *Folio Weekly's*. The alternative to *The Florida-Times Union*, a few of which are also on the table. The local papers all bare her face above the fold. Pictures of her walking into court with James, sitting at the table, on the witness stand, standing before the judge. The headline on the paper on top of the stack reads: **Ebony Jones convicted in March murder of Judge Barker Gordon.** It is only the subtitle that calms the salacious overtones of the headline: **Facing three-to-five years for culpable negligence.**

"Dr. Edwards, is there something you want to say to me?" Ebony asks.

Johnnie stews in her own truth. The truth she's held since March. The truth she refused to admit to when she was confronted. The truth she denied before she was thrown out of the hospital locker room by the Dean of Medicine who had trained her since her residency. The truth she barely admitted to sitting outside a historic church, with a choir singing, the city in mourning, and a preacher preaching that to be absent from the body is to be present with the Lord. The truth she halfway admitted to her friend who works in the news. Johnnie stews in what she's only been able to say in parts. Her confession of "I killed a man" to Nathan was dismissed as doctor snark. She doubled down on Dawn in frightened self-preservation, pontificating that a medical professional is rarely brought up on charges for trying to save a life. Now she faces the dark-eyed, brown-skinned, curly-haired woman, whose entire stature screams power, and whose stone face detects bullshit.

"Medically speaking," Johnnie begins, "I think Barker could have survived the bullet."

"But he didn't."

"Again, medically speaking, he should have."

"Johnnie, whatever you're trying to tell me is not coming out clearly. I don't have time for games. What happened? Or rather, what did you do?"

"Not what I was supposed to," she mutters.

"What does that mean?"

"Shit," Johnnie sighs.

She wipes her sweaty palms on her thickened thighs. The material of her black shorts cuts through her flesh. She pulls at the T-shirt clinging to her new midsection.

"I need something stronger than water."

Ebony lets the confession fall in the silence of the room. She waits, staring at the woman beside her. The woman who is mostly a stranger to her. Two chance meetings, once before Barker was shot, and once after, and weeks of support in court, and she still doesn't really know the woman sitting in front of her. The woman who showed up because she doesn't have her number. The woman whose heart is apparently burdened with a confession she can't evince. Ebony waits beside her, her own arms at rest, her fingers still, her heart calm, her ears perked for whatever is to come next.

"The day Barker came into the hospital," Johnnie starts over, "I was supposed to be taking Dani to the zoo on her class field trip. I was off, and I got called in."

"Okay," Ebony says rolling her eyes.

I don't have time for more stories about your kids.

Johnnie continues, "I got to the hospital late and I was pissed and not at my best."

"So, your anger killed Barker?"

"No, what I did to alleviate my anger, may have contributed to my slow response in the operating room."

"And what was that?"

"Drinking."

The admission settles between them with no reaction from either woman. The truth in all its power when it's withheld is anti-climactic once it is released. Johnnie focuses on her hands pulling at the hem of her shorts, to loosen the cut in her thighs. Her subconscious is silent, her mind no longer racing. It is empty of pent up angst, and waiting for a reaction to signal what to do next.

Ebony stands up from the couch and walks into the kitchen. She bends down beside the cabinet next to the fridge and retrieves a tall bottle of brown liquid. Grabbing a checkerboard tumbler from the cabinet, Ebony pours the liquid into the glass, sans ice,' and brings it to her lips, still holding on to the bottle.

"Want some?" She offers toward where Johnnie still sits on the couch.

"No. I'm good."

"Are you an alcoholic?"

"High functioning."

"So, what you're saying is if you hadn't have been drunk, Barker would've lived."

"There's a high probability."

"So why are you just telling me this now?" *Why the fuck didn't you say something before?*

Silence descends between them. Ebony blinks. Her hands are around Johnnie's neck. Squeezing. Shaking. Committing a murder she would have no problem being convicted of, not feeling the scratches of the nails from the woman she's trying to kill, fighting for her life. Her voice is elevated, yelling, screaming, "You did it. You did it. It was you the whole time." Johnnie's eyes roll into the back of her head as her head bobbles. Her grip loosens arounds Ebony's strangling hands as life begins to leave her. Ebony blinks.

Her hands are to herself. Johnnie is still sitting across from her alive, well, and unharmed. Her eyes are frozen and glazed over, her lips as straight a line as they can be, with her pronounced cupid's bow. Ebony's gaze demands an answer to a question she never would have known to ask without the overwhelming power of Johnnie's guilty conscience. She is expressionless, despite the war of words doing flip-flops in her head.

You had a lot of fucking nerve to be in my house talking about you support me, in court every day, knowing the whole time this shit wasn't even technically my fault.

"What's happening to you isn't right," Johnnie begins. "Not when I know I could have done my job better, and that might have saved his life and prevented you from being in this mess in the first place."

"And where was all this guilt and sympathy when you came to my house with Soleil before the trial?"

Johnnie doesn't respond. She doesn't have an answer for why she didn't come forward sooner. She doesn't have a response for why she didn't save Ebony from her misery in March. They sit in their silences, both knowing the woman with the gun makes a better suspect than the woman on the bottle. They both know crime can be punished, while addiction, when seen as addiction, is treated. They both know someone had to be the sacrificial lamb and Ebony was offered first, found first, turned herself in first.

Ebony nods her silent understanding and takes another swig from her glass. The doorbell resounds in the house and the front door opens. The sound of rubber squeaks across the hardwood floor.

"Hey," James says, coming into the open living area.

"Hey," Ebony says. "Dr. Edwards came by."

"Oh. Hey," James says, turning toward Johnnie in the living room.

"Hello."

"What's going on here?"

"I just came by to visit Ebony and see how she's holding up." Johnnie stands from the couch. "I should get going. The kids will be getting out of school soon. It's an early release day."

"I'll walk you to the door," Ebony says, putting the bottle down on the peninsula.

She sips from the glass as she follows behind Johnnie. At the front door, Johnnie turns the lock and lets herself out.

"Thanks for telling me the truth," Ebony says, searching Johnnie's face for motive.

"I don't know if it helps, but you needed to know he didn't have to die."

"I'm probably better off that he did. He couldn't use his influence or tell his side of the story."

"I still wanted you to know."

"Why now?" Ebony asks again.

"It's never too late to tell the truth."

"I guess."

"Have a good rest of your day," Johnnie says.

Dazed and unable to unleash her inner rage, Ebony watches Johnnie step off the porch, march down the walkway, and chirp her car. She closes the front door without waiting to see her drive out the neighborhood. She closes the door with what she left behind. The truth she's been tasked to hold. Ebony walks back to James in the kitchen, laden with someone else's burden that is now for her benefit. Arms heavy, she lifts her glass to her lips and takes a sip of the brown liquid. It burns down her throat just like the new truth burning in the pit of her belly.

13.

"What's that?" James asks nodding toward Ebony's glass.

"SoCo. Your favorite." Ebony takes a sip.

"I thought you didn't want anyone to drink it."

"I have the right to change my mind, and it's not like you listened anyway."

James rolls his eyes at her accusation. "What was she doing here?"

"Dr. Edwards came to tell me she was drunk when she operated on Barker," Ebony says, her voice shaky, still in disbelief. "She said he probably could have survived the two gunshots."

"Are you serious!"

Ebony takes another sip from her glass as James stares at her, wide-eyed and incredulous. She sees the color return to his gaunt and ashen face. He almost looks like himself save for the weight he still hasn't gained back. The missing pounds make his extra-large T-shirt fall away from his body like he's a wire hanger. She can tell he's actually wearing a belt in his dark wash jeans to keep them up on his waist. She looks over him from his head to his light-colored, sun-shamed feet, before she nods to confirm she is serious; to communicate to him that what she said is real. That she is telling him what he's always asked of her. The truth.

"This is good news, Baby."

"Oh, I'm Baby now?"

"Don't do that," James admonishes. "We can work out our shit later. You just got a lifeline."

"How so?"

"If she admits to being drunk during the operation then even though you shot him . . ."

"I didn't shoot him, James."

"Whatever. You know what I'm saying. Even though he was shot, his death is the result of medical malpractice."

"Isn't that only a civil case?"

"Only if Mrs. Gordon makes it one. For us, it's reasonable doubt and grounds for an appeal, if not an entirely new trial."

"How are you going to convince the judge to even hear your new argument. Johnnie told me she hasn't worked since March."

"You let me figure that out."

"You got it." Ebony takes another sip.

"You know getting drunk while on house arrest won't help your cause."

"I should be saying the same to you."

Ebony sits on the bar stool Johnnie vacated, and sets her glass on the table. She stares at James, daring him to answer her challenge.

He says, "What are you talking about?"

She laughs. "I'm talking about the fact this bottle was damn near full when we got home Monday. Two days later, and there's only one drink left. And I've only had two."

"What's your point?"

"Don't play coy."

"I'm not playing anything. I drank it. What's your point?"

"I guess I don't have one then."

"Good. I gotta go."

"You just got here."

"And now I have to go. I'll be back."

"Whatever."

"You're so fucking ungrateful."

"How am I being ungrateful? You come and go out of here as you please. In and out of the bed when you feel like it. Drink the liquor and leave pissy drunk, just like he used to, and I'm being ungrateful. These are the worst days of my life and I'm the ungrateful one. Don't do that. Don't even try it. In two months, I'll be out of your hands and out of your hair, and then you can do whatever the fuck you want to do, because my ungrateful ass will be locked up. Is that what you want, James?"

"If you calm the hell down, and chill the fuck out, you'll see everything I'm doing is for you."

"How is you getting drunk for my benefit?"

"First of all, I'm never drunk. Secondly, I never leave here drunk. And thirdly, why does it matter how much I drink? I'm dealing with your shit, too, and you don't even give a damn."

"How do I know what you're dealing with? You don't say shit to me about it."

"Because you don't give me a fucking chance to, Ebony, you just start jumping down my throat."

James steps back into the flip-flops he slid off when he came into the kitchen. He marches toward the front door, leaving Ebony sitting on the bar stool nursing her glass.

"Where are you going?" she yells.

"To clear my head, and work on your appeal."

"Mhmm."

"Thanks for the information."

"Tell your mother I said, 'Hi.'"

The door slams shut behind James. Ebony picks up her glass and drains the uncomfortable contents of southern whiskey. She drowns her misdirected anger in alcohol. Staring out the glass doors, she tries to imagine the smell of the grass, and the feel of the dirt on her bare feet. She tries to imagine the feel of the sun on the skin of her arms and legs. Her eyes squint until she sees red checkered blankets and a full picnic spread laid out on top of them. Her ears perk until she can hear the slight breeze rustling the grass, and feel the sting of red ants biting her feet. Her feet escape the ant hill. They escape their rest on the bar stool. They carry her to the sliding glass back door until her face is pressed against the glass.

Her body acts of its own accord. Hands reach for the latch. The door is unlocked, the glass is pulled back, and then the screen. Outside is upon her. The cool breeze from the shade of the covered porch. She can smell outside. She stands in the doorway of her prison, arms outstretched among the sliding glass doors. Her right foot, the one unshackled, and not monitored, steps down on to the concrete beneath her. It is not grass but it is outside.

Ebony straddles the threshold between freedom and being held captive, between emancipation and prison, and leans against the open door frame. Her hands crossed beneath her breasts, her fingers raking the backs of her hands, she closes her eyes and recalls the memories that are halfway her own. The picnics, the water gun fights, the games of tag because there was nowhere to hide for hide-and-go seek. She recalls the wide open space of the small yard, of her neighbors next door when she was a child, that made her buy this home. It was their influence that put her in the second house from the entrance. It was their influence that left her vulnerable to every stranger who dropped by unannounced with a message, or a confession of their own. She sees them as clearly as the day they left her alone with Ayana to drive to their deaths. The pang of grief she felt seeing their crumpled car on the news strikes her all over again. Instead of incoherent sobs, she whispers into the breeze, "I miss you, Mrs. Marilyn."

The home she mirrored after the family she chose does not provide the peace their's did. Her home is now her own personal hell, much like Ayana's was when she was child.

Ebony stands with one foot on the ground outside her back door, in the gap between liberty and death, with her revolution in the hands of a man transforming into the ghost of the man she's accused of killing. She chooses the temporary permanence of purgatory and brings her free foot back inside. She closes the door on the outside, on the memories that were not hers to keep, and on the family that left her. She walks back to the bar stool, drains the remaining contents of the bottle into the glass, and takes the drink like a shot, relishing the fire it stirs in her soul. She numbs the violence she saw flash before her eyes as Johnnie spilled her guts. She welcomes disorientation, for her daze to turn into mind-swimming dizziness. Ebony relaxes in her limbo, stares out at her yard, and allows the games of her youth, with the twins she wished were her sisters, set her free — for now.

126.

14.

"Mama, it's me," James says, turning the key into his childhood home.

"Two days in a row, this is a surprise."

"Mama, don't start," James admonishes, sidestepping into the kitchen.

"I'm not starting nothing," Rachelle says, reaching up slightly to hug her son around his neck. "I'm just saying I'm surprised to see you two days in a row."

"After yesterday, I know I need to try and come by every day and see Pops."

"Just because you're here now doesn't mean he's going to remember you any better than he did yesterday."

"Mama, that may be true, but I gotta try."

"Alzheimer's is a progressive disease, Baby."

"I know, Mama."

"As long as you act like you know. I don't need you in here crying and carrying on trying to make him remember what he done already forgot."

"Mama!"

"Don't Mama me."

James sighs. "What are you cooking?" he asks letting her go.

"I'm fixing these greens that girl you brought in here messed up."

Rachelle walks back into the kitchen to an oversized silver pot nearly bubbling over with pot liquor, meat, and stewed greens. She picks up a wooden spoon and stirs and stirs. Satisfied with her distribution, she pulls out the drawer beneath her and grabs a double-sided plastic baby spoon. Her tasting spoon. The spoon that used to be his when he was a child, and then was Joey's spoon when he got older. The spoon that is now reserved, mostly for Joey's children. Mostly.

Rachelle dips the spoon into the pot, careful not to drop her hand in too low or she'll burn herself on the scalding liquid. She brings up one collard leaf, a shred of meat, and a bit of broth on the tiny spoon. Taking a sip, she smacks her lips and works over the flavor, and texture, until she makes a face at the spoon and then the pot.

"What's wrong with Laverne's greens?" James asks, coming close to the stove.

"I think she put hot sauce in them to cook, instead of just the vinegar like I told her. Now it's too vinegary with the white vinegar, and the apple cider vinegar, and I can't fix it."

"Put some sugar in it," James suggests.

"Boy, get out my kitchen with your no-cooking behind. I see that thing you with ain't taught you nothing about the kitchen. Don't look like she feeding you no how. You walking around here all skinny, pants falling off your behind, shirts and suits don't fit. I raised you better than to be walking around town like you don't have no home, or people who love you."

"Mama, first of all her name is Ebony."

"I know what her name is, James."

"She's not a thing. She's my girlfriend."

"I don't see why, with her convict self."

"And she's the reason I came over here to see you today."

"Oh really? Is she going to prison early?"

"No, Mama."

"Okay," Rachelle sighs, "spit it out."

"I'm going to file her appeal."

"So you made a final decision on it that fast, huh?"

Rachelle drops the baby tasting spoon into the sink catty-corner to the small four burner electric stove. She dries her hands on the front of her pink terry cloth housecoat and walks out of the kitchen, past James, and into the living room. She takes her seat on the couch, nearest her puzzles resting on the leather arm. An empty plastic bag that used to hold curtains is produced from the floor by her feet, along with a comb, brush, and a small bottle of white cream. Rachelle runs her fingers through her hair, snatching out the pink and blue wet set rollers. She drops the curlers into the empty bag after separating them from the end papers, she balls up in a trash pile beside her.

"What made you decide to go forward with the appeal, James?" Rachelle asks as she works.

He watches her tousle the curls of her hair, she probably washed the night before. She opens the nondescript jar and puts a quarter sized amount of cream into her hands. Rubbing them together like lotion, she spreads the product through her hair. James watches his mother, as he's watched her since he was a child, massage product into her scalp, fluff and primp curls into place, and then brush around her edges until her short cut is perfectly coiffed, all without a mirror.

"Are you going to answer my question? Or are you just going to stare at me? I ain't no circus animal. And this ain't the zoo."

"Dang, Mama."

"Language."

"I didn't even curse."

"You were close enough."

"Anyway. Ebony received some new information today that may actually clear her name completely."

"Oh really. She tell you it's the hospital's fault she killed that man?"

"Yes, she did, actually."

"And you believe that?" Rachelle asks looking up at James. "Then you as big a fool as she is."

"Hear me out, Mama."

James moves away from where he leaned against the post separating the kitchen and dining area. A relic of the era the house was built in. He takes a seat in the recliner, leans on the lever and flips up the footrest.

"The doctor, who actually operated on Judge Gordon, told Ebony today she was drunk during the surgery."

"Really," Rachelle says, setting her hair materials on the couch beside her. "I'm listening. Just gotta throw these end papers in the trash."

James waits until his mother comes back from the kitchen.

"Keep going. I'm listening," she says sitting back on the couch.

"Yeah. The doctor. Her name is Johnnie."

"What kind of name is that? You said it's a woman, right?"

"Yes, Mama."

"You sure? You know they have them . . . what's it called . . . transgenders now."

"Mama. That's rude."

"They do!" Rachelle picks up the remote and turns on the television.

James waits to speak until he notices, it's already on mute with the captions scrolling. "I'm sure she's a woman. It's Johnnie, short for Jonelle."

"Jonelle is such a pretty name. Why would she want to go by Johnnie?"

"Mama, that's not the point."

"Okay. Okay. Okay. Tell me the rest of the story."

"She stopped by Ebony's house today and told Ebony she was drunk during the operation. I walked in on her as she was leaving."

"So you didn't actually hear this Johnnie woman say she was drunk during the operation?"

"No."

"Then, Son, you don't have shit. Excuse my language, Lord." Rachelle looks up at black Jesus to absolve herself.

"What do you mean, Mama?"

"What do I mean? Son, you should know better than I do that Ebony being told somebody else is responsible for her crime that she was convicted of, is hearsay. I didn't go to law school, but I paid enough attention to the lessons you brought home, since you was spending my money for three more years of schooling."

"It's not hearsay if I can prove it," James says quickly.

"And how are you going to do that?"

Rachelle stares at her son waiting for an answer. She holds the gaze in the masculine face that looks just like her own. She watches his earnest eyes roll inside his lids to rack his brain for all the knowledge he can muster to convince her of what he couldn't convince a jury. She stares at him, waits for him, and allows the blinks of her eyes to be the counter of the seconds that pass by and turn in to minutes, as he tries to come up with a viable, plausible answer.

"I can ask the judge to exhume the body, and get an independent autopsy to prove there was medical malpractice."

"You still need to have a solid piece of evidence to convince the judge to allow the exhumation. You can't just go digging people out the ground for no good reason."

"I have good reason."

James blows the air out of his nose. His bouncing foot shakes his left leg all the way up to his knee. Rachelle watches him wipe the backs, and then the front, of his hands against his jeans as he waits for her admonishment or her approval. She gives neither.

She says, "You know, when you were a baby. No, a toddler. About one or so. You would be in the class with the other kids your age. Of course, you were the first one there, and the last one to leave, because I'm your Mama and I owned the place. Anyway, you'd be there, and your favorite toy was this big square thing that teaches shapes and sizes. You'd sit on the carpet with that thing between your legs, and all the pieces around you in reaching distance, working to figure out which piece goes where. You'd get the star. The heart. The circle. The triangle. The octagon. The diamond. You would get all of the shapes right, except the square and the rectangle."

"Mama, what's your point?" James asks, bringing his hands to his face.

Rachelle rocks back and forth on the saggy sofa with a fond smile. "I mean, this went on for weeks. You'd put the rectangle in the square and it wouldn't go, no matter which way you turned it. You'd put the square in the rectangle, but it wouldn't go, no matter which way you turned it. Sometimes you'd get so frustrated you'd throw the toy across the room. I just watched you to see if you'd get it. And one day you did. One day you put the square with the square and the rectangle with the rectangle."

"Mama, what's your point?"

"My point, James, is that even when you were a baby working your own puzzles, you always had all the pieces right in front of you, you just had to figure out where they go and how they fit."

"What does that have to do with Ebony's case?"

"You have all the pieces right in front of you, you just need to know how they fit."

"So you think my plan could work?"

"Does it matter what I think, James? You're going to do what you want to do anyway. You'll figure it out."

James doesn't respond. He leaves his face in his hands, fingers steepled, pointers resting against the center of his forehead. He breathes through his shroud, absorbing his mother's anecdote, trying to separate out the practical use of the story. His own breath comes back at him, hot from the enclosed space he makes with his hands and the baggy neck of his shirt.

"I think this could work, Mama." James says looking up.

Rachelle is not across from him. He turns his head toward the kitchen. He doesn't see her, but he can hear her. The sound of her low hum. He knows it's a gospel song, but he can't catch which one. The sound calls to him from the kitchen. James stands from the recliner and goes back to where his visit began. He goes back to where his earliest memories begin. In the kitchen with his mother, on the floor wrapped in her skirts, as she stood before the stove, a song in her heart manifested in the hum of her lips. James leans against the post and watches her move about the kitchen. Washing, drying, wiping, straightening, until the small space is spotless. She grabs a chipped stoneware plate from the plastic drying rack in the sink, along with a serving spoon. Heaps of rice and gravy are piled onto the plate, followed by a braised chicken leg quarter, creamed corn from a small pot behind the greens, and cornbread in a cast iron skillet next to the them. She does not add any greens to the plate.

Rachelle hands it to him after she's covered the pots and sets the serving spoon on the spoon rest. James takes the plate with a rushed, "Thank you, Mama," and sits down in the space they called the dining room. It wasn't a formal dining room. It wasn't even a separate room. It was just a space on the other side of the half wall enclosing the kitchen, without living room furniture. An invisible line of demarcation ran horizontally along the floor as the boundary of the dining room and the living room. The living room began with the recliner. Any toys, papers, homework, magazines, books, or games found on the wrong side of the recliner was grounds for a fussing. Any food found on the wrong side of the recliner was grounds for a beating. James snickers at the memory as he sits down at the table in the place he's sat since he was a child; close to the wall, looking out over the dining room and the frames of his family, the First Family, the holy, and the righteous.

"Mama, let me get some of those greens," James calls.

"You don't want them nasty ass greens, Son."

"Mama!"

"I'm sorry. That's the one thing Laverne can't cook. She might as well stop trying. Boy, I know you better bless that food before you eat in my house."

James looks to Jesus on the wall, bows his head and mumbles a prayer.

"Where's Laverne, Mama?" James asks looking up.

"She went out to the store to pick up some more things for your daddy. Diapers and such."

James nods. Picking up his fork he asks, "You think I can convince the judge to exhume the body?"

"I don't know, James. You almost convinced the jury that girl wasn't guilty."

"I know," he answers with his mouth full of food.

"I don't know why you let her embarrass you the way she did. I always told you be prepared for what you didn't prepare."

"I know, Mama."

"Then act like it."

"I am."

"How, Son."

"I'm drafting the appeal. I can argue battered woman syndrome for the stalking part."

"So now the girl sick in the head."

"If it will get me my appeal she will be."

"I hope she knows all this."

"She will."

"Alright then," Rachelle says, sitting at the head of the table. "What's the rest of your strategy."

"I'm still working on it." James shovels another spoonful of food into his mouth. "But I was thinking about requesting an independent autopsy. I can have Barker's mom approve it, even if the judge doesn't, since it's her son's remains."

"She was good on the stand. That's good, baby. Real good. I don't know what it would be like to be a mother with no love lost for your dead baby. I just can't imagine."

"That's because you got me." James smiles.

"Boy, chew your food."

He swallows. "Anyway. I can get the exhumation, the independent autopsy, and if it shows medical malpractice, then I may even get her conviction overturned."

"That sounds like you paying for the results you want. With what money?"

"A fund-raiser ."

"You think people are going to give you money for a guilty woman? Boy, you really are crazy."

"Mama, she didn't do it."

"You and her really believe that, don't you?"

"She does."

"You in here defending her to my face. You must believe it too."

"It doesn't matter what I believe, Mama. I'm the lawyer. I have one job. Defend my client."

"That's why you lost the case the first time. If you don't know what you believe, how is the jury supposed to believe you?"

"Rachelle."

The voice croaks from deep in the bedroom across the hall from the kitchen.

"That's your daddy," She says, standing up from the table.

Slippered feet carry her quickly out of the dining room and into the bedroom. Her lingering, accusing, questioning gaze is gone. James is left at the oval shaped table of his teenaged years, alone with his thoughts and her words. *If you don't know what you believe, how is the jury supposed to believe you? How is anybody supposed to believe me, and I'm not sure she didn't kill him?*

Thoughts, tactics, transitions, and schemes change with each bite of his food. Consumed by his own pending strategies and possible outcomes, he doesn't hear his mother in the next room assuring his forgetting father that there is not a burglar in the house. He doesn't hear or see her struggle to raise him from the bed. He doesn't hear the commotion they make to get James Senior to brush his hair, put in his teeth, and wipe the cold from his eyes. James chews away his doubt. He swallows his own disbelief, clears the comestibles, and leaves only his self-assured assumptions in the crumbs he couldn't gather on his fork. Standing from the table, plate in hand, James takes it to the kitchen and drops it in the lukewarm dishwater, he knows his mother ran shortly after she woke up this morning.

He remembers her saying when he was a child, "If you wake up cleaning, you don't have to do it later when all you want to do is sleep."

James washes his fork and plate and places them in the drying rack beside the barely soapy water. He turns ninety degrees and grabs a can of iced tea out of the refrigerator.

Another ninety degrees and he is face-to-face with his ailing father.

"Rachelle. Who that?"

James Senior asks the question with his finger pointed. James nods at the man he calls Pops. The man who used to push his stroller, now being pushed in the wheel chair. The man who used to wipe his butt, sitting upright in his own diaper.

"Hey, Pops," James says.

"Rachelle. Who that?" James Senior asks again.

"Jamie, that's Junior. Our son."

"Joey, our son."

"And so is James."

"I'm James," James Senior points to himself.

"Yes, Baby. Come on let's get you over here so you can watch your stories."

Rachelle maneuvers the modern, narrow wheelchair James bought for just this occasion around the cramped living room to the side of the sofa where no one sits. She takes a fleece blanket from behind the sofa and lays it across his lap.

"Your stories are on, Jamie."

Rachelle points to the muted television where Judge Mathis stares back at them. His words flashing quickly on the screen in the half captured closed captioning. She sits back on her end of the couch, and grabs a puzzle book and pen from her arm rest. James joins his parents on the sofa. He sits in the sagging middle cushion, his body toward Rachelle, and his feet toward his father.

"How long you staying, Baby?" Rachelle asks her nose stuck in the puzzle book.

"I don't know, Mama. I just need to clear my head."

"Take your time, Baby. Take your time. We ain't going nowhere no time soon."

James leans his head against his mother, crosses his arms across his chest, and closes his eyes. He tries to conjure his own memory to teleport him back to daycare. Back to his mother's care when he played with a block puzzle, and got it wrong, over and over again until he got it right. His mind won't take him back. His memory fails him. James opens his eyes to his father's profile, his eyes intense on the silent television.

"Rachelle, that woman's guilty."

"Yes, Jamie, I know," she answers without looking up.

"I wish court was as fun as these clowns make it look on TV," James mutters.

He closes his eyes once more and wills his mind to work for him. He wills himself to revive a memory that's not his, to conjure a connection his brain was too young to retain. His eyes open to his father's profile. The grown man living his second childhood in reverse. Benjamin Button in the brain. James watches the man losing his mind stare at the TV judge he mistakes for his own son, until his own eyes get heavy, lids droop, and the emptiness of no memories and no dreams takes over. In the silent understanding between his parents, only one memory is allowed to linger on for his father. The memory of his wife. James falls asleep in the quieting, calming comfort of the first woman he ever loved, grasping for an obstreperous memory that won't come, to pull the wisdom he didn't know he had, to save the woman he's in love with.

"Rachelle, he's guilty too."

"Yes, Jamie. I know."

15.

"Right now on *Dawn in the evening*," Dawn says into her camera. "Inside the deliberations. Our coverage of the Ebony Jones trial continues tonight with Ora Ellison, who served as the jury forewoman, and Milton Tobin, who also served on the jury."

"Thank you for joining us," she says, facing her guests who sit across from her.

They both say thank you as they shift uncomfortably on the stiff, white leather couch. Dawn traded the stark glass news desk for the in studio interview set, to make her hesitant guests feel more at ease.

"Ora, let's begin with you," Dawn says. "What was the atmosphere inside the room when deliberations first started."

"Tense," she answers.

Dawn smiles at her to encourage her to say more. "Tell me . . . how did the other jurors come to select you as the forewoman?"

"We didn't." Milton interjects. "She just took over and we went with it."

Dawn takes a beat to study her guests. The only African-American woman who served on the jury, the forewoman, who she begged to come on her show after finding her, and the large white man who eagerly said yes. She intended for Ora to do all of the talking and Milton to offer perspective. Intentions she realizes will not come to fruition. She focuses on Milton in his short-sleeved white button down shirt closed over his turkey neck, and directs the next question toward him.

"Was it a relief to have Ora take charge."

Milton looks to the skinny woman beside him. She gestures her hands forward as if giving him permission to speak.

"It was. Nobody wanted to be there. Nobody knew what to think after closing arguments. We just wanted to come to a unanimous decision, so we could go home and get back to our normal lives."

"So, how did you all do that? Come to a unanimous decision."

"We took a vote," Ora says.

"A vote on what?"

"To see where everyone stood on the case."

"And where was that?"

"On the second degree murder charge, we were split four for conviction and two for acquittal."

"But you all acquitted her of second-degree murder."

"Yes," Milton says. "That happened Saturday during deliberations after our first question."

"Nobody would budge on their positions," Ora says, "so we asked the judge if we could consider lesser charges."

"So how did you all acquit her of manslaughter as well?" Dawn asks.

"We took another vote," Milton answers.

"What was the outcome?"

"Five-to-one," Ora says. "Not guilty for the majority."

"That's a big change," Dawn remarks.

Ora nods her head at the anchor she knows is not much older than her. She fidgets with the hem of her forest green pencil skirt, and her black blouse. Her hands come to the straight cut wig, and accidentally knocks against the mic.

"Sorry," she mumbles.

"How did you guys go from four ready to convict on second degree murder, to five ready to acquit on manslaughter?" Dawn asks, setting her notes beside her.

"We went back to the evidence pictures," Milton said.

"And what did you see?"

He clears the phlegm from his throat and swallows. "It was the picture of her car."

"Ebony Jones's dented black Acura?"

"Yes. We looked at those dents, and then the pictures of her the police took when she turned herself in. Even through all that hair she had a bloody scalp, we concluded that was from being thrown into the car."

"Not just that," Ora says with manufactured depth to her voice. "We talked about what we would all do if we were in that situation."

"And what's that?"

"It had to do with the gun. The fact, she never took it out to let him know she had it. If she truly wanted to shoot him, she could have done so when she said he grabbed her by the neck. But she never did."

"And what did that mean to you?"

"That her intention was never to kill him," Milton says.

"Then why did you all not acquit her entirely?" Dawn prods.

"Because the juror who wanted to convict on second-degree murder, and manslaughter, still didn't believe the rest of us and our theory."

"What did he believe?"

"He thought she made those dents herself with a hammer," Milton scoffs.

"Why is that?"

"He said because she left the shooting scene and didn't turn herself in for eight hours, that she and her attorney could have done all that damage themselves."

"His real problem was with James," Ora says in her normal high-pitched speaking voice.

"What was the issue with attorney James Parnell?"

"The way he acted when the state attorney started questioning Ebony."

"What do you mean?" Dawn asks.

"He was falling all over the table, sweating, mumbling, crying when the state attorney asked her about following the Judge and that other girl . . . the girlfriend . . ." Ora snaps her fingers three times in succession. "What was her name?"

"Sola," Milton says trying to help out.

"Soleil St. James," Dawn answers.

"Yes. Her," Ora says. "As the state attorney asked each question he just got worse and worse. He looked like he was hearing all of this for the first time. Like he never considered Ebony to be a stalker, or to have been following people for as long as she had. Even the judge yelled at him to straighten up."

"And what did that chastisement mean to you?"

"Nothing, personally," Ora says. "I know as women we don't always tell our men everything about ourselves. It keeps the mystery. If they don't know we've been hurt by someone else before them, or even that there was someone else before them, it keeps the relationship easy. Whatever she did to cope with how the abuse affected her life, is her business."

"Milton?" Dawn encourages.

"It made her look guilty in my eyes," he answers. "He was losing his cool in the courtroom because he didn't believe her. I'm a man. I know what that looks like. It made me feel like if he didn't believe her, and that's his client *and* his girlfriend, why should I?"

"So what changed?"

Milton sighs, "I'll be honest. I was one of the four who wanted to convict on second-degree murder. But Ora here changed my mind when we looked at the pictures."

"But that's not where the deliberations ended. How did you go from manslaughter to culpable negligence."

"The gun," Ora answers.

"What about the gun?"

"In the jury instructions it talks about proper gun ownership and what's considered reckless behavior. No matter how we all personally felt about the case, we all agreed she was reckless with the gun."

"What do you mean?"

"She may not have meant to kill him," Milton begins, "but she did."

"Okay . . ."

"That's the definition of reckless," Milton says.

"But Ebony Jones said during her testimony, she didn't pull the trigger."

"It doesn't matter, he's still dead. I might say I don't eat cake, or brownies, or ice cream, but I'm still fat. Just because you say you didn't do something, doesn't negate the outcome of what happened."

"Are you satisfied with the verdict, Milton?"

"I think we did justice by the Judge and by Ebony, considering everything she said happened. Not like we could ask the dead guy his opinion."

"What about you, Ora. Are you satisfied with the verdict you all reached?"

"Am I satisfied that we reached a verdict? Yes. Am I satisfied with the outcome of the trial? No."

"What do you mean?"

"She had a concealed carry license. She had a right to have a gun. We saw she was beat up pretty badly. Fresh blood, fractured ribs, bruised appendix. Even if the doctors said they couldn't be one hundred percent sure her bruises were fresh, the other evidence picture, the one with you in it . . ." Ora nods at Dawn, "shows there were no bruises on her four days before the shooting."

"Ora, we couldn't even see her whole body in that picture. You don't know if she had bruises then or not," Milton argues.

"We have the picture," Dawn says. "Let's pull it up if we can in the control room."

Dawn turns away from her guests and looks at the screen below her teleprompter. The television screen showing their interview and what's on air, in real time. Their faces and the couches disappear as the picture is punched up.

"Is this the picture in question?" Dawn asks, not turning away from the screen.

"Yes," Milton answers.

"For full disclosure I must say this picture was taken the Saturday before the shooting death of Judge Barker Gordon at a luncheon thrown by the mayor that I hosted. In it are the Judge, his date, Soleil St. James, Ebony Jones, who we know is now convicted in Judge Gordon's death, and her boyfriend James Parnell, who was at the time an assistant state attorney. I took this photo with the group after meeting

Ebony and Soleil, and learning Ebony was a fan of the show."

"Milton," Dawn says turning back toward him, "what is your issue with this picture as it relates to the facts of the case."

"It doesn't have any facts that go to the case," he says. "All we can see is her face and part of her shoulder. I don't know if she has bruises on her back, or not."

"Ora?"

"As a woman, I still say that if you've been beaten up, or you've fallen down, and your body is covered in bruises, you're not out and about in stilettos and a bandeau dress, giving Kool-Aid grins to the cameras, no matter who you're a fan of."

"We don't know that," Milton argues. "You ask me, she should be going to prison for a lot longer than three-to-five years. You ask me, she should be in prison now, instead of sitting at home on house arrest until her sentencing."

"Milton! I thought you said Ora convinced you otherwise?"

"She convinced me to see the woman's point of view. That brings reasonable doubt, which means legally, the prosecution didn't fully convince me of their case."

"And personally?"

"Personally, you don't get to stalk someone, pick a fight with them, and kill them because you lost the fight."

"George Zimmerman did," Ora says.

"George Zimmerman didn't leave the scene of the shooting for eight hours either. If she didn't do anything wrong, why did she run?"

Dawn leaves Milton's question unanswered. Distracted by the buzzing of her phone on top of her notes beside her, the ringing bell for her to ask about the conviction is ignored. She illuminates the screen.

"That's a great question, Milton," Dawn says, trying to mask her gasp. She sets the phone down in the lap of her pale pink skirt suit. "But if you feel so strongly about it, why didn't you stick with second-degree murder, or manslaughter?"

"For the greater good," he answers with a smug smile.

"What's that?"

"If me and a few others didn't give on the first two charges, that woman would have walked out of court scot-free, because we would have deadlocked."

Ora adds, "Second-degree murder and manslaughter were nonstarters, but culpable negligence, everyone could agree on, no matter their personal feelings on the case."

"It may not be over yet. When we come back, breaking news on the next steps in the Ebony Jones case. Attorney James Parnell responds in his own words to the jurors questions, accusations, and when he plans to file his appeal. That's next on *Dawn in the Evening*."

16.

"Boy, are you texting the news lady while she's on TV?" Rachelle asks James who's still buried in his phone.

"I'm getting ready to call her, too, Mama."

"You just don't know when to leave well enough alone, do you?"

"I already told you I was going to file the appeal."

"And now you've told Dawn, who told the whole world."

"The whole world doesn't even get this channel, Mama."

"Ain't no time for you to be joking. Messing up your life, that's what you're doing," she humphs.

"Mama, I got this," James says confidently.

"Kelly and Jennifer," Dawn says aloud in the studio.

"That was an abrupt tease," Kelly says in her ear.

"Thanks for going with me," Dawn says. "James just texted me. I need you to make a full screen of what he said."

"I'm ready," Jennifer says into Dawn's ear. "What does the message say?"

"It says: I thank the jury for their service and their honesty on your program tonight, but my client and I disagree with the jurors that justice has been served. Whatever my shortcomings were during the trial, does not negate that my client, Ebony Jones, was afraid for her life, and nearly killed, while trying to help a friend in need, the best way she knew how. We disagree with the jury's assessment of the facts and the case law. Additionally, in light of new evidence, I will be meeting with the state attorney and Judge Marisol Shaw tomorrow morning to discuss full vindication and an acquittal for my client, Ebony Jones."

"Okay, Dawn," Jennifer says. "That's way too much to fit on this one full screen. Can you email me that message, and I'll try to get it done before we come back from break."

"How much time is left in the break?"

"A minute," John says from the floor behind Dawn's camera.

"I'm sending it to you now, Jennifer."

"Dawn, the phone's ringing back here," Kelly says with slight annoyance.

"It's James. I sent him a number to one of the phone lines. Put him through. We can talk to him, and he can talk to Ora and Milton."

"Are you guys okay with that?" Dawn asks her guests.

"Fine with me," Ora says.

"I have some questions for him anyway," Milton answers.

"Good."

"Thirty seconds," John yells aloud.

Dawn picks up the mirror she removed from the set desk and places it on the floor beside her feet. She fluffs her growing bangs and moves hair out of her eyes, except for one or two wisps. Two fingers smudge the smile lines in her makeup around her mouth, and dab at the extended cat eye she made with eyeliner.

"Fifteen," John yells.

Dawn straightens the collar of her black button-down over the collar of her matching pale pink suit jacket.

"Ten, nine, eight . . ."

She smudges her lips together once more, and then sets the mirror back at her feet.

"Here we go," she says to Ora and Milton.

"Three, two, one. Cue, Dawn."

"Welcome back to *Dawn in the Evening*. We are following breaking news tonight in the Ebony Jones case. Jones's attorney, James Parnell, is live on the phone with us tonight. James, I'll go ahead and let you break the news to the people."

"Good evening, Dawn," James says, sitting beside his mother and sleeping father, while staring at the muted television.

"Good evening," Dawn says into her camera. "What is this big development you're telling us first tonight on *Dawn in the Evening?*"

"I can't go into great detail right now," James begins, "but what I can say is I have received new evidence in the case, and I have requested to meet with the state attorney and Judge Shaw tomorrow morning."

"James, can you at least allude to us what this new evidence entails?" Dawn pries.

James smiles at the television watching Dawn move to edge of her seat hoping to entice more out of him than he wants to say.

"Not specifically," he answers. "But I will say that if Judge Shaw and the State Attorney agree with me, Ebony Jones will be a free woman."

"That's a pretty bold statement, James. What if they don't agree with you?"

"If they don't see things my way, there is another tactic I can use to still introduce the new evidence, and make sure Ebony never sees the inside of a prison."

"You seem pretty confident things will go your way, no matter what."

James pauses until he sees her finish settling back into the leather cushions of the small set sofa, then says, "I am confident things will go my way."

"Were you this confident going into Ebony's trial?"

"I decline to answer that question."

"I'm not sure if you've been watching, James . . ."

"I've been watching."

"Good. Then you know we have two of the jurors here with us who served during Ebony's trial."

"I'm aware."

"Then let's loop them in to the conversation. Milton and Ora, do you have any questions for James while we have him on the phone, or vice versa?"

James waits for the questions to come through the receiver of his cell phone while watching the TV. The shots jump from Dawn, to the two jurors, to a shot of the three of them on the set, to a shot of two boxes with the three live people on one side, and a picture of James, from his official city picture when he was an ASA, in the other box.

"Why do you think your girlfriend deserves to go free?" Milton asks. "She shot a judge."

"Thank you for your question, Milton. The loss of Judge Barker Gordon is a terrible tragedy for this community, and for myself personally. I worked side-by-side with him for many years and counted him as both my mentor and a friend. However, there are things about him that I did not know until recently. As hard as those sordid details of his life are to reconcile with the man I knew, I cannot deny that the women around him, who knew him best, one of whom just happens to be my girlfriend, knew a different man altogether. They knew a violent man. They knew a batterer, an abuser. I'm not saying Ebony Jones deserves to go free because she's my girlfriend. I believe Ebony Jones deserves to go free because she is a victim who has been abused not just by someone who was supposed to uphold the law, but by the entire justice system itself."

"James," Dawn interjects, "since you were watching earlier, you know the issue some of the jurors had in the case was the presence of the gun, and the fact Ebony fled the scene of the shooting and didn't turn herself in for eight hours."

"I heard."

"Do you have anything to say to that point?"

James sees Dawn at the edge of her seat again. "I hate to disappoint you Ms., Anthony, but all I will say to that point is that it is not illegal for Ebony Jones to have a concealed weapon on her person."

"You have nothing to say about her fleeing the scene?" Dawn presses.

"Only what you already know, and that is, I am the one who brought her in to the police."

"James, what about the jurors observation you lost it in court during the cross examination of Ebony Jones?"

"I believe I addressed that in the statement I sent you. No matter what my shortcomings are, they don't negate the fact Ebony was afraid for her life, and trying to help a friend in need."

The statement comes up on the television screen with his picture beside it. The full screen of his own words hides Dawn and her guests. It hides the accusatory stares into the camera from the white man who tried to hide behind the forewoman as the verdict was read. James remembers his red face and denim button down as clearly as he sees it on the screen when the camera cuts back to the seated trio. He remembers the pained expression of the juror he assumed was constipated during the verdict reading, and the cool vibe he received from the forewoman when he stared at her before she opened her mouth to speak. It is her who he focuses on now, as he watches the exchange he is both a participant in, and an observer to, play out on the standing fifty-eight inch flat screen he bought his parents one Christmas.

"You addressing your shortcomings for your loss of composure in court, does that mean you failed to fully vet and prepare both Ebony Jones, and yourself, before trial?" Dawn asks.

"It means I'm human," James answers. "Emotions are high for me in this case both professionally, and personally. I am also not a defense attorney by nature. I am a trained prosecutor. I am also a man, in love with his client. Did I have blinders on during the trial? Perhaps. Have I learned from what you all call my mistakes? I have."

"I have a question," Ora says looking directly at the camera.

James stares back at her through the television. "Ms. Ellison, is it? Go ahead."

"Did you know about Ebony's relationship with the Judge before trial?"

That's not any of your business. James silences what he wants to say and stares into Ora's slim face, with the shifted wig that reveals a lighter color of hair at her natural hairline. He searches her wide, round Diana Ross eyes, but sees

149.

nothing that should make him hesitant about the words he should choose to answer her question. James stands up from where the couch sucks him in, maneuvers around an old wooden coffee table, covered with old issues of *O!* magazine, *Ebony* and *Essence*, and walks directly toward the television. He stands in front of the screen studying the woman who volunteered herself to be the forewoman. The woman who naturally took charge of the deliberations and the outcome of the verdict. The woman who understands women keep secrets from men, and that abuse is processed differently between victims.

"I knew," James answers.

"Move, Boy. I can't see the TV," Rachelle yells at James.

"Is everything alright, James?" Dawn asks. "I hear yelling in the background."

"Yes. It's just the neighborhood I'm in. It should be better now."

He cuts his eyes at his mother and brings his index finger to his lips.

"Piggy-backing off of Ora's question, If you knew about Ebony's relationship with the late Judge Gordon why did it seem the questions from the state attorney during her cross examination, caught you by surprise?"

"I'm not the one on trial. I decline to answer that question."

"That's because he didn't know his girlfriend as well as he thought he did," Milton says. "And if you didn't know she was a stalker, there's probably a whole lot else you don't know about her either, like maybe she did pull the trigger, and has just been leading us on this whole time with the gun-went-off-by-itself bit."

"Mr. Tobin, if that's your opinion of me, my client, or what you believe to be the facts of this case, then you are entitled to it. However, none of us were there the day Judge Gordon died, none of us own the gun that killed him, and none of us stood trial for his murder. We can armchair quarterback what Ebony, or even I, should have done over these last six months all evening long, but it won't change what's happened."

"Typical lawyer. Not answering the question."

"Mr. Tobin, you didn't ask me a question. You offered your opinion. I countered with one of my own."

"You know she did it," Milton accuses directly into the camera.

"I don't know that, any more than you do. And if that's what you truly believe, you had a chance to express that in your verdict."

"I did."

"If my memory serves me correctly, I believe you began to change your mind because of Ms. Ellison's arguments."

"I believe in the justice system. I believe in what our country stands for. I believe if there is reasonable doubt, that should not be ignored, no matter what my gut tells me. The system works."

"And for that, Mr. Tobin, my client is facing three-to-five years in prison. Thank you very much for your contribution to the system."

"Well," Dawn says quickly. "We need to take a break. When we come back, my final thoughts in "Sound Off.""

"I guess you told them," Rachelle says as James pulls the phone down from his ear.

"We'll see how it plays out tomorrow. None of this matters unless I get what I want."

"You've always been so intractable that way."

"Intractable, Mama?"

"Stubborn. Bullheaded. Hard-headed."

"I know what the word means, Mama. I'm just surprised you're using it."

"I know words, boy."

"I know, Mama. It's just . . ."

"What? I don't talk like I'm educated."

"Nothing, Mama."

James allows his silence to be the apology for the unintended insult. He walks from where he was standing by the television to where his father sits sleeping in his wheelchair. He touches the back of his hand to his father's forehead. His father's skin feels cool and clammy. The skin rough with stubble that's grown in over the course of the day, has lost the rich blackness of its color James remembers from his childhood. The skin that darkened even further in the summertime, when he would spend hours in lumber yards picking out wood pieces to cut down and create something beautiful. James pulls the sweater tighter across his father's frail body, and tucks in the blanket tighter beneath his thighs where he sits in the wheel chair. He steps over his father's feet and flops back down into the sagging center cushion beside his mother.

"What's another word for stubborn?" She asks, not looking up from her word puzzle.

"Intractable," James says.

"You ain't funny. It has to start with the letter O."

"Obstinate," James answers.

"Thank you, Baby."

"You're welcome, Mama," James, says standing back up with a smile, aware of where his mother's growing vocabulary is coming from. "I guess I better get back home. It's late."

"You going to your house, or hers?" Rachelle asks putting her puzzle down.

"Does it matter, Mama?"

"Boy, don't question me. Everything you do matters to me."

"Probably her house."

"You be careful. You hear me."

"Yes, Mama."

"I love you, Baby."

"I love you, too, Mama."

James bends down and kisses his mother on the forehead. He walks past the TV he bought and follows the hallway wall to the front door. He turns the handle at the same time as someone else on the other side.

"Laverne! Hey. Let me help you with the bags."

"Hey, James. I just heard you on the radio."

She hands him the bag in her arms, and readjusts the bag on her shoulder across her pastel, floral print scrubs as she steps into the house.

"You heard me on the radio? How is that?"

"They said you were on TV talking to Dawn Anthony, and then they played the segment with you arguing with the people from the jury."

"That was fast."

"Mmhmm," Laverne says closing the front door behind her.

"I wasn't arguing."

"Sounded like arguing to me."

"Whatever." James rolls his eyes. "You've been gone a long time," he says.

"No. You were sleep a long time," Laverne says, pushing her square rimmed glasses further up her nose.

She stops rummaging in the kitchen for Tupperware containers to put away the food she cooked in the morning.

She says, "I came back this afternoon and you were passed out on the couch with your head in your Mama's lap, mouth all open, like a milk drunk baby."

"I didn't even hear you."

"I know you didn't. I came in, gave your daddy a bath, changed his clothes, and rolled him back out to where he was, and left again to get my kids from school, without you so much as rolling over."

"My bad, Laverne. I didn't mean no harm."

"I take my job seriously."

"I got it. That's why I keep you around."

She turns away, giving him her curly afro to stare at, and begins using the utensils left on the spoon rest to put away the food.

She says, "Then you better remember that, the next time you want to question my comings and goings."

"I won't question you no more," I'm gone.

"Did you tell your mama, Bye?"

"I told her bye before you came in the house. She over there nose deep in those puzzles. She ain't paying me no attention."

"Boy, you know I can still hear you, even if I don't say nothing to you, you know."

"Yes, Mama. Bye, Mama."

James turns the lock on the front door again. Again it is being turned from the outside. He pulls it open wide.

"Uncle James!" His niece shrieks in the doorway.

"Hey, Joanna," James says lifting his arms above his head as his niece wraps herself around his waist.

"Girl, is that the only person in this house you see?" Rachelle stands up from the sofa.

"Grammy," Joanna shrieks, releasing James and running toward his mother.

"Hey, Uncle James?"

"Hey, JoJo," James says slapping his nephew's hand. "Where's your dad."

"He's getting Jessica out of her car seat?"

"I guess I better stop putting the food away then," Laverne says, dropping one of the half-filled Tupperware bowls on the counter.

"Ooh, Laverne, you cooked?" Joey asks coming in the house.

"You know I did; that's why you here, ain't it?"

"Mama invited us," Joey says nodding toward the living room. "Hey, James. I heard you on the radio."

"So I've been told."

"You sounded good, Bruh-Bruh."

"How is the princess?" James rubs the back of Jessica's sleeping head.

"Knocked out. Thank the Lord," Joey sighs. "This girl wore me out."

"Give her here," Laverne says with her arms outstretched. "You can make JoJo and Joanna's plates."

"She's all yours."

James looks on from the doorway as Laverne takes the sleeping 10-month old baby. She rocks Jessica gently in her arms, pressed close to her bosom. Sure the baby is good and sleep, Laverne removes her pink sneakers, carries her into the living room, and sets her on the sofa in the sagging spot James left.

"I'm gone, y'all," James says, turning the front door handle for the third time to leave.

"Hold on, Bruh-Bruh."

"What is it, Joey?"

Joey puts down the paper plate he started to fill with food for one of his children. He wipes his greasy hands on the back of his khakis, and then reaches into his back pocket for his wallet. He flips it open and pulls out three crisp one hundred dollar bills.

"I'm paying you back early," he says, pride tinged in his voice, "what I owe you, and then some. Call it interest."

"I meant it, Joey. Keep it for next time."

"You sure?"

"Yeah, I'm sure."

Joey puts the money back into his wallet without giving James a chance to change his mind.

"Where'd you get it from anyway?" James asks. "You said you don't get paid until Friday. I hope you didn't go to one of them check cashing places."

"Hell no! Charlene came through for me."

"Who is that?"

"A lil' honey I'm seeing."

"She know about all of this?" James asks gesturing to JoJo, Joanna, and Jessica.

"Just Jessica. She saw me one day picking her up from daycare. You know the ladies love it when they spot a supportive daddy."

"And she just gave you three hundred dollars."

"Don't worry about all that."

"Strap up before you have another baby."

"Damn that. I'm getting fixed. The only person I want having my babies is Laverne," he nods toward the living room. "You hear that, Baby."

"Fool, ain't nobody paying you know attention. I can't have no more babies, and I wouldn't have yours even if you paid me."

"Damn, Laverne. I thought we had a good thing going here."

"We don't have nothing going on. Not even the rent."

"I'm gone y'all."

"Bye, Baby," Rachelle calls from the living room floor where she sits with JoJo and JoAnna by her side and a book spread across her lap.

"Bye, Uncle James," the children call.

James pulls open the door and steps out into the cooling night air. He appreciates the temperature drop to about seventy degrees, even if it is still warm by other state standards. He gets into his car, turns it on, and backs out of the driveway.

We have a clip of Attorney James Par . . .

He turns the radio off before the announcer finishes his name, not wanting to relive the impromptu interview he gave to the whole city, and quite possibly the entire country.

"That was a helluva show you had tonight," Boyce says to Dawn as she walks off the set.

"Thank you," she says.

"Where are the jurors?"

"Jennifer and Kelly walked them to the door."

"How did you get the attorney to call in?"

"I sent him the phone number."

"Wow. It was awesome. Good TV," he says following her on the short walk to her office.

"Thanks."

"You want to debrief with Linden before the eleven?"

"I'll talk to him."

"Make sure you run a good chunk of that sound. Especially the argument between the attorney and that juror guy."

"Milton."

"Yeah, him."

"We will."

"What do you have planned for the rest of the week?"

"Tomorrow we're recreating the shooting. Friday we're going to have a sociology professor from UNF on why this black woman was convicted when so many white men have gone free."

"You know the reason, right?" Boyce goads.

"Because they're police officers and she's a civilian?" Dawn stops inside her office door.

"Exactly."

"But if they can hide behind the badge and claim they were scared for their lives, when they carry a gun and are trained to use them, why can't she?"

"She picked a fight and she lost, Dawn. She got angry, killed out of anger, and tried to blame the victim instead of herself."

"Police do the same thing all the time. If saying she was scared for her life and doesn't remember firing her gun doesn't work for Ebony, it shouldn't work for the police."

"Just make sure you tell both sides of the story on Friday. And have a second expert to balance out the one guy's opinion."

"It's a woman."

"Whatever, just have balance," Boyce demands.

"We will."

"I sent that draft to your lawyer and your agent," Boyce says softening his voice.

"I know."

Dawn walks completely inside her office. Boyce follows behind her and closes the glass door. It clangs as the lock clicks. She sits in the high-backed Italian leather chair, and kicks off her heels under her desk. She slips her feet into her nearby furry boots and waits for Boyce to make clear why he's in her space.

"I spoke to them today and they seemed to think the deal was pretty good."

"They told me."

"But I guess that means you have other thoughts."

"Five years is too long, Boyce," Dawn says flatly. She leans as far back as the accordion recliner will allow her. Eyes closed, she waits for the rebuttal she knows is coming.

"Okay," he says eagerly. "Three years."

"That's still too long. I'm a woman of a certain age, at a certain point in my career."

She doesn't open her eyes, but she knows Boyce is nodding his begrudging understanding. He leaves the silence of her admission unfilled. The next move on the board is hers. The next sentence in the conversation is hers. She is at the helm of this tête-à-tête, plotting a grand slam worthy serve in the conversation.

"I was thinking," she begins, "Just one year."

"Extend my current contract one year without changing my title or what shows I do on paper. That allows Julia's review to go forward and if the research shows she's missed, she can come back to the chair she loves. If it doesn't go well for her and the research prefers me, *and* it works for me, I'll sign a four year deal and you'll get me for the full five with only a network out."

Dawn opens her eyes to see Boyce nodding this time. His fingers are wrapped beneath his nose, around his lips, and down to his chin. She waits for him to meet her gaze. He looks up from where he stared at the floor.

"Julia's already out," he announces.

"That's not my problem. I still only want one year."

"That's not fair to us, Dawn," Boyce whines.

"Aren't you grooming Tarren Tyler for my chair? Why isn't that fair? It's not like you don't already have somebody waiting in the wings. Isn't that what you told me a few months ago?"

"Dawn, you're a valued asset of the 9 News Now team, and you know that."

"Julia was a valued asset going on four decades and she's not here anymore."

"Blame the business. I didn't want to let her go."

"But you did. Which means the same can be done to me."

"I wouldn't do that to you, Dawn."

"Yes, you would."

"Two years."

"One."

Boyce shoves one hand in his pocket, and pulls the door handle open with the other. "I have to run it by the folks upstairs."

He steps out of the office, his suspendered stomach, over a shirt that nearly matches Dawn's pale pink suit, leading the way. She watches him until he disappears past the glass of her office toward his own. With the door closed and her television off the newsroom is nearly silent. The only noise that remains is the click-clacking of someone in the octagon of the assignment desk area typing, and the eerie ringing of white noise when rooms get too quiet. Dawn looks down at her desk. Her phone, her laptop, the keyboard to her computer, her framed Post-it Note.

I am not your enemy.

She smiles at the reminder and puts her head down on her desk.

James fights the urge to rest his head on his steering wheel as he drives the last miles to Ebony's house. He turns on the radio, hoping to fill the stillness of his car with a noise other than the sound of momentum wind, brushing past his Impala.

About two hours ago, former Assistant State Attorney, James Parnell called in to Dawn Anthony on Dawn in the Evening.

He turns down the volume on the car radio. Still unwilling to relive the recent past he flips the station from the controls on his steering wheel until he gets to Pandora.

He turns the volume back up. Marvin Gaye's silky voice comes through the speakers mid-song. "Trouble Man." He catches the lyrics at the beginning of the singing rap, and adds his voice to the mix.

"I know some places and I've seen some faces/I've got good connections they dig in my directions/What people say that's okay/They don't bother me."

James let's his voice taper off, turns up the volume, and allows the classic song to fill the space of his car until it is a full aural assault on his ears. He sings along. The swinging rhythm, the steady snare, and the smooth vocals send chills up his exposed arms. The bumps from his shaken spirit by the truth in the late singer's song, stay with him long after he's parked his car in Ebony's driveway. He waits until the final notes of the song resound before turning the car completely off. It hums as it settles in its parked position. James opens the door. His phone rings. He looks at the screen, declines the call, and puts it back in his pocket.

He closes the car door and walks slowly toward the house. He feels the buzzing of his phone in his pocket before the ring sounds. He pulls it out, flips the switch for vibrate, and drops the phone back behind his butt. James doesn't waste his time ringing the doorbell at this late hour. He knows Ebony is asleep. She's been going to bed at 9:30 every night since the verdict, to prepare herself for prison when she will be forced to wake, eat, shit, and sleep on a schedule. He thumbs past his car key, his own house key, and the key to his parent's house until he gets to Ebony's front door key. Inside the dark house, the security system beeps twice. That is all. The alarm is not on. James closes the door quietly behind him. He takes off his shoes and walks barefoot in the darkness past the bedrooms at the front of the house, into the open space at the back of the house. He knows her house the way he knows his own. Ignoring the incessant buzz in his back pocket, he makes his way around the peninsula toward the refrigerator. It is the cabinets he is after. Hands and fingers move by memory opening doors, retrieving a glass and a bottle. It is different from the one he had been drinking out of. The one he watched Ebony finish. He pours the contents of the liquor into the glass until it spills over onto his fingers and the counter. He closes the bottle and puts it back in the discreet lower cabinet. Lifting the drink to his lips, he sips the new brand of whiskey.

James takes his 'drink to the couch and feels around the cushioned suede for the remote. He finds it tucked between the seat cushions. He powers on the cable, and is not surprised when he sees his picture staring back at him. He knows she went to bed after watching *Dawn in the Evening*, after she saw the interview with the jurors and his exchange with them. James mutes the promo as it goes off teasing more of what he said on the phone hours earlier for the 11 p.m. newscast, as if it was new. He mutes his own words like the television that stays muted at his mother's house for his father's sake. The working theory that the less stimuli he has to process, the slower his current memory would leave him.

James sips the drink until the alcohol is gone and the glass is empty. He sets it down by his feet and waits for the headiness of drunkenness to overtake his senses. He waits for a blackout to take his mind away from his mother, away from the interview, away from the jurors and Dawn's fixation on how he acted during the cross examination. But their accusations sprint across his thoughts one after the other. *If you don't know what you believe, how is the jury supposed to believe you? He didn't know his girlfriend as well as he thought he did. Did you know about Ebony's relationship with the Judge before trial? If you knew about Ebony's relationship, why did the state attorney's questions catch you by surprise?*

James picks up the empty glass and sets it back down again. He waits for the under of nothingness to take his mind off the Hail Mary he threw by calling a meeting with Judge Shaw and the state attorney on TV, instead of through formal channels. He waits for the darkness of dreamlessness to take him away from his own troubled feelings; his love, his regret, his sex-driven ego, his instincts, his guilt. He waits to not feel what it feels like to know he could have done more to save the woman practicing, sleeping on prison time, in the other room. He waits to feel the weight of his obligation, to her and the law, lift. He waits to feel the facetious questioning of his impossible plan dissolve. He waits for her conviction to become a nightmare he couldn't sleep through to dream. He waits to not feel the choleric consumption of his emotions, but all that meets him is a silent TV without the captioned subtitles, and buzzing in his back pocket.

He reaches his heavy arms behind him to grab the phone. He answers without looking at the caller ID. It is the same caller who has been trying to reach him since he left his parents. He answers the phone, but doesn't speak first. She summoned him, she must state her intent before he decides to participate.

She doesn't keep him waiting long.

"James," she snaps. "Did you see that interview?"

"Yes, Ayana. I saw the interview."

17.

"So, what are you going to do about it?"

James doesn't answer the question. It is leading. Baiting. He lets it hang in the air between them. He clicks the TV off, stands up with the phone to his ear, his empty glass in hand, and walks back to the kitchen. He walks back to the lower cabinet near the refrigerator where the liquor is kept. He sets his glass on the floor, opens the cabinet, and pulls out a different bottle. He pours until the liquor settles at the rim. James lifts it gently from the floor to his lips, standing upright, sipping from the glass in one hand, holding the bottle in the other.

"Hello," Ayana says into the receiver. "Hello."

"I'm here," James answers between sips.

"Did you hear me?"

"As loud as you are? Yes, I heard you."

"Then what are you going to do about it?"

"Do about what, Ayana?"

"What they said about my baby."

"I can't do anything about what they said about, Ebony. They have a right to their own opinions. The trial is over. They're no longer jurors. They can say whatever they want, just like everyone else in the country."

"So you're just going to sit back and let everyone in the country think my baby is a crazy stalker, who carries a gun around for fun."

James sips from his glass until it is empty. Standing alongside the refrigerator, he grabs the bottle by the neck and turns it up to his lips. He hoists one butt cheek on to the counter, and then the other. Leaning against the humming appliance he let's the stainless steel machine hold the weight of his head. It is slightly cool against the side of his skin. He cradles the bottle in his lap, stroking it's neck; he runs his fingers over the feathered geese on the front. The movement comes from his wrist. It lifts until the lip of the bottle is at his lips, and liquor is flowing down his throat.

"James!"

Ayana demands his attention. Her normally husky voice is high and shrill. Agitated and aggravated. He has never spoken to her like this. He has never seen this side of her. Manic in her concern, frenzied in her questioning, questioning him when just months ago, she didn't even know he existed. She had no idea he was dating her daughter. Likewise, he didn't know her either. He thought her name was Marilyn and her husband Ivan. He thought she had three other children who all ostracized the woman he was with. But that phantom family are part of the reason he didn't know she was around. Part of the story he knows he will never get the whole story out of between her, or Ebony. He gave up trying before he started, and got to know the woman on the phone for who she presented herself to be. A month of talking, five months after he first found her in a manila folder from a background check he requested, he believed Ayana to be a wise woman. Wise from the lessons she learned in life. Wise from the mistakes she was forced to correct. Wise from the outcomes and circumstances she had to live with, because of her own actions and indiscretions. In all that wisdom he found her to be a mild-mannered woman, animated in language only when absolutely necessary, missing the child she never got to raise, longing to be friends with the adult she's been blocked from knowing. James figured Ayana was supportive because of her strong maternal instincts despite her shortcomings, and genuinely agreeable and accommodating to whatever he asked of her during the trial. The crazed woman on the phone is one he does not know. One he does not know how to answer. One he does not want to deal with. He rests his head on the side of the refrigerator and waits for her to rant and rave and hang up, or just hang up, unable to breakthrough his prolonged silences.

"James!"

She does neither. Instead, she does the opposite. She gets louder on the phone, calling out his name as piercingly clear as possible.

"I knew I was going to regret calling you from this number," James mutters.

"Too late now."

"What do you want, Ayana?"

"I want to know what your next move is to keep my baby out of prison. You know she didn't kill that man unless she had to."

"Now all of a sudden you know her motives?"

"I'm her mother. Even as a child she didn't do anything unless she had to."

"Does that include choosing another family over you, because you were unfit to raise a child."

"I was waiting to see how long it was, before you threw things you don't even know anything about, in my face."

"I know plenty."

"Only what Ebony told you."

"When it comes to you, her point of view is the only one that matters. She was the child."

"Whatever, James. You still didn't answer my question. What is your next move?"

"Clearly, you didn't watch the whole program. If you had, you would have heard my next move."

"All I heard you say is you requested a meeting about some new evidence. You don't even know if they will see you. That's not a next move, James. That's a moon shot."

"You don't know what the evidence is," James says.

"And I get the feeling you don't know what you're doing. Once a prosecutor, always a prosecutor."

"That's unfair."

"I call it like I see it, James. I call it like I see it."

"Then call this. Ebony says you're a drug-addicted bitch who only cared about herself. So who the hell are you to call me out about something you don't know shit about?"

"You're drunk."

"Not yet. But getting there."

"I know high when I see it, hear it, or smell it. You're drunk."

And you're a crackhead."

"Crack was never my thing."

"Whatever, Whitney."

"I don't know what she sees in you."

"You don't have to. Just know it's a helluva lot more than what she sees in you."

James lifts the bottle by the neck, and swigs until he can't guzzle the vodka as fast as it pours, and pools in his mouth. He gulps hard. Audibly. Intentionally. Repeat. He makes sure the sound of him drinking comes through the phone. He smacks his lips and sets the bottle down beside him. His eyes cross. His vision blurs. The bottle wobbles on the counter. He steadies it with both hands before it falls over. The phone drops out of his hand and falls to the tile of the floor. James slips his butt off the counter and drops to all fours on the ground. He lays on his side and puts his ear to the phone that fell upright. He catches Ayana mid-rant.

". . . It makes sense my child would fall for broken people. First an abuser, and now a drunkard. If she didn't have to see me in my mess, she probably wouldn't be in this mess in the first place. Sins of the mother."

"Shhhhhhhhh . . .," James purrs into the phone.

"This is not going to work."

"That's better, Ayana. Inside voice. What are you talking about?"

"You are not fit to represent my child. Thanks for trying in the first place, but she needs new representation."

"Oh really."

"Yes, really."

"Good luck with that. She has too much for a public defender, and not enough for a defense attorney."

"I hope she didn't pay you."

"No, she did not. We're both going to end up broke and out on our asses if my plan doesn't work, so you better hope it does."

"What's the plan, James?" Ayana demands.

"A fund-raiser ."

"That's not a plan," Ayana mutters. "You don't even have a plan," she says loudly in the receiver.

"And you don't have a daughter."

"Are you going to throw our relationship in my face every time I say something you don't like, to point out this long shot you just assume is going to work, when six months of trial prep didn't work the first time?"

"The second time's the charm," he says, rolling over onto his back and bringing the phone to his ear.

"It's the third time's the charm," Ayana screams. "Put the bottle down."

"I already did."

She doesn't respond. They sit in the near silence of each other's breath, holding the phone to their ears, waiting for the other person to say something first. They wait for each other, not knowing what the other is thinking, not knowing how to respond to the virtual stranger on the other end of the line they are forced to assume a familial closeness with, because of their connection to the one who binds them. To the one who brought them together. They wait. James on the floor with his eyes closed, the phone laying next to his head, so he can hear; Ayana in her small apartment, her phone laying face up in her breakfast nook, on speaker.

Ayana speaks first. "You have to fix this."

The normal timbre of her voice returns; deep, thick, and choking. Restrained with anguish and unexpressed emotion.

"I'm trying to."

James places his hands over his face. He creates more darkness in the pitch black of Ebony's unlit home. Blinds and curtains drawn, lights off, he lays in the darkness, covering his face, away from the urging of what Ayana wants him to do, of what she has asked him to do. He hides in the darkness away from what his own mother wants him to do. He hides away from what his own body is telling him to do, from what his gut, his heart, and his brain have yet to agree on. James creates his own darkness in the blackness of Ebony's house, breathes on the phone with her mother, and waits for what he knows won't come. He knows he cannot go backwards, no more than Ayana can go backwards. He knows he cannot rewind time. He cannot climb out of the hole he's dug. The hole Ebony put him in. He can only keep digging and mine his way through the obstacle, through the problem to the other side, that does not guarantee victory. He can't go over, he can't go under, he must go through without any assurances he will be successful, without any affirmation he will even make it.

"You have to fix this," Ayana repeats. "She's all I got."

He nods his confession before throwing another jab, "And you don't even have her."

"You're a mean and angry drunk."

"And you're a poor excuse for a mother."

"But I'm still her mother. I will always be her mother. She was in me when I was in my own mother. She was in me before I knew myself. She came from me. She will always be mine. Our souls are intertwined."

"That's some deep spiritual shit. Souls intertwined. Which religion did you get that from?"

"Good night, James."

"Don't hang up now. I want to hear how you found Jesus after you stopped finding drugs."

"Good night, James. I'll talk to you when you're sober. I won't tell Ebony this happened."

"Tell her. It's not like she's going to believe you. Even if she does, it's not like it matters."

"You're the worst kind of person, you know that. You blame other people for what you do, how you feel, your problems, and your issues, but then still want to show up and be the hero. Do yourself a favor and save yourself before you try to help my baby."

"Your baby? Let me guess, did you try to save yourself at the bottom of a prescription bottle that wasn't even yours."

"I tried to save myself in a lot of ways. It wasn't until I put the bottle down that my own rescue began."

"Well, I'm just getting started."

"You're the worst."

"Like you were *ever* any better for her."

"Good night, James."

"See you at the fund-raiser ."

The line clicks without a comeback. The black screen of the former phone call in progress, alights with the white brightness of the keypad screen of calls to come. James takes one hand from his face to turn the phone over. It sends him back into darkness. She is gone, but her intrusion on his evening is not over. Her accusations are added to the rest still sprinting the track in his mind.

If you don't know what you believe, how is the jury supposed to believe you?

He didn't know his girlfriend as well as he thought he did.

Did you know about Ebony's relationship with the Judge before trial?

If you knew about Ebony's relationship, why did the State Attorney's questions catch you by surprise.

You're the worst kind of person. You blame other people for what you do but then still want to show up and be the hero.

James turns over and presses his face to the tile of the kitchen floor, his hands to his ears, in a futile attempt to stop the voices in his head and silence his critics. The criticisms that influence his own questions about his ability to defend the indefensible. He concentrates on the blackness around him. Without sight or sound, he welcomes the tar of the atmosphere. The sunken place he can't escape. The black hole he relishes in. *You're the worst kind of person. You blame other people for what you do, but then still want to show up and be the hero.* He is haunted by her words, her characterizations, her depictions, his truth.

He runs deeper into the darkness covering his mind, and welcomes the foggy obscurity clouding his judgement. He runs into the deepest end of the ocean where light doesn't reach, until there are no dreams, no visions of joy, no manifestations of other lives, or other worlds, or wrinkles in time. Passing the snailfish and giant crustaceans in the Mariana Trench, he drowns his mind and body in what he hopes is the bottom of the Earth. He runs in the blackness, tunnels through the darkness, and digs down in to depths he didn't know he could reach, depths he didn't know existed, with no thought, no care, no worry or wonder to look back. He runs.

18.

Running in her sleep is how he finds her when he walks into the room. She runs through the sheets, tangling them around her ankles. He watches from the doorway, leaning on the doorframe, his head heavy with the banging aftermath of alcohol. James stumbles barefoot to the bed she's turned into a track. The mattress that's become her course. The sheets, blankets, pillows, and night time accoutrements her dreams transform into a trail.

He strips. On his side of the bed he drops his jeans, pulls off his shirt, and steps out of his underwear. He sits in the bare space of the fitted sheet and lets his head hit the pillow first, before swinging his feet into the bed. He uses his toes to bring the top sheet to him. It takes more than one try. More than two tries. But he tries in earnest, through his stupor and her racing, he tries until the top sheet is in his hands, her legs still running their course through her unconsciousness. He covers them and grabs her around her waist. Pulling her small body into his, he tightens his grip around her until her legs settle. His arm is her anchor, her support. Her limbs stop their twitching. Whatever she was running from is no longer a nuisance.

She whispers, "What time is it?"

"Late for me. Early for you."

Her question didn't require an answer, though he gave her one. She was sleeping peacefully before he finished his sentence. Her question was only a break to take her from a nightmare to a dream. He lays on his pillow, her uncovered hair splayed on the satin bed pillow beside him. His nose to her scalp, he breathes in the essential oils coating her strands. The tea tree and peppermint oils cut through his haze. He inhales her hair until the bottom of his nose becomes greasy, until whatever she layered on her tresses covers the bottom of his face, and moisturizes the prickly hair he never lets fully grow in. He inhales until all of her subsumes all of him; her hair and its products, her drama, her body, her essence, her soul. Like Ayana, her spirit is tied to his. Not through the bonds and life blood that create mother and daughter, but through the same bonds and ties that were formed to create life. He lays behind her naked, his arm around her waist to rescue her from the hell her imagination creates. With her ass in his lap, he is restless for more than what sleep can offer. Her body folded in his, softer than what it used to be, thinner than she used to be, he envelops her in his body heat, and waits for her to arise from her slumber.

He waits for her to awaken, but doesn't want to disturb the peace that's fallen over her face. Looking down from the crown of her head at her closed eyes, lashes resting on her cheeks, nose flaring with even breaths instead of anxiety or anger, he sees the woman he met outside his job, before he knew she was there to see someone else. In her state of rest, he sees the confident creature who leaned on her car, a spectator to the circus of news performed in front of her. She took his blunt observation as an insult, proffered one of her own, and made him stumble all over himself when she asked for a card. When he first approached her, he didn't notice her; not her body, and her face was turned away from him. He didn't know he would be disarmed when she snapped her head to find out who was judging her appearance. He didn't know he would be rendered inept when she offered her hand and it was soft and warm, nails neatly manicured, even if they were cut short. He didn't know that when he found his bravado again, she would break him down just as easily; that when he showed himself off in jest, she would do the same, giving him a glimpse of everything she worked for at work.

She laughed at him as he fumbled to find a pen after producing his card. It was a giggle meant for little girls, but didn't seem out of place in the grown woman it was coming from. It's a sound he hasn't heard in months. Her laughter is elusive, and giggles are completely ghost. Laying a head above hers, folded into each other, he sees what they have lost since her crusade to right wrongs against her and others. In both their physical posture and treatment of one another, they have lost.

James lays in the bed beside her, a radiating heater of warmth and emotion ready to course correct. Ready to tunnel backwards, to dig up instead of out, to climb instead of rappel, he is ready to be what they were when they met. He lifts her tank top and places his hand to her belly beneath the fabric. He can feel her body breathe with each contraction of her abdomen. She turns toward him.

"You're not asleep," he says.

"How can I with your friend there poking me in my back?"

"Sorry."

"No, you're not."

"You're right. I'm not."

He lowers his body, so they are eye to eye. Closing in on her face, he allows his lips to lead. He kisses her nose and then her lips. It is his undoing. It has always been his undoing. No matter how many times he's kissed her, no matter how many vile and nasty things they've said to each other, a kiss against her down pillow soft lips, always erases whatever damage has been done, it always clears any salt from a wound. He lingers against their softness, his hands flirting with her night clothes. She leans into him, presses her face to his and kisses him back.

Hands grip the cotton fabric covering her, and pull. Ebony pulls her knees into her chest and wiggles her feet out of her underwear. He pulls the tank top completely over her head next. She is as naked as he. He kisses her again. And again. And again until their lips part, and they dance with their tongues waltzing and whipping a foxtrot, and a tango. Bodies pressed together, faces smashed into one, heat rises between them, wetness drips between them, lust and power build between them, but they don't give in to the greed of their hormones. His hands palm the deflating muscles of her ass. Fingers disappear into the fat as he pulls her as close as possible, while still being apart.

They kiss until they are panting. They kiss until they are forced to break and breathe. Not wanting to be apart, not wanting to separate, James rests his lips on her nose, then drags them backwards across her flushed face to that space on her neck just below her ear. He kisses. He sucks. He bites. She climbs up the pillow to run away from his tongue. He pulls her back and wraps her body in his arm. On her side, her back to his chest, he enters her from behind. Her gasp is open mouthed and audible. He pulls all the way out and repeats. He breaks through the tight walls he's been denied for weeks by his own lack of libido, and the stress of the trial. He breaks through the warmth of her inner sanctum, searching for what wild cookies can't give. He breaks through a third time to enter in to her secret place, catching the rhythm of the roll of her hips against his body.

She uses his arm around her waist as a support as she throws everything inside of her into him. Baring down on his body, she straddles one leg backward over both of his, trapping him in her vice. She pliés from where she lays, widening her womanhood to accept everything he has to give. He strokes her in successive, syncopated rhythm, playing a staccato beat on her three tiered drum. His aim is the center as he wrenches through the sides, stroking, beating, banging, pounding out his own problems. She throws him anxiety, and he thrusts her with anger, she rolls into him frustration, and he drives her with determination. She rocks him with fear, and he levels her with lies.

She pushes her upper body out of his grip to slam back down on his dick. They beat each other's skin with their bodies. His arm loosens and becomes slack around her waist. His hands hang on to her breasts, rolling and pinching at her nipples. She turns her head back toward his face and masters his mouth. He melts in her tongue and she belabors the kiss, elongating the sensation, begging not to come. She kisses him to ride the wave of denied satisfaction, but it is of no use. Their wet bodies do what they want. They slip and slide along the other, finding familiarity the longer they're aligned.

Ebony breaks the kiss. His fingers find her mouth. She sucks his index and middle fingers as he drills into her deception and deviousness, indecision, and devotion. She expels his digits, dripping her saliva over them as she breathes through her mouth. She unstakes her leg from over his and puts it between him. He takes her hand and folds it into her belly. They run a three-legged race through the tangle of sheets toward the finish. They are in sync and in step, working together to the end. Tied at the legs, the hands, the heart and the soul, he delivers one last drop of wrought passion, and she throws one last curve of hallucinogenic bliss. They finish in a burst of their bodies. He into her and she along the sides of him. They are together, refusing to separate, connected and intertwined in the bonds made to create. Knotted in limbs tighter than the cord that joined daughter to mother to grandmother, they are in and within each other still running, still dancing, still tied at the legs, the hands, the heart, and the soul. They are still giving and receiving in their laps around the bed track, still taking and delivering in their sprints around the trail, still adding and subtracting in their jog through the course as they push, and they pull, and they pulse everything out of themselves into the other, until they've mastered what it means to combine, bind, connect, and tie up two souls into one whole.

They fall asleep without letting go.

19.

Ayana tries to let go of the past in her lap, but she can't leave it alone. The photo album of memories she will never be remembered for capturing. The pictures that start with her pregnant. Pictures taken by Ebony's father when she had barely begun to show. Pictures taken before the bigness of her belly belied the baby she was carrying was real, and was going to cry, eat, and shit for the first year of its life without a care of whose schedule she interrupted and whose life she inconvenienced. Ayana looks back on the pictures of her textured hair in a jheri curl. She looks at the pictures of herself in pleated shorts that stop just above her knee, and A-line maternity shirts that made her look bigger than she was with a first time baby.

She flipped through the pictures in the hospital she took with the doctors and nursing staff, who became her support system for the three days she was under their care and supervision. The only other visitors she had in the hospital were Marilyn and Dr. Ivan, with a toddling Isaiah in tow. Marilyn was still pregnant with Monica and Monique. That was all they had in common. Eight years apart in age, Marilyn was her reluctant, surrogate big sister for twelve years when she moved in next-door to Ayana and her parents, before they died. She moved in with her new husband and started a family. She visited when she found out Ayana's parents were killed in a crash, leaving her pregnant and alone. She visited when Ayana had her baby. Then she took her baby in as her own when Ayana couldn't muster the energy to mother. It is the one place in the photo album where the picture can't tell the story of more than one thousand words. There is only a dated caption and dried glue stains from where the picture used to be. The picture she threw away after she worked so hard to get clean, and Ebony still preferred to play with the girls she saw in school every day and their mother, who didn't belong to her. The lamenting poetic irony their entire family was killed in a crash like her own parents, was not lost on her.

Ayana flips through the sparsely populated photo album. After Ebony's newborn photos, the next ones don't surface until her first birthday party. There are no pictures marking each day until she made a week, or each week until she made a month, or each month until she made a year. There are newborn pictures, and then one-year-old pictures. Only two of those to be exact. One from her birthday party held at a fast food restaurant with no one else to celebrate, and another from a babysitter Ayana hired when she tried to find work. Pictures for birthdays to mark ages two, three, and four are missing. The pictures begin again at age five, when Ebony was in public school and had picture day. Ayana doesn't have a series of shots and poses from kindergarten through twelfth grade. The pictures are static poses without personality, of a little girl with big hair, and dark eyes staring boldly into a camera. Across the front of her face is the word proof, until Ebony was in seventh grade. That is the year the pictures stopped saying proof. It was after the Washingtons were killed in a crash, and after Ebony cried for months about her loss. It was when Ayana finally decided for herself to be the mother she had, the one she always wanted to be.

For ninth grade, tenth grade, eleventh grade, and twelfth grade, there is only one picture, one pose to mark each year. Ebony's hair just as wild and free, her eyes just as penetratingly deep, with a smirking smile to pierce hearts, because you could tell from looking at her face, she always knew something the one taking the picture did not. After twelfth grade the pictures stop. There are no mommy-and-me photos other than the ones from when Ebony was a newborn. There are no snapshots at church of them dressed alike in pastel Easter dresses, the only difference being the height of their shoes. There are no pictures of them candidly hanging out in their house, and backyard, before the bank took it back, or in their apartment, just the two of them, once they were forced to move. There is a page of baby pictures, minus the missing one with Marilyn, a first birthday, and school-issued pictures, the majority of them with the word proof written across the face.

The pictures don't pick up until four years after Ebony's high school graduation, at her college graduation. The graduation she still doesn't know Ayana attended. The graduation Ayana had to beg for a ticket for from another family, who happened to have an extra the day of the ceremony. Ayana stares at the picture of her daughter in her black gown, her neck draped with cords from honor societies and service groups, her butt pronounced in the oversized gown because of the six-inch heel of her shoe. She stares at the picture of her daughter with her hair pressed straight. It's styled long and sleek, to fit beneath her cap, and drapes down her back to where her bra strap would be. Ayana stares at the blurry photo that doesn't show Ebony's face. She stares at the photo taken from a distance. The photo capturing a moment of motion in time. Ebony's legs were spread because she was walking, her arm extended in gratitude toward the dean to accept the stand in for her real diploma. The diploma Ayana never got to see, because Ebony never had it mailed back to the home she refused to return to.

Three-and-a-half years in college and she never came home. Not for summer, not for spring break, not for Thanksgiving, or Christmas. It was an arrangement Ayana was forced to accept. Ebony sent an "I'm alive" text once a week, and a copy of her grades once a semester. If Ayana wanted to know anything else, if she was dating, whether she'd lost her virginity, how she was doing in her classes, she had to make an inordinate amount of calls to campus, and RAs who preferred to party than assist, or apartment office managers, who didn't double-check after getting their rent check.

Three-and-a-half years of missing pictures save for one shot from graduation followed by a postcard Ebony sent from Jacksonville with no return address that read, "I'm here. I'm alive. I've moved. I'm working." Where she moved to, or had begun working, Ayana did not know. Most days she told herself she didn't have a daughter, if her gaze lingered to long on the bookshelf that held the photo album of no memories.

Ebony's room in the two bedroom apartment was closed and locked. What was left in there Ayana had long forgotten. She told herself it was a door to nowhere, a room that held the air conditioning unit with a filter that never needed to be changed, and the water heater that never needed to be checked.

In the twelve-hundred-plus square feet of living space, Ayana told herself she needed every square inch because she deserved it, and not because she hoped her daughter would one day come home and spend the night. She cleaned both bathrooms because she used both bathrooms. She cooked large meals because she liked eating leftovers for days on end. These are the stories she told herself, the mental barriers she constructed as to why she didn't downsize, even though the rent kept going up. These are the lies she told herself as to why she didn't move into a new space, a home of her own, to make new memories.

She told herself she liked being cooped up in the apartment with the same decor from decades before. Peach curtains hanging in front of the sliding glass door onto the deck. An iron-worked book case with flourishes and embellishments too close to antique to be appreciated by a time in design where classic lines are preferred over intricate detail work. She tells herself she deserves to be lonely. She deserves to be friendless and childless because of what she did to her child, and how she treated the woman who was her friend.

The friend who didn't call the department of children and families when she found out where Ebony got her lunch money from, or why the child slept in the car some nights. Marilyn didn't confront her until the third time it happened. Ayana remembers answering the doorbell after it rang at least eight times. Marilyn stood in front of her dressed in a simple skirt and blouse with sensible shoes and a block heel. The most glamorous thing about her were her wedding rings and her makeup. Her face was beauty personified, even with just light powder, eyeliner, mascara, and lip gloss. Ayana on the other hand, knew she was disheveled. She had to tuck her breast back into the tattered full slip, and her breath was rank when she finally said, "What do you want," after Marilyn just stood there staring at her.

"I want to know why Ebony keeps sleeping in the car when you seem perfectly able to get into the house every night?" Marilyn had asked her.

"She slept in the car?" Ayana asked still high.

"You didn't know?"

Ayana shrugged, "I guess not. Are you taking her to school with the twins?"

"Don't I always."

Ayana started to shut the door, but she remembers Marilyn shoving her foot inside to leave it open. She stepped close until she was nose to nose with Ayana's foul stench and said, "The next time I see her get out of the car in that Princess Jasmine nightgown because she just woke up, I'm calling DCF, and then I'm going to take her in as a foster child, and adopt her. Get your shit together, Ayana."

Marilyn pulled her foot out of the door and left Ayana slack-jawed, wide-eyed, and open-mouthed. She got in the van that was loaded with children, rolled the passenger window down as she pulled away from the curb, and threw out a sugary southern, "You have a nice day now. Get some rest."

Ayana remembers how kindness coated her concern and her threat. Friend is the only way she can describe the woman who raised her daughter from afar as best she knew how, because neither of them were prepared to cope with the clinical sadness new moms can now label as postpartum depression.

Ayana lives in the past without acknowledging that it happened. She lives in the past pretending her future will be a do over of what she didn't do the first time. She dwells in what happened before, instead of trying to build her after. Ayana flips, and flips, and flips the few filled pages of the book, seeing the memories she's missed in all the empty slots for pictures she didn't take with disposable cameras she didn't buy.

She hears the rain falling before she hears the blow of the wind. The last summer rain, just days from the beginning of fall, beats at her covered porch. Ayana sets the photo album to the side and stands up from the striped upholstery on the sofa. Her feet carry her to the sliding doors. She pushes through the curtains, flips the lock, and steps onto the wooden deck. It is damp with the spray of water against her bare feet. She tiptoes to the edge and lays against the banister. Bent at the waist, she rests her head and chest across her forearms, and lets the rain spray her from whatever angle it takes. She waits in the water hoping the wetness against her skin will find its way into her bones and manifest itself in a cold, or the flu, or pneumonia. Something to take her away from the mess of a life she's created, into an afterlife where she no longer has to pay for her mistakes in the grams, ounces, and pounds of love she didn't freely give.

Ayana rests her eyes in the rain until her shirt sleeves are soaked and her feet are cold. Only then does she step back from the protective rail meant to keep people like her from jumping when they're dispirited and inconsolable. She turns around and walks back into her apartment. The sheer peach curtains drag and stick to her wet body as she walks right through them without parting a way. She strides to the small kitchen. The wet soles of her feet make a squishing noise against the vinyl floor that looks like hard wood. She ignores the sound and continues her countertop beeline. A glass covered dish in the corner near the stove is her destination. It is where she left the cake she baked to mark her own recent birthday no one called or texted to help her celebrate. Her birthday she mostly spent in court, on the second row on the defense side of the room, sitting in the corner with three other women. She was within a stone's throw and a hair's breadth of her daughter, but still more out of touch, and out of reach than the strangers who cackled like sisters, and objected way more than James did.

Ayana opens the glass top. The aroma of a lemon pound cake with drizzled glaze icing greets her nose. She reaches above her head and gets a small salad plate from the cabinet, though she rarely has salad. A wedge shaped cake cutter is already sitting beside the cake. She cuts a large chunk, heaps it on the plate, and places it in the microwave. She stares at the cake going around in the artificial heat for forty seconds, refusing to let her gaze drift to anything she opened or touched, that would trigger a memory she doesn't want. The glaze of the icing drips into the firm center of the moist cake.

The microwave beeps.

Ayana uses only the tips of her index and middle fingers on her right hand to remove the hot plate. She wipes her burning hand on her tan slacks, then opens a drawer to get a salad fork. She slices into the cake before her hurt hand cools off, and savors her own creation, satisfied by her success.

A lemon pound cake. It is the first cake she learned how to make in her spare time, when Ebony first left to go off to college. She took a cooking class, and then a baking class, to improve the skills she didn't have when she should have had them. Convinced she was going to prepare feasts for the holidays for the two of them, she learned how to make sauces; beurre blancs and hollandaise, alfredo and pesto, béchamel and rouxs. It was dessert that became her favorite. Cakes, and cookies and pies, and souflee's if she was feeling fancy. But her holiday feasts were only a fantasy, a phantom never to come true. Instead, she feasted every day of the week on one decadent meal, and one delicious dessert she told herself was just as amazing on day seven, as it was on day one.

Ayana finishes her cake and is warmed from the inside out, but still shivering from the outside in. She places the plate that held her high into the sink with the fork that fed her both white sugar and brown sugar; key ingredients in any drug meant to addict. She leaves the plate and fork unwashed, just as she left the photo album opened on a random page on the couch where she sat. Walking to her bedroom at the back of the apartment, she unbuttons her blouse as she goes. She drops it to the ground, and then shimmies out of her Dockers, underwear, and bra. Those are left on the floor as well. In her closet, Ayana catches a glimpse of her body in the mirror. Seeing herself always catches her by surprise. Each time she passes a mirror, she sees the face of the daughter she does not allow herself to face. She sees the body she gave her child. Taut and thick, round and shapely, and well maintained, save for the pot in her belly that proves she gave birth and delivered life. It is her testament to the one thing she did right, even if she did it wrong in the end.

Ayana clothes her stretch-marked nakedness with the nightgown hanging on the back of the closet door. She walks through her trail of clothes back into the living room, and flops on the couch she's had since the '90s. Ayana turns on the television standing in the middle of the entertainment center, from the remote control sitting beside the open photo album she doesn't look at. She doesn't look down at the memories of her undoing, of her years of being unfit, and neglectful. She presses power on the television to watch the one channel she's been fixated on, since she saw what looked like her younger self smiling in an orange jumpsuit charged with murder. She turns on to the pretty brown-skinned anchor who's taken over for the white woman she grew up watching, when her parents were alive.

Tonight on 9 News Now at 11...

Inside the minds of jurors.

The reason biases they didn't know they had, may have played a role in the conviction of Ebony Jones in the death of Judge Barker Gordon.

In a preview of our exclusive interview tomorrow night on Dawn in the Evening...

Our expert weighs in on why race and gender make all the difference in the outcomes inside a courtroom.

Ayana settles into the lumpy couch cushions and watches the television rapt and with attention. She watches to

183.

see if there are any new pictures of her daughter, any new video of her baby, any new news on what's next, besides James's insufficient answers and his lack of plans. Ayana sits back and watches the news, waiting to face the woman who doesn't want to see her, thankful for the crime she didn't commit, for connecting them again.

Part 2

"There are those who hate the one who upholds justice in court and detest the one who tells the truth."

— Amos 5:10

"If you are silent about your pain they will kill you and say you enjoyed it"

— Zora Neale Hurston

20.

Victor pulls Dawn by the tips of her fingers into the ballroom of the Jacksonville Marriott. She follows behind him, reluctantly, her head buried in the screen of her phone reading and scrolling, scrolling and reading.

"Great. You guys made it," James says, approaching them across the carpet.

He is the only other person there, so far, for the black tie gala he's holding to raise money for Ebony's legal defense.

"Good to see you again, man," James says slapping Victor's hand, and bringing him in close for a hug.

"You too," Victor says. "Though we really didn't meet last time."

"I guess not." James nods.

"Yeah. I'm the only one not in that picture."

"Ha. Be thankful. That picture is more trouble than you know."

"I think I know how much trouble it's been." Victor nods toward Dawn.

She doesn't look up from her phone. She doesn't acknowledge that she's been acknowledged. That it's her turn to enter the conversation. To add to the conversation. To do what she does best, what she is trained to do, what she is paid to do, what she is there to do. She ignores the men staring at her because she doesn't see them. She doesn't hear their small talk, the chatter of men connected by the women around them, one of whom is not with them. The one who cannot be with them. The one who is forbidden to leave the house. She does not take the natural opening to fill-in the conversation, to ease the awkwardness, to assuage the disquietude. Scrolling, reading, clicking, Dawn flies through sites, timelines, feeds, tweets, and trolls, reading and consuming page after page of content.

"I thought we'd set the podium and the band up over here." James points across the room. "Kind of like last time."

"Uh huh."

Dawn walks in the general direction of where James pointed, still more engrossed by what's in her hand than the duty she's been asked to perform.

"Thank you," James says. "For doing this. I really appreciate it, and I know Ebony does too."

"Anything. Anytime. You've helped me. I'm helping you."

She sets the small pearl clutch on a shelf inside the podium. "What time is everyone expected to arrive?"

"Eight thirty," James answers. "The silent auction starts at nine."

"What are you auctioning off?"

"Wine, art. It'll be here shortly. Ms. Gordon is bringing it."

Dawn looks up from her phone to face James. Her eye contact makes him stumble backwards. He catches his footing and stands as straight as possible. He adjusts the skinny white tie knotted at his neck. It lays brilliant against the purple of his suit. The color he asked all participating, volunteering, and helping in the fund-raiser to wear. Dawn waits as he makes his adjustments. She is slightly taller than him due to the height of her heels. With one hand she pushes her wispy, long bangs out of her eyes, to see him more clearly. To see if he said what she thought she heard.

"Ms. Gordon, as in Judge Gordon's mother Ms. Gordon?" Dawn asks.

"The one and only," James answers.

"I met her briefly at the funeral. Why would she be coming and bringing art?"

"Because she believes in Ebony. Don't you?"

"My job is to be objective."

"And, yet you're here hosting a fund-raiser for Ebony."

"Your point?"

"Your bias is showing."

Dawn raises one corner of her mouth in a smile before looking back down at her phone, scrolling and reading. James walks away. Victor walks over. Dawn doesn't look up. She leans against the empty platform that will serve as a stage for the band to set up. Perched on the cushion of her butt, legs stretched in front of her and crossed at the ankles, she consumes the media she seeks, before time will force her to put the phone down and engage with those around her.

"What's got your attention tonight?" Victor asks sitting beside her.

"This story out of Cleveland."

"Why do you care so much? Victor asks.

"It's 100 miles away from my last station," Dawn says briefly lifting her eyes to see his face. "I still get the alerts."

"Okay." With reluctance he asks, "What happened?"

"Twelve-year-old boy was shot by a cop?"

"Did he die?"

"He's in surgery."

"I hope he makes it."

"Me too."

She clicks a button and darkens the screen on her phone. Standing up straight she plays with the leather tassels of her earrings. She adjusts the backs until she can no longer fidget with her ears. Dropping her hands to her sides, she smooths the wrinkles that aren't there, adjusts the fall of the fabric against her body, and picks away lent she rolled off before she ever left the house. She knows Victor is looking at her, watching her, reading her movements to discern her mood.

Bringing him was a bad idea.

Dawn shakes the thought away and looks up into his eyes, and then away. She avoids his gaze, to deny the need in his burning brown eyes that long to ask her personal questions, relationship questions, questions about them, where they stand, what they are doing, why they are doing it?

He grabs her hands away from her fidgeting. He lets his fingers massage her palms until he can feel the stress move from that part of her body, until softness replaces the rigidity that set in from scrolling and reading. She still does not look at him, though she allows his fingers to work their magic on whatever part of her body they happen to touch. He places her hands at her sides, but he does not release her. He runs his palms over the oiled and buttered backs of her hands, past her wrists, up the length of her arms, until he reaches her shoulders. His left hand holds steady on her right shoulder, his right hand moves from her shoulder, tracing the bare skin of her collar bone, over the strap of the halter dress, up her neck, until it reaches her chin. Heat radiates from her body. He lifts her head to meet his. He blows a stream of breath to separate her bangs and expose her forehead.

"What's going on in there?" he asks, touching his thumb to her naked skin.

"Nothing," she answers. "Just keeping up with what's going on in the world."

"You don't have to do that tonight."

"Maybe not tonight, but Monday I will need to know."

"It's not Monday yet."

"I know."

"Then act like it."

"Excuse me?"

"Calm down." Victor raises both hands in surrender. "I only mean you agreed to do this, to help out because you wanted to. No one is forcing you to be here. Not even your job. So be here."

"I am here, Victor. The event hasn't even started yet."

"Your body is here, but your mind is elsewhere. You haven't spoken to me since we got in the car, and you barely spoke to James."

"I was reading up on the situation in Cleveland. And again, the event hasn't even started yet. When people get here, I'll be Dawn Anthony, in full anchor drag. Is that what you want to see?"

"I didn't say that."

"You haven't said anything, Victor."

"I don't even know why you invited me to this."

"I asked you if you wanted to come. You said yes. You don't have to be here."

"It's time to spend with you. I figured why not, even if you are somewhat working, maybe we can still have a good time. I didn't know you were going to be rude, and ignore everybody until you had to do your job."

"Tonight is not about you, Victor. I don't understand why you're tripping."

"I'm not," Victor says.

He walks away from Dawn. She watches his long-legged stride across the ballroom carpet to the double doors leading to the other parts of the hotel. She watches as he stops at the door to hold it open for the large canvas works coming in one by one. Twelve pieces of art are marched in by bellhops in matching uniforms. Only after the last one breaches the doorway where Victor is assisting their entry, does she see the regal woman she remembers from the funeral. The woman in the white linen suit, opaque stockings, and kitten heels, with a bustling cream and gold scarf, and silver hair glinting in the sun. Standing in the doorway of the chandelier lit ballroom, she is just as regal in a purple off-the-shoulder gown with a beaded bodice, that flows into layers upon layers of a floor-length chiffon skirt. Her hair is tucked, pinned, shaped, and molded into a bouffant of victory rolls, showing off her face that shows little sign of her age. Her neck is bare, and the scar Dawn first saw when she took the witness stand gleams with the rest of her skin.

Dawn crosses the room to where she stands. She can see her mouth telling Victor thank you for holding the door. As she nears them, Victor disappears into the bowels of the hotel. The door closes with a loud click and clasp, as Dawn gets to where he was.

"Ms. Gordon, how are you? I'm Dawn Anthony."

"I remember you," Ms. Gordon says taking her hand. "I'm well."

"I told James I was surprised when he mentioned you were coming tonight, and donating the work for the silent auction."

"This all comes from Barker's personal collection. He was a horrible human being, but he had an eye for beautiful things, even if he didn't deserve them, or always know how to treat them."

"Wow."

"What? You never thought you'd hear a mother speak so frankly about her dead child?"

"James told me you supported Ebony, and you didn't seem to be grieving at the service, I just didn't expect . . . I didn't know what to expect."

"Every day I'm alive on this Earth, every day I wake up alone, every day I look in the mirror is every day I'm reminded I survived the trauma and the violence of my marriage. Barker may have been my miracle baby, but in his life, he was no one's blessing. He was the same pain his daddy produced; only he had power."

Dawn nods in empathetic understanding. She nods because she has no personal experience to add to the texture and tone of Ms. Gordon's story. Her biggest concern walked out of the door, and she is trying to deny the fact she is grateful for the solace of her own company, and the wisdom of the elder woman in front of her. Dawn nods and stares at Ms. Gordon, holding her gaze, willing her eyes to stay on her face, instead of traveling down to the scar she knows she is no longer ashamed of. No longer covering up. No longer hiding.

The double doors behind them open, breaking the turgid silence subsuming the one-sided conversation. James and Victor walk in with full arms. They each carry several easels. The sticks and legs that must be setup to hold the artwork, to display the pieces James hopes will sell and generate enough money for both Ebony and himself. He and Victor cross the floor quickly to the stage where the canvas paintings are propped. Ms. Gordon follows behind them, and Dawn behind her. She studies the older woman as she directs

James and Victor on what to do with each painting, how they should be organized, lined up, and displayed.

"If I had the money, I'd buy one of these myself," James says.

"I don't think Ebony would like that," Ms. Gordon says.

"You're right. She probably wouldn't. And I like living."

"Don't say that," Ms. Gordon chastises.

"It's just a joke," Victor says.

"That kind of levity is uncalled for when it's her life you're joking about."

"At least she's living," Victor says.

"You're right," Ms. Gordon begins. "At least she's living. There are so many like her who are not. Who don't get out. Who don't leave. Who don't have friends that make them leave. When I was married, I wish I'd had a friend like Ebony to rescue me from my hell. Laugh at her. Call her crazy, stalker, obsessive, but know this, she is no killer. She did what needed to be done to rescue a friend. James, you did what needed to be done by representing her. And now we're all here doing what needs to be done because we all know, she does not deserve to rot in prison for protecting herself and her friend against my son."

"Yes, ma'am," Victor says.

The double doors to the ballroom clank and open. The two women and three men of the five-piece band, walk in carrying their instruments. They make their way to the stage where James and Victor set up the last pieces of art work. The doors clank again. The waitstaff comes in with trays of hors d'oeuvres. They set up platters and tasting plates along two rows of tables lining the back wall of the ballroom. The rolling aluminum shutter of the bar rumbles from the pull of the bartender behind the counter. Dawn stands at the stage watching the activity around her. The ballroom buzzes with the last-minute makings of the affair she is hosting, despite blowback from Boyce. Victor is nowhere to be seen.

It's probably best if he left anyway.

Music begins, suddenly interrupting Dawn's thoughts. She steps away from the stage covering her ears, ill-prepared for the decisive chords of the band she thought would be playing quiet jazz. The doors clank once, and then twice. The center set of double doors are opened and locked into their permanent position, encouraging everyone invited to enter the atmosphere, to experience the evening, and the cause for which it was curated. People trickle in slowly. Soleil is the first person Dawn recognizes. She waves at the woman dressed in a brilliant red. She is fire in the somber room, a light to the collected collective of people supporting the woman accused of a crime she says she did not commit. More people stream in. Dawn sees dresses in black, navy, forest green, and more purple, and other subdued jewel tones to match the mood of the evening. The men who are present are dressed in black suits or tuxedoes, dark ties, and dark shirts. Her eyes come back to Soleil as she goes to the podium. The woman in red is her light and reference for how she hopes the evening will go.

Dawn looks to James standing with Victor at the back of the room near the opened doors.

He came back.

She smiles as he nods. The band fades out their music. Dawn grabs her pearl clutch from the shelf in the podium, pops it open, and pulls out a folded sheet of paper. She shoves the purse back on the shelf and lays the yellow legal paper flat in front of her.

Dawn adjusts the mic to her level and says, "Good evening," in a voice too loud for the speakers projecting her sound.

A creaking sound is emitted along with her voice. She waits until the feedback passes before speaking again.

"I am Dawn Anthony, from 9 News Now, and we are all hear tonight to support Ebony Jones ahead of her appeal of her conviction for culpable negligence in the death of the late Judge Barker Gordon. Her attorney, James Parnell, is here with us as well. He will speak to you in just a moment, but first a word from the woman of the hour, Ebony Jones."

The lights dim in the room and a white projector screen behind the band comes alive with a video. Ebony appears on the screen. Her hair is curly and wild, and fills most of the projector frame. Dawn sees a light sheen of gloss on her lips, eyeliner and mascara pop her eyes, taking away from the gaunt chisel at her cheeks. Dawn sees the weight loss in her face, the purple peasant top that floats away from her skin, and the severe pronouncement of her collarbone. She sees how much thinner she is now, than when they first met, how much of a toll her trial and circumstances have taken on her. She forces herself to listen to the video her team recorded at Ebony's home a week ago, to make it look more professional. James wanted Ebony to Skype in to the fund-raiser live. Dawn vetoed the idea and pushed for the recorded version to make it more smooth, contained, and to eliminate the possibility of people asking questions, or reacting in a way for Ebony to respond.

The short clip ends with Ebony's excessive thanks. The lights return. Dawn steps back to the podium.

"I want to echo Ebony's thanks, and say it myself, thank you to everyone for being here with us tonight. As you already know, Ebony and James really appreciate it. And I'm also encouraged by your presence to support these two, with everything going on in the world over the last few months."

Dawn veers away from her prepared remarks. She looks up from her paper. Her eyes scan the room until they find their light. Soleil in red. A beacon for defiance.

Dawn continues, "As you know, before Ebony was convicted, we mourned and we protested the loss of Eric Garner, Mike Brown, and Michelle Cusseaux. After the verdict in Ebony's trial was delivered, many of you marched right here in this very city. Some of you even called in to my show in the week after the verdict to express your outrage. One caller said live on air 'Ebony is being punished for doing the right thing, the wrong way.' Tonight as we gather to uplift, support, and fight for Ebony, I want to tell you there is another fight going on hundreds of miles away from here."

Dawn pauses before continuing. She lets her eyes look around the room at the faces looking back at her. Her beacon still shines brightly from the center of the room, unaccompanied by anyone who would encroach upon her effusive brilliance. Beside her is stately royalty, comfortable in her quiet power, short but towering over everyone in the room, with her scar face forward and her chin lifted toward the heavens.

Dawn focuses her eyes on them as she says, "Hundreds of miles away from here a little boy is fighting for his life. He was shot by a police officer. He is only twelve-years-old. So tonight as we gather to mix and mingle, and bid on wine and art, let us remember there is a reason for our gathering. There is a reason our demonstrative show of support is necessary. It is for the lives that were lost. Those taken too soon by a system that sees justice only as a sword or gun to wield in punishment, instead of as a shield to save, preserve, and protect those who need it most. As we make small talk and decide on which work will look best in our homes and offices, let us remember this evening is not just a gala to attend, a silent auction to boast about, or an opportunity for networking. This evening is about showing up, and showing out for what is right; and tonight that happens to be for the appeal of Ebony Jones."

Dawn steps away from the podium, the folded yellow paper of remarks balled in one hand, her pearl clutch gripped in the other. Applause surrounds her as she walks toward the women who nodded their approval at every word. She stops when she reaches their duo. They embrace her. Another hand is on her back. Their trio is now a quad. The hug continues. The spread of emotion is distributed. Another pair of kitten heeled feet approach them. The embrace is opened and closed around them. The affecting sensation is spread even further. Hair is smashed, makeup is smudged, scents are mixed, involuntary tears are dried, arms are loosened, hands drop from backs and waists. Dawn stands in the middle of the semi-circle, surrounded by four women.

21.

"That was a helluva speech you gave up there," Ayana says.

"Thank you," Dawn says. "How are you doing? I haven't seen you since the trial. How is Ebony?"

"I'm doing alright, and Ebony is Ebony. I've seen her once."

"Ayana, have you met Ms. Gordon?" Dawn asks.

"No, I haven't. Though I will say this is awkward. The mothers of the suspect and the victim together like this."

"It's only awkward if we make it awkward," Ms. Gordon dismisses. "Call me Nona."

"Ayana."

"And you remember Johnnie and Soleil from our row at the trial, right?" Dawn asks.

"Yes, I do. Nice to see you all again."

"Now, Ayana," Dawn begins, "I asked you at the trial and you said no, but I'm going to ask again since you liked my impromptu speech so much."

"Yeah . . ."

"Would you consider coming on the show some time?"

"Why not," Ayana answers quickly.

"What about Monday?

"Damn, I didn't think you'd try to book me that fast."

"Don't underestimate, Dawn here," Johnnie says. "She's quick to put a story together."

"I see." Ayana nods. "I'm not doing anything else Monday. I don't see why not."

"Thank you," Dawn says. "I guess I'll go find that man of mine." She sighs.

"He's back there with Danielle, Nathan, and James," Johnnie points.

"Oh, you brought Dani?"

"She wouldn't let me leave her. Tyler didn't want to come."

"Let me go see her then," Dawn cranes her neck to the back of the room. "Oh, Johnnie, she's so cute in her little dress and heels."

"That was leftover from Easter; so thankfully she's getting a second wear out of it."

"If you all will excuse me." Dawn backs away from the group of women.

"It's been lovely meeting all of you," Ms. Gordon says. "I'm going to greet some of the other guests."

"I'll come with you, Ms. Nona," Soleil says.

Soleil and Ms. Gordon disappear into the crowd. Dawn moves toward the open double doors where the trio of men stand, two of them identical in black suits and purple ties. James is the peacock among sparrows in purple and white. Ms. Gordon and Soleil float through the crowd chatting with people, encouraging them to visit the bar and to open their wallets. The mingling leaves Johnnie and Ayana side by side in the crowd of networking social climbers fooling themselves they are gathered for philanthropy, and not their own selfish opportunities. They scan the room, leaving the reticence of strangers between them.

They nod their heads to the music, pat their feet to the beat, tap their hands on their gowned sides, and check their phones. They create comfort in the uneasy atmosphere of their proximity. Johnnie turns her head. She looks away from Ayana, back behind her and over her shoulder. She looks at the bar. She counts the people in line waiting to do what she cannot, what she no longer allows herself to engage in. Eleven gowned and suited people wait for wine glasses, champagne flutes, tumblers half-filled with amber liquid, or pastel cocktails in straight glasses with a toothpick of kabobbed fruit.

Johnnie sighs at the steady moving line.

"I wish I could drink," she says.

"How long have you been sober?" Ayana asks, turning toward her.

"It will be eight months in six days."

Johnnie swallows hard and stares at the growing crowd lined up at the bar, waiting to replenish their glasses. The crowd of people imbibing away their insecurities, and becoming more attractive to those around them with every sip of sweet or savory liquid. She stares at them as they laugh, fall into one another's shoulders, spill liquid over the rims of their glasses and down the sides of their fingers. Johnnie looks at them and remembers when she used to be them. She remembers when she floated across this very same ballroom just months before, with red bull and vodka in her hands, alcohol fueling her anger at her husband who smelled like another woman. She remembers when she teetered across the ballroom to accept her award from the mayor for being a trailblazer in medicine, for her groundbreaking skill in surgery, outfitted in a dress that gave her a coke bottle shape, and the illusion of an ass. The dress that kept her flat mommy stomach sucked in to the form of her pre-baby body.

Johnnie fingers the flirty ruffle hem of her peplum top, covering the weight she's gained since she switched from alcohol to carbs. She adjusts the waistband of the long A-line skirt that pulls away from her body. The skirt with a slit to her upper thigh that still allows her to own her sex appeal, even if she doesn't feel sexy, because her body has changed out of necessity from leaving behind bad habits.

Ayana says, "I wish I could tell you the first year is the hardest, but as you already know, every day is hard."

"What did you quit?" Johnnie asks, turning back toward the older woman.

"Pills."

"How long have you been clean?"

"Twenty-one years, seven months, and three days."

"That's very specific."

"Just like your soon to be eight months in six days."

Johnnie nods.

"Mama, Mama, Mama," Danielle says rushing over to where Johnnie stands.

"What do you say when mama is talking to someone?"

"Oh, sorry. Excuse me, Mama."

"Yes, Dani."

"Daddy, let me get a drink from the bar."

"Did he now?"

"Yes. It's a Shirley Temple. You want one?"

"No, Baby. Where is your daddy?"

"He told me to come find you. He said he had to go to the bathroom."

"Oh. Say hello to, Ms. Ayana."

"Hi," Danielle says stepping closer to Johnnie.

"How are you doing?" Ayana asks bending down to Danielle's level.

"Good," Danielle says.

"How old are you?"

"Six."

"Nice to meet you, Danielle." Ayana extends her hand.

Danielle takes it. "Nice to meet you too. I like your glasses."

"Thank you," Ayana says, pulling them from her face to give Danielle a closer look.

"They have cheetah spots."

"I guess they do." Ayana turns the glasses around to look at them, as if she's seeing them for the first time.

"Hey, Ms. Ayana, guess what?"

"What's that?"

"I saw a cheetah at the zoo when I went with my class."

"Did you see it run?"

"No. It was sleeping," Danielle answers. "But Miss Jessie said the cheetah is the fastest animal in the world."

"Okay, Dani, that's enough. Ms. Ayana doesn't want to hear about your trip to the zoo."

"But, Mama, I was just telling her what Miss Jessie said about the cheetahs."

"Nobody cares about what Miss Jessie says, Dani."

"But Mama . . .,"

"No buts Danielle. Go find your Daddy."

"But Mama . . ."

"Gooooo . . ."

"Go on, Danielle," Ayana says gently. "Do what your mama says."

Danielle darts between where Ayana is still bent to her level, and her mother's tapping feet and shaking thighs. She watches the little girl run to the back of the ballroom near the double doors where she stood before near James. Ayana stands up and smooths out the wrinkles of her own dress. It is simple in comparison to the others in the room around her; a deep purple, nearly black, suit. The skirt comes to her calf, and it came with a bodice and matching jacket. Conservative, cheap, and the right color she found from a back rack in Ross.

"I have a headache." Johnnie sighs.

"I don't even remember when Ebony was that age," Ayana says.

"That girl knows she loves her daddy."

"Try as I might, I just can't remember what it was like when she was six-seven-eight years old. You're so lucky."

"Lucky enough to have a daughter who loves her daddy, and the teacher's assistant from last year's class, more than she loves me."

"Is that who Miss Jessie is?"

"The other woman my husband claims isn't the other woman."

"I guess you do need a drink."

Johnnie nods her agreement gazing again at the movement of the line of people gathered at the bar. Some order drinks for themselves. Some order drinks for others. Some get their drinks and walk away alone, or to rejoin a group. Johnnie looks from the length of the line at the bar, to the scant line at the back tables filled with untouched hors d'oeuvres. The tapas that will go cold until fifteen minutes before the night is over when the bruschetta, cheese, crackers, and assortment of fruits, will be consumed in earnest to soak up the pools of alcohol sloshing in empty bellies.

"It's been my experience," Ayana says following Johnnie's gaze, "men are the least trust worthy of all the species on Earth. Even a snake is more reliable. If you get a python as a pet, it lets you know when it's ready to turn on you by laying next to you vertically. It's measuring how big it has to be to eat you. Even a snake is more honest in its deceptive intentions than a man. Men think they're doing right, and being right, when really they're stringing you along, wasting your time, and making you think you're fucked up for feeling some kind of way."

"I take it you're single," Johnnie says.

"I'm too damaged and got too much baggage to date somebody just as damaged and loaded down with baggage as me."

"Never married?" Johnnie asks.

"Nope."

"I've been married sixteen years," Johnnie says. "In the beginning it was easy. With Tyler it was easy. It was just the three of us. We had what we needed, and love filled up any empty spaces we felt. With Danielle it's been different. I swear a second child, especially so far after the first one, will test everything you're made of."

"I wouldn't know. Ebony is all I have, and I barely have her."

"What happened?"

"After the pills . . . a never ending roller-coaster ride of resentment. When she needed me I wasn't there. When I was ready she turned her back on me, and picked a dead family over me."

"You're here now."

"It doesn't matter. This is my penance. The least I can do."

Johnnie doesn't respond to the woman beside her. The woman in sensible square-toed shoes, and a block heel. The woman with the short salt and pepper curly fro and the cheetah print glasses. Golden rosebud studs in each of her

201.

ears, and eyes slightly squinted with knowledge beyond her years. Johnnie looks at what comes with age, and sees herself in another ten or fifteen years. She sees what she could become if she allows bitterness and resentment to rule her world.

She shifts her focus from her companion in sobriety back to the bar, and then to the double doors. Nathan nods to her. She gives him a thumbs up. Danielle is in his arms. Her bunned hair askew from laying against his shoulder. James is beside him. Johnnie scans the length of the room. Beyond the table of uneaten snack food, down the short edge of the ballroom in a corner behind the band stage, she sees Dawn and Victor.

Dawn stands eye level with Victor. Her face is pleasant, her smile false, her eyes ablaze. His lips are pursed in frustration. They are square to each other, but only his back is visible to most of the crowd. Only he can be seen if a disturbance is created. Only his actions can be accounted for by the throngs of witnesses if their argument escalates.

"I should have left a long time ago," he sneers.

"But you didn't. You stayed. So obviously you want to be here."

"Dawn. How many times do I have to tell you? I only want to be with you."

"And I've told you being with me means being with all of this. I'm not just some regular woman you found off the street."

"I never said you were."

"Okay, then. Then what are we fighting about?"

"It's not a fight. I walked away for you to do your thing. I helped James and Ms. Gordon set up, and hung out in the background. You're the one who thinks I'm upset. I'm good."

"I only think that because you questioned why I invited you tonight."

"I did. But you're the one who said tonight wasn't about me. So stop making it about me, Dawn. Go work."

"Don't dismiss me. I came to check on you. Came to check on us. Don't do that."

"No, you came to make sure I didn't ruin your little image. I'm good. Go work."

"Whatever, Victor. You can go. I'll Uber home."

"Bet. I'm gone."

"Don't show up outside my door either."

Victor doesn't respond. He walks away from Dawn, cutting diagonally across the ballroom. She watches his deliberate stride. The determination in his walk as he breezes past the band, and bumps through couples and groups to make his exit known. To make it so people realize he is walking away from the host, the anchor, the news lady, the Dawn Anthony. *I knew this would happen* she thinks to herself as she watches him make a scene with his abrupt exit. He throws a hand up at James when he reaches the double doors to signal his goodbye. It's the only sign of respect he's shown in his disrespectful escape. Dawn watches until well after he's left through the open double doors. Doors she's thankful will not clink and clang to mark his departure with a resounding exclamation point to her embarrassment.

She opens the clutch dangling from the chain hanging on her arm and pulls out her mirror compact. *Just because I've been jilted doesn't mean I have to look the part.* She uses the pads of her fingers to dab at the cat eye lines of her eyeliner that smudged from the tears that threatened to fall. She smooths out the creases around her mouth from where she's been smiling and posing for pictures; schmoozing with guests to encourage them to do more than to pay lip service about black lives matter and to open their wallets and express their progressive opinions, suggestions, and recommendations with their money. Dawn blinks at herself in the mirror, tousles the front of her hair until her bangs fall in a frame around her face, the edges of the wispy fringe tickling the curled hairs of her eyelashes.

She closes the compact and is confronted by another face. The face of a friend walking directly toward her. Dawn drops the round mirror back in her purse and snaps it shut.

She turns up the corners of her mouth to resume the pleasant playacting she's performed all night, ready to do another scene, for another audience of one, in a crowded room of watchful eyes and listening ears, where they can't be themselves.

22.

"Where's he going?" Johnnie asks once she reaches Dawn in the corner of the room.

"Home. I guess. I don't know," Dawn answers. "I don't care either."

Johnnie nods, "He should take Nathan with him."

"I thought you guys were trying to work it out."

"You can't work anything out if one person refuses to admit they did something wrong."

"That's still going on?"

"He says it's not. That it never happened. I don't believe him."

"Why?"

"Because he stopped wearing Old Spice. You don't just change deodorant, soap, lotion, and everything else you've been wearing since you found your first pube above your dick, unless some woman tells you to."

"Okay. Tell me how you really feel."

"Then he had the nerve to ask me why I'm going gray. Hell, he's the reason these gray hairs are here in the first place."

"You hide it well," Dawn says.

"I can do anything with some Eco-styler, and some extra-long hair pins."

"I see. This updo is beautiful."

"Thank you. How have you been?"

There are not enough hours in the day to answer that question. Dawn sighs and turns her head. She expels as much air out of her body, shrugs, and sighs again.

"I've got a lot to decide," she answers.

"Like what?"

"Just, what to do next. I saw you talking to Ayana."

"She's a nice lady. Sad though."

"Why is that?"

"You'll find out Monday during your interview."

"I guess I will. What, did she find out?" Dawn asks with a knowing look.

"I didn't tell her."

"Why not?"

"Because I already told the one person who needed to know."

"When did you do that?"

"A couple months ago. After you replayed your interview you did with her that day we all came over."

"Good for you," Dawn says, flashing an encouraging smile.

"We'll see. James still hasn't announced yet what the basis for his appeal is, but I have a funny feeling I already know."

"Don't worry about it. The judge delayed her sentencing so whatever it is, it's got to be solid," Dawn reassures.

"Blaming the drunk surgeon and not the person who pulled the trigger sounds pretty solid to me."

"I told you to stop drinking a long time ago."

"I should have stopped drinking after we met," Johnnie answers. "That's when it really started anyway."

"What do you mean?"

"Nathan and I have been having problems for years. Even when you first came to SENT and we gave that testimonial, things were starting to unravel then."

Dawn nods, remembering the night three years ago after she followed one of Boyce's suggestions to attend an event under the guise of building community relationships. The event turned out to be a matchmaking seminar for the single, ethnic, and not taken. At the door she met the eager founder who had been anticipating her arrival at events and panels for months. In the audience she listened to Johnnie and Nathan, who were then still strangers to her, expound on the virtues of a good marriage. During their talk, they flashed pictures of their family. Pictures from their small beach wedding, baby pictures of Tyler, family pictures of the three of them, and pictures of Johnnie pregnant with Danielle.

Their talk ended with a picture of all four of them on the screen, Tyler was eleven at the time and Danielle was three. They finished their talk by discussing the sacrifices they made for each other, and their children. Nathan had recently left his job to look after the family as Johnnie's ascent at the hospital took off. Dawn remembers Johnnie saying, ". . . sacrifice and spice. *That* is the key to marriage." She nodded from her seat in the back row of the small conference room of another hotel. As people stood to applaud the brave couple, the ideal couple, the couple SENT was built on, Dawn tried to make her way toward the door. She knew before Johnnie's coup de grâce line they both were lying, but Margo Westscott cornered her in her escape route, wrapped an arm around her shoulder, and ushered her to the front of the audience and the growing crowd around the imperfect couple.

"I remember," Dawn says. "That's why I never came to another event. You were nice, but you were lying."

"I was. I was drunk by the end of the night, and according to Nathan, a drunken zombie for the last two years. Three, if I'm being truthful, but he wasn't paying attention in the beginning."

"Men never pay attention until it's the end."

"Is that why Victor stormed out of here?"

"Victor left because he can't handle everything that comes with me. He's cool as long as I'm the one on his arm and not the other way around."

"It takes a very secure man to be okay being an accessory."

Dawn nods. "Even though I knew you guys were lying way back when. I still admired Nathan for taking a step back to let you do your thing at the hospital."

"That's probably the only reason we're still together now. He's a good man at his core, and a damn good father. He's just got shitty tendencies right now."

"Or maybe he's just impatient waiting for you."

"Waiting for me to do what? Finish my career. Tag him back in? What?"

"I don't know." Dawn shrugs.

"Well, he's not waiting anymore," Johnnie crosses her arms. "I'm not working. Don't even know if I can go back to my job, and he's back with the city engineering whatever the hell that needs some ingenuity around here. So he's in, and we're still in a shitty place."

"I've never made it that far in a relationship to know what to tell you to do."

He was my first real relationship since I've been in this city. It's been at least six years since Greg and I broke up.

Dawn keeps her thoughts to herself and Johnnie doesn't pry. She lets the pain of her friend's confession settle between them. The pain of her own confession is stacked on top. They are connected by the toils, trials, and tribulations of what it means to be single, and what it means to be married. What it means to walk in this world as a powerful, successful, talented woman and still be looked at as less than for a lack of marital status. Or to walk through this world pitied and patronized for not knowing your place, emasculating the man in your life, and setting a poor example for a son who doesn't know any better than his mother works, and his father stays at home. They stand side by side in their own thoughts connected by an invisible string of what their womanhood means, and why whatever contributions they've made for their sex, for their gender, are not enough to compare with the men who decided to be apart of their lives.

"I think it all comes down to not wanting to see other people win," Dawn says.

"What do you mean?" Johnnie asks.

"It's like sports. You only root for your team. Same thing in life. You only root for your team. If you're black you root for black people. If you're a woman. You root for the women."

"What about the Olympics?"

"Same concept applies. We may talk about this country like a baldheaded stepchild, but every four years we're just as nationalistic as anybody else saying America first, but even then, we're really only rooting for Gabby Douglas or the women's track team, and maybe Michael Phelps."

"So you're saying we have relationship problems because Nathan and I don't want to see each other win?"

"Jealousy and competition," Dawn surmises. "It goes for you and Nathan, and me and Victor. But what do I know. It's not like I can keep a man anyway."

"No. I think you might be on to something."

"Men love to compete, even if they say they don't want to compete against their partners, they always want to win."

"What are you guys talking about?" Soleil asks walking up to Dawn and Johnnie.

"Men," Dawn answers.

"That's the only reason I'm here tonight," Soleil says. "And he's dead."

"No new love interest in your life?" Dawn asks.

"Not here. I can't go anywhere. I can't do anything because people recognize me. His funeral was front page in the city and all over the Navy Times. And who was photographed sitting on the front row of the church? Me."

"You looked fabulous though," Johnnie says.

"Thanks."

"For right now, for me, self-love is the best love."

"That's all well and good until you need something more than yourself." Johnnie smirks.

"In that case I have a detachable shower head, a vibrator, and a very capable dildo if I just have to get it in."

"There's no substitute for the real thing," Johnnie says.

"Agreed." Dawn adds.

"Let me be the judge of that," Soleil says.

Johnnie quips, "You can't judge what you ain't getting."

"Last time I got some, I got more than what I wanted."

"He doesn't count," Dawn says.

"Why not?"

"Because his ass is dead," Johnnie says.

"Tell that to my memories."

Johnnie and Dawn's quick comebacks are ground to a halt by the woman in red standing in front of them. The woman whose six months of trauma and pain they learned about in court. The woman who brought them all together by what she endured in silence and a made up face. They don't tell her to try to forget what they know she can't. They don't ask her to have amnesia to a life she's lived. They can't beg her to develop dementia to erase what happened. They wait to follow her lead, in her own life, about what's appropriate to do, to say, to become next.

Johnnie looks away from her confidantes back toward the bar, her every thought on the drinks she can't have. *Ugh, this day is made for alcohol.* She sucks her teeth in disgust at the dwindling line. She turns her head to the other side of the room to see people lined up at the table holding the large plates of little food arranged more to be photographed than consumed.

"I'm going back to school," Soleil says.

"For what?" Dawn asks.

"A Masters in Social Work. I've already got the experience from the victim's side of the equation, and from teaching. Might as well put it to some use."

"Not enough people go into that," Johnnie says. "Half the people who come through that ER wouldn't be there if they just had one line of defense in the system before they got to me. Well, before they used to get to me."

Dawn nods.

"It just makes sense," Soleil says. "Start over. Do something different. Reclaim my life. My time. I'm tired of always being labeled as Barker's girlfriend, or ex-girlfriend, or alleged abuse victim. I have my own name, my own job, my own identity outside of him."

"Unfortunately, that's not what people know you for," Dawn says. "So that's not how they're going to see you."

"I know," Soleil says sardonically.

"It's the infamy of fame. Even in Jacksonville."

"I could have it worse," Soleil says. "I *could* be Ebony."

"This *is* where we all met!" Johnnie exclaims. "We were on dates then."

"I wouldn't call mine a date," Soleil says. "More like held under duress."

"Okay, maybe not," Johnnie agrees.

"And, we're still missing one person."

"That we are," Dawn says. "Even if James gets her off, her life will never be the same."

"Neither will mine," Johnnie mutters.

"She should be here," Soleil says.

Soleil opens her mouth to say something else but refrains. She refuses to verbalize the dark thought that crosses her mind every time she goes home to her apartment and looks at the peeling patch job over the hole in the wall, where her headboard used to be, and the globe light that covers where the fan used to hang. The hole in the wall he made with her head, the fan that fell from spinning to fast, mostly, usually over their violent affairs. She stops herself from thinking of where she would or wouldn't be if it weren't for Ebony approaching her in this very ballroom, from dragging her through the double doors and out to the valet stand. She shudders to think where she would, or would not be, if it had not been for Ebony trailing her, stalking him, and confronting him.

I owe her my life.

Soleil looks away from Dawn and Johnnie toward the front of the ballroom. From her vantage point all she can see are the brown backs of the canvas paintings she has no desire to see again. The paintings that covered the walls of Barker's Queens Harbor home. The abstract images of color she used to see behind her own eyelids when he'd slap her face, or grab her by her cheeks and chin. The random dribbles of electric color, the splotches of hue and tint left in uncoordinated patterns; paintings that were as engaging as they were confusing, as beautiful as they were frustrating, as complicated as they were simply misunderstood.

Soleil looks to the front of the room where she sees James walking toward the podium. He stands between two of the largest paintings. The paintings she remembers hanging in Barker's bedroom, covering the back wall of his master suite. She only saw them from upside down, from beneath him, from where she was trapped until she accompanied him to an event, and met a woman who knew his capability for brutality.

I hated those fucking paintings.

James clears his throat.

Soleil whispers, "Ebony is here, because we're all here."

23.

"Today, I'm here to tell you about the appeal of Ebony Jones," James says adjusting the mic.

He stares out over the crowd of the well heeled and socially mobile in front of him. The crowd he used to be apart of at private parties, and city government functions, galas, and conventions. He looks out over the men in their tailored tuxedoes, and the women beside them in their off-the-rack gowns made to look like custom designs, as he adjusts his own suit. The new suit he bought specifically for the fund-raiser. The new suit that is nearly two sizes smaller than what he used to wear. Slim fit pants, and a three button, side vent jacket that fits snug at his armpits and restricts his range of motion, is what he broke the bank for and dropped half his mortgage payment on, just to look the part amongst his former peers.

He says into the microphone, "More than two months ago a jury found Ebony Jones, my client, guilty of culpable negligence in the death of Judge Barker Gordon. They said she was criminally irresponsible with the weapon she legally owned and was licensed to carry in the great state of Florida. Obviously my client, who also happens to be the woman I love, who many of you have seen me with over the last year-and-a-half, believes differently. She believes she was armed to protect herself as some of you in here are now."

James pauses and looks up to see the men he knows are second amendment defenders, shift uncomfortably, as they tell everyone in the room they have stashed away in their waistbands, ankle holsters, and even their pockets, the fruits of their license to conceal and carry. He doesn't see them but he knows there are .22s and .357s and maybe a slim Glock 9 among the men, and even some of the women he stands in front of.

"My client and I also believe that despite Judge Gordon's injuries from the shooting he provoked, he could have survived. In fact we know he should have survived."

Johnnie bumps Dawn's elbow from where they stand in the back corner of the ballroom. James doesn't see the movement taking place behind him. The glancing side-eyes being shared between the women.

He continues, "With the permission of the decedent's mother, Ms. Nona Gordon, whom many of you in here also know, I will have Judge Gordon's body exhumed and examined by an independent medical examiner. The doctor who will perform the second autopsy will look for any signs of medical malpractice due to human error. We know this will prove that not only should Judge Gordon have lived to defend his despicable actions against my client, but also the trajectory of the bullets into his body were only due to the close contact he had to my client when he choked her, and slammed her so hard against her own car that her 125-pound body left a dent, and shattered the tempered glass."

Soleil claps from the corner beside Dawn and Johnnie. They join her as do a few others in the large ballroom. James turns and nods his head in her direction, grateful for the show of support, even if it is pitiful in measure against the blank black, brown, white, and some red faces, who stare at him as if he is the chimera from Ebony's nightmares.

He waits until the hollow skin slapping dissipates. James licks his lips, then swallows loudly in the mic.

He says, "I will not bore you by arguing the points of this case or our appeal before you tonight. Tonight is about generating enough support from you who are here. You see this beautiful artwork in front of you tonight, it was donated by Ms. Nona Gordon for our silent auction. And if the artwork is too rich for your blood, we have some wine baskets as well. Now I ask you to keep drinking, and when Ms. Nona gets up here, to dig deep, and buy something some of you were always mad Barker had that you didn't. Thank you."

James steps away from the podium with resounding applause and a few chuckles at his dry joke. Ms. Nona replaces James at the podium. He makes the diagonal walk to the corner of the room where Dawn, Johnnie, and Soleil remain. He stands beside Dawn as Ms. Nona adjusts the microphone to her own mouth. She smooths the beaded bodice of her dress, and then runs the fingertips of both hands across the smooth scar beneath her collar bone. Her delicate fingers linger on the marring of her own skin like some women who nervously finger their strands of pearls, or diamond necklaces.

She looks out over the audience with her fingers paused on her purposely exposed body. Poised and posed like black and white photos of high fashion models, she slowly brings her fingers away from her body and sets them on the wood of the podium.

She says, "My son was a judge, but you know that already. My son was also an abuser. Something you maybe didn't know. Or maybe you did. He was an abuser like his father. You see the proof of my testimony in front of you. That is why I take the side of James and Ebony. That is why I have approved the exhumation of Barker's body. It is why I am taking the valuable assets of my son's estate and putting them up for auction to be used for the good of the woman who's life he damaged, even in his death."

James turns his head away from Ms. Nona to the women beside him.

"Dawn, Johnnie, will you be bidding for anything tonight?"

"My walls are full," Dawn says.

"If Nathan wants to, I don't see why not," Johnnie answers.

"Maybe you can convince him," James says. "You've been such a big supporter of Ebony . . . Especially since the trial."

"I was just following my heart to do what's right."

"I know Ebony appreciates your help. Even if it is a little late."

"Better late than never, right?"

"Not always. But I'll try to make it right."

Ugh, I need a drink. Johnnie watches James move along the perimeter of the ballroom. He ignores the table of picked over finger food and goes back to the open entrance. Nathan stands leaning against one door with Danielle in his arms asleep on his shoulder. She watches James greet Nathan. They slap hands into a grip, and come in for an awkward hug with Danielle between them. James claps Nathan's back with one hand and runs his hand across Danielle's back with the other.

"You alright?" Dawn asks beside her.

"What was that about?" Soleil asks.

Johnnie doesn't answer either question. She squints her eyes to sharpen her focus on James and Nathan across the room. She ignores the sea of people separating them, the art explaining voice of Ms. Nona, the light playing of the band, and the murmurs of the crowd. She watches their body language and reads their movements. *Shit, he's going to tell him.* Every tilt of James's head, every shift of Danielle in Nathan's arms, their nods, their smiles, their pleasant listening faces that neither alight with joy, fear, or concern all tell her she should have told Nathan more clearly the first time.

"Soleil, would you come up here please." Ms. Nona beckons toward the trio.

The woman's waving arm and effusive face breaks Johnnie's gaze. The old woman's request ruptures her line of sight. It interrupts the conversation she imagines James and Nathan are having. Soleil's breach of her vision tears her focus from the back of the room to what is happening in front of her. She watches Danielle's former teacher float toward the podium in her red dress. Her hair is down, curly corkscrew ringlets float around her shoulders.

"I don't think I've ever seen her without her hair pulled up in that messy bun she always wears," Johnnie says.

"Oh, you're back now." Dawn says.

"I never left."

"Your body didn't, but your mind did."

"I was just listening to Ms. Nona describe the artwork."

"Bulllshit," Dawn says.

216.

"If you know so damn much, then what was I doing, Dawn?"

"I saw you staring at James and Nathan. I take it you never told Nathan why you were really suspended from your job."

"I told him the day it happened. The day he had that woman in my house. The day he took my children and left. I told him."

Dawn ignores the stutter in Johnnie's voice. The pain in her words. The request for grace, mercy, and understanding, in the rehash of her recent history.

She asks, "What did you say?"

"I told him I killed a man."

"You told Soleil and I the same thing, but then said you were trying to save his life. Which one is it?"

"Just like I told you then, I tried to save his life. He died. I wasn't good at my job. I feel like I killed him."

"Then why is James exhuming the body to look for signs of medical malpractice, if you only *feel* like you killed him?"

"Because I told Ebony what happened, and apparently she told James, and I guess he thinks it's enough to get her off."

"There's something you're not saying."

"I need a drink."

"I thought you were sober."

Johnnie leaves Dawn's litmus test for her innocence unanswered in the corner.

She follows the path James took toward Nathan. Head down, her feet walk the perimeter of the ballroom until she gets to the table of what's left of the food. Small plate in hand she loads it up with crustless ham sandwiches, bacon wrapped scallops, and stuffed button mushrooms. Johnnie doesn't pick up a fork. She pops a mushroom and then a scallop into her mouth, then adds two more of each onto her plate. Barely chewing, swallowing chunks of food without tasting, she focuses on her plate as she passes the gang of doorways, including where James and Nathan stand.

Don't look at them. Stay cool. Eat something else. She passes them without looking, without acknowledging them, without trying to intrude on their conversation. Johnnie walks with the dwindling tower of food, popping appetizers in her mouth, to the other line in the ballroom. The line that's been consistently long and steadily moving. She takes her place at the end and eats.

Johnnie gobbles her way through the mushrooms and the scallops until all that's left are the sandwiches. She eats them slowly as she shuffles her way to the front of the line. Bite for bite, she indulges in the toasted buttery bread, spread with dijon mustard, and layered with thinly sliced honey ham, and what she thinks is provolone cheese. She finishes the first sandwich in three bites. The last sandwich in her hand, she takes even smaller bites, willing her mouth to obey her mind, she nibbles at the sandwich smaller than the width of her hand until she is one person away from her destination. She puts the rest of the sandwich in her mouth, chews twice, and swallows.

Johnnie places the empty plate on the bar. "Shirley Temple, please. Virgin."

The bartender in his black and white, and gel spiked hair, doesn't question her order. With the deadened eyes of someone who knows they've worked a dead-end job for too long, he produces a wet glass from beneath the bar. He drops square ice cubes with rounded, water wet centers into the glass with the stainless steel scoop. Two nozzles in his hand, he sprays the glass with the liquid of the kiddie cocktail, threads a plastic toothpick with cherries, and drops it inside and pushes it toward Johnnie. She pushes the plate toward him and grabs the drink.

"Thank you," she says.

Johnnie ignores the thin straw and sips the drink straight from the lip of the glass. She savors the attempt of well-meaning adults to make ginger ale take the place of vodka. The attempt to make children feel grown is her saving grace. She relishes the movement of bringing the cocktail glass to her mouth more than the calories added from the sugary fizz barreling down her throat.

"What are you guys talking about?" she asks, walking up to Nathan and James.

"Nothing," James answers. "Nathan's just catching me up on all the gossip in City Hall since I've gone rogue."

"Is that right?"

"What do you have there?" Nathan asks, pointing at the drink.

"Shirley Temple. Virgin. Danielle offered me some of hers and I didn't want any. Thought she might want some of mine."

"She's knocked out."

"I see."

"She's a beautiful child," James says. "I'll catch you later, man."

James slaps Nathan on the back and they do an awkward finger entangling handshake. Johnnie stands in front of Nathan where James stood. She watches him walk and stop at a few standing couples. He smiles, he shakes hands, he laughs, he claps backs, he moves on. He is the minister of money in the church of perceived upward mobility. He entices check books and credit cards with the promise of donation-based tax write-offs, and the feeling of supporting a good cause and doing the right thing.

Still looking at James glad-handing his way through the room, she asks Nathan, "You bid on anything?"

"There are a few pieces I like, but it all seems too rich for my blood."

Johnnie nods. "I'm ready when you are."

"I would have bid on the wine baskets, but that may be too much temptation for you, and I don't like drinking alone."

"Wine isn't really my thing. Only a last resort."

"Like this Shirley Temple?"

"I'm trying."

Johnnie drains the glass, walks it to the bar, and sets it down.

"Give her to me," she says opening her arms.

"She's heavy."

"You've held her all night. Let me help."

Nathan transfers Danielle into Johnnie's arms. She holds her around her knees, Danielle's head rests safely on her shoulder.

"You ready?" Nathan asks.

"I'm ready," Johnnie says, walking through the open doors of the ballroom.

Nathan looks in James's direction and raises his hand once he gets his attention. Johnnie doesn't see James wave back. She walks out of the ballroom, kicking through the fabric of her long purple skirt so as not to trip, or stumble over her own feet with Danielle in her arms. Nathan jogs to catch up with her. They make their exit, heels clicking on the glossy tile as they stride through the lobby, out of the automatic sliding doors, and to the valet stand where they wait, side by side, Johnnie shifting Danielle's dead weight in her arms.

"The last time we were here is when you met Ebony for the first time," Nathan says.

"Yeah, it was." Johnnie nods.

"And now she's brought us back here again."

"She did."

"I guess some people just have that power to bring others together."

"Seems like it."

"Even if they can't be here themselves."

The valet pulls their 4Runner up to the curb.

Right on time.

Johnnie steps forward and waits for the driver to make it around to the passenger side and open the back door. She is grateful Danielle is in her arms. Grateful to be able to put her sleeping body in her booster seat and strap the seat belt around her fluffy dress. She is grateful Nathan is no longer beside her. Grateful to be rid of his small talk filled with loaded questions that question her. Johnnie closes the door on Danielle and walks to the valet stand. She pulls a wad of bills from her bosom, rolls back a twenty, and hands it to the professional car sitter. She doesn't hear his thank you. Lost in her own thoughts and out of delays, she picks up the middle of her skirt and gets into the awaiting SUV. The valet slams her door shut.

Maybe they talked about golfing.

"Mama, where are we going?" Danielle whines awake.

"Home, Baby. We're going home."

"Is daddy there?"

"I'm right here, Dani," Nathan says, turning around to look at her in the back seat. "Daddy's right here. I'm not going anywhere."

Johnnie feels Nathan's glare burning into the side of her face as he puts the truck in drive.

Shit.

She looks straight ahead, out of the windshield, and waits for the confrontation to come.

24.

"So are you going to tell me what James said, or are we going to act like this isn't happening?" Johnnie asks as Nathan exits I-295.

"Seems to me like you already know what James said."

"It's nothing I haven't already told you."

"Johnnie, you didn't tell me shit."

"I told you I was suspended after he died."

"You told me you were suspended, but you didn't tell me it was because of how he died."

"He was shot."

"And you were drunk."

"Barely," she says to herself, looking out the window as Nathan makes a right at the corner by the elementary school with a giant apple and an A plus on the marquee.

"I wasn't drunk," Johnnie says.

"You for damn sure weren't sober. You were wasted when you got home that day. What do you mean you weren't drunk?"

"What I was when I got home, has nothing to do with what I was when I was at work."

"So much for the rules of AA."

"What the hell is that supposed to mean?"

"Didn't you tell me the first step is admitting your baggage and bullshit. You told Ebony you were an alcoholic and drunk in the ER. You haven't told me any of that."

"I did tell you I was an alcoholic, and you tried to get me to stop saying it."

"You never told me, you were drunk during the man's surgery. Hell, Johnnie, you just denied it a second ago."

"It's not easy to admit, Nathan. Just like you still haven't admitted you cheated on me with the teacher's assistant."

Johnnie's accusation rings loudly in the car. *Checkmate.* He doesn't respond as he turns into their aging subdivision. He winds the SUV through the worn asphalt of the streets until they make their way deep into the bowels of urban planning. Johnnie stares out at the looming old trees whose roots have ripped through the pavement. Despite the late hour, she watches as children on bikes, and the teens in charge of them lag behind walking. They pass by the house where the tree has been torn down, and their grass replaced with dark brown mulch and spider plants. She knows they are on their block. Johnnie looks out the windshield. She watches as Nathan creeps up the block to their house in the cul-de-sac.

She says, "Every time I drive home and get close to the driveway I always hold my breath to see if I'm going to see her car. She had a lot of fucking nerve."

"I told you she was just here to drop-off Danielle."

"Dropping off doesn't require parking, coming inside *my* house, and watching *Frozen* with *my* child."

"She was just being nice."

"You have an excuse for everything."

Johnnie unlocks her own door before Nathan hits the button to close the garage behind them. She jumps down and picks up her shoes from the floor of the SUV where she kicked them off. She slams one door and opens the other. Her fingers work quickly unfastening Danielle's seat belt and lifting her out of the car. She is around the front of the family truck and in through the back door of the house as Nathan closes the door to the driver's side of the SUV.

Inside, she disarms the alarm before it goes off. Shifting Danielle in her arms Johnnie walks through the kitchen, past the living room and down the hall toward the front entrance. Marching is how she moves up the single flight of steep stairs directly into Danielle's room. She lays her down on the bed covered in a pink Minnie Mouse spread, and leaves her in her dress and shoes from the fund-raiser.

Johnnie walks barefoot down the hall. She stops in the room for her son Tyler. Now fifteen, she sees him sprawled across his bed, headphones on, phone next to his hand, fast asleep. Johnnie turns the light off in his room, pulls the door closed and continues the short walk down the hall into the master suite. Nathan is already there sitting on the edge of the bed waiting. She sucks her teeth, drops her shoes, closes the door, and walks past him into the closet. *There's no sense in talking if he's just going to lie.* Inside she strips out of her long skirt, peplum top, Spanx, bra and panties. She balls up the clothes to drop them in the dirty clothes hamper beside the shower.

In the warm water, Johnnie sits on the marble bench as the spray soaks her body. It sprinkles her face and wets her hair still molded and sculpted into a twisted creation atop her head. The water runs until her face is covered with grease, cream, and gel from her hair products.

Slouched against the marble wall of the shower Johnnie waits until the lines in her body from the cinching shape wear, the underwire in her bra, and the lace imprint of her thong disappears into her expanding cellulite. She jiggles her thighs and the fat of her belly disgusted with her own body. *I need to go to the gym.* Stretching her back she spreads her legs and leans forward. The water beats against her spine and the top of her butt. She webs her fingers through her toes and then slowly rolls upright. She stares down at her breast, her nipples rest on the upper plump of her stomach. Johnnie stands up from the bench directly beneath the water. She pulls in her belly and looks down. She lets it go. Tears fall from her eyes and mix with the water of the cooling shower.

Sixteen years, two kids, and we don't have shit to show for it.

The tears she didn't cry in the emergency room, or the locker room after the botched surgery fall. Tears she didn't cry when she put all the pieces of her and Ebony's intertwined story together roll down her cheeks. Tears she didn't cry at the funeral she forced herself to attend even though she was loaded with the same liquor that left her jobless, husbandless, and filled with guilt, regret, and remorse stream into the drain with the softened and filtered city tap. Johnnie grabs the loofah from the bath caddie, and a bottle of berry scented body wash. She pours an exorbitant amount of soap into the dried out sponge and washes her body until the water is cold, and her skin is raw. It is her form of flagellation, punishing herself for what she didn't do and what she didn't say months ago. She lathers, washes, rinses and repeats, until her tears are dry, her skin hurts, and her hair is soaked and falling out of the bobby pins no longer gripping her scalp.

Johnnie turns the handle of the shower, steps out of the glass doors and drips water as she walks through the bathroom, past the closets and into the bedroom, where Nathan is still waiting. He's still dressed in his tux, shoes still on, tie not loosened. She walks past him naked to the chest of drawers.

"What are the chances they charge you if they find medical malpractice once they exhume the body?" Nathan asks.

"I don't know. I guess we'll find out together."

"Johnnie, that's not funny. You could put us all at risk?"

"How?"

"I'm your husband. I work for the city. The kids go to public school. We're visible. Vulnerable. If they come after you, they could come after all of us."

"How? Ms. Nona is only exhuming the body because she wants to help Ebony. I doubt she's going to file civil charges against me because her woman beating son is dead."

"You don't know that."

"And you don't know that I *will* be charged."

Johnnie snatches underwear and a satin romper out of the dresser and steps into both. She walks toward the closed bedroom door.

"What happened to 'First, do no harm?'"

"That's not apart of the oath, Nathan."

"Treading with care in matters of life and death is though. What happened to that?"

"What happened to for richer, for poorer, for better or worse, in sickness and in health, until death do us part?"

"I'm still here. And we're still married."

"That doesn't mean you didn't break a vow, Nathan."

"I could say the same about you."

"I always tread carefully in the matters of life and death. If it is given me to save a life, all thanks. But it may also be within my power to take a life; this awesome responsibility must be faced with great humbleness and awareness of my own frailty. Above all, I must not play at God," she says, finishing the Hippocratic oath. "I know my vows, Nathan. Both sets."

Johnnie turns the handle of the bedroom door she's been holding, and steps out and leaves Nathan sitting on the bed fully dressed. The romper clings to the meat around her legs and sticks in some places to her still damp skin. The new fat of her thighs rubs together as she jogs down the stairs. She holds her unbound chest to keep her breasts from flopping around. When she reaches the bottom she lets herself go, and crosses the white tile of the dark house, avoiding walls, and furniture. Johnnie ends up in the kitchen, in the refrigerator. She grabs the pitcher of water, and a carton of strawberries and butter. Johnnie moves quickly, opening cabinets for a glass, plugging in the toaster, and opening the half eaten loaf of bread. She pops in two slices, pours a glass of water and brings it to her lips, sips, and smacks "aah." Johnnie drains the glass, refills it, and replaces the pitcher back in the open refrigerator. It beeps from being open too long. She ignores the noise and pops open the plastic carton of fruit. The bread jumps from the toaster. She rummages in drawers until she finds a butter knife to slather the bread. Snack made, Johnnie runs the open carton of strawberries beneath the water from the sink in the island to rinse them off. She stands in the light of the refrigerator, her wet hands dripping onto her bare feet and bites into her toast. Bread, fruit, water. She eats. She drinks. She chews. She swallows.

Johnnie decides against making more toast. She unplugs the toaster, closes the carton of strawberries, and puts it and the butter back in the refrigerator. The only light source in the house disappears when she closes the stainless steel door. Nathan's shadowy figure is behind it.

"What?" Johnnie snaps.

"You can't eat your way out of this, just like you couldn't drink your way out of whatever it was you were trying to escape from before."

"So I'm fat and an alcoholic? Great. Thanks. That makes me feel amazing."

"I didn't say you were fat and I didn't call you an alcoholic. I'm saying you can't keep running from shit that won't go away."

"Like you?"

"What the fuck is that supposed to mean?" Nathan snaps back.

"Just what it sounds like. You ran away. You left. Look at you now. You're still dressed like you want to run away again. You want to go so bad — leave."

Nathan loosens the purple tie at his neck and unbuttons the top button of his shirt. He does not take off his jacket, or his belt, or step out of his shoes.

He says, "I'm not going anywhere, Johnnie."

"What do you mean, you're not going anywhere? You just got back."

"Yes. I left. You needed to get yourself together. Hell, I needed to get myself together. I didn't want my kids around an alcoholic. They don't have to go through the shit I went through when I grew up. I got my job back. And I came back."

"And while you were out getting your shit together I was here, at home, alone, abandoned, without my children who are the only reasons why I work like a Hebrew slave, so they can have everything I didn't. Everything *we* didn't when we were growing up, including at least one parent who would always be with them, no matter what."

"The only one who needs steady parental presence, Johnnie, is Danielle," Nathan says. "Tyler's fifteen. He's going to be leaving soon. Danielle is six and the only person she wants to be around is you. And you're never here."

"I have to work," Johnnie says.

"Not all those crazy hours you don't."

"And what would we do if I didn't?"

227.

"We'd figure it out."

"Saying 'oh, we'll figure it out,' is what people say when they haven't figured shit out. But no worries. I figured it out for us. I work, you decided to stay home because you were burnt out from all the political bullshit, and the shit was handled."

"Everything accept your drinking. When did that become your escape, instead of me?"

"I don't know."

Her honesty disarms him. Johnnie moves past Nathan standing beside the refrigerator into the living room. She falls onto the old couch and lays down on the flat, decorative throw pillows. Covering her face with her arm she waits for the conversation to continue or end. She waits for Nathan to make the decision for the both of them; disinterested in doing anything that requires thinking.

She hears his shoes as the heels click from the tile, and then become muffled in the carpet of the extra-large area rug marking off the living room. He sits on the edge of one of the matching arm chairs.

He says, "Johnnie, talk to me."

"For what? It's not like you listen to me any way. I can't drink, now I can't eat, might as well lay here and sleep."

"Johnnie, what's wrong with you?"

"If I knew, I'd tell you, but I don't. So now what?"

"I don't fucking know. Leaving's not the answer, but I don't know if staying is either."

"So you want to separate, get divorced, what?"

"I don't know."

"Then what the fuck do you know, Nathan? You're full of suggestions and no fucking solutions. Why are you even here? What are you good for, but to accuse me of shit, and blame me for shit, like you're so fucking innocent."

"I didn't do shit."

"You're right, you *didn't* do shit. All the hours I worked, and I still had to come home and cook and clean and help with homework, and then find time to cater to you when you've been in the house all day. And then when shit got a little rough you left for the fucking teacher's assistant. Her ass might be big, but I doubt if it's even real."

"This conversation is going nowhere. You're not an angry drunk, you're just belligerent."

"And you avoid anything you don't want to admit to, so I guess we're perfect for each other."

"You need to figure out what you're going to do about this Ebony situation," Nathan says, standing up from the chair.

"Just add it to the list of all the other shit I have to figure out by myself, since I clearly don't have a partner, or a helpmate around here."

"Good night, Johnnie," he says, walking out of the living room, down the hall toward the steps.

She hears his feet above her, walking toward the bedroom. The door closes. The alarm beeps once. The system is armed.

"Good night," she mutters, turning her body into the couch cushions.

25.

The alarm beeps twice as James steps in to the laundry room from the garage. He closes the door behind him, arms the system, and heads into the bedroom.

"I thought you'd be asleep," James says, stopping in the doorway.

Ebony puts the book in her lap face down on the nightstand. She says, "No need, since my sentencing's been pushed back. How was the fund-raiser?"

"Good. We sold all the artwork and the wine, so I'd say it was successful."

"How successful?"

"About forty-five thousand dollars' worth of success."

"People paid that much for art and wine?"

"They did."

James comes fully into the bedroom. He slips out of his shiny shoes, loosens his belt, and drops his pants. His suit jacket, tie and shirt follow. He leaves a pile of clothes on his side of the bed, the side closest to all the doors, the entrances and exits. He tosses the decorative pillows Ebony piled in his place to the floor, pulls back the covers and slides in the bed in his underwear. He pulls off his dress socks once he's seated on the soft, pillow-top mattress. They fall from his hand on top of the clothing already on the floor. If there's a fire he might have a chance to get dressed before choking on the smoke versus Ebony, who insists on sleeping in underwear and wife beaters nine months out of the year, if not more than that. Her bedroom attire is wholly dependent on whether winter makes Jacksonville a stop on its cross country tour or not.

"So what else happened?" she asks.

"Johnnie and Nathan were there."

"What did they say?"

"Your girl didn't say much. She knew she was wrong. I don't even know why she was there."

"To support to the end, even if it means her end, I guess."

"Maybe, but when I talked to Nathan, he was just shooting the shit with me after I talked about the appeal, like he didn't know his life was about to get wrecked. He even asked me, 'What new info did you get to exhume the body?' I just looked at him at first, and then I told him to ask his wife."

"You know they haven't been together since Barker died. That's what she told me when she came to visit. She said he cheated on her but won't admit it, but she still took him back because he's moved back in."

"They were there with their daughter like one big happy family."

"Let me guess, you ruined that for them?"

"Why'd you say it like that?"

"Because you sound excited."

"I'm not excited. I didn't ruin anything for them. He asked me what new evidence we had, I told him to ask his wife. He asked me what did that mean, and I told him what you said she told you."

"That's a lot of he said, she said going around, Counselor."

"It wouldn't have to be if she had told the truth from the beginning."

"The truth is hard when lies come so quickly."

"I know, and now Nathan knows too."

"What's that supposed to mean?"

James slides underneath the covers until his head hits the pillow. *I hope she just drops it* he thinks, punching each side to fluff it beneath his head. He rolls over onto his stomach, looks toward the door, and closes his eyes. He ignores the woman waiting for him to answer her leading question. He knows he's said too much, been too candid, and now Ebony, sensitive and defensive, is offended. He keeps his eyes closed to refrain from seeing her face glaring into his, but it is no use. He can feel her gaze roaming all over the covered form of his body, beside her, in her bed, in her house.

"Turn the light out, please."

"Not until you answer my question."

"Ebony, I don't want to fight with you. Tonight was a good night. Everyone loved the video Dawn's crew recorded of you. She gave a good speech, I gave a good speech, Ms. Nona and Soleil worked the crowd, and gave good speeches, and we have forty-five thousand dollars to show for it. It was a good night."

"Was is the operative word."

"Ebony, don't do this. You said it. I just agreed."

"Whatever, James. It doesn't even matter. I did say it. The truth is hard, and yet I told it to you every step of the way."

"Okay, now you're making stuff up," James says rolling toward her. "Anytime you told me the *truth*, is because I forced you. The shooting, your mom, the stalking. You only told me because you had to, and by the time you got around to filling me in on your side of the story, I already knew."

Ebony's arms are folded beneath her breasts, her fingers shoved tightly beneath each armpit. She's trying to resist the urge to scratch an itch that's not there; to pick at herself, her skin, her scabs, and her scars in the name of something to do. She holds her breath, counts to ten, and then sighs to alleviate the anxiety behind her nervous habit. It doesn't work. She tries again. Deep breath. Hold. Ten seconds. Release. Her hands are no longer pretending to be perspiration pads beneath her arms. They caress one another as she folds them, over and over, in front of her body. Still resisting the urge to scratch what isn't there, she folds her hands until the urge has passed, until holding her breath and sighing works. Until the willingness of her mind has conquered the easy habit of her flesh. She shoves her hands beneath her butt, not trusting herself to let them alone at her sides.

James asks, "Why haven't you ever gone to therapy for that?"

"For what?" Ebony snaps.

"The scratching."

"Ayana says I've been scratching since I was twelve. Since the accident. She didn't put me in therapy then because she probably didn't think about it. And if she did, she didn't have the money. It's better to ignore it, than dwell on something you can't fix."

"Okay, but you're not twelve anymore. You're not in Ayana's house anymore. Why didn't you ever go to therapy for it."

"Because I only scratch when I'm upset. It's not a problem."

"I'd disagree."

"Yeah, well we disagree on a lot of things."

"Seriously, you need help. The scratching, your issues with Ayana, the following people, the shit with Barker."

"It's not like I can go anywhere with this thing on my leg. So I'll just keep getting along, like I've been getting along."

"It's not working."

"What else do you want me to do? It's not like you care."

"What do you mean, I don't care? Am I not still here, still with you, still beside you fighting for you. Defending you. Raising money for you? Stop being so fucking ungrateful."

"Do not curse at me."

"Don't start that bullshit. We're in too deep and too far beyond it. You know I don't mean no disrespect. You're just fucking difficult." James shakes his head. He mutters, "I should have just listened from jump, and I wouldn't even be here."

"Listened to who?"

"It doesn't matter. I'm here."

"The only person I know you listen to is your mother, and she hasn't liked me since the day she met me."

"Drop it, Ebony. It doesn't matter."

"I won't drop it. You brought it up. I'm just finishing it. You say if you had listened to your mother you wouldn't be here. James, you act like you're not here. You realize this is the most you've talked to me in months. The most conversation we've had since the trial ended. Hell, we haven't even had sex in months."

"I swear, we keep having the same damn conversation and argument over and over. I already told you I've been working, and most of that work has been for you."

Ebony yells, "I don't see you, I barely hear from you. The only reason I know you're still working for me is because Dawn always has some kind of update on the news. The only person you talk to is her, and apparently Mrs. Rachelle."

"Leave my mom out of this, Ebony."

"You put her in it."

"I'm serious."

"And so am I. You say you love me. How can you love someone you don't talk to? You don't say shit to me. You stare at me like I'm some kind of deformed zoo animal you can't help but look at. You come and go as you please, and that's cool, this is *my* house, but to pass by me like I'm not here, like I'm not struggling with all this shit, to not even ask me how I'm doing . . . Then you want to come in here all charming and self-righteous because you had a good night at the fund-raiser, ruining someone else's life, that's fucked up."

"You've got to be fucking kidding me," James says sitting up in the bed. "You throw my feelings for you back in my face, and you've never even said the fucking words."

Ebony jumps down from the bed. She walks over to the door frame, arms beneath her chest, fingers scratching the back of her hands.

"Where are you going?"

"I'm not going anywhere, but you're not going to yell at me, and curse at me in my bed, and I don't have anything to protect myself with."

"Oh, so now you want to shoot me?"

"I didn't say that."

"Good, because that's what got you in this mess in the first place."

"I didn't shoot him!"

"Yeah, I know. I'm just trying to make everybody else believe your bullshit."

234.

"It's not bullshit. It's the truth. And the jury would have believed every word I said if you hadn't melted down in court."

"So it's all my fault now?" James asks incredulous. "*I* followed Judge Gordon for months. *I* confronted him at his job. *I* took a gun he didn't know I had to meet him. *I* provoked him. *I* shot him. *I* fled the scene of a crime. *I* confessed to all of this watching the news. *I* turned myself in, and *I* represented myself at trial and lost. *I* did all of this. Ebony didn't do anything. Ebony is innocent. Get the fuck over yourself. It's me you're talking to. I've seen the best of you and the worst of you, and I'm still here."

"Your body is here, but that's about it. You come to bed late, if at all, and you leave before the sun rises. You're gone all day. You don't call, you don't answer. I don't know what you're doing. All I know is what you say."

"How about what you see. You're not in jail. You haven't been sentenced. You've got forty-five thousand dollars in donations to keep your bills paid, a roof over your head, and food in your refrigerator. Judge Gordon's body will be exhumed Monday morning, and the pathologist will conduct the autopsy as soon as the body is out of the ground."

"I didn't know that."

"You didn't give me a chance to tell you that. I told you I've been working. You're not paying me, and I'm not taking a fee from the money we raised tonight. I've been doing some consulting work on self-defense cases for attorneys across the country. Some prosecutors, some defense attorneys. The interview you did with Dawn has had my name everywhere and my phone ringing off the hook."

"I didn't know that."

"No, you didn't know that," James snaps. "Because all you think about is yourself. I know you're going through a lot, but you're still free and you're home. How about the shit I'm going through because of you, for you? When I leave here in the morning, I go home and feed and walk my dog. I go see my parents because, in all the months of trial prep, my father forgot me. When I first went to see him after the verdict, he thought I was Judge fucking Mathis."

Ebony laughs.

"That's not funny," James says, losing the edge in his voice. "I spend time with them for most of the day. I usually leave once my brother gets there. I go back home. I feed Caesar, I walk him, I play with him, I watch the news, I work on your briefs for court. Then I come back over here. That's my day. Every day for the last two months. The consulting just started. The money's barely coming in."

Ebony comes back to the bed. Disarmed, she sighs and gets under the covers. She waits for her rage to dissipate before she asks, "Why didn't you tell me?"

"What could you do about it? What can you do about it now that you know? You're dealing with your own shit, and I'm dealing with mine."

"You're right, I can't do anything but be a listening ear. The same way you can't change my circumstances either."

"What do you mean, I can't change your circumstances? I'm changing your circumstances. Look past that ankle monitor at the bigger picture."

"I didn't mean it like that, James. I'm just saying, everything I feel on the inside . . . you can't change that, nor can I change what you're going through. The least I can do is be here for you and listen."

"I'm good. I need to focus."

"And there you go, shutting me out again."

"I'm not shutting you out."

"Yes, you are. That's the reason we keep arguing about the same shit over and over again. Nothing gets resolved. You just shut down."

"I'm not shutting you out or shutting down. It's late. I'm tired. It's been a long day and I have to go by and spend the day with my parents tomorrow, since I didn't see them today."

James slides back down in the bed and covers his body with the sheet and comforter.

"You're not in a relationship with your parents," she says looking down at him.

"I'm not, but they gave me life, and I'm going to be there for them at the end of theirs."

"You know good and well, your mom is not dying no time soon."

James sighs, "Maybe not, but my father will."

"James . . ."

"What?"

"I'm sorry."

"Yeah. Me too."

Ebony clicks the switch of the bedside lamp and shrouds the room in darkness. She lays in the bed remembering the woman she met more than a year ago. Short and stocky, plain brown skin, clear face, a few wrinkles, tight roller set curls, arms that jiggled, a belly that didn't, and a voice that was strong and southern sweet. The kind of voice that sang alto in the church choir; deep, distinctive, and pronounced. Ebony lays in the bed and remembers the woman who shook her hand and squeezed her in for a hug before offering her a plate of food on chipped stoneware from Dollar Tree. The woman who was fiercely protective of her first born, doting toward her husband, and suspicious of any other woman who dared to try to set a permanent foot between her and her men.

26.

"Mrs. Rachelle, do you have any hot sauce?" Ebony asked from where she was seated at the small dining room table beside James.

"What do you need hot sauce for, Baby?" Rachelle asked.

"These greens. They're good, but I like a little more kick in mine."

"James, you heard your lady. Get her the hot sauce out of the cabinet in the kitchen," Rachelle demanded.

"Mama, you're right there."

"I am, but she's your guest, boy. Get her some hot sauce."

Rachelle lumbered over to the glass table and took a seat beside Ebony.

She had only been dating James three months when he insisted she meet his family. He insisted at two months in, and she had only been able to delay his eagerness a few weeks. He picked her up on a Sunday afternoon in the last days of spring, when the heat outside was hot and still kind of dry. The air hadn't developed the humid wetness of an impending hurricane or a daily afternoon storm. He picked her up in his freshly washed and waxed gold Impala, and they drove with the windows down from Mandarin to the Northside. They drove I-95, crossed the bridge, and maneuvered through the lazy Sunday traffic on the side of town where everyone was in church until at least two in the afternoon. Everyone except Rachelle, who had forgone attendance at Sunday's service to slave over a feast for her family.

When Ebony walked into the small family house, she smelled scents she only imagined from watching reruns of *Soul Food* on her worn out DVDs. Macaroni and cheese was in the oven, along with a pan of cornbread, and a dish of candied yams. Greens were boiling over in a large pot filled with fresh seasoning and smoked neck bones, both turkey and pork. Chicken was turning golden brown in the deep fryer, and catfish fillets were doing the same in the cast iron skillet on the stove. Rachelle greeted them with words only, her attention focused on the various states of done of the different dishes. It wasn't until James said, "Mama, I want you to meet someone," did she turn around.

She wiped her flour dirty hands on a red apron that said, "What would Jesus cook?" The question was answered "soul food" just beneath a caricatured plate of fried chicken and waffles. Rachelle opened her arms to embrace Ebony, forgoing a formal handshake.

She said, "James hasn't told me much about you. That means he likes you a lot."

"Oh, really?" Ebony asked playing along.

"Yes, chile. You can call me Mrs. Rachelle. Go on over there and have a seat. Food'll be ready in a little bit."

"Mama, you don't mean little bit like little bit on Thanksgiving do you?"

"Boy, don't you rush me. It's done when it's done."

"Yeah, but we're hungry now."

"Ebony may be hungry, but I know you ain't. I ain't never known you to miss no meals, snacks either."

"Ebony's helping me get in better shape. I'm down ten pounds, Mama."

"You ain't vegetarian, or what they call them people now, vegan, are you?"

"No, ma'am. I'm Duval born and bred. I like meat, bread, and cheese. I just work out so I'm not as big as a house."

"James did tell me something about you being in the gym all the time. How do you have time to do all that and still go to work?"

Ebony laughed from the table before answering. She said, "My work is the gym. I get paid to be fit. I'm a walking advertisement for my training services."

"Is that right?" Rachelle asked clanging pots in the kitchen.

"Yes, ma'am."

"Us ladies at the church used to have a walking group. We'd walk around here or go over to the school and walk the track. But between the arthritis and the shootings, we didn't last very long. It would be good to get somebody to teach us aerobics or something, maybe in the church."

Ebony nodded but didn't answer. She knew the tidbit of information was more than just a story to share. She knew Rachelle was testing her to see how quickly she would jump at the chance to spend time with the mother of the man she was dating. She knew agreeing to teach aerobics to a group of holy rolling church mothers would either endear her to Rachelle, or make her seem desperate. Ebony didn't want to find out which side of the equation she ended up on.

"What do you say?" Rachelle pushed.

Ebony cut her eyes at James.

He said, "Mama, let us get through dinner first and see if she decides she wants to come back."

"Why wouldn't she want to come back?" Rachelle asked. "I birthed you. Anything she like about you, she's gon' love about me."

"If you say so, Mama."

"What I do say is this catfish is ready. Y'all come on in here and fix your plates."

"I got you, Baby," James said. "What do you want?"

"Everything," Ebony answered.

"That's my kind of girl right there," Rachelle shouted from the kitchen. "You might be alright. You might be alright."

"Well, I'll take that as a compliment, Mrs. Rachelle. Thank you."

Ebony sat at the table listening to mother and son fuss in the kitchen about whether to use paper plates or real plates, paper napkins or cloth, and whether to drink soda out of the can or out of a glass with ice. She listened to them bicker content to have a front row seat to their expression of love and affection. It was one of the few times she let her feelings of missing Marilyn move over to a yearning for a better relationship, or any relationship, with Ayana.

James came out of the kitchen with her plate piled high, a silver fork holding all the food in place, and a Chek peach soda in his hand. He handed her the plate and the paper napkin beneath it. She quickly made the sign of the cross, bowed her head, and blessed her food.

"Ebony, you're Catholic?" Rachelle asked, peering through the lunch counter cut out in the wall that separated the kitchen from the dining area.

"No, ma'am. My neighbors were Catholic. I used to always see their kids make the sign before praying, and I guess I just picked up on it."

James returned with the hot sauce and sat down beside her. He blessed his food without reverence for the crucifixion and began to eat.

Rachelle asked, "What church do you belong to?"

"Bedside Baptist," Ebony answered.

Rachelle didn't laugh. She didn't smile or smirk. Ebony shoveled food in her mouth as Rachelle looked at her with pursed lips, and tight eyes. She knew she'd made a mistake. She should have known better than to joke about Jesus with a woman who just asked her to teach aerobics to the mother board. Ebony focused on her plate more than the woman glaring at her. She said between mouthfuls, "Mrs. Rachelle, this is amazing."

"Thank you, Baby," she answered. "I take it you don't cook, with your having to be in the gym all the time."

"No, I cook, but it's been a long time since I've had some good down home cooking like this. It's been years."

"Well, I'm glad you enjoy it."

The smile returned to her voice. Her dissatisfaction with the joke about her God was almost forgotten.

Rachelle said, "Tell me about your parents."

Ebony doesn't answer. James barely had the chance to skim the question with her before she shut him down. She looked to him. His scraggly face not yet trimmed, combed, or groomed to sideburn and goatee perfection. She looked at him for a lifeline and knew he had none to throw her. He waited as expectantly as his mother. She looked from one to the other. *Damn,* she thought as she looked between James in his tight T-shirt, and Rachelle in her hot pink lounge wear. She looked from his face to her face. The face they shared, only one was more chiseled because of testosterone and cardio, while the other was round and aged, even if it didn't look the double digit figure it was.

This is exactly why I didn't want to come. I can't meet his family without talking about mine.

Ebony gulped down the peach soda, her thirst still unquenched. She dry gulped until she felt like she was going to heave. She placed the empty can back on the table and put her arms in her lap working to keep from scratching in public.

She said, "Oh, my family is just your average family," Ebony offered without explanation.

Rachelle didn't press. A gift she knew Ebony was thankful for. She continued the line of conversation on her own, watching as Ebony picked over the food she previously had a voracious appetite for.

Rachelle said, "I don't know if James told you, but family is very important to me. I take care of my husband Jamie, since he's been diagnosed with the Alzheimer's. And my other son, James's brother, sometimes stops by on Sunday with his kids. He's got two now JoJo, short for Joseph Junior, and Joanna; and quiet as it's kept, he's got one on the way."

"Don't look at me like that, Mama," James says.

"Why not? You didn't tell me your brother got another one of these girls pregnant, even though you been knew."

"Mama, it wasn't my place to tell you. When Joey wants you to know, he'll tell you."

"Well, I'd had rather you tell it to me, then to have to find out like I did last week in Sunday service from Mrs. Hattie Jenkins. You know she think she all that because her son is a doctor up in Chicago. Said he work at the same hospital where Michelle worked before her and Barack got in the White House."

"Mama, it's not my fault she knows Joey stays out in the streets after these women."

"Young fast-tailed heifers." Rachelle humphs. "I love my grandbabies, but I didn't want them like this. Ebony, you want kids?"

"No, ma'am," she said.

The swift decisiveness with which she answered left the room silent. Rachelle stood from the table. James dropped his fork. Ebony stopped pretending to still be hungry after the family question. She knew she had made her second mistake despite the introductions going so well. Not having a church home, and not wanting kids went against everything Rachelle stood for and believed in. Ebony listened to her bumping around in the kitchen, scraping neckbones, chicken bones, and forgotten pinbones from the fish into the garbage can.

"Ray-shhhhhhelllll," a raspy voiced called from a room not seen.

"Hold on, Jamie Baby, I'm coming."

Ebony exhaled as Rachelle scurried out of the kitchen and into the back bedroom to attend to James Parnell, Senior. She wheeled him out in his chair, pulled back the cushioned seat where she had been sitting, and pushed him to the table.

"Hey, Pops," James said.

"Son. Rachelle, who is this?" He asked pointing at Ebony.

"Jamie Baby, that's James's friend Ebony."

"What you do?" he asked.

"I'm a personal trainer."

"You take a personal train to where now?"

"Jamie Baby, she said per-son-al train-er," Rachelle enunciated slowly. "She teaches aerobics, and jazzercise or something."

"Actually, I'm a boxer," Ebony corrected.

"But you're so little."

"And I still have to know how to defend myself."

"I guess. James, don't let this little bitty thing kick your behind now."

"I won't, Mrs. Rachelle."

"Mmhmm. Until something happen you don't like, and you'll be ready to fight. Just know this, something happens to my boys . . . I fight back."

"Mama!"

"I'm just letting her know, Baby. If you don't tell people who you are, what you're about, and how to treat you in the beginning, they just walk all over you. Jamie Baby, let me get your plate."

Rachelle disappeared behind the wall into the kitchen once more. She returned quickly with a small plate of food, separated like a child's so none of the items touched the others. Ebony watched as Rachelle helped James Senior eat. She was the steady hand around his shaky arm. She dabbed at his mouth with a napkin when he forgot to use the one he insisted on putting in his lap, and she brought the can of soda to his lips when she realized he was thirsty but couldn't remember the word to express what he needed. Ebony sat at the glass dining room table watching the two of them. She watched what could have been the aging romance of Marilyn and Dr. Ivan, had they not been snatched from her. She watched rapt and at attention learning lessons in both love and patience. Her enamored trance is what allowed the question born out of curiosity to roll off of her lips.

Ebony asked, "Mrs. Rachelle, have you ever thought about getting some help around here, so you don't have to do so much cooking and cleaning by yourself."

She realized her mistake after she had already made it. The insult she had lobbed at her gracious host she'd already offended twice, with her unconventional sensibilities. Rachelle didn't break. She kept whatever ill thoughts to herself, caged by her teeth. She cut her eyes away from Ebony and didn't engage her in anything, not eye contact, not a smile, and no more conversation. James stood from the table and cleared both of their plates. He walked them around the recliner, past where his mother was feeding his father, and into the kitchen. Ebony heard it again. The sound of scraped plates, the running water of the sink, and then the silence Rachelle insisted they exist in.

"Mama, we're going to go," James said stepping out of the kitchen.

Ebony popped up out of her seat, grateful to be put out of her misery. She followed James's earlier path around the recliner toward the mostly open wall leading to two of the three bedrooms in the house.

She said, "It was great meeting you."

Rachelle said nothing to Ebony. She didn't even look in her direction. Instead, she turned to James Senior and said, "Say goodbye to your son, Jamie."

James Senior mimicked Rachelle and said, "Goodbye."

"I'll call you later, Mama."

"Okay, Baby. I'll be here."

Rachelle did not turn away from her husband to look at James or say goodbye. James grabbed Ebony's hand and pulled her the short distance to the door. He turned the simple lock and opened it, stepping outside just in time to see his brother pull up. James marched them toward his car, but his brother's children were already out and running toward him.

Ebony watched as they screeched, "Uncle James, Uncle James, Uncle James."

She laughed watching them jump all over him. He fell to the ground as if they had taken him down.

"Who's that, Uncle James?" Joanna asked.

"That's Ms. Ebony," he said.

"Is she your girlfriend," JoJo said clearly, despite the stutter of his toddler voice.

"You have to ask her, JoJo," James said, turning the kids around to face Ebony standing in the doorway of the car.

"Are you my Uncle James's girlfriend?" JoJo asked.

"Yes, I am," Ebony answered with a big smile, happy to impress someone in James's family.

"Okay, kids," James said standing up. "Uncle James and Ms. Ebony have to go. We gotta pull out so your daddy can pull in."

"Okay."

Ebony laughed louder hearing the immediate sadness in JoJo and Joanna's voices at their pending departure. She slid into the car and closed the door. James got in beside her.

"Your mother hates me," she said as he turned the ignition.

"She doesn't hate you. She just didn't like your question. Why would you ask her that?" James asked backing out of the driveway.

"I don't know. I was just watching her do it all. She missed church to cook all the food. She waits on your dad hand and foot because she has to. That's true love. I just wondered, stupidly I guess, if she had ever considered getting any help."

"My mother is a proud woman. Too proud for her own good. All that bible reading she does and she has yet to realize her pride is a sin."

"I think it's admirable."

"Too bad, she doesn't think that about you."

"I told you she hates me."

"She doesn't hate anybody," James says. "If you ask her, she'll tell you she loves you. But right now I'd say you were in the strong dislike column."

"I'm sorry."

"You don't have to apologize to me. I like it when my mother doesn't like my girlfriends. That means they're really in the relationship to be with me, and not to rush me into marriage and kids like that knucklehead right there," James said nodding toward Joey pulling into the driveway.

James honked his horn twice to tell his brother, niece, and nephew, he was leaving. He saw Joey raise a thumb up in the air as he pulled away from the house. His phone vibrated seconds later. James picked it up and looked at the screen.

I hope you know what to do with all that azz

246.

James put the phone back down, rolled down the windows, and cut the radio on high. His phone vibrated again. He looked at it. Another message from Joey.

Yo, Mama hates your girlfriend. That was the first thing she said to me when I walked in the door

James cleared and then deleted both messages as he maneuvered the traffic to get back on the highway. He grabbed Ebony's hand and brought it to his lap on his upper thigh. She smiled her gratitude. They rode in silence across the bridge back to her house. The radio sang to them, the wind blew on their faces, their thoughts traveled to other places, and other people. James's mind ran back across the bridge to the home of his youth, and Ebony's untimely question about help. He mulled it over in his mind, thinking it wouldn't be such a bad idea. He smiled to himself as he drove, pleased with her concern for his mother and father's well-being. He smiled not know knowing her stale, blank face, was a mask she wore to cover her pain. The pain she felt being rejected by James's mother matched the pain she always carried from being rejected by Ayana, and left by Marilyn. Ebony rode in silence, holding James's hand, the wind blowing on her face, the radio singing sad love songs as she resolved to release yet another woman who could've been her surrogate mother.

27.

Ayana rings the doorbell and waits for an answer. She stands on the small porch, in front of one of the smaller homes in the neighborhood and waits. The warmth of the weather and the moisture in the air form sweat beads beneath her breasts and arms. They hang at her side. Fingers lightly tap the thin material of her cropped jeans. The linen of her butter-yellow blouse suffocates her body as she waits for someone to come to the door, to accept her presence, and to allow her inside.

Her hands move from her thighs to the back of her neck, smoothing, patting, and disturbing the freshly sponged curls of her teeny weeny afro. She takes one coil near her ear and twists it around and around until the curl is elongated into a lock. She grabs another coil beside the one she twisted and rolls it until it's straightened. She takes a third and fourth piece of hair and does the same. It isn't until she has four locks laying against the back of her neck and a fifth coil in her hand that she sees movement on the inside of the house. Ayana quickly loosens her busy work and sloppily tries to reform the tight curls on the stretched pieces of hair.

The door swings wide open. Ebony stands in front of her, her red painted toenails touching the front edge of the threshold. Ayana looks in her younger face with the wild curly hair, and braces herself for rejection.

"You're here."

"I told James last night at the fund-raiser I would come by today."

"He told me."

"I would have told you, but I still don't have your phone number and he won't give it to me."

"I know."

"Are you going to let me in?" Ayana asks looking directly in the eyes she gave her daughter.

"Come in," Ebony says turning away from the door.

"You look nice," Ayana says closing the door behind her.

"Thanks."

Ayana follows Ebony along the cherry hardwood into the kitchen that's become more and more familiar to her with each visit. She doesn't see Ebony's satisfied smile from her benign compliment. She doesn't know the contentment she provided to her daughter by caring. She doesn't know she imbued happiness with her attention.

Ebony says, "Would you like something to drink?"

"Water please," Ayana says. "Is that one of your dresses from the trial?"

"It is," Ebony says smiling to herself.

She gathers together two wine glasses and pulls the pitcher of water out of the refrigerator. She places everything on the peninsula in front of Ayana and pours.

"It looks better without the jacket."

"Thank you," Ebony says.

She conceals her smile by turning around to put the pitcher back in the refrigerator. She moves in slow motion; turning around, resting her elbows on the granite countertop, bringing the wine glass of water to her lips, taking a sip, and swallowing. She relishes in the silence with the stranger she knows, the mother she doesn't, and the woman James told her she should just treat as another woman, one she can decide whether or not to befriend.

"I told James this dress looks better without the jacket, but he didn't want anybody to see my arms or my ass."

"You wore sleeveless to court before though. And I'm sorry to tell you, you can't hide your behind no more than I can hide mine. It runs in the family."

"I know. He just didn't want them to look at my body and see its power and not feel sorry for me."

"Is that why you were always buttoned up to your neck?"

249.

"Yup."

"And it was his idea for you to straighten your hair."

"Yeah. Especially since my mugshot looked crazy."

"I liked your mugshot . . . As a picture I mean."

"Thanks."

"It was the first time I had seen you since . . ."

"Since I left for college."

"No, since your graduation," Ayana says softly.

"You weren't at my graduation."

Ebony stands up straight from the counter. She picks up the glass and drains it. Ayana takes another sip never breaking Ebony's gaze. Trying to impart to her the truth that she was there. She saw her walk across the stage. She shouted for her. She took a picture and kept it all these years in the baby book that is more of a standard photo album. The pictures that don't span an entire lifetime but give snapshots of some moments. Including her mugshot. The mugshot Ayana found online and printed. The picture of her daughter with wild, glass streaked hair, smiling freely, eyes ablaze, in an orange-red county issued jumpsuit.

Ayana says, "I don't know what you were wearing since all I could see was your black gown, the silver shoes you had on, and your butt sticking out because of how high your heels were."

"Maybe you were there," Ebony says going back to the refrigerator for the pitcher to top off their glasses.

"Your hair was straight then, like it was at trial. And you had all those cords around your neck. I remember there was a gold one, a black one, and a blue one."

"There was a white one too."

Ayana nods.

"I can't believe you came to my graduation. How did you even find out?"

"You sent me your grades every semester, so I knew you were on track to graduate on time. I called the registrar and they told me you applied for graduation, and the date, and I drove up there that morning to see you walk across the stage."

"Wow. How did you even get in? I sold all my tickets for twenty-five dollars each."

"I asked this white family if they had any extra tickets outside the civic center. They did. So I got in."

Ebony nods. *Maybe she does love me.* She drinks the water processing what she's learned. The woman she'd tried to forget, didn't forget her. The woman she'd put out of her mind, didn't do the same to her. The woman she blamed, the woman she hated, took it all on herself without complaint. She swallows the last drop and pours the rest of the water from the pitcher into her glass. She moves away from Ayana, away from the revelation, away from what can only be described as a mother's love. She takes the pitcher to the sink and fills it up from the filtered faucet.

Taking it back to the refrigerator she asks, "Why didn't you try to find me after the ceremony?"

"You didn't want to see me. If you wanted me there, you would have invited me. I wanted to be there to see you for myself, so I did, and then I left."

I guess I got what I wanted. Ebony nods again. *I wanted her gone. I pushed her away, and she stayed that way. Mission accomplished.*

Ebony swallows, lifts her glass, and drinks the water, blinking rapidly. She remembers the joy she thought she felt when she would text Ayana once a week, "I'm alive." How she would roll her eyes at her phone from the varied responses. The replies that said "K" or "I love you," or "Be safe." It was the "be safe" message she liked the least. The message that made her humph in her cynicism the hardest. The message that felt most like mothering from the woman she believed was never fit and never wanted to be a mother.

"Why are you here?" Ebony asks more sternly than she intended.

Ayana nods and smiles knowing Ebony is warring with what she feels and how she wants people to see her. It is the way she remembers her acting from a child. The tears Ebony didn't know Ayana heard her cry at night versus the washed face and surly attitude she presented in the morning after the Washingtons' died. The stories Ebony used to tell

251.

her stuffed animals she named Marilyn, Monica, Monique, Isaiah, and Dr. Ivan, when she was alone in her room, she never thought Ayana heard. The hair cut she got in high school to mimic the mother she claimed but passed off as just something she wanted to do. Ayana smiles at the daughter who may never call her any form of the word mom accepting that maybe she doesn't even deserve it. She smiles at the daughter who keeps her at arms distance not knowing she is always with her even when she pushes her away.

"I wanted you to know, I'm going on Dawn's show tomorrow."

"Tomorrow is going to be a busy day," Ebony says.

"Why is that?"

"They're exhuming the body and doing the autopsy tomorrow."

"That's fast. He didn't say which day everything was going to happen when he laid out his plan at the fund-raiser."

"I don't know why not. That's one of the reasons we needed the money. Ms. Nona knew, too, I'm surprised she didn't say anything."

"She seemed like a nice lady."

"She does."

"I saw your friend," Ayana says.

"Who."

"Johnnie. I met her at the trial. She was on the row with me and Dawn every day, and that other girl Sol . . ."

"Soleil."

"Yeah, her."

"Soleil is sweet, but I wouldn't call Johnnie my friend."

"Why is that? She was at the trial every day but verdict day, and you said she's come to visit you, and she was at the fund-raiser. Sounds friendly to me."

"That's only because she feels guilty for what she did."

"What's that?"

"She was the surgeon operating on Barker. She said he could have lived if she wasn't drunk."

"Well, damn."

Ayana soaks up Ebony's words. She sees a defeated expression she's never known, in the times she's known her.. She takes in Ebony's nearly closed eyes, turned down lips, and flattened nose. Her face resigned and acquiescent to someone else's chosen future for her, instead of the one of her own making.

"That's fucked up," Ayana says loudly.

"I know."

"Seems like James is trying to make things right since the doctor spilled her guilty guts."

"We'll see."

"He says you'll be free soon enough. That you'll be able to come out of that anklet and rejoin the rest of the world. Start boxing, training, eating."

"I wouldn't hang my hat on what James says." Ebony sighs.

She walks away from the peninsula leaving Ayana staring at the refrigerator behind her. In the living room she takes a seat on her white suede couch. She piles the canary, salmon and marine colored throw pillows on her body and lays down no longer caring about whether or not her dress gets wrinkled. Ayana turns from facing the kitchen to looking out over the living room. She can't see Ebony wallowing on the couch.

"Why don't you trust what he says?" Ayana asks.

"Because he said I wouldn't even be here. Trial, acquittal, that was it."

"He also didn't expect to be blindsided in court."

"You're taking his side?"

Figures. Ebony sits up on the couch and stares at Ayana. She dares her to repeat what she said, to pick the word of a stranger over the daughter she birthed. She stares daggers into her mother waiting for her to say something to ruin the fragile balance of the relationship they've built over the last two months.

"He's just trying to get you out of the mess you've both gotten yourselves into. You've tunneled too far to turn around and go the other way. Now you have to keep tunneling through until you get to the other side of wherever the hell it is you're going."

"That's prophetic."

"It's life. Fucked up situations and all."

"Seems like my whole life has been one big fucked up situation after another. You, the accident, you, Barker."

"That was mean," Ayana says.

"It's true and you know it."

"I always hated that about you. Your need to hurt people you feel have done you wrong, even when they're trying to do right by you."

"The only person I do that to is you."

"And James," Ayana says.

"You don't even know him. How can you say what I do or don't do to him?"

"Because, I know you."

"Barely."

"So much for our nice visit." Ayana stands up from the bar-stool at the peninsula.

"We can't pretend to be the Brady Bunch forever and act like the fucked-up shit in my life never happened."

"I didn't say forget, Ebony. I suggested working through it and moving on."

"I got too much baggage to move on."

"Girl, I got a barge load of baggage and some extra containers at Jaxport waiting to get on board. But eventually, you gotta put that shit down and move on."

"How can I move on? I have no closure. You won't even fucking apologize for the shit you did."

"I did a lot of bad shit, Ebony."

"Exactly my point. You've never even said sorry for it. How many nights did I sleep in the car, huh? Because you were too trifling to wake me up and bring me inside because all you wanted to do was pop them damn pills in peace. Peace I would ruin if you had to do anything for me."

Ebony's honesty stuns Ayana into silence. Memories her daughter has that she doesn't. Memories she will never have. Memories she erased with illegal medications because at the time she didn't want to think, she didn't want to feel, she didn't want to raise a child, alone, in the house her parents left her.

Ayana stands between the bar-stools and the couch. Her toes press into the thin soles of her costume jeweled flip flops. Her hands find their way to her head. To the nape of her neck. To the coils she stretched and re-curled. The strands of hair she rolled into locks as she waited to be rejected. The same rejection she felt years ago when Ebony picked the Washington's over her, is the same rejection she feels now for being put off, put out, by the woman she's no longer allowed to access as a daughter.

Ayana drops one hand from her hair to wipe her eyes. Warm, unfettered tears run down her raw cheeks. She dabs at her face with the back of her hand in silence drawing no attention to her overflow of emotion, to her own sadness, pain, and torture, haunted by the nightmares that she tormented the one person she was supposed to love. Ayana cries alone in her daughter's home, not knowing Ebony is blinking back her own tears on the couch. They let the silence subsume them in their equal obstinance.

Ayana breaks first.

"I'm sorry I left you sleeping in the car and for every other horrible thing I did that I can't remember."

It's too late now. Ebony keeps her body pressed into the couch, curled around the cushions, still dissatisfied.

"I didn't deserve you," Ayana continues. "And when I thought I did, you didn't want me. It used to kill me to watch you playing with them in their backyard, on their blankets, during their family picnics. I used to watch you watching them from the back porch until you worked up the nerve to ask if you could go outside. Then I'd watch you from the backdoor laughing and playing and trying not to get on anybody's nerve before they sent you back to me. As much as I wanted to come outside and get you, and play with you myself, I knew you wouldn't have me. So I'd take the pills and go lay down and start the shit all over again."

Ebony lays on the couch remembering those picnics. The Washingtons' red-checkered blankets. Their water gun fights. Marilyn's desserts she made from scratch. Her sweet potato pie and New York style cheesecake with a fresh watermelon drizzle instead of the traditional cherry. Ebony cries more salty tears into her pillows remembering the life she lost when the Washington's lost their lives.

"It should've been you," Ebony croaks. "It should've been you that died in that crash. Not them. They didn't deserve it."

Ayana feels her bottom lip trembling. She gets up from the bar-stool and gathers her purse as tears stream down her face. She doesn't question Ebony's wants; what she's wished for all these years.

"Why now?" Ebony cries from the couch. "All the years I wanted a mother, needed a mother, just wanted you to act like you gave a damn and you didn't. Why now?"

Ebony's sobs into the couch overtake her voice. She doesn't look up to see Ayana in her own agony. Battling the enemy of her inner me Ebony wails into the pillows until her sobs are so heightened they drown out Ayana's "I'm gone."

Ayana walks toward the door quickly. She turns the handle to step through the threshold as James comes in the back door off the garage.

"Hey." Ayana's voice comes out in a strained croak.

"Hey," James says. "I didn't realize you were still here."

"We had a longer visit today."

"Are you crying? Is she. . . Is she crying?" James asks.

"Yeah. We talked about what happened. Some of it . . . Anyway . . . Wrecked both of us."

"Why's that?"

"Let her tell you," Ayana says.

"I guess I have to wait for her to shoot somebody else before that happens."

Ayana chuckles through her own tears. "I'm gone. I said what I had to say."

"And what was that?"

"I'm going to be on Dawn's show tomorrow. Just wanted her to know before she thought I was trying to blindside her, hurt her case, or any other crazy thing she might come up with."

"Good to know," James says.

"Goodbye."

"See you on TV."

Ayana walks out Ebony's front door and does not look back. She doesn't wait to hear if James clicked the lock. She doesn't text him to see if Ebony is okay in her absence. *I can't fix this*, she thinks to herself as she gets in her old LeSabre and drives away from the neighborhood that looks like the one she grew up in with her own parents. She drives away from the side of town where she lived the majority of her life, and where Ebony had spent the happiest years of hers making memories without her. Ayana drives away from Mandarin, on the highway, racing through construction zones, ignoring troopers sitting in plain sight waiting to catch certain profiled speeders.

I can't fix this.

It is her consistent chorus as she zooms across the three-mile-long Buckman Bridge. She crosses the river shining brightly against the blue November sky until she reaches her part of town. Her county away from the trauma of childhoods and young single parents. *I should have never gone to see her in the first place. Should have told James to never call me again after he found me. I could have stayed dead to her. That's what she wanted anyway.*

Ayana hears Ebony's shrill cries of "it should've been you" as she drives the quaint streets of Orange Park. A fresh set of tears fall as she waits in the bumper to bumper traffic on roads jam-packed with strip malls, and tightly packed cars trying to get to the one decent shopping center for the area. She drives fighting the tears, telling herself to hold her composure, and to practice for TV where she will have only her truth to tell.

28.

"We're following breaking news right now on *Dawn in the Evening*," Dawn says into her camera. "A second autopsy is underway on the body of the late Judge Barker Gordon. 9 News Now brought you live coverage starting just after ten this morning when crews, authorized by Judge Gordon's mother, began to exhume the body. Tonight we're getting reaction from those close to the case and the appeal of Ebony Jones. Joining me right now is Ayana Jones, Ebony Jones's mother, in a 9 News Now exclusive interview. Ayana, how are you?"

"I'm well," Ayana says rubbing her hands on her thighs beneath the desk.

"How is Ebony?" Dawn asks.

"She's as well as can be expected. Anxious mostly."

Ayana resists the urge to turn away from Dawn's face and look into one of the three cameras surrounding the glass desk in the cold studio. She feels air and heat at the same time from the open vent and the burning lights. She smiles tightly holding Dawn's gaze, listening for the next question.

"Do you think the exhumation of Judge Gordon's body will benefit your daughter's appeal effort?"

"I can only hope so," Ayana says.

"Do you think your daughter was unfairly convicted?"

"I'm not sure you want me to answer that question, my opinion is obviously biased."

"Is that a yes, you think your daughter was unfairly convicted?"

Dawn told her she would push her with questions she didn't have to answer. Ayana sits at the desk a mask of pleasantness waiting for her to move on. To realize this is one of those questions she will not be forced, baited, or coerced into answering.

Dawn tousles her bangs with a shake of her head and leans her face and upper body closer to Ayana. She can smell her own perfume and lotion combination through the v-neck of her kelly green and gold flecked blouse. She smiles widely with her teeth barely touching, partially toward Ayana, and partially toward the camera.

"It seems to me," Dawn begins, "A conviction on a charge of culpable negligence is a slap on the wrist considering your daughter killed a judge and fled the scene."

"She was abused, and she turned herself in."

"She claimed she was abused."

"You were in court beside me. You saw the same blown up photos of Ebony's injuries that I did."

"So did the jury."

"What's your point?"

"My point is that, despite the powerful imagery, Ebony has still been convicted of a crime."

"But not the crime she was originally charged for. She was convicted of being reckless with her gun. But I don't see how."

"So you disagree with the jury's point of view?"

"Absolutely."

"Why is that?"

"She has a concealed carry permit. There was nothing reckless about her having it in her hoodie when she went to meet him."

"But he was killed."

"He died."

"From a gunshot wound. From bullets that matched your daughters gun."

"A gun that fired when he slammed my daughter so hard against her own car she dented the door, shattered the glass, and cut her scalp despite all the hair on her head."

Ayana holds Dawn's gaze and resists the urge to fan her face or wrap her arms around her body. She resists the urge to show she is weak, any less strong than the woman sitting across from her. *You will not win this* Ayana thinks as she waits for Dawn to ask another question.

Dawn turns her head and then her body away from Ayana making sure her swivel is deliberate. She makes sure her body language communicates to the woman beside her and those watching from their side of the television that she is still in control, that they are still watching her show, Dawn in the Evening, and she is still, Dawn Anthony.

She says with a slight smize into the lens, "We'll be right back with more from Ayana Jones."

Dawn gives a sultry stare into the camera until she hears her mic click in the studio.

"What the hell was that?"

"Kelly, we needed to go to break and regroup," Dawn says aloud in the studio. "Just add the time to the next segment."

"There wasn't supposed to be a next segment with Ayana," Kelly whisper-yells through Dawn's ear piece.

"Well, now there is."

Ayana watches the one sided tete-a-tete unclear whether the conversation is about her.

"What about the other guests?"

"Send Jennifer out to tell them we'll do the other topics with them tomorrow if they can come back."

"Can't," Jennifer says walking into the studio. "How much time is left in this break, John?"

"Ninety."

"What is it?" Dawn asks.

"We've got breaking. I saw this come in through email and printed it. Thought it'd be better if you just read it and got a natural reaction from Ms. Jones."

"What is it that it requires so much secrecy?" Dawn asks.

"Just look it over." Jennifer hands the printed email to Dawn and walks out of the studio.

"Thirty," John yells aloud from the floor.

"Anything you can let me in on so I don't make a fool of myself?" Ayana asks craning her neck to read the sheet of paper sitting in front of Dawn.

"The autopsy results came in," she answers.

"Ten seconds."

"What do they say?" Ayana asks.

"We're about to find out."

Dawn pulls out her mirror from beneath the desk and shakes her bangs, purses her lips to spread the color of her lipstick, checks her teeth for stains, and then puts it back as John's hands reach zero.

Her mic clicks.

"Breaking news right now on *Dawn in the Evening*. In the last two minutes, we received an email from James Parnell, the attorney for Ebony Jones. It includes the preliminary results of the second autopsy on Judge Barker Gordon, conducted this afternoon. The handwritten report, which I have here, from the independently hired medical examiner says Judge Gordon's body does show evidence of the possibility of medical malpractice during the surgery to remove the bullet and repair his wounds. However, Doctor Belinda Little says she can't say with certainty if the discrepancy in Judge Gordon's treatment is due to intentional ill will, or just gross negligence on the part of the presiding surgeon."

Dawn takes a beat to let her words sink in to the audience and to Ayana beside her. She swivels her seat, so her body turns first before her head snaps to the other camera that will capture her and Ayana together. With one eyebrow raised she looks between the long layers of her hair and then turns to Ayana with a smirk of a smile.

Halfway to the camera and halfway to her guest she says, "If you're just joining us, the mother of Ebony Jones, Ms. Ayana Jones is here with me tonight. Ayana, you just heard the findings of Doctor Little's autopsy this afternoon, right here on *Dawn in the Evening*. What do you think about the report from her procedure."

"I want to know if what she says is right, how come the first medical examiner didn't find the same thing."

"Are you pleased with Doctor Little's report?"

"I won't be pleased until Ebony is truly free. For now this is just another Doctor's theory of what happened. Right now it don't mean sh. . . Sorry. Right now it doesn't mean anything until the judge says it does."

"Do you think Ebony is happy with the outcome of the doctor's autopsy."

"If she's anything like me, she's probably pissed?"

"Why would she be angry?"

"Because she said she didn't kill him in the first place. She was convicted of a crime she didn't commit, and damn near, excuse me, went broke trying to prove she was telling the truth the whole time, and she's still waiting. Yeah. If she is anything like me, she's probably pissed."

"One minute left in show," Dawn hears in her ear.

She nods at the camera to let Kelly know she got the message and then turns back to stare directly at Ayana. She gives the audience her complete profile, the first mistake you learn not to make in a broadcasting class.

"One last question," Dawn says.

"Go ahead." Ayana gestures with open palms.

"What do you think it will take for your daughter to be a free woman again?"

Ayana waits for what seems like minutes before answering the question. *I gotta take my time with this one.* She sees the large white man on the floor of the newsroom make a weird symbol with his hand she assumes to be another time cue.

She exhales deeply and says on the end of the breath, "Understanding."

"Understanding," Dawn repeats with a double nod before turning away from Ayana. "Thank you, Ms. Jones, for joining us tonight, and to medical expert Doctor Elias Atterby who was with us in our first half hour. And to you at home, thank you for watching, I'm Dawn Anthony, and *this is, Dawn in the Evening.*"

Dawn's microphone clicks in the studio.

"That was great. Thank you for coming," Dawn says.

"You're welcome," Ayana answers.

Ayana watches Dawn untangle herself from the cords that keep her broadcasting over the air, thinking *this was a mistake.* She watches as she unthreads the microphone cord from where it is clipped to one of the lapels of the v-neck in her blouse. She pulls it from around the back of her neck until she can lay it freely on the glass desk in front of her. *I should've known she only cared about making herself look good and not Ebony.* Dawn removes the battery pack from the waist band of her skirt and lays it on the desk.

"Do you treat guests like this all the time?" Ayana asks hopping down from her swivel chair.

"What do you mean?"

"I mean, be all nice to them before they get here, when you're asking them to come on your show, and then flip the script and act like a bitch once the show starts."

Dawn smiles with her lips only as she steps down from the desk.

She says, "My job is to tell stories that matter and make great TV. Tonight you were part of that. Like I told you in the beginning, I will ask anything I want, but that doesn't mean you have to answer."

"Maybe not, but you push until you get the answers you want anyway so what's the point in even giving that little speech in the beginning."

"To prepare you for what is to come." Dawn sighs. "Look, your answers were great. You protected and stuck to the story Ebony and James have been telling since the beginning, and your reaction to the autopsy report was great. You did a great job tonight for yourself, for Ebony, and James. You stayed on message. Consider it a success."

"It wasn't a message. It was the truth," Ayana says walking out of the studio.

"Let me walk you out."

Dawn trots to catch up with Ayana. Once they're in step, Dawn increases her pace slightly to show her through the newsroom, and down the hall past the bevy of sales offices for those who focus on bringing advertisers in to keep the news on. Dawn leads her through the tiled front office, filled with real plants of varying sizes, the desk from where the receptionist has already departed, and an unarmed guard standing outside the sliding glass doors in the parking lot.

"Thank you again for coming," Dawn says.

"The pleasure was all yours," Ayana says leaving.

Dawn watches her walk away from the building, and across the parking lot to the old Buick that still looks in pristine condition, at least from the outside. She sees the last of Ayana's picked out hair, and her purple blazer from the fund-raiser that she wore over a white shirt, and black pants, disappear inside the car. *If I had been nice and asked softball questions the interview would've been boring, and I wouldn't be where I am.* Ayana's engine rumbles to life, she pulls forward and waits for the wrought iron gates to open completely before driving through. *Somebody has to ask the hard questions. It might as well be me.* Dawn waits until Ayana's car disappears around the corner away from the station before she turns around and walks back to the newsroom.

She walks quickly to the set where her crew is waiting on her to tape three promos for the next day's show.

"There you are," Boyce says, confronting her as she enters the large empty newsroom.

"I didn't know I was lost."

"I want to introduce you to somebody," he says motioning toward the woman beside him.

"Hello. I'm Dawn Anthony."

"I know," the woman says in an accent Dawn can't immediately place. "I was watching from Mr. Butler's office. Your show was great. Especially your interview with Ebony's mom. That was awesome."

"Thank you . . ."

"Naomi," the woman says. "Naomi Grace."

"Naomi is interviewing with us today and tomorrow," Boyce says. "Right now she's reporting in New Orleans, and anchors on the weekends, but she's looking to make a move."

Dawn nods and smiles with her wide anchor grin.

"Good luck to you," she says.

"Oh, Dawn," Boyce calls her back. "I want her to shadow you for a moment. She can watch you tape your promos, go to your post meeting and ask a few questions. I know we'll be busy in the morning and she has an early afternoon flight back to the Big Easy."

"Oh. Well, follow me."

Naomi shifts the weight of her aqua tote bag on her shoulder and walks behind Dawn past the desks of the producers who are there putting together her 11 p.m. newscast. Dawn gets to the edge of the newsroom and steps from behind the backdrop on to the set.

"This is it," Dawn says.

"It's beautiful. Smaller than it looks on TV though."

"Pardon?"

"I watched your coverage of the Ebony Jones case online back at home. The set looks a lot bigger on TV than it does with me standing in it now."

"The magic of television, I guess."

"Dawn, your mic is still on the table where you left it," John says from behind the camera.

"Naomi, that's John our floor director. My producers, Kelly and Jennifer, are upstairs in the control room. I'm going to get hooked up to tape these promos. If you want you can watch from the couches of the interview set, or from the weather office in the back. It's right behind the cameras through those frosted glass doors."

"I'll wait on set, if that's alright with you."

"Be my guest."

Naomi walks over to the couches and sets her bag down before she sits beside it. Dawn busies herself with reattaching her microphone and battery pack. Her head down to the floor, she fidgets with the clips and cords until she is ready to record. She reaches under the desk and grabs her mirror. Turning her body slightly she looks through the glass at her own reflection and the golden-brown skinned woman behind her. The woman in the white sheath dress and the blue topaz belt demarcating her small waist from the rest of her body.

He thinks he's so slick. Like I wouldn't remember he did this when he brought me in.

265.

Dawn looks at the woman sitting where she sat more than four years ago when she came in for her own interview from Toledo. Then she wore a plain black suit. Boyce brought her in, introduced her to Julia, Julia took her to set, and she like Naomi opted to sit on set instead of waiting in the weather office. Four years later Julia is gone, and Naomi sits on the couch watching, waiting, ready, and eager.

"Dawn, are you ready?" She hears through her ear piece.

"One second."

She looks at herself in the mirror her irritation apparent on her smooth licorice skin, bobbed hair, and fading makeup. *I called it. So much for being a valued asset of the 9 News Now team.* Dawn grabs the compact she keeps under the desk, when she's on set, opens it up, and powders her face full of foundation until the shine is gone and the richness of her color restored. She shakes her hair, parts her long bangs, purses her lips, and smiles to check her teeth. Dawn places the mirror and compact back on the shelf inside the desk.

"Ready," she says aloud.

John holds up his hands. "In three, two, one, cue, Dawn."

The mic clicks.

29.

Johnnie clicks off the television mounted on the wall in the bedroom. She stares at the black abyss of the screen in front of her. The screen that was previously illuminated with Dawn breaking the news of her failure. Her mind thinks the worst as she sees her impending arrest, trial, conviction, and imprisonment flash before her eyes; the loss of Nathan, Tyler, Danielle.

"Danielle," she whispers aloud.

Johnnie jumps out the bed. The new fat around her belly jiggles more than it did last week. More than yesterday. She walks out of the door and down the hall. The fat of her legs at her inner thighs rubs through the material of her blue scrubs she used to wear at the hospital, in the operating room, doing only what she used to be able to do, save lives.

She pushes the door open to Danielle's room. The Minnie Mouse night light plugged into the wall creates an amber, angelic glow across her face. She's fast asleep, her face pressed to the pillow, eyes squeezed tight, mouth open, butt hiked in the air. Johnnie walks into the room and switches out the light. She moves Danielle's body back to the middle of the bed to keep her from falling out, then pulls the sheet and comforter that matches the nightlight, pillowcase, and curtains over her body. Johnnie leans over and kisses Danielle on the forehead then turns to walk out. She leaves the door cracked behind her.

In the next room Tyler is sprawled across the bed. Noise canceling headphones on his ears, his phone in his hand, a girl on the screen.

Johnnie pulls up one ear of the headphones.

"Maaaaa."

"Who are you talking to?"

"Amri."

"Well tell Amri goodnight. It's after nine o'clock. You don't want her parents to think you don't have no home training."

"Alright, Mama, I will."

"Right now, before I tell her good night for you."

"I'll talk to you tomorrow," he ends the call on the phone. Happy now?"

"Don't get an attitude with me . . . before you're on punishment for the next month."

"Sorry, Mama. Goodnight."

"And don't call her back again. You can see her at school tomorrow."

"Alright, Mama."

Johnnie closes the door to Tyler's room and stops at the banister. She considers going downstairs to talk to Nathan. She considers it but decides against it. She walks back to her room and closes the door. She is left in darkness, blinds and curtains closed, the television off. She stares at the black screen and remembers why she left the room. *I can't lose my kids.*

Johnnie sprawls across the bed. Her body hits something hard. She pulls her phone from underneath her back. The screen illuminates from her touch. She has three missed calls. They are from Taylor. Her teacher. Her mentor. The Dean of Medicine at the illustrious University of Florida Health hospital where she used to work.

Johnnie slides her finger across his name to dial the number. The call barely rings through her ear before his anxious voice comes through the phone.

"Did you see the news?" He asks breathlessly.

"I should be asking you the same question. He was my patient."

"I fixed it for you. Signed my name on the death certificate instead of yours. I didn't think anyone would ever find out. How the hell did they find out?"

Johnnie remains silent on the phone knowing she should tell the same truth to Taylor she told Ebony and Dawn. She hopes her silence is answer enough, that her non-denial is confirmation enough. Johnnie waits with the phone suspended on her shoulder, barely touching her ear. She waits for Taylor to gather what she's not saying, for him to surmise the answer to his own question, to assume what he thinks about her and believe in its truth.

"What's next?" Johnnie asks.

"In the morning I will tender my resignation effective immediately."

"I doubt Ms. Nona sues."

"That's good news for you, Johnnie, but somebody's head will have to roll for this, and it looks like it's going to be mine."

"I'm sorry, Taylor."

"It's not your fault, Johnnie. I've been in medicine a long time. I was just trying to help you out because I know how these mistakes get made. I know what burnout looks like. I just always thought I'd die in the hospital at my desk."

"That's morbid."

"No, Johnnie. That's real. If it's not a career you would die doing then it's not a career and it's not worth it."

"You said that to me when I first started."

"I meant it then and I mean it now.

"Thank you, Taylor."

"You're welcome. You should be able to get your old job back whenever you're ready, though my recommendation won't mean much after tomorrow, I never told them why you left."

"You blamed it on burnout?"

"Like I said, I know what it looks like."

"Thank you, Taylor."

"Goodnight, Johnnie. You take care of yourself."

The line clicks. The phone drops from her shoulder and lands behind her head. She doesn't bother to move it despite all the studies about cell phone radiation and cancer.

"Wooh!"

She exhales. As quickly as she imagined herself being carted off to prison, she now imagines herself returning to the hospital. *I can't wait to get back to work.* Her mind's eye imagines herself back in the operating room, the bright round lights beaming down on her as she stands in front of an open body in an effort to preserve limbs and life. She sits up in the bed. The action takes extra effort. The once flat muscles of her abdomen are soft and pudgy, covered in the fat of her stress, the comfort of food, her replacement for vodka, gin and if she was desperate wine. The bottom of her belly rests on her legs like it did when she was pregnant. *I have got to get this off of me.* Johnnie stands up from the bed before the contact of her skin produces heat and sweat in the least attractive of places.

Johnnie crosses the room, opens the door, and walks out into the darkened hallway. She flips the wall switch on the staircase and descends. Each step brings her closer to Nathan. She can hear the television playing from the living room. A game show is on from what she can tell by the hoaky music and the unnatural cheeriness of the host's voice. Nathan is sprawled across the couch, a book across his chest, glasses he just started wearing on the floor beside the remote control, and a half full bottle of beer.

Johnnie picks up the bottle and walks it to the kitchen. She can smell whatever mixture of grains and hops was used to make the liquid in the green bottle. The smell of the beer nearly makes her wretch. She holds her breath as she empties the bottle into the sink. Johnnie quickly runs water to chase the alcohol down the drain, then pours dishwashing liquid and bleach behind that to replace the smell of the beer in her nose with an antiseptic that has the hint of lemon. Only once the sink is clean and the smell of beer no longer a nauseating trigger of how she used to get sloshed, does she stop breathing through her mouth and inhales through her nose. Johnnie leaves the beer bottle on the counter above the space where the trash can goes. She will make Tyler take it and the pile of recyclables out to the canisters in the garage in the morning.

With tentative steps she walks back over to Nathan. She doesn't want to wake him, but she does. She doesn't want to argue but she wants to give him an update. She looks down on his sleeping frame. The couch he's taken to since the fund-raiser. The spot he's occupied to avoid her and her assumptions of infidelity. She removes the book from his body and puts it on the floor beside his glasses. Hands pick up the remote and mute the TV. It is a glowing beacon of silence. Johnnie pushes his feet off the couch to make room for herself to sit down.

He startles awake. "What are you doing?"

"Did you see the news?"

"I saw it."

"You didn't say anything."

"You haven't spoken to me in two days. I'm not trying to argue with you."

Johnnie stills her voice and blows air out of her nose. "I'm not trying to argue now. I came to tell you I spoke to Taylor."

"And?"

"He's retiring."

"What does that have to do with what the doctor found out about the body?"

"I never signed the paperwork for the surgery or the death certificate. Taylor did. He signed his own name. So he's retiring in the morning and I can go back to work."

"Is that something you want to do?"

"It beats sitting around the house all day cooking, cleaning, eating and get fat. I do more of the last two than the first two anyway."

"You can be at home and not eat as much," Nathan says.

"Thanks."

"I didn't mean it like that."

"Yes, you did, but it's cool. I'm getting too damn big anyway. I'll work on it. Work on me. Just like everything else."

Nathan asks, "Are you going to find time to work on us?"

"What?"

"Are you going to find time to work on us?"

"I heard what you said the first time. I just don't know what you mean."

"We can't keep living like this, Jonelle."

"I'm not going to let you sleep in my bed and you're lying to me every day."

"Johnnie, I'm not lying. I didn't fuck Lisa."

"I don't believe you."

Nathan opens his mouth to speak but doesn't. He tries again but nothing comes out. Even in the semi-darkness of the TV lit room he still knows what her face looks like. He knows how her eyes droop when she is tired, how her temple pulses when she is angry, and how her entire face seems to sag when she is resigned; when she has given up. It is this last look he knows she has now. He can see it from the shadows in her face beside him. He knows she's giving up on him and their marriage. Ready to live life apart, in separate beds and in separate rooms. *This would be so much easier if I had just cheated.*

He stands up not knowing what else to do. Disarmed by her vulnerability, her admitted lack of trust and belief in his word, he walks around the sofa and into the kitchen. He opens the refrigerator. His hand touches a bottle of beer first before moving to a plastic water bottle. He pulls it out, twists the top, and takes a gulp inside the doorway. He closes the refrigerator. She is still there, sitting in her silence, in her disbelief, waiting for him to make it right.

"Johnnie," he says. "I was wrong for having her in the house with Danielle that day. I didn't think you'd be getting back so soon."

"So you're only apologizing because you got caught. Nathan, that's even more fucked up."

"Johnnie, that's not what I mean."

"Then say what you mean," she says crossing her arms.

"I mean Danielle invited her inside after she dropped her off and I didn't say no, because I didn't want to hear her whine for not getting her way."

"Oh please. Be an adult."

"I am, Johnnie, if you'd just listen. Damn."

"I'm listening."

"The first time I took Dani to the zoo, Dani saw her and wanted us all to walk together. She was there with her niece or nephew or sister something. I don't know. So we walked together and did all the stuff at the zoo together."

"What does that have to do with her being in my house, laughing and joking with my husband, and my daughter, like I didn't even fucking exist."

"I just told you Danielle invited her in and I didn't tell her no. When you walked in you saw the end of the tickle monster game, and that's why we were all laughing and rolling around on the floor."

"So you left the house for six whole months because Danielle invited the teacher's assistant inside? Bullshit."

"I left because you were drunk. I left because you needed help.

"You abandoned me, didn't tell me where you were, what you were doing, where my kids were even living, and it's all my fault. I'm done, Nathan. I'm sober. I can go back to work, continue making my living, and you can do whatever the fuck it is you want to do with your precious Lisa."

"Johnnie, stop. She's not precious anything. If I wanted to fuck Lisa, I would've fucked Lisa. It's not like she wasn't trying to throw ass my way. I just didn't catch it."

"Don't act like you're doing me any favors."

"I'm not acting like anything. I'm telling you the truth. You had been around here hiding your drinking for years. Years. The only reason you stopped is because you got caught at work and Taylor told you to take a break. I had to standby and pretend like I didn't see all the bottles in the recycling bin. Like I didn't know what you used to keep in that white water bottle. Why you lost your shit when you caught Danielle drinking from it when she was three. You needed a wake up call and losing your job because you killed a man wasn't enough. I'm not going to have my children around somebody drunk and belligerent, I don't care who they are."

"Are you done?"

"Yeah, I'm done."

"Good."

Johnnie turns to walk away.

"You don't have anything else to say?" Nathan asks.

"Nope."

"You think I'm still lying."

"Nathan, I know you're still lying. You can blame me. You can even blame Danielle for your transgressions. You can say it was about my drinking or whatever else you want to make it about, but it still doesn't explain why you were walking around smelling like fucking lemon grass and jasmine for months. For months before the field trip, when in all the years I've known you you've only worn Old Spice."

"Johnnie . . ."

"Don't Johnnie me. You say she threw you ass. I know she did and you caught that shit without question."

Johnnie walks away from Nathan. She turns and goes back up the stairs, down the hall, and into her room closing the door behind her. Splayed across the bed, her phone in her hand, there is one more person left to call. One more person to talk to about her future or her fate. She finds his name and dials. The line rings, and rings, and rings. . .

"Hello."

"Hi James, this is Dr. Edwards."

"Who?"

"Dr. Edwards. Dr. Johnnie Edwards."

"What can I do for you?"

"I'm calling because I of course saw the news. Congratulations, I guess, on finding the smoking gun, so to speak, to help Ebony."

"We couldn't have done it without you."

"It was the right thing to do."

"Yeah. Better late, than never. Right. Isn't that what you said."

"I just wanted to make it right."

"Thank you. You did. Is that all?"

"Well . . . No . . . I was calling to find out whether . . ."

James interrupts her broken train of thought, "We're not coming after you, Dr. Edwards. No one knows it was you but that fella who signed all of Judge Gordon's paperwork. Ms. Nona doesn't want to hurt anybody, she just wants to help Ebony and be done with all of this."

"I understand."

"The only way you'll get in trouble is if there's an internal review at the hospital and that has nothing to do with the legal system."

"Thank you."

"You're welcome. Goodnight."

"So what's next for Ebony and the case?" Johnnie rushes before he hangs up the phone.

"We wait," James says. "We wait on the courts. The never swift hand of justice."

Part 3

"When justice is done, it brings joy to the righteous but terror to evildoers."

— Proverbs 21:15

"If you want to say that I was a drum major, say that I was a drum major for justice. Say that I was a drum major for peace. I was a drum major for righteousness."

— Martin Luther King, Jr.

30.

Friday, April 17, 2015

Breaking news right now on Dawn in the Evening. A judge with the first district court of appeals in Tallahassee overturned the conviction of Ebony Jones on culpable negligence in the death of Judge Barker Gordon. The court ruled Jones is to be released from house arrest immediately after examining the findings of independent medical examiner, Doctor Belinda Little, who suggested there was evidence of medical malpractice. In the opinion the appellate judge in the case ruled, the findings of Doctor Little create more than just reasonable doubt but point to an entirely different suspect who has yet to be held responsible for the death of Judge Barker Gordon. It goes on to say Ebony Jones, a licensed gun owner, has been wrongly convicted and is guilty of nothing than for failing to protect herself against an abusive man of the law. The court wishes her it's sincerest apologies.

"You should be all set, ma'am," the geeky man says as he gathers his bag of tools from the countertop.

"Thank you," Ebony says, still holding on to her unshackled ankle.

"I'm going to make my way on out."

"I'll go with you."

"You sure you want to do that, ma'am? There's whole teams of reporters out there swarming your yard."

"I haven't been outside this house unless it was for court in more than a year. I don't care who's outside. I'm going."

"Suit yourself, ma'am."

"I will. Follow me."

Ebony stands up from the couch where she sat clutching her newly freed leg. She walks onto the hardwood floors and leads the way to the front door. She doesn't pause or hesitate to open the door and greet the people doing their jobs who have been trying to talk to her for months. She pulls the door back and deliberately steps outside in her bare feet to allow the technician from the department of corrections to leave with his bag containing her former ankle monitor, and the monitored alarm system that was supposed to sound anytime she crossed a threshold to the outer world she was barred from entering for thirteen months.

She hears questions flying at her as the reporters crowd her small porch. In the background she sees James waiting to turn in her neighborhood.

"Please make some room," she says.

The corrections technician takes a tentative step down off the porch. The six reporters surrounding her split half and half to allow the man in the blue work jumpsuit, with greasy hair to pass through. It takes the camera men longer to adjust. Ebony watches James turn into the neighborhood and then in to the driveway and into her garage. She knows he is anxious to stand beside her to monitor what questions she answers. She waits while the technician maneuvers his body and his bags through the crowd. He squeezes through the men loaded down with cameras, backpacks that produce live signals, and boom mics with fluffy ends that will pick up the slightest sound from Ebony breathing too loudly.

"What are you doing?" James asks, stepping out the front door.

"Waiting for you."

"Ms. Jones, how do you feel now that you're a free woman."

"Good," Ebony answers.

"Attorney Parnell, will you and Ms. Jones file suit against the hospital for their part in her wrongful conviction?"

"No."

"Attorney Parnell, I'm Naomi Grace from 9 News Now. You obviously had a close relationship with Judge Barker Gordon and knew his family as well. Are they still seeking justice in his death?"

"If you're referring to Judge Gordon's mother, Ms. Nona Gordon, the answer is no. She is not looking to press charges against the doctors, hospital, or medical staff for the death of her son. She told me months ago that she is ready for this to all be over."

"Will the state attorney be going after the hospital?" Naomi asks.

"You'd have to ask the state attorney."

"Do you plan to return to your former job as a prosecutor with the State Attorney's Office?" Naomi follows up.

"At this point, I don't know what I plan to do next," James says to the reporters rapt with attention. "I started my career as a prosecutor and have proven to be an okay defense attorney considering the circumstances. The only thing I want to do right now is eat and take a nap. Thank you."

He turns around to go back in the house. Ebony follows.

"Ms. Jones, one last question," Naomi says before Ebony shuts the door completely.

"Go ahead."

"What do you plan to do now."

"Take a vacation."

Ebony closes the door and turns the lock. She walks into the bedroom where James is sprawled across the bed. She lays down beside him, curls her legs and wraps them around his body, rubbing against his side.

"Somebody's happy," he says rolling over to face her.

"Got that damn thing off my leg. I'm super happy."

"Good for you."

James rolls onto his stomach. He plants his face in the covers. Ebony taps him with her free ankle again. He lifts his head.

"Thank you," she says.

James rolls back to face her. Her face is stress free, no longer wracked with worry about sentencing, and prison. She is no longer watching episodes of *Orange is the New Black* to glean what prison life will be like from Taystee, Poussey, and Black Cindy. He pulls her closer to his face until they are nose to nose. Until they are breathing the same breath and their foreheads touch. With her legs still wrapped across his body and her face against his, she reaches for his hand. She flattens it on the bed and places her hand on top of it.

"Thank you," she says again.

"I told you I'd get it done as long as you told me the truth."

"I know."

"Now you know."

"Okay. Now I know."

"Your head is as hard, as your ass is big," he says slapping her butt.

"I know. All the weight I've lost, and this thing ain't going nowhere."

"I'm glad," James says.

He closes his eyes and exhales away what stress he can get rid of. He tries to enjoy the moment. To keep the question of *what's next* from running over and over in his mind. To not think about his own affairs. His mortgage, his mother, his father, his future. He tries to push back any thoughts that will make him angry, defensive, but one won't leave him alone. One thought nags at him and nags at him. He opens his eyes and looks up at the tray ceiling. The ceiling he's stared at so many times as she's laid beside him sleeping, dreaming, wrestling with her own demons. He traces the pattern of the layered boxes that remind him of the inside top of a coffin until he's been nagged enough by his own mind that he has no choice but to speak out loud.

He says, "The last time we were like this I told you something and you didn't respond."

"What are you talking about?"

"You said, 'wait until the jury delivers a guilty verdict and see how much love we have for each other then.'"

"I did."

"You've been convicted, and now that conviction is overturned."

"It is."

"You're free."

"It doesn't feel like it. Even going outside just a minute ago didn't even feel real."

"But you are, and it is."

"Just like your love for me?"

"I've got more than love for you, Ebony. I said I love you. That's a whole different configuration of words."

I love you too is not enough.

Ebony sighs in no rush to untangle her complicated feelings for James. She doesn't want to talk. She doesn't want to fight. She doesn't want to ruin the moment of their victory, her freedom, with words that will become misunderstood, and broken hearts that can't be put back together. Instead she moves her legs from across his body and puts her knees against the zipper of his pants. She closes whatever space is left between their faces and kisses his lips. Softly, at first. Gently, until he allows her the space and time to kiss away his questions with her actions. He allows her to erase his curiosities with the comfort of her tongue. She kisses him and works her knees against his pants until he kisses her back.

He kisses her back with the force of the love his words did not convey. His hands tangle in her hair as he rolls her on her back. His body flat against hers, entwined at the mouth they kiss, rolling tongues until they are forced to break apart and breathe. They're breaths are short. They're break insignificant. They rush back to each other hungry to express what words cannot. Kissing, biting, lapping, her hands work at his waist unbuckling his belt, unbuttoning his pants and pulling his zipper down. She works the bunch of his encumbered clothes down his hips until he sprints his legs free and pushes his feet out of his socks. He presses into her. His growing erection lays on the belly of her white dress. The white dress she wore when Dawn interviewed her months ago, and that she wore on her first day of court. The white dress she wore as the corrections technician removed her anklet, and took the alarm sensors out of her house. It is the same dress she wore to greet the reporters. The white dress that was supposed to convey her innocence from the first time she put it on.

James lifts the hem of the dress and pulls it up over her body. It goes without protest even though she is supposed to be zipped in and out of it. He drops it to the floor and stares a moment at her body. He can see all the weight she lost. All the weight she dropped from stressing and not eating, and not eating and stressing some more. He lowers his body once again to hers and kisses her navel. He hooks his thumbs into the stringed sides of her lace thong and pulls it down her diminished thighs, over her knees and off her ankles until it drops to the floor with the rest of the clothes. Rushing back into her body he kisses her navel again and then moves his intentions lower. He kisses over her mound urging it to wake up, to respond to him, to his touch, to his warmth, to his breath. He kisses her at first with just the wetness of his licked lips and then with the water of his entire mouth. He gives her suction, over, and over, and over until Ebony sits up on her elbows in the crush of pillows and pulls her legs in so she is sitting upright.

He doesn't let her run. He follows her body, what he's claimed as his. With both of her knees pulled into her chest he spreads her legs until her petals bloom and he can drink from the pink pistil inside. Prostrate before her he laps at her pleasure center until it drools for him. He kisses her crown jewel until it vibrates against his skin. Until the bundle at the division of her joy streams heaven's elixir that creates the mud to make men. James rubs two fingers across her clit. He feels the activated explosion and her shudder.

She drops her arms tired from holding her knees while he tortured her with his tongue, and then her legs to his delight. James straddles Ebony who is still sitting upright, smashed between the half dozen decorative pillows and enters her sanctuary. He pulls her close to the base of him and unhooks the bra she still has on. She runs her fingers through the top four buttons of his shirt until she has undone enough to pull the rest of the starched fabric over his head. Naked, trunk to trunk, small breasts to deflated chest, his arms around her neck, and hers around his waist, they move in time to their own rhythm. They create their own beat. Building heat she throws as much of her weight into him and forces him on his back. She rides her own waves of passion and lust, and confused complicated love. He pulls her body forward and takes a breast in his mouth. Suckling one and then the other he alternates his attention as she rides every inch of his dimensions throwing her ass around his length and girth so that it is never without her warmth. Up, down and in circles, over and under, Ebony rocks and rolls on James throwing what she cannot say, what she did not say into her movements hoping her motions convey her twisted emotions.

Reaching for her face he brings her back to him. He restores the connection that initiated their tryst. Forehead to forehead, nose to nose, mouth to mouth they kiss life into an out of each other steadily rolling and rocking, building the intensity of their concupiscent heat. His fingers again find his way into her curls. It is the only thing the stress didn't take away. Her mane. He grabs and grips more of her soft length she maintained despite the wasting away of the rest of her body. They trade places. He rolls her onto her back and pulls her legs up to his shoulders. His hands at her waist he pulls her light body into him keeping her strokes into his body short, successive, and succint. The slapping of her smooth, waxed skin, against his stubble adds another element to their soundtrack as old as Adam and Eve. He pulls her into him over and over, tightening his grip on her waist until he feels the seed of his own satisfaction pass out of him into her. He pumps his own body in double time wrenching every drop until he collapses.

They are warriors who've ended at a draw, a match made even. Their panting proving how much they are willing to fight for the other no matter how much they fight. Her breath normalizes first. Ebony stays quiet and waits for James to come down. She waits for his heart rate to match hers, for his breath to become normal, than lazy, and then sluggish with the necessary craving of sleep. She waits for him to wrap-up behind her, for them to scoot as one out of the way of the wet spot, pull the edge of the soiled comforter over their sweat wet bodies and shroud them in a thick sleep.

James begins to move and Ebony shifts with him until they are covered, his chin in her hair, their eyes closed.

"I love you," he says sleepily.

Ebony yawns. "I know."

"And you love me too."

Ebony sighs. "I know. I've always known."

31.

Ebony knew the first time they were together, naked together, in bed together, sleeping together, that he would be the one she would love. The one she would try her hardest not to mess up. The one she would try to keep. The one she wanted to stay.

Two years ago, when they'd only been dating a month James invited her over to his place for dinner. He offered to cook. She said she would eat. He told her to arrive at 7. She got there at 6:30, purposely early to see how he responded to her. She wanted to know if he was as addled by her presence as she was by him. She wanted to know if he would still stumble and fall all over himself around her like he did when they met. Like she was starting to do when she thought about him. The random thoughts of him that would enter her mind. When she was with a client at the gym and he would appear in her head and the client would land a lucky shot against her in the ring because she was distracted. Thoughts of him would find her in her kitchen while she was getting a glass of water or taking something out of the oven. She had burned herself twice from not paying attention and shattered one glass she overfilled with water. It slipped out of her hand when she chose to save the glass pitcher instead of her cup. She pulled up to his home in a subdivision just off San Jose Boulevard and waited until her heart rate stabilized before getting out of the car.

In a long sleeved black dress, that hugged her body, Ebony walked to his front door sans underwear. She came for dinner with the intention of leaving full. His dog barked when she rang the bell. It ran to the door and peaked through the mosaic shapes wagging its tail behind him. James lumbered up behind the dog seconds later. He opened the door with an apron tied around his neck and waist, and one hand still gloved in a pot holder mitten.

"I told you seven," he said.

"I know. I'm sorry. I couldn't wait to get here."

"This is Caesar. I told you about him."

"Does he bite?"

"He has teeth."

"So do I."

"I think he'll definitely bite you if you bite him first."

"Ha, ha, ha."

"Come on in," James says stepping out of the way of the door and holding Caesar by the scruff of his neck.

"Thank you."

Ebony stepped into the house and immediately smelled candles burning. She detected the smell of black currant and roses. James led her from the front entrance that opened immediately into a family room to her left. She passed through his office space, and then his dining room into his long galley kitchen that still had enough width for the both of them.

"Since you're early I'm putting you to work," James says, washing his hands at the kitchen sink.

"Okay."

"You *can* cook, right?"

"I've been cooking for myself for the last thirteen years. I'm comfortable in a kitchen."

"Good. Some women today just don't know what to do over a stove."

"It still doesn't look to me like you've missed any meals, and with that apron I'm sure you're grubbing on more than Chef Boyardee."

"I can do a little sumn, sumn."

"So what are we making?"

"Jerk chicken, red beans and rice, and cornbread."

"Jiffy mix or scratch?"

"I'm a real southern boy. From scratch, cast iron skillet, in the oven."

"Impressive. So what do you need my help with."

"Make the salad."

"Oh, you got jokes."

"You're a personal trainer. I didn't want to ruin your diet with my gluttonous ways. So I figured I'd pick you up something I know you'd eat."

"I'm a trainer because I eat. And today's my cheat day."

"Is it really?"

"It is now."

"I still need you to make the salad. It's the first course. I started the prep right here on the counter by the sink."

"What's for dessert?"

James looked her up and down in her black dress with her pretty toes sticking out of her gladiator sandals. He didn't say anything to answer her question. He turned back to the stove to tend to his pots. Ebony turned away from him and washed her hands in the large white sink. When she finished with her hands she then rinsed the spinach, arugula, and kale. She picked up the knife resting on the cutting board and cut the greens into small, bite sized pieces. Once that was deposited into the glass bowl he'd already set out she rinsed the cherry tomatoes. She cut them in half, and then half again, until she had enough to populate the greens. She started skinning and slicing the cucumber next.

Ebony asked, "Who taught you how to cook?"

"My mother," James answered. "I need to go outside and check the chicken on the grill. Excuse me."

"Go ahead," Ebony said.

James dusted his hands on the front of his apron and then disappeared out of the kitchen and through the dining room where he'd brought her from the front entrance. Ebony stayed put in the kitchen. She finished the cucumber, and then cut up the boiled eggs that were sitting out. She saw an avocado, a bag of chopped pecans and shredded parmesan sitting on the counter. The Mexican staple fruit was ripe. The large seed fell out once she sliced through it and twisted it open. She scored it in the skin, and then scooped out chunks of avocado with a spoon that was already on the counter. Ebony followed that up with a sprinkle of two handfuls of pecans and one handful of parmesan. All of the ingredients added she looked for something to cover the salad but didn't see anything. She dusted her hands into the sink, rinsed them off with water, and shook them to dry.

Stepping out of the kitchen she followed to where she thought she saw James disappear to. She passed through the formal dining room with the wooden table for six, and the office with the glass desk and leather rolling chair, tilted in a permanent recline. She was back in the living room, facing double doors to a patio. Moving between the leather sofa, love seat and arm chair, Ebony maneuvered her way to the doors and out onto the back porch.

"You have a beautiful home," she said.

"Don't tell me you're one of those women that goes snooping when left alone."

"No. Calm down. I finished the salad, didn't see any foil, and you hadn't come back yet, so I came back to where I started and saw you out here."

"Just joking, girl. You don't have to explain yourself."

"It's cool. I can understand not being comfortable with people in your space."

"Is that why you haven't invited me to your house yet?"

"You haven't asked to come."

"I didn't know I needed to."

"I'll return the favor soon."

"Is that a soon that means never? Or a soon that means someday, or a soon that really means soon."

Ebony laughed. "I really mean soon."

"Okay. Don't get a brother's hopes up and you're not serious."

"I'm serious. Soon means soon."

James didn't say anything else. He focused on flipping the chicken leg quarters that were still pink and covered in the gunk of spices that would make the heat of the chicken sing on their lips.

"I really do like your home." Ebony said watching him. "Reminds me of the house I grew up in."

"Really. Your family still live over here."

"Not anymore," she answered.

Ebony looked around the yard closed in with a white fence. She stepped away from him and leaned on the post of his lanai. Her feet in the freshly cut grass, her body slanted against the vertical support beam, she didn't hear him come up, but felt his presence, and smelled the food he'd prepared emanating from his skin.

He asked, "Why are you so quiet? What are you thinking about?"

"Your house. It just reminds me so much of where I grew up."

How I tried to lay out my own.

He stepped close to her and pulled her waist back against him. She pulled her feet out of the grass and leaned her weight into him instead. He became her post. She rested in his embrace. His hands politely sat on her waist and then her hips discovering her secret.

He said, "I need to go check on the food inside and turn it down. The chicken's going to be another 30 minutes."

"Okay," Ebony said.

James stood up straight and backed away from Ebony. She followed him and walked through the door he opened for her. She made her way to the kitchen knowing he was behind her, his eyes on her body, his thoughts no longer on the food. She moved all the way down to the far end of the kitchen where she hopped on the granite countertop and sat.

"So you just make yourself comfortable, huh?" James said.

"I did."

"Okay, okay."

She watched him turn the knobs of the stove until all the lights went out. The burners on top of the range as well as the oven beneath it. He untied the apron from behind his back, pulled it over his head and set it on the counter behind him, beside the salad Ebony prepared. He walked down to where she was sitting on the counter with her legs crossed, and her feet bouncing against one another.

"Just how comfortable do you plan on getting?" He asked stepping close to her, so she was forced to uncross her legs.

"As comfortable as I can?"

"Oh really."

"Yes. Really."

James stepped closer until she was forced to part her legs. She held on to the edge of the counter as he pulled her body forward until her knees touched the fabric of his shirt on his chest. He stepped back only to pull her down to the ground. She was shorter than him, but he couldn't tell through all of her hair. He leaned his face to hers. Forehead to forehead, nose to nose he brought his lips close until she met him halfway. Their kiss was familiar and new at the same time, not a first kiss, but not a kiss of old lovers that had been together for years.

He broke first. "We should eat," James said stepping away from her. "You want to grab the salad."

"Not really," Ebony said.

"You don't want to eat?"

"Not hungry for food."

"Are you sure?" He asked.

"I'm sure."

James closed the cabinet he opened to get the plates. He walked back toward the end of the kitchen and grabbed Ebony's hand. She came easily, willingly, following behind him out of the kitchen, through the dining room, past his office, the living room and to the other side of the house where the bedrooms were tucked. He pulled her to the back of the house, to the back bedroom. His master suite with its own set of French doors leading to the patio and the grill where the chicken burned. They never made it back to the salad, or the red beans and rice, or the cornbread made from scratch. They began and ended the night in his room, in his bed, she trying to hold back feelings she was sure he didn't have.

They laid there and ordered in. Pizza. With no TV in the room they were forced to talk. Forced to have the conversations that bring people close together. The kinds of conversations that create binding ties between two naked bodies and open souls taking the relationship ladder rung by rung from acquaintance, to like, to love.

It was some time that night or early the next morning James said, "I want to meet your family."

Ebony didn't answer, and he didn't elaborate. He continued in his heady voice drunk with sex thick sleep and said, "I want you to meet mine too."

She nodded her head yes even though her mind immediately screamed no.

He said, "I'm serious."

She said nothing.

He said, "Soon."

She said nothing. She didn't protest against what he wanted and didn't fight whatever it was he was feeling. She didn't even fight her own feelings. She ignored the voice that told her to get up before she had to tell the truth, disregarding the suggestion to leave before she fell in to deep. Laying in his king sized bed, snuggled under his arm, her head on his skin in the heart-shaped space between his pectorals and the paunch of his grown man weight she slept knowing soon she would have to manufacture a family for him, a story to ease his questions and to keep his curiosity satisfied. She slept knowing soon she would have to show him who she really was. Soon she would have to reveal what she'd never told anyone before. She would have to share what she had never stayed in a relationship long enough to give up. Her truth. She knew soon he would demand she give her heart as he had given his. She just didn't know how soon, soon would come.

32.

Soleil rings the doorbell and waits for an answer. From close inside the house she hears Ebony call "coming" shortly before the door opens and she steps outside in her bare feet to hug her.

"How are you doing?" Ebony asks.

"I should be asking you the same thing, but I guess I already know being free to go and do what you want to do when you want to do it suits you well."

"Hell, yeah." Ebony says.

"Come in, come in."

"I'm coming," Soleil laughs stepping through the house.

She hears music playing in the living room. It's loud enough to make her dance, but not loud enough for her to discern the song, artist, or break out into a body roll. Ebony leads her to the glass sliding doors off the kitchen and living room at the back of the house and out onto the patio. There are two wicker love seats and a sofa set up in a semi-circle with navy blue cushions. A matching ottoman is in the center. Ebony sits in the center of the outdoor sofa and stretches her legs until her back is reclined on the cushions and her feet are firmly crossed at the ankles on the ottoman. Soleil sits beside her on one of the love seats, kicks off her no-name, open back canvas tennis shoes, and curls her legs beneath her like a cat.

She says, "This is a nice setup out here, I've never noticed it before."

"That's because when they put me on house arrest, I had James to move all of this stuff into the garage. No use looking out the window daydreaming about sitting outside on the pretty furniture when I couldn't even go outside."

"I get it. The mind games and the lies we tell ourselves to cope with whatever we're facing."

"Exactly."

They sit in quiet stillness listening to the rustle of the wind blowing through the yards knowing the lies they've told, and the stories they've concocted to cope are lies and stories that tie them together. The lies Ebony didn't want to admit to, the stories Soleil didn't want to reveal, their shared pasts with the same man that left one of them in hiding and the other on the prowl.

"Would you like anything to drink?" Ebony asks. "I have water and sweet tea?"

"Water is cool."

Ebony bounds up from the sofa, opens the sliding door and steps inside the house. She barely closes the screen door behind her leaving room for flies and mosquitoes to make it inside. Soleil smiles at Ebony's happiness seeing the woman she first met at a luncheon a year ago who just wanted to introduce herself at their table of lawyers, judges, and their wives. Then she barely raised her face. Then she barely spoke above a whisper, consumed by the fear that he was always with her, always watching, even if he wasn't close by. A fear she later learned gripped both of them but manifested itself in different ways. A fear she learned Ebony chose to confront while she chose to cower. A fear Ebony rejected with attitude and violence. While she tried to appease, to acquiesce, to turn the other cheek in the name of peace. Remembering Ebony that day before their worlds collided, and seeing her return to herself now, she knows Ebony's confrontation, the shooting, the trial, the appeal was all worth it, if for nothing else than to be free in spirit. Soleil wipes her eyes and turns her head out over the yard as Ebony comes back outside. She carries a silver tray with two glasses filled with ice cubes and a pitcher of water stuffed with an assortment of greenery and fruits.

"The water is infused," she says setting the tray on the table. "I hope that's okay."

"Infused with what?"

"There's fresh basil leaves in there, mint, rosemary, cucumber, lemon and strawberries."

"Basically an entire garden."

"No. Just the freshest selection from the Publix produce aisle."

"Thank you," Soleil says as Ebony hands her a glass.

"You're welcome. So what's going on with you?"

"I applied for a couple online programs to get a MSW. I just found out I got in to the one at Central Florida, but I'm waiting to see what Florida State says."

"Go to FSU."

"Why, because you went there?"

"Yeah. We can just keep living this parallel life we've got going so far."

"It won't be exactly the same," Soleil says. "I'll still be here teaching until I finish and graduate, but I think once I'm done I want to move."

"Where?" Ebony asks.

"I don't know. Just away. It would be a good time to start over. New degree, new career, new life . . ."

"New man?" Ebony asks raising her voice.

"I'm not even thinking about that," Soleil says. "If it happens it happens but I could very well be single for the rest of my life and be okay with that."

"Don't let him keep taking life away from you from the grave."

"Is he really taking anything from me if it's what I want?"

"Would you really want to be single for the rest of your life if you had not been in a relationship with him?"

Soleil doesn't answer because they both know the answer is no. She faces the woman who rescued her, who freed her from her own hell as she relishes in her new found freedom. The woman with skin the color of brown olives dipped in brown sugar, whose fluffy mane frames her face with a bold center part that shows off the scar they share. The jagged half-moon he marred them with when he ran his backhand across both of their faces with his spiked titanium ring. The scar Ebony told James was a birth mark before she was forced to tell the truth. The scar Soleil will tell the next man, if there is a next man, is a birth mark refusing to ever tell anyone else this part of her story, her history.

"May I ask you a question?" Soleil asks.

"Should I be nervous?"

"I don't know, maybe. You got your interrogation at the luncheon. It's my turn."

"That wasn't an interrogation. It was more like, 'Hey, sis, I see you."

"I guess, but something has been bothering me this whole time."

"What's that?"

"When we met, you already knew me. You had been stalking him, and me and you never came up to me before the luncheon. You let him beat me, abuse me, and you never thought to come up and say any earlier, 'Hey girl, you need to get out of this relationship."

"Would you have listened if I did?"

"You could have at least tried."

"I did. I came up to you at the luncheon, pulled you to the car, talked to you. Told you to leave. And you never did. You just went to work in big glasses, your hair down, and a bunch of makeup."

"You saw me at my job?"

"I had to. I had to know what he did to you. I wanted to see the damage he left."

"That's a fucked up thing to say. To see the damage he left. Are you saying I'm damaged?"

"You just said yourself you're ready to go the rest of your life without any kind of relationship. Life is short, but it ain't that short, and it's going to for damn sure feel long if you're alone the whole time. If that's not damaged, a damaged mentality, then I don't know what is."

"I guess then I have you to thank for those six months of ass kickings, and my damaged mentality, since you could have done your 'Hey Sis, I see you' bit the day I met him at Cracker Barrel."

"Again, would you have even listened?"

"Again, you could have at least tried."

"I shot him, didn't I?"

"I thought you didn't shoot him?"

"Whatever. He was shot with my gun when he banged me up against the car. He's dead."

"Why?" Soleil demands "Because you felt like he was going to come after you again, or did you just feel sorry for me?"

Does it even matter.

Ebony doesn't answer. She stares at Soleil and watches her work through her feelings. She watches her process all that has happened in the months since their meeting. The actions she took to help her unappreciated. Soleil's anger, bitterness, and resentment born out of her rejection of the titles of helpless, hapless, and victim. She is self-righteous in her belief she could have saved herself, rescued herself, delivered herself, freed herself. Ebony does not intrude on her thought processes or correct her conscience. She waits, as she waited to meet Soleil, as she waited to confront Barker, as she waited for trial, as she waited for the jury, as she waited to be sentenced, as she waited for the appeal to either be won or lost. In the last year she has learned life is a series of seasons of waiting so she may as well learn to wait well.

Soleil says, "After you finally introduced yourself I took an ass kicking for your half assed confession about what he was like to you. For three days straight he beat me. Even in my face, which he rarely did, because you know he was all about appearances."

"And now he's dead and can never hurt you again, and most of your scars are gone."

"There are scars I will always have. Pain I will always carry. Bruises I will always remember. The shit I have will never go away. So what you shot him."

"I have those same scars, pain, bruises, shit that will never go away, and I nearly went to prison for it."

"Your decisions not mine," Soleil says.

"You're right," Ebony says setting the glass she'd been holding down on the ground. "They were my decisions, but you know good and goddamn well you would have been with him until he beat you to death. Say it's not true."

Ebony waits for an answer that doesn't come. She waits for an answer Soleil can't give.

She says, "You didn't want to leave him. I gave you no choice. The least you could do is say thank you."

"How can I say thank you for something I didn't even ask for. Barker's dead for my benefit, you nearly went to prison for it, but you didn't. How can I say thank you or that we're even, when we're not even close. I have to start over. You can just go back to your life as if nothing ever happened. Just pull everything out of the garage and return to what you used to do before you ever met me."

"The only thing I pulled out of the garage is the patio furniture. I have to start over just like you. I don't even have a car. I don't have a job. And I've got the most recognizable face in the city so who's going to hire me to be a personal trainer when all they're going to see is the woman who killed a judge. I have to start over just like you."

"Then maybe you should move to," Soleil suggests.

"I'm not running. My life is here. I will be here. Everybody else will have to deal with it."

"You think I'm running?"

"Aren't you?"

Soleil doesn't the answer. They both know she is. They both know she stayed when she should have left, and now she's choosing to leave when she has won the right to stay.

"Three years," Soleil says.

"What happens in three years."

"If I get in to the program at FSU I will be here for three more years."

Ebony nods.

"That's enough time for me to decide whether I'm going to stay or go."

"Time heals all wounds. Isn't that how the saying goes."

"Yeah that's it."

Soleil slips her feet back into her shoes and stands up. She places her empty water glass with the melting ice cubes and the soggy fruits and herbs on the tray atop the ottoman. Ebony follows her lead and stands as well. She walks her around the patio furniture to the sliding doors. The wind, the birds, and the ducks in the distance provide the noise to break up the silence of their dead conversation. Ebony slides both doors open and let's Soleil pass through first. She steps up into the cool house and follows the straight path of the cherry hardwood floors from the back door to the front door. Soleil turns the lock, opens the door, and steps outside on the newly placed welcome mat.

She looks at her friend in a loose yellow tank top and ripped jeans and sees the happiness she didn't have all those months before when she lived in sweats, and wife beaters, and the occasional white outfit when she was going to court. Soleil looks down at her own clothes. Shorts and a white tee. Something she never would have worn if she was still with him for fear the marks on her legs, and arms would show. She appreciates the levity of her appearance even if she doesn't feel it.

"I'm sorry," Soleil says. "With everything that's happened I can't decide if I'm angry or grateful or both."

"It's okay to be both," Ebony says. "Feel what you feel, and know it all works out for good."

"Another saying."

"The Bible. This lady I knew used to say it all the time when I was a kid."

"Smart lady."

"She was," Ebony says quietly.

"I'll see you later," Soleil says.

"Yeah, you too."

Ebony watches Soleil walk to the curb to where her little blue Honda is parked. The alarm chirps. Ebony begins to close the door as Soleil gets in the car.

"Ebony," Soleil yells from the curb.

She pokes her head out.

"Thank you."

33.

Ebony hears the garage door lift not long after she's closed the door on Soleil. She walks back to the front of the house from where she was sitting in the living room watching TV. Through the laundry room she opens the door and waits as James parks, lowers the garage door, and gets out of the car. She watches, leaned against the doorframe as he takes his time getting his briefcase out of the back seat, closing the door to the Impala and walking around to her. He gives her a brief peck on the lips before stepping into the house.

James moves in silence through the laundry room, down the hallway, and into the kitchen. The briefcase is dropped in the corner by the peninsula. His movements are rote, by memory. Into the kitchen, opening the cabinets, grabbing a tumbler. He sets it down on the counter beside the refrigerator and keeps on moving. He bends down and grabs the first bottle his hand finds. He pulls it up and twists the cap. Brown liquid falls smoothly from the lip of the bottle into the awaiting cup. James fills it halfway before returning the cap and replacing it in the cabinet.

He takes a sip. Ebony watches from the arm chair in the living room. She watches him take tentative sips of the brown liquor under her knowing gaze and judgmental eyes. She watches him enjoy the whiskey he gulps from the glass. He finishes the rest of his drink like a shot, guzzling with his head tossed to the back of his neck. James bends down again and comes up with the bottle. He twists, he pours, he twists, he replaces, he lifts the glass and sips. He sips, and sips, and gulps and guzzles. The glass dings when he sets it back on the counter.

"It's a little early for that don't you think?" Ebony asks from where she's perched in the arm chair.

"No," James answers. "I don't have anywhere else to go."

"I'm glad, because you wouldn't be of any use to anybody like that."

"I'm not even tipsy. I just had a hard day with my parents. Why was Soleil here?"

"She came to visit. Wanted to see how I was doing newly free and what not. And to yell at me."

"Yell at you for what?"

"For not letting her make her own choice to leave Barker. Now she's planning to run away again when there's no reason to."

"You can't save everybody."

James moves toward the couch. He throws the pillows on the floor beneath the cracked glass coffee table and stretches his body out across the three cushions of the white suede sofa. One arm behind his head, and one arm over his face, he closes his eyes to rest.

She says, "Present company included."

"Huh?"

"You said I can't save everybody. Are you referring to yourself?"

"What are you talking about? I don't need you to rescue me or save me from anything."

"Are you sure, because I sure as hell can't tell."

"Says the woman who just had her entire case thrown out, her conviction overturned, and her house arrest anklets and monitors removed. But no, you did that yourself."

"I didn't say that."

"You sure as hell didn't say thank you, either," James says.

"That's a lie and you know it. I've thanked you multiple times *and* in multiple ways."

"Fine, whatever, you said thank you. I still don't need you to rescue me."

"Keep telling yourself that and you'll end up just like Johnnie."

"No, I won't. I only drink when I'm at home. And I know when to stop. She was drunk all the damn time."

"I'm sure she didn't start off that way."

"I guess we'll never know."

James rolls over on the couch and buries his face in the cushion. Ebony takes the hint and turns back to the TV. She turns back to the national news that's no longer about her. The broadcasters are now focused on another name, in another city, and another outrage. A seemingly unlawful arrest, and a mysterious ride in a police van, that left the suspect-victim with a nearly severed spinal cord, and crushed voice box fighting for his life. A life no one but his family seemed pressed to save, until they realized they couldn't save him and he died still in his coma.

James rolls over on the couch and turns to face the TV. He watches what Ebony watches. He follows her head and hair movements as she reacts in silence to the scenes she sees.

"Why are you watching this?" He asks.

"Because it's crazy. Doesn't make sense."

"I'm sure the police have an explanation for what happened?"

"Not a plausible one," Ebony says turning around to face him. "You don't just end up dead riding in the back of the police van."

"You didn't have a plausible explanation for what you did and yet here you are."

"That's different."

"How?"

"It just is. I'm not the one charged to protect and serve. They were. Hell Barker was. They're held to a higher standard."

"That's hypocritical. Morals are morals." James sits up on the couch. "If it's wrong for the police or a judge to abuse their power and hurt and abuse people, it's just as wrong for everyday people to hurt and abuse other people, even those in positions of power, for the sake of evening the score or exercising their agency."

"Exercising their agency. Is that what you think I was doing?"

"I don't know."

"No, you don't because you never asked."

"I didn't want to know. Didn't need to know if I was going to defend you."

"Do you want to know now."

"Ebony, it doesn't matter now. You said you confronted him because he was beating Soleil and you brought your gun to protect you, that's good enough for me."

"No, it's not and you know it."

"Ebony, it doesn't matter anymore. The case is over. It's closed. What you did, and why you said you did it, the only person that needs to know the difference between those two is you."

"What happened to always telling you the truth?"

"I've learned some things are better left as lies."

"You don't believe that."

"It doesn't matter what I believe anymore. Right now I don't have to believe in anything but God, taxes, and death."

"So you're determined to just waste the rest of your life away until you die."

"I didn't say that."

"You haven't said anything."

"Because I don't know what the fuck I'm going to do. Can I just not know shit for awhile?"

James stands up from the couch and walks back into the kitchen. He pulls the glass he had out of the sink rinses it out, and then pours out the excess water. He repeats his steps by the refrigerator. Bottle, twist, pour, twist, replace, sip, drink, gulp, guzzle. Repeat.

James brings the glass with him into the living room. He sits down on the couch with it clutched between his hands and sips while the TV tells them things they've already heard, dubious facts they're all learning at the same time.

"And you say you don't have a problem." Ebony says looking away from him toward the TV.

"The same way you didn't think you had a problem when you were following people around every chance you got like you were Inspector Gadget."

"That's fucked up."

302.

"Well, Ebony, you've taught me the truth sometimes is fucked up."

"How long are we going to keep doing this?" Ebony asks.

"Do what?"

"Playing pretend that this works. That we work without the drama of everything around us."

"I didn't know we were playing at anything," James says. "We're having a conversation you don't like."

James sighs. *What are we doing?* He takes a sip from his glass. Ebony maneuvers her feet from under her butt and crosses them across her knees in the chair. Her legs are in lotus as her nails attack the back of her hands. He drinks, She scratches. He gulps. She scratches. He guzzles the last of the liquid and then sets the glass down on the table.

He watches Ebony do the only thing he's always known her to do when she's processing information she doesn't like. He watches her scratch her feelings into her hands, so she doesn't have to speak them aloud. *Maybe I was stupid to think this could work. She still didn't say it, I had to say it for her.*

James watches her claw at her own skin in an effort to avoid the truth that's already been told. His eyes scan her body as she works her nerves and stress into peeling healed scabs because she's been knocked off her throne of self-righteous self-importance and her own spotlight has been turned back on her as an interrogation lamp.

"Stop that," James says.

Ebony digs in her skin one final time before bringing her hands under her butt. She sits on the itch that isn't there and turns back to the TV.

"Why didn't you ever get help for that?"

"You've asked me that before."

"You didn't answer."

"I did."

"No, you avoided the question."

"I didn't. I told you I couldn't leave to get help if I wanted to."

"Now you can."

"I'm good."

"Look at the back of your hands. I don't think so."

"I could say the same thing about you. Look how much you just drank out of that bottle. Look at your empty glass. We all have flaws, James. You've got your vices and I've got mine. Johnnie has hers and Ayana has hers."

"You need to work that out in therapy too."

"Is that your answer for everything now? Go to therapy?"

"It could help free you from your demons."

"Freedom is a farce."

"Tell that to the women you didn't join in prison."

"We're doomed to whatever lies we all choose to believe."

"Like the fact you don't need help. Is that the lie you're believing today?"

"I'll go to therapy for Ayana and the scratching when you join Johnnie for an AA meeting or whatever the hell she's doing to stay sober these days."

"I don't need AA. I haven't been drinking and hiding it as long as Johnnie has. Hell, I don't even hide it. You just don't like it. I only do it when I'm here or at home. Chill out."

"Ayana used to do that. Always make an excuse for why she didn't need help, why whatever intervention the Washington's thought up was an overreaction. She always had a reason for why she left me sleeping in the fucking car."

"I'm not Ayana."

"And I don't need therapy."

The television blares loudly between their denials. They zone out on the moving pictures and the broadcasted information. They stare at the screen to keep from staring at each other, to keep from looking at each other, blaming each other, accusing each other of old sins, and old crimes.

James's phone dings. He pulls it out of his pocket and reads the message. Ebony's phone resounds next.

"Ayana is on her way," he says.

"I know. She just texted me."

34.

Ayana is armed with a box when Ebony opens the door for her. She steps inside and walks to the back of the house toward the kitchen without saying a word. Ebony closes the door behind her and follows her lead. Ayana stops and begins unpacking the box on the kitchen counter, but Ebony keeps walking. She pulls open the sliding glass door, and the screen protector to lead onto the patio. Ayana sees her, puts the few items she'd removed from the box back, and picks it up once again. They step outside and Ebony takes up her spot on the outdoor sofa where she lounged earlier with Soleil. James is already outside. He stands up to take the box from Ayana.

"Good to see you again," He says hugging her.

"You too," she says. "And under much better circumstances."

"What's in the box?" Ebony asks.

Ayana sits down and begins unloading her items until she gets to what she's really looking for. She pulls out two old, worn photo albums and hands one to Ebony. She watches as Ebony tentatively takes the book. She handles it as if it is fragile, as if it will fall apart at the seams, or turn to dust.

Ayana says, "You didn't seem convinced when I told you I attended your graduation."

"So what's this?"

"Proof."

Ebony fondles the front edge of the book debating whether she wants to open its secrets to find out if Ayana is telling her the truth. She lifts the heavy front cover and closes it again without looking at the first page.

"Go on," James encourages.

Ebony lifts the front cover and opens it completely until it lays flat against her lap. She turns the first protective page until she is face to face with a page of baby pictures.

"Is this me?"

"You're the only baby I've had. Who else would it be?"

"Where are your friends?"

"When you're twenty-two and pregnant, you kind of lose friends. They had their lives and I had you."

"What's supposed to be right here?" Ebony asks, her hands fondling the dried glue stains in the place where the missing photo used to be.

"I threw that one away."

Ebony sets the photo album to the side and stands up. She side steps around the ottoman and James's stretched out legs from where he reclines on the love seat opposite Ayana. She walks around the back of the furniture, opens the sliding doors, and disappears into the house. Walking to her bedroom, she moves with purpose to the night stand and opens the bottom drawer on the mini bureau. She lifts out tin boxes and oddly shaped containers filled with the random knick knacks of her life she's refused to throw away. Keys to doors she no longer has access to, thin papers from old fortune cookies whose version of her future she preferred, and notes with phone numbers, and online passwords to access her various accounts. She pulls out what she put away to hide her past from herself. At the bottom of the drawer she finds the square polaroid, laying face down. She pulls it out, stands up from her squat in front of the drawer and takes it outside to where James and Ayana wait.

Ebony sidesteps her way back to where she sat. She picks up the photo album she set aside and places it back in her lap. Turning over the photo she pulled out of her room she presses it on to the dried glue into the place where it used to be.

"I should have known you had it," Ayana says.

"I saw it in the trash when I was like eight. You gave me ravioli for dinner. I finished eating and I was about to scrape my plate when I saw the picture in the trash. I took it and I kept it."

"Figures."

"Who is that?" James asks.

"Marilyn, Dr. Ivan, and Isaiah," Ebony answers.

"She looks like Diahann Carroll," James says.

"She did," Ebony says. "But even prettier."

"Where are the girls?" He asks.

Ayana answers, "She was still pregnant with the twins. Ebony was a few months older than them."

"Oh."

"Why did you throw it away?" Ebony asks.

Ayana closes her eyes and sighs. *Where do I even begin.* She closes her eyes and recalls her state of mind that led her to throw the picture Ebony's cherished all this time in the trash. The months she spent shaking, dry heaving, gagging, sweating, crying, doubled over in front of the toilet with nothing left to empty, nothing left to hurl. The months she spent in withdrawal trying to hide it while she looked for jobs to put her nursing degree to use. The degree she hadn't used since she earned it because her parents died, and then she got pregnant, and was deserted by the man who was supposed to be there for her, for their new family. The degree that after Ebony's birth always got her in the door for an interview. Her experience in the UNF campus clinic, and volunteering at Wolfson Children's Hospital always made the potential employer eager to see her, eager to schedule an interview after speaking with her on the phone. They always ended up disappointed after she showed up in person, with her hair unwashed, clothes wrinkled, face not made, shoes sometimes not matching, eyes glassy, and breath foul.

She remembers the day she threw the picture away was different. She hadn't heaved in days, hadn't felt the urge to run to the bathroom and empty the contents of her empty stomach in days. She had stopped sweating at night, stopped shaking, stopped gagging at the smell of sugar, and she had an interview where her reputation for blowing it in person hadn't preceded her. The day she threw the picture away she had gotten the job at a nursing home. She had been hired to start immediately. Happy for her own success, her own accomplishment, Ayana arrived to Ebony's school when Marilyn did, and told her she would bring the kids home. She waited in the snaking parent pick-up line for the bell to ring and the kids to come outside. She was excited to do something she hadn't done in years, pick Ebony up from school. She usually rode the school bus and walked home from the neighborhood bus stop or piled in with the Washington's. Ayana remembers being excited to have her old Buick in the pick up line to transport Ebony and their neighbors. Ebony's face was less than enthused when she pulled up to the curb. Ebony asked, "Where's Mrs. Washington?" Ayana remembers she didn't even listen for her answer, didn't ask about her day after she asked the kids about their day. Ebony rode in surly silence home, whispering to Monica and Monique every once and awhile, apologizing Ayana had to pick them up, and that they had to ride in the old beat up car.

Ayana remembers when they got home Ebony scampered out of the car and rushed to the Washington's front door with Monica, Monique, and Isaiah. Ayana called her back, but Ebony whined. Ayana forced her to come home, forced her to come inside with her, forced her to do her own homework while she monitored, observed, and checked it over. She remembers Ebony finished her homework and then went in her room. She moved from her room, to the living room, to standing at the backdoor watching her friends have a water gun fight in their back yard that was not fenced off away from their own. She remembers watching Ebony longingly look out the back door and all she could do was say, "Go on, girl." She remembers the finite slam of the door. The slam that still sounded in her ears when she walked over to the bookshelf in the living room, pulled down the photo album, and snatched out the picture of the surrogate family she was disowning.

Ayana sighs as she opens her eyes. "I was angry you chose them over me."

"You left me no choice," Ebony says.

"You were a child. I never thought you would choose them over me."

"You left me no choice. You left me asleep in the car, cold. They saw me get out in my nightgown while they were getting ready to go to school. I'm surprised they never called DCF on you."

"Ivan wanted to, but Marilyn wouldn't let him. She always looked out for you. She wanted to adopt you, but I told her no. The year she said that is when I got clean. On my own. No rehab. I got a job, and I picked you up from school and you looked at me as if you didn't even know me. As if you were embarrassed by me. Even at eight I could see in your eyes you were only tolerating me until you could get away from me. That hurt."

"Not as much as your own mother rejecting you and you don't know why."

"I didn't know how to take care of you. Didn't know what to do. You were a colicky baby. You cried all the time. You wouldn't latch on, and by the time you did I wasn't even producing milk, because I was barely eating. I tried hard to do all the things I thought mothers were supposed to do. Baby talk, tummy time, story time, but all you did was cry. I couldn't handle it. Marilyn would come over and get you and you'd just coo at her. She'd put you down with Monica and Monique and you'd just giggle and smile at her and at them, and all I did was sleep."

"Sounds like you had postpartum," James says.

"That's what they call it now. Nobody talked about that after I had Ebony. I thought something was wrong with me. I had some of the pain killers left over from right after I had you to make it easier to cope with the stitches and I would take those to help me sleep when Marilyn would come get you. Just one. At least that's the way it started."

"I'm sorry," Ebony says.

"It's not your fault. I managed. I guess. I kept the job at the nursing home and just drank at night. Tried cigarettes but didn't like them. Pills and booze until they died."

"That's when you stopped everything," Ebony says.

"I didn't know you knew."

Ebony flips the pages in the photo album still open on her lap.

She says, "I knew because you started buying my school pictures. You had money for stuff."

"Everything but the mortgage," Ayana says. "I refinanced the house when you were like six and blew through the money. With them dead there was no one buying you what I didn't or giving you what I couldn't. I tried but it just wasn't enough."

"It's okay," Ebony soothes. "I turned out alright . . . Well, if you don't count the murder charge."

Ayana laughs first. The song of her relief comes out in a deep throaty chuckle until it is a full on cackle of a laugh. Ebony joins in.

"What else do you have there?" James asks.

Ayana wipes her eyes and hands Ebony the other photo album. She reaches inside the box and pulls out a stack of cards wrapped in a rubber band. She hands the stack of cards to James.

"When she went away to school I started writing her post cards, but she always sent them back." Ayana says. "I kept them."

"I was so angry," Ebony says. "I just wanted to get rid of you, but you wouldn't go away."

"Are you still angry now?"

"I don't know what I am?"

"There's birthday cards in here," James says flipping through the stack.

"Christmas cards, Easter cards, Juneteenth cards," Ayana says. "Any reason I could find to send more than one, I found it."

"Why did you keep sending me stuff if you knew I was just going to send it back."

"Because a mother never gives up on her child. I couldn't give up on you. I had no right to since I was the one that was wrong. And I knew that you read them, even if you were being evil."

"How did you know that?" James asks.

"Because she took the money out of the real cards," Ayana says.

"That doesn't mean I read them."

"It doesn't, but that's not what I told myself. And if you didn't read them then, you can read them now."

"What am I holding?" Ebony asks lifting the second photo album in her lap.

"Open it and see."

Ebony flips open the heavy, navy flap and turns to the first page of pictures. She sees a little girl with long curly hair, brown skin, and skinny legs. A woman is beside her with a gap toothed grin and hair just as long pressed straight. Ebony turns the next page. More of the girl and the woman. In a few of the pictures Ebony sees a man in skinny pants with bell bottom legs, and a tight t-shirt, with a perfectly round Jackson 5 afro.

"Who are these people?" Ebony asks.

"Who do they look like?" Ayana says.

"That looks like me and you, but I know that's not us. You rarely straightened your hair."

"It's me when I was a girl. That's my mom and dad. You never got to meet them."

"You told me when I had to do my family tree project in school you didn't have any pictures I could use."

"I didn't want to give them to you."

"Why? It was for school."

"Because I didn't want them to get lost or messed up."

"You know you could have copied them down at Kinkos and kept the originals."

"I know."

"I got a C on that project because I didn't have any pictures," Ebony says.

She turns more pages of Ayana's growth and evolution from a wiry kid, to a teen with weight everywhere, to a young woman who grew into her butt, and breasts, and had lost the chubbiness around her waist and in her cheeks. Ebony sees herself. She flips the page and sees Ayana with a group of women and men, all smiles with alcohol squinted eyes.

"Is this when you were in college?"

"Yeah."

"Any pictures of my sperm donor in here?"

"At the back."

Ebony bypasses the pages in the middle of the book and flips to the back. There in matching Osprey sweatshirts, shorts and tube socks, Ebony sees the love that created her. Ayana curled beneath his arm, her curly hair in a bushy ponytail fanned out over the shoulder of his sweatshirt. The picture is blurry from his apparent thumb print, but his face is clear. She sees where the other side of her comes from. Though she looks like Ayana she sees where he played a role in her phenotype.

"What is his name?"

"Kayo. Kayo Spencer."

"Kayo," Ebony whispers to herself.

She pulls the picture out of the cellophane wrapping protecting it in the book and brings it closer to her face. Inspecting his face she can see the faint freckles under his eyes and across the bridge of his nose. His hair is cut low, eyebrows thick and striking, nose wide, but fitting on his face.

"Have you ever looked for him?" James asks.

"If he wanted to be found he'd find me," Ayana says. "He knew I was pregnant. He knew my parents died. He left anyway."

"Even now. You haven't tried to search him on Facebook?"

"No."

"What about the property appraiser?" Ebony asks.

"No. He wasn't from Jacksonville. He was from somewhere out in the panhandle. Bay County I think. He didn't want to go to FAM or State but didn't want to go too far so he chose UNF."

"I can run a search for him if you'd like?" James offers.

"There's no need." Ayana says. "With all the press Ebony's gotten, and even the little interview I did with Dawn that everybody's picked up, I'm sure he knows we're here. If he wanted to know his daughter, he would have showed up like I did."

"Is that why you showed up? You want to know me now?"

"I showed up because you were in trouble. Whether you allow me the chance to continue to get to know you is on you."

"I gave you my phone number."

"I know. And you have mine, and my address."

"I know."

Silence marks their stalemate. Face to face, eye to eye, woman to woman they communicate what they won't say aloud. Refusing to force the issue of who they are and what they will be to each other, reconciling their pasts with their presents, they acknowledge the feelings each of them has felt directly caused by the other. There are no grand apologies or grand gestures to share, only mutual respect and a silent agreement to take things as they come, day by day, hour by hour, minute by minute, second by second, fleeting moment by fleeting moment.

"Why don't we go inside," Ebony suggests standing up. "I'll cook."

"I'll help," Ayana says.

"When did you start cooking? If it didn't come in a bag, box or a can you couldn't fix it."

"I told you I have cable now. Food Network has been helpful. I like that Barefoot Contessa lady."

"Well let's see what you can do."

"I'll eat," James adds.

"I bet you will," Ebony says. "You're getting too damn little anyway."

"I'm not the only one."

"Y'all have been through a lot," Ayana says putting the photo albums and the stack of cards back in the box.

"I'll get that," James says.

Ayana passes him the box and then follows him and Ebony inside the sliding glass doors. James sets the box on one of the bar-stools and makes way for Ebony and Ayana to get into the kitchen. He walks over to the sofa, flops down, and clicks the remote to turn the television on. They catch it in the middle of a commercial.

New name.

New host.

The same news you need.

Naomi Tonight, Tonight at 8. Only on 9 News Now.

"Isn't that the time Dawn is supposed to come on?" James asks.

"It is?" Ebony says.

"Seems like your girl lost her show."

"Let's find out." Ebony pulls her phone out of her back pocket and types a message:

> Who is Naomi
> ?
> New girl
> Did you get fired?
> No
> I'm leaving
> Where are you going?
> Atlanta
> I've been meaning to get in touch with you. Just been busy.
> U busy now?
> No
> Come over
> Have dinner
> My mother's here
> I'll be there in about an hour
> See you then

35.

The smell of food greets Dawn before she ever sets foot in the home. She rings the doorbell and hears her stomach grumble. She looks down at her t-shirt covered belly and waits for the door to open. Dressed in sneakers, jeggings, a long, black graphic tee, jacket, and baseball cap, Dawn waits to make a social visit to the woman responsible for advancing her career. The woman she was able to make her name off of, and position herself as an elite journalist, amongst the glorified anchors of cable and broadcast networks.

The door opens, and laughter spills out of the house.

"Come on in," Ebony says.

"Thanks for having me. It sure smells good, I can smell the food from the porch."

"Nothing major. Just some grilled salmon, pasta with a lemon butter sauce and capers, garlic bread, and some salad."

"Sounds delicious."

"We'll see. Ayana can't cook."

"I can too."

"And we've had wine," Ebony excuses.

"I could use a glass myself," Dawn says.

"I can make that happen."

"Dawn Anthony, how are you?" Ayana asks.

"Just, Dawn, is fine."

"I see. You in hiding or something. You don't have on your news lady clothes, or your bitch face."

"No, Ms. Jones. Not in hiding. Just packing."

"Ebony, said you were going to Atlanta," James says sitting up from the couch.

"Yeah. Next week. I start Monday."

"Where are you going?"

"NNC. National News Corp. They're letting me keep the show. Same time. Same me. Just different channel and a different city."

"So did you give the new girl . . . What's her name, Baby," James asks.

"Naomi," Ebony and Ayana answer together.

"Yeah," he continues. "Did you give her your job, or did she take it from you."

"It was mutual. Her getting hired gave me the confirmation I needed to know it was time to go."

"Is that why you're here all dressed down, and incognito, because it's time for you to go?" Ayana asks.

"A little. When I don't want to be seen, I make sure I blend in to the background. Sometimes it works. Sometimes it doesn't, but I also came to say thank you."

"It's good to see you looking like a regular person," Ayana says. "Let's people like me know you don't take yourself too seriously."

"Thank you. I think."

"Red or white?" Ebony asks. "What do you mean you came to say thank you?"

"Red, please."

"You'll get the last glass of this bottle."

"Thank you," Dawn says. "I came to tell you thank you because I wouldn't have the opportunity at NNC without all my coverage of you."

"You did the work," Ebony says. "I'm just grateful all your coverage worked in my favor. So, thank you."

"Then, you're welcome," Dawn says.

She moves the cardboard box off one bar-stool and on to the other and sits at the granite peninsula. Ebony sets a rinsed glass of red wine in front of her. Dawn wipes the dripping droplets of water off the sides of the glass with her finger and then picks it up by the stem. She balances the lightweight goblet made to look like Olivia Pope's infamous wine glasses between two fingers. Dawn takes a sip and then just holds the glass in her hands. She looks around the room. Mother and daughter in the kitchen together cooking, laughing, drinking, and teasing. James on the couch flipping between sports and NNC. Dawn looks around the room at the people inhabited in the spaces beside her and sees what she doesn't have, what she didn't see during her first visit. Where her walls are filled with art and culture to ease the silence inside her condo, the walls of Ebony's home are filled with cases of books and magazines, framed photos of herself, selfies and candid's of her and James together, and the sound of familial love. Infectious laughter, jesting sarcasm, and a few harmless dozens are traded back and forth between Ayana, James, and Ebony. Dawn sits perched on the stool, the monkey in the middle of their game of petty shade. She ignores the personal digs she doesn't understand and turns off her instinct that the scene before her is fueled by the empty wine bottles behind her. She disregards the fact that Ayana's laughter is a little more forced than Ebony's and that James only chimes in when a tense thickness begins to descend and erase whatever tone deaf joke didn't land as it was supposed to. Dawn ignores her natural curiosity that's accelerated her career and gives in to the side of her that she neglects. The side of her that needs feeding. The side of her that simply wants to belong on the same level as the subjects she covers.

"How long have you two been together now?" Dawn takes another sip from her wine glass.

"More than two years now," James says without looking up from the couch.

"That's amazing."

"Is the guy who came with you to the luncheon and the fund-raiser going with you to Atlanta?" James asks sitting up completely.

Dawn counts the number of times his fingers drum the back of the sofa before answering. She brings the glass to her lips, sips, and then sets it on the counter.

"No."

"Why not?"

"We broke up," Dawn sighs. "You could say we broke up at the fund-raiser. That's the last time I've seen Victor."

"Oh, no. Why?" Ebony coos.

"He was a cutie," Ayana says.

Dawn holds up both her hands. She tells them to stop before they break their necks to dote and fawn over her. She gives them the universal girlfriend's signal that she is okay.

"I don't want to talk about it," Dawn says.

"My man seemed nice," James says. "He helped me out when I needed him. He was a keeper in my book."

"But this ain't your book," Ayana says flapping one hand in his direction.

"It's okay," Dawn says to Ayana. "He was nice," she says to James.

"So what happened?" He asks.

"Damn, you act like you're on deadline with all these questions."

"We learned from the best," Ayana says.

"Well, thank you."

"No problem," James says. "Now answer the question. Why'd my man leave."

"Because he didn't realize my life is about me."

"That's no way to have a relationship," James says.

"And that's why we're not together."

Ayana, Ebony, and James are silenced at Dawn's frank admission. She sees James slowly turn back toward the TV. Ayana and Ebony's, loud, playful cheeriness drops to a whisper behind her. Dawn doesn't look at them. She stays on the bar-stool, wine glass in her hand, eyes focused on the swirling liquid inside. She takes a sip and places the glass on the counter where she picked it up from. Eyes down, navel gazing and fiddling with her fingers she offers no apologies for her own behavior, for knowing who she is, and not being flexible enough to adapt to what someone else wants her to be. Relentless in her ambition and her dogged pursuit of her ever evolving definition of success she thinks about the note she used to stare at on her desk. The framed yellow Post-it in the faded red scrawl. *I'm not your enemy.* It motivated and inspired her to do all that she's done. Have her own show, replace Julia, move on to network. She hoped the same catalyst for success that it inspired in her transferred to Naomi.

Dawn presented Naomi with a note of her own on her last day. She didn't leave it anonymously like the one had been left for her. She approached her desk, placed her hand on her shoulder, set down the frame, and said "this is for you." A yellow Post it, the red scrawl written in her own hand that read, *Know yourself. Know your enemies.* Naomi asked her what the note meant, and all Dawn offered her was, "you'll figure it out soon enough." She left the young woman, sitting at her desk, perplexed, as she walked off to the set for the final time, to do the show she was hired to do, the show she created, the show she would be taking with her to Atlanta.

"Are you ready to eat?" Ebony asks.

"Sure," Dawn says.

"James, come on," Ebony calls.

Ebony walks the box of mementos to her room and comes back into the kitchen. She rummages through the cabinets until she produces four plates. She passes them one by one to Ayana who heaps food onto them, and then passes them back to Ebony. She sets the plates in front of Dawn and James who sit at the counter, then the two others opposite them for herself and Ayana. They stand while James and Dawn sit. Wine and water is poured to refresh mid-level to empty glasses. Forks scrape plates, teeth chew, and lips smack. They eat in a comfortable quiet each consumed with their own thoughts. Each of them eventually subsumed by their unlikely gathering and the circumstances that brought them together.

Dawn takes a sip of her topped off wine glass and places it back on the counter. It clinks against her plate.

She asks, "So what are your plans now?"

"Who?" Ayana asks.

"All of you."

Ebony puts her fork down and swallows the food in her mouth.

She answers, "To live."

Ayana and James nod their agreement with the simple answer to the loaded question. The two word answer that sums up whatever their future may hold.

Breaking News Right Now on Naomi Tonight.
Anger and outrage in Baltimore following the death of Freddie Gray.

"You want me to turn that off?" James asks.

"No," Dawn answers. "She's pretty good."

"She's green," Ayana says.

"I was green once," Dawn answers.

"Why is she on, on a Sunday?" Ebony asks.

Dawn says, "It's the way they roll out new anchors. Sunday nights when people are home watching. They don't really know the weekend anchors that well so seeing a new face isn't weird. If people watch and like her, it will make her transition tomorrow a whole lot easier."

"I guess," Ayana says.

Dawn continues eating. She savors the pasta and salmon along with the wine as she watches Ebony's and Ayana's faces react to the news playing behind them. She watches them listen as the story unfolds about how a 25-year-old man died while still in police custody. Their faces contort in emotion as Naomi lays out what is known about the case and what still has to be discovered. Dawn listens to Naomi's crisp pronunciation, and where she inflects emotions into the words she's reading. She hears her stumble over sentences not written for her, by producers who don't know her voice, her style of speaking, or the rhythm of her delivery.

"This shit just keeps happening," Ayana says over the television.

"What?" Ebony asks.

"These kids getting killed," she says.

"Seems like it," Ebony says.

"Ain't no seems," Ayana says dropping her fork. "It is. It's happening and there ain't shit being done about it."

James says, "As long as we keep making the same mistakes and not learning our lessons it's always going to happen."

"You're not saying it's his fault, are you?" Dawn asks.

"Put your guard back down," James jokes. "That's not what I'm saying."

"Then what are you saying?" Ebony demands.

"I mean this stuff has been going on long before surveillance cameras and smart phones. Some cases we've known about and some we haven't. Look at Fred Hampton, Eleanor Bumpurs or Rodney King. But as a country we keep making the same mistakes, so it keeps happening."

"So what's the solution, Counselor?" Dawn asks.

"To just keep living," James answers. "Just like Ebony said."

"But we're not all given the opportunity to *keep* living," Ayana says.

"No, we're not, but for those of us who are, we have to keep going for those whose life was taken away from them."

Forks scrape plates as another round of agreement and grumbles passes between the four of them. The news continues in the background. Dawn recognizes the voice of one of the experts she used to book for round tables and discussions when it was her show. She left Naomi her list of Jacksonville specific contacts to help her round out her in depth coverage until she was able to build relationships of her own. The only name and number she did not leave was for Victor. If Naomi needed an architect, she would have to find one herself.

"To life," Ebony says lifting her glass in the air.

Ayana drops her fork. She looks at Ebony and sees the resolute resolve in her face. She lifts her glass, and with a smile only Ebony can see, she says, "To life."

James and Dawn follow their lead. They drop their forks, lift their glasses, and ignore the noise in the background. They ignore the news of another man's death, and the tinder box of another city's impending destruction.

Three wine goblets, and a water glass raised in the air, they clink and toast to honor the men and women robbed of the opportunity they have been fortunate to keep.

"To life."

On July 10, 2015 Sandra Bland was pulled over for a traffic stop in Prairie View, Texas. The encounter between her and the police officer went from routine to violent in a matter of minutes. She was found dead in her jail cell on July 13, 2015.
#sayhername
#sayhisname

#SayTheirNames

#KeithScott
#TerrenceCrutcher
#PhilandoCastile
#AltonSterling
#ChrisTaylor
#JamarClark
#CoreyJones
#SandraBland
#RekiaBoyd
#TamirRice
#RenishaMcBride
#EricHarris
#WalterScott
#TheCharleston9
#FreddieGray
#EricGarner
#TrayvonMartin
#JordanDavis
#SamDubose
#OscarGrant
#SeanBell
#AmadouDiallo
#JonathanFerrell
#MikeBrown
#PrinceJones
#LaquanMcDonald
#AkaiGurley
#JohnCrawford
#MichelleCusseaux
#StephonClark
#FredHampton
#EleanorBumpurs
#TanishaAnderson
#

Author's Note and Acknowledgments

If you're reading this because you finished, *Four Women*, and wanted to know what happened next — now you know. If you're reading this and you're like, "*Four Women*, what's that?" I need you to go back and catch up. Please and thanks.

As I began to outline this novel in December of 2017, I had to think about the timeline of Ebony's case as it would have unfolded in the real world. *Four Women*, was intentionally and specifically set between the two trials of Michael Dunn, the man who killed Jordan Davis. During that time Eric Garner and Mike Brown were killed. With, *The Appeal of Ebony Jones*, the timeline of the novel unfolded against the backdrop of the real world killings of Tamir Rice, Michelle Cusseaux, and Freddie Gray.

It was always my intent with, *Four Women*, and now for this novel, for it to be my comment on the state of race in America as it relates to policing and the criminal justice system. This is my expression of the pain we collectively felt watching cities burn, protesters scream for justice, and grand juries refusing to hand down indictments in case after case after case. As a journalist these novels have been my way to release the stories I've covered day in and day out, that never leave me, even after I've left the newsroom.

I hope you enjoyed the story, and most of all I hope these characters made you think differently about this America we call home, and who is allowed to live their lives with liberty and in the pursuit of happiness. Thank you.

And very quickly . . . Thank you God for getting me through this novel and for the gift that flows through me. All praises be to the most high Father in Heaven. I'd also like to thank Dale Carson for explaining the appeals process to me so that I could make this story as accurate as possible. Thank you to my editors Roy and Arvita Roberts-Glenn for pushing me to explore these characters more deeply than I already had, and for catching all my mistakes. Gisette Gomez, thank you for another dope book cover. You brought Ebony to life in all of her sexy, fine, mean and aggravating glory. But most of all, thank you to you the reader. This book would not exist without you because I truly had no plans to write a sequel. Until next time . . . Peace.

— Nikesha Elise Williams

About the Author

Nikesha Elise Williams is an Emmy award winning news producer and author. She was born and raised in Chicago, Illinois, and attended The Florida State University where she graduated with a B.S. in Communication: Mass Media Studies and Honors English Creative Writing. Nikesha's debut novel, *Four Women*, was awarded the 2018 Florida Authors and Publishers Association President's Award in the category of Adult Contemporary/Literary Fiction. Nikesha lives in Jacksonville, Florida, but you can always find her online at www.newwrites.com, Facebook.com/NikeshaElise or @Nikesha_Elise on Twitter and Instagram.

www.ingramcontent.com/pod-product-compliance
Lightning Source LLC
Chambersburg PA
CBHW030623110726
47901CB00002B/285